in our
hands

in our hands

larissa c. moyer

BOOKLOGIX
Alpharetta, Georgia

ISBN: 978-1-6653-0635-5 – Paperback
eISBN: 978-1-6653-0636-2 – eBook

These ISBNs are the property of BookLogix for the express purpose of sales and distribution of this title. The content of this book is the property of the copyright holder only. BookLogix does not hold any ownership of the content of this book and is not liable in any way for the materials contained within. The views and opinions expressed in this book are the property of the Author/Copyright holder, and do not necessarily reflect those of BookLogix.

Cover Designer: okaycreations

First printing edition 2023

☉This paper meets the requirements of ANSI/NISO Z39.48-1992
(Permanence of Paper)

032023

disclaimer

Otis is a Deaf character, but the rest of the cast are hearing. The dialogue in his scenes uses American Sign Language but it is not a direct translation of the language, as it has no written form because it is a visual language. Sometimes the signing is indicated in the dialogue and sometimes it is not. But for an immersive reading experience, please assume that the characters are signing while conversing with Otis, unless otherwise indicated.

And while I have you: go learn ASL and thank me later!

When we love, we strive to become better than we are.
When we strive to be better than we are,
everything around us becomes better too.
—Paulo Coelho, *The Alchemist*

prologue

evelyn

My feet carry me right past him and I don't look back. It's like I'm in a trance. No, not a trance; it's like I'm possessed by a ghost who's in so much pain they wish they were *more* dead.

Buried deeper underground, breathing less than no air, like a person who never existed at fucking all.

Somehow, I end up on the Southbound L train. Reality starts to return to me slowly as I look around at all the people on the train and I'm in such a hopeless place that I truly wish I was any one of them.

That woman probably hasn't been slowly dying inside for the last three months. That man probably has a best friend; one who didn't lie and betray him.

I see a couple sitting next to each other. They each have an earbud in one of their ears and the girl's chin is resting peacefully on the guy's shoulder as they watch the city from above out the window.

Ugh, we get it. You're in love.

They're probably on their way to dinner or a museum or maybe just back to one of their apartments for a cozy night of togetherness.

Must be fucking nice.

My mind has been cycling through its own stages of grief since this morning when my already fragile world got knocked out of orbit completely.

Agony. Denial. Numb. Repeat.

I'm lingering between numb and agony as I reach the Granville stop. I step off the train even though this isn't where I live because I can't keep watching the high and mighty train people.

Standing there on the platform like a lost toddler.

Someone tell me what to do, someone tell me where to go.

But I'm not a toddler. I'm a twenty-three-year-old college graduate and no one is going to help me.

I walk down the steps and out onto the busy Chicago sidewalk and wander aimlessly around Edgewater. I walk toward the lake, passing by an Italian restaurant. As the door opens, the divine smells of oregano and garlic waft into the air.

If I felt like I could eat anything, I'd go in. The building is kind of cool. It looks old, but it's made with black brick and there's ivy twining up the wall, and the smells lead me to believe it's the real deal, full of old family recipes.

But I trudge on toward Lake Shore Drive, hoping Lake Michigan will give me some peace.

She doesn't. The vast sight of the lake feels taunting; telling me that this torment is never ending. It's like the opposite of Mufasa telling Simba that "Everything the light touches will be yours" in *The Lion King*. Lake Michigan is telling me, "Your pain has no end in sight."

We used to be friends, Lake Michigan.

I wander a few blocks down and away from the water when I suddenly realize I know where I am. I see the old dive bar I used to go to with . . .

Fuck. Him.

I step through the door and the familiar smell hits me like a concrete wall. This place always smells like a toilet that was rolled around in a litter box.

Denial takes over. I avert my eyes from the booth I used to sit at with him and slump onto a bar stool.

The booth is behind me. It doesn't matter. It doesn't fucking exist.

Denial is the best stage; denial led me to alcohol.

"What can I get ya?" the bartender asks.

The bartender is kind of cute. He has light blonde hair and dark blue eyes. The total opposite of—

Bitch. We're not thinking about him right now, remember?

It doesn't matter. I'm in my oversized gray sweatpants and a dirty white t-shirt. I didn't put on deodorant or brush my hair this morning because who needs hygiene when your world is crumbling? I probably look and smell like a sewer right now and I honestly don't care.

"A beer and a shot of tequila, please."

I pull my card out of my wristlet and hand it to the cute bartender and he gives me a knockout smile.

"You want to start a tab?" he asks.

I want to buy the fucking bar but I can't let Brad Pitt-wannabe know that so I just nod, trying to quirk my mouth into something resembling a smile.

He takes my card and I sit awkwardly on the stool. I've never been to a bar alone before.

"You Belong with Me" by Taylor Swift blasts at an absurd volume for a near empty bar at four o'clock on a Wednesday.

The song is mocking me, and it's a dumb fucking song.

I immediately scold myself for criticizing T. Swift. At least she turns her pain into chart topping hits.

Maybe I should write a song. What rhymes with "AUUURRR-GHHH?"

Pulling my phone out of my pocket, I cringe at my background picture. A sweet memory of him and me cuddling in bed at the beginning of the school year, right after we moved in together, stares back at me.

The bartender brings over my drinks with perfect timing and I give him an appreciative closed-mouth smile.

I will tip you well, Brad Pitt.

Knocking back the shot and taking a healthy swig of beer, I quickly replace my background photo with a picture I took of a sandwich I had a few months ago.

Grilled cheese never lets me down.

The sun has disappeared as well as my ability to sit up straight. I have no idea how much time has actually passed but it's been long enough that there's now two of Brad Pitt behind the bar.

They come over with a tall glass of tequila and I give them what I'm sure is a dopey smile. I take a big gulp and realize it's water.

"Do you have a ride home?" they ask.

My chin drops, trying to nod, even though it's not true and I take my phone out, scrolling through my messages.

Can't call him, he left me.

Can't call them, they're in Pennsylvania.

My thumb hovers over my messages with my best friend. Even though I stormed off on him earlier, the alcohol has lowered my in-hibitions enough to believe he'll come get me.

Even in my hazy state, I feel a pang of guilt at how I left things with him.

He's always honest with me, even when it's hard.

My thumbs tap the screen and I send him a text:

Me: Can you ride me home?

chapter one

evelyn

seven years later

I t's 6:00 a.m. and I *should be* out the front door. But naturally, I'm tearing through my studio like a malfunctioning claw machine game, grabbing things aimlessly.

I whip a t-shirt off my desk chair—where I keep all my clothes that are too dirty to fold back up and put in my dresser but too clean to wash—and I shove it over my head.

Fishing out a second pair of socks from in between my loveseat cushions, I slip them over my first pair of socks, already on my feet, as I hobble toward my small kitchenette and grab a banana.

One arm wiggles its way into the sleeve of my zip-up and I jam my finger on the doorknob.

"Fuck!"

Shaking my finger, I open the door, holding my banana and keys in the other hand and quickly close the door then lock it behind me.

The small hallway that leads from my studio apartment to the set of stairs of my daily commute are just a few feet away.

Thank God.

I stare down the small hallway to the stairs that will bring me down to the back office of my coffee shop, and I do what any normal, grown-ass woman, who is still a little afraid of the dark does: I run.

My morning cardio.

I push open the door to the stairwell, then barrel down the steps with the grace of a newborn giraffe. My fingers move to unlock the office door and then immediately lock it from the other side. It's the only way to access my apartment so I like to make sure it's secure before I start the day.

The perks of living just upstairs from your business are exceedingly helpful when you are someone who struggles to manage personal time. And someone who struggles to put things away. Someone who struggles. *Period.*

When I finally saved enough money to open Bohemia, there was no way I could afford the rent of *two* properties. The landlord, Sal, took pity on me and gave me the studio above the storefront for a small amount more than I was already paying and the rest is history.

My hand pushes through the swinging door, bringing me behind the counter of the small café and I flip on the lights. I swear, every morning I have this feeling: I can't believe this is *my* place. This business is *mine.*

It's a dream I never knew I wanted, but it's my pride and joy. I might be a hot mess in the life department, but I take *care* of my business. As a small, neighborhood café, I know nearly all of our customers.

Chicagoans take a lot of pride in their neighborhoods, and my shop was coined "An Edgewater hidden gem" last year. Since then, we've seen some new faces here and there but mostly it's our local regulars and the students at the University just up Lake Shore Drive that keep us comfortable.

Walking to the far end of the wall behind the counter where the tablet we use to ring up orders sits, I power up my playlist of '80s Rock Anthems. "We're Not Gonna Take It" by Twisted Sister blasts through the speakers.

Oh, hell yeah.

I was a theater major and the loud singing and spontaneous dancing came with the degree. It's physically impossible for me to stand in the produce section of the grocery store and *not* soft shoe while I contemplate actually buying vegetables.

Once the music is going, I weigh out a full batch of coffee on the scale for the drip brew. The low rumble from the grinder coupled with the rich, caramelized smell of the freshly ground coffee is like a warm morning hug. It might be my favorite part of the day—almost as good as the first cup of the day.

Almost.

The hot water bubbles in the brewer and the coffee starts dripping into the empty urn, so I walk back through the swinging door to check my calendar. I click on October 3rd and see that the only thing I've got down is that Dean will be by to drop off this week's order at ten.

I wonder if there will ever be a day when the thought of Dean doesn't make my heart roll over. He's one of the head roasters at Red Line, one of Chicago's elite coffee roasting plants. But he also happens to be my ex-boyfriend. We were together through three years of college and broke up right after we graduated seven years ago.

The end of our relationship was . . . messy. Actually, the end of our relationship was like trying to outrun a fucking cyclone, but it seems too early in the day for such dramatic thoughts.

Suddenly, the bell above the front door jingles.

"Holy feck—it's cold!" Mary's muffled shriek is audible from the back office.

My mouth curls up as I walk back through the swinging door, already chuckling at the scene unfolding.

Mary locks the door behind her and hugs her small body, dressed in a giant puffy coat that she named Fiona. Her hood is lined with some kind of faux fur and encases her whole head, so I really only see her nose and mouth, which is muttering other obscenities in a faint Irish accent. She's from Ireland, but she's lived here for thirty-years or so with her husband, Jim. Her accent is only noticeable when she's drinking and cursing.

Belligerent babble.

She finally removes her hood and gives me a tight smile.

"Good morning, love," she says, teeth still chattering.

"Is it?" I laugh.

Her tiny frame twitches as she shivers and groans.

"There's a fresh pot," I offer, pouring some for myself.

Mary shuffles toward the mug wall and retrieves the bell-shaped mug I bought her for Christmas the first year we opened. I lean against the counter and watch her shuffle toward me, giving her a small smirk.

"Such a beautiful smile, you've got." She grabs my chin and wiggles it back and forth in perfect doting fashion.

I love this woman *dearly*. She's like a mother to me. She and Jim are *both* family, honestly. Mary doesn't *need* to work. Jim makes enough money to provide for them both comfortably, but she chooses to spend her time at Bohemia with me and I am so grateful.

She pours herself a cup of coffee from the urn and cradles the beverage in her hands, seeking its warmth. I watch her take a long inhale as she savors the smell and rising steam, her eyes closing and crinkling at the edges from years of warm smiles.

I love watching people enjoy their drink, especially their first one of the day. It's a small, but gratifying pleasure in this line of business.

Mary takes one sip and appears to thaw a little bit. She slips out of Fiona and hangs her up on one of the hooks by the office door, shivering once more.

She grasps my arm affectionately as she passes by me, picking her mug back up.

I move to the espresso machine and start to dial in.

Grind, tamp, brew.

I repeat the process several times while the machine warms up.

"Red Line gets here at ten today," I tell Mary, over my shoulder.

"Hmph! Is *that boy* making the delivery?"

I nod my head, keeping my eyes on the espresso shot slowly dripping from the portafilter.

Dean always brings our delivery but Mary just can't resist an opportunity to voice her disapproval.

"You know I don't like him," she warns and I snort a small laugh. "Can't Otis bring us the order? God, I love *that boy.*"

Jesus. She shifts moods like a damn Sour Patch Kid and I can't keep up.

"Mary . . . Otis doesn't work at Red Line." I adjust to a coarser setting on the espresso grinder, trying to speed the shots up.

"I bet he'd do it for you if you asked," she sing-songs at me.

I breathe a laugh and roll my eyes while my attention turns back toward the espresso machine.

Why are these shots not cooperating?

Grind, tamp, brew.

Mary *loves* Otis, Dean's brother. I love him too; he's my best friend. I was worried that Dean would get him in the settlement when we parted ways but Otis has stuck by my side. We became close while Dean and I were still together, and just like Mary and Jim, he's become family.

I watch as the espresso shot pours steadily and blondes just as it finishes pulling. I tap the glass on the tray of the machine and watch the shot's layers settle from golden to dark brown.

Fucking finally.

I pour the shot in my mug and take a victory sip, then look over to Mary. Her salt and pepper bobbed hair bounces wildly as she scrubs the cold brew container with aggressive purpose. I cradle my mug in my hands and walk past the urns, then use my backside to push open the swinging door to the back office. Placing my mug on the desk, I dig my phone out of my bag, scoring a slightly squashed granola bar in my search.

I unlock my phone and see a new message.

Otis: They're building some shitty fast food place on the corner of my block. I'm moving.

Hah, yeah right.
Otis wouldn't move—he loves his place and this neighborhood.

Me: You can always go back to Evanston!

It was an ongoing joke when we were in college. Otis went to Northwestern and Dean and I used to correct him anytime he'd mention he "goes to school in Chicago."

"No, Otis. You go to school in Evanston," either Dean or I would say.

I follow up my message with the laughing face emoji just to rub in my snark. He has a strange hatred for emojis and I have a certain love for getting under his skin.

I sit down at the desk, taking another sip of my drink.

Damn, that's good.

My calendar is still pulled up on the screen and my eyes zone in on Dean's name blocked out in red next to the 10:00 a.m. tab.

It was early afternoon and I was laying on the couch watching Boy Meets World *reruns when I heard my cell phone buzz.*

"Dean?" I answered.

"Hey baby . . ." he said so quietly I wasn't even sure he really said it.

"Are you on your way home?" I sat up and ran a hand through my matted hair.

"No . . . I'm . . ." he trailed off and I heard a muffled intercom announcement in the background.

I thought maybe he was on L, but we usually couldn't get decent service when we were on it.

My heart sped up and a cold sweat broke at my hairline.

"Where are you?" I asked.

"I'm at O'Hare."

The airport? Why was he at the airport?

"I'm gonna go to Colorado, Evie," he said, and I stood up on shaky feet.

"Colorado?" I echoed.

He cleared his throat and let out a pained exhale. "Yeah. Collin hooked me up with a job at his dad's coffee farm, so . . . I'm gonna go."

I felt like I was floating away, like a lost balloon just about to pop from the altitude.

"You're . . . you're leaving?" My voice was a whisper and my breath caught in my throat.

I was starting to panic. He couldn't just leave! We lived together, for Christ's sake!

He sighed again, saying, "I don't know what else to do, Evie . . . I . . ."

"You're leaving me . . ." I cried. "All fucking alone . . . right now?!"

My legs gave out and I sank back to the couch, choking on my sobs. He was leaving me, and he didn't even have the decency to tell me to my face.

"Baby, don't cry. Please . . . I know that this is so fucking hard but . . . I just can't do this anymore. I can't be . . ." he cleared his throat again. "I'm so sorry, Evelyn. I love you. I know you hate me, but I love you."

Call ended.

"Love!" I jolt at the sound of Mary's call from up front. "These feckers are gonna start a riot if we don't open up the doors soon. Ya ready?"

I take a steadying breath; my hand tremors as it grabs the mouse and I click out of my calendar.

"Open up!" I holler back to her.

chapter two

otis

My biceps shake and my stomach tightens, letting out a labored exhale.

I drop down from my lifting bars over my bedroom doorway, then hold the frame as my mouth hauls in some heavy breaths.

Feelin' old today.

A tired groan rumbles my throat and I grab the towel off the back of my desk chair, wiping the sweat from my neck as I walk over to the fridge and grab a water bottle. I pick my phone up from the counter and see a couple messages from Evelyn.

Evanston. She's hysterical—And we've talked about the emojis.

I click on my baseball app, mostly out of habit.

But it's a sad day for Cubs fans—we're out for the season. I read over the article detailing the loss of their last game like it's an obituary.

Isn't it, though?

Another groan escapes me as I drop my phone on the counter, then gulp down some water.

After a quick shower, I throw on some jeans and a gray thermal shirt.

My hair is unruly, so I sift my fingers through it with some expensive product my friend Reggie gave to me for no occasion at all—just winked and said my hair had "Prince Eric potential."

Whatever that means.

I gather my laptop off the desk and some notes I might need in case I actually get to work on my book today.

Writing bullshit columns for a local paper isn't exactly fun, but they only need me to go into the office a couple times a week when they're handing out stories and finalizing that week's issue, so most of my work is remote.

The articles can feel soul-sucking, and the pay isn't great, so I have to pick up other freelance work. But sometimes the flexible schedule gives me time to work on my book of short stories.

A gust of wind greets me as I open the door to my building and I bow my head, taking off toward Bohemia. It's only a five-minute walk, made even faster by my long, hurried strides.

Rounding the corner street market, the smell of fog and fish from Lake Michigan becomes particularly pungent and my eyes flick up to see the black, brick building just a little further ahead. Another billowy wind increases my pace before I quickly push inside the door, finally pulling my chin up.

Warmth immediately floods me, and it's not from the heat.

The space has worn wooden floors with vintage-bulb lights strung along the ceiling. The curtains on the windows are a mix of sheer purples, reds, and yellows, so the sun still shines through even when they're closed.

Local artists' work hangs on the walls, and black and white photos of different customers hang between all the artwork. Evelyn installed a mug wall where the regulars' mugs hang on small hooks.

This place *is* Evelyn.

It's all about the people. She always wanted it to be a place for the locals in the neighborhood to meet and work and talk. It will be a goddamn institution one day.

My spot is open, so I claim the table, placing my coat and laptop bag on the small bench attached to the wall, then I grab my mug.

My mug is *hideous*.

Evelyn made me go to one of those pottery painting places and paint our mugs for the wall together. My mom spins her own pottery, so I've done it before, mostly when I was a kid. And I never half-ass anything, so I took my time and made clean, geometrical lines with colors that I like.

She painted her whole mug one color then dipped three brushes in three different colors and splatter painted it, which was really just her wiggling the three brushes erratically at the mug.

"It's abstract!" she claimed.

Anyway, she liked the way mine turned out more and asked if we could switch. I told her no way, but every damn morning, she's sipping from *my* masterpiece. So, I'm always stuck with *this* monstrosity.

I begrudgingly bring the mug up to the bar when Mary quickly scurries out from behind the counter, quickly hugging me tight around the neck.

This is how she greets me every time she sees me. I chuckle and hug her back because you *never* turn down a Mary hug.

She pulls back but keeps her hands on my shoulder.

"Hello, love," she says clearly.

Smiling, I sign, "Hi, Mary."

"Americano?" she asks, taking my mug with a bright smile.

Mary doesn't know sign language but luckily, our routine has been the same every morning for three years: hug, hello, Americano and sometimes another hug to round out the exchange.

I nod, then point to the office, silently asking if Evelyn is back there. Mary understands, nodding, so I start toward the swinging door.

When I step through the entry, Evelyn's back is to me, sitting at her desk with her ear buds in. She's looking at a selection of mugs on a local potter's website while a half-eaten banana sits next to the keyboard. I tap her on the shoulder and she jumps but settles when she sees it's me.

"You scared me!" she signs, plucking her ear buds out.

"Now you know how I feel," I sign back, chuckling.

She playfully smacks my arm and stands. "Want to get dinner later? I hear they're building a swanky new restaurant on the corner of your street."

I roll my eyes, dragging my palms down my face, irritated by the reminder.

"How was your date with Lexi last night?" she signs, trying to wiggle her eyebrows at me, but she can't wiggle her eyebrows.

I don't know why she keeps trying. Her face is incapable.

"Good. It's always a little weird trying to get to know someone who doesn't know how to sign. But it was nice."

"You didn't take her to the library, did you?" She makes a snoring face for dramatic effect.

I shake my head and laugh.

Brat.

"We went to Grasstropub," I sign.

She raises her eyebrows and shakes her right hand out, signing, "Wow."

I'm not sure if she's making fun of me or not—it's hard to tell sometimes. Grasstropub is a vegan place. I'm not a vegan, but Lexi is, so I figured it was a safe choice.

"Your brother should be here in about an hour," she signs, then returns her attention to her computer.

Damnit.

I was too busy mourning the Cubs that I forgot it's Monday. I usually avoid coming here when Dean drops off the order.

My chest always caves a bit at the reminder that Dean and I have ended up in this place—this reality where we're acquaintances when we used to be inseparable. We actually met Evelyn on the same night, together.

Dean had come up to Northwestern to grab lunch with me and caught wind of a party over at the Arts House and forced me to go.

Almost immediately after arriving, he quickly abandoned me to go have a cigarette out back and I stood awkwardly in the living room.

I remember thinking: what do people do with their hands at a house party when they're not groping each other or dancing?

I settled on holding my beer and picking at the label just as a seat opened up on the couch and I graciously took it.

Only a moment later, I noticed a girl with wavy brown hair, wearing a simple, form-fitting gray dress. She was jumping up and down with a tall guy that had curly, black hair. The strained muscles in their necks indicated they were yelling to whatever song was playing over the speakers.

Their jumping became more erratic and the girl started holding the hem of her dress flat against the side of her thighs. I assumed, in an attempt to not flash the rest of the partiers. The rest of the room was dry humping their dance partners but the two of them appeared to be dancing to an entirely different song.

I chuckled, casting my eyes down at my bottle with part of the label removed when suddenly, the jumping girl plopped down on the couch next to me. The dark room's only light was a small disco ball swirling around flashes of white light.

Theater kids . . .

The girl's chest was heaving up and down as she leaned her head back on the couch before she finally lifted her chin and glanced over at me.

"Hi," I think she said.

I gave her a tilted smile and a small wave.

Smooth.

Just then, Dean found me on the couch and signed, "They're setting up a slip and slide in the backyard—want to go?"

I squinted my eyes in confusion and maybe mild irritation.

A slip and slide?

His focus shifted to the jumping girl who was now glancing back and forth between the two of us. I saw Dean reach his hand out and introduce himself. He must have told her my name too because she turned to face me.

I shifted to face her too and she smiled nervously.

She raised her left hand up, parallel to the ground with her palm facing up toward the ceiling, swiped her flat right palm forward over the left, then raised her two index fingers and circled them around to meet each other and then pointed at me with her right index finger.

She had signed, "Nice to meet you."

That was . . . unexpected. It wasn't often that I met a stranger with even basic ASL literacy.

"What's your name?" I signed back.

She fingerspelled, "E-V-E-L-Y-N."

Evelyn is staring at me expectantly.

"What?" I sign.

She narrows her eyes. "I knew you weren't listening!"

"You talk a lot," I tease.

She shoves my shoulder, still smirking. "Can you come lock up on Thursday? Reggie is moving into his new place and can't possibly survive without my muscles."

She flexes, and even though her arm is small, she does have a bit of a bicep. She *is* freakishly strong.

I nod then point at the door letting her know I'm going out to get to work and she follows me. Mary is standing suspiciously close to the swinging door and my eyes squint curiously.

She hands me my Americano with a small grin and I lift the mug appreciatively, then continue around the counter, glancing back at her . . . still confused.

What a strange woman.

As I reach the seating area, I notice a few more tables have been taken. I place my mug down and take my laptop out of my bag then plug it into the outlet on the wall under the table. Scooting in on the bench, I finally take a sip of my drink.

Damn, that's good.

I notice Evelyn eyeing me from the counter, wearing a small smile. It's only for a split second and then she shifts her focus back to the customers.

My head shakes, breathing a small laugh. She loves to watch people enjoy their drinks. She loves to watch people enjoy anything, really.

I open my laptop and get ready to start on my story for the paper. This week's breaking news involves a woman who left an alligator at the airport.

So many questions.

I open my email to see if any of my sources have responded to my inquiries about the alligator when I notice an email from Lexi:

> Hey Otis,
>
> Just wanted to let you know that they're cutting off electricity in our building for a couple hours today. I guess they're doing work on a building at the end of the block but they have assured me it will be back on in a "timely manner." I know you work from home so I just wanted to give you a heads up :) Unless they've already shut it off in which case— sorry.
>
> -Lexi

Lexi also happens to be my landlord.

Her parents own a few properties throughout the city but she lives across the hall from me. I have no complaints for her as a landlord. She lets me know what shit is happening, when and gets maintenance requests filled quickly. She's also pretty damn cute. She even brought me a space heater the night my radiator stopped working on one of the coldest nights we had last year.

I shoot her an email back and then my procrastination runs out as I have no more excuses to avoid this fucking absurd article. Taking one more sip of my drink gives me some fuel and then I wiggle my fingers on top of the keyboard, like stretching before a tedious workout.

chapter three

evelyn

L istening to Reggie drone on about how much he hates Carol
Greer, or as he refers to her: "The Greer who stole *my* clients"
is exhausting.

Cute pun, though.

"She's a bitch!" he whines.

I groan as we head through the back door that leads to the alley.

"She's just doing her job," I remind him.

Reggie is a real estate agent and the market can be really competitive. I
might be a little biased because he's my other very best friend, but I have a
hard time believing anyone is as personable or as charismatic as he is.

We met our freshman year of college at a theater showcase the department held for the incoming class. I'll never forget Reggie's flawless
tan complexion and sparkling white teeth when he sauntered up to me
after my performance.

"Girl!" he barked, looking me up and down. "The sock boots have
got to go, but the voice is *perfection.*"

I threw out the sock boots and friends we have been ever since. He comes to the café a couple times a week to provide free labor and witty, sarcastic commentary on all things.

He shoves a heavy crate in front of the door to prop it open and glares at me through his gray eyes.

"What?" I'm afraid to ask.

His eyebrow raises. "Baby girl, did you get laid?"

I snort a laugh. It's a bit sad that the suggestion warrants such a laughable response.

My last date was over a year ago and . . . well, I tried.

His name was Evan and he had just bought a house from Reggie. He was actually really nice, but I was just too wrapped up in my own head to really enjoy myself. I just don't think dating is for me, honestly.

And casual sex is *definitely* not for me. I *do* have a pretty steamy relationship with my vibrator, Melvin, though.

He gets me.

The alleyway is creating a bit of a wind tunnel on an already blustery day. My feet start to bob in place in an attempt to keep warm, and maybe settle my nerves. I glance down toward the street looking for any sign of Dean's pick-up. He should be here any minute.

I turn my head back toward Reggie and see that he's still eyeing me down.

A scoff escapes as I roll eyes. "No Reggie, I did not get laid."

"A psychotic break?" he asks.

"Not today!" I joke. Kind of. "What's with the psych eval? Are you in the middle of another true-crime obsession or something?"

"No. You just seem so . . . level-headed lately. It's freaking me out."

I'm winning at life.

My best friend is *worried* about me because I'm acting fucking normal, for once.

As my right hand hangs down at my side, it starts to fingerspell different objects in the alley way:

Crate, brick wall, gravel . . .

Grounding is the clinical term, I believe. It gives me something to do with my hands, helps me to focus on something else when my anxiety starts to rise.

Traffic cone, door . . . truck.

Dean's pick-up slowly backs into the alley and the hazard lights start blinking as it pulls to a stop.

My breath stutters in my chest and my jaw tenses as my mouth pulls into a fake smile. Dean hops out of the driver's side and rounds the bed of the truck, smiling warmly at me.

"Hey Evie."

"Hey," I say, shuffling my feet. "Were you able to roast more Honduras?"

He unlatches the bed of his truck and steps in, starting to hand Reggie and I the big sacks of beans.

"Yep, I've got it." He hands me one burlap sack.

"Awesome!" I grunt as I turn to carry the heavy bag back through the door.

"Hi, Helen. Nice beard," I hear Reggie say dryly to Dean, behind me.

I drop the bag on the floor in the back office and use the opportunity to expel a heavy exhale.

It's always a little weird hearing Reggie call him by the nickname he gave him back when we were all in school together. It disrupts my delicate balance of keeping those two worlds separate. Actually, it disrupts my attempts to deny that *that* world existed at all.

One night at a party, Reggie claimed that the name *Dean* "didn't suit him."

"Well, what do you want to call me?" Dean had asked, slurring.

Reggie then grabbed Dean's face between his palms and rotated his head, inspecting his features.

Always, with the dramatics.

"Helen of Troy: the most beautiful woman in the world!" he announced, and then fell into a fit of laughter on top of Dean on the couch.

The nickname stuck but Reggie never rekindled his friendship with Dean after we broke up. In fact, it wasn't until Dean helped me out with my coffee supply that Reggie even considered *playing nice.*

Dean hands me another sack and I carry it through the door.

"So, how's it going?" Dean calls out from the truck.

As I sit the bag down, Reggie eyes me deviously.

"Good!" I call back to Dean, giving Reggie a *behave* look.

The gravel crunches under my steps as I walk back outside to see Dean hopping down with the last bag.

"Oh, I can take it," I offer.

"Nah, I've got it," he says.

I follow behind him, asking, "How are things with you?"

He drops the sack and turns back around. "Good . . . busy. Marnie's sister came to stay with us for a few days so it's been . . . it's been going." He laughs and then scoots past me to go back outside.

Ah, yes. Marnie. Dean's wife.

They got married three years ago, right around the time I was opening Bohemia, actually.

When I was getting ready to open, Otis cautiously reminded me that Dean might be a good person to contact since he worked at Red Line. They have the best whole beans in the city and I wanted my shop to be a success.

Otis offered to talk to Dean *for* me, but I refused to put him in the middle of anything having to do with Dean and me. Well, I refused to let it happen any more than it already had, anyway.

I emailed Dean that night, thinking that would suck the least.

Hi Dean,

How's it going? I hope you're doing well.

Otis told me you're roasting at Red Line - Congratulations! That's really cool.

So, I'm opening this shop off of Granville and I'd really love to brew Red Line. Thing is, looking at your prices . . . You might be a little out of my price range. Is there any sort of deal you could give me if you left the beans in the sacks to save on packaging? Maybe I could pick them up myself to save on delivery?

Anyway, let me know what you think.

All the best,
Evelyn

I mentally patted myself on the back for my maturity and then physically smacked myself in the head.

I didn't have a car! Why the hell would I offer to go pick up heavy bags of coffee with no mode of transportation? An image of me trying to haul a cart full of coffee sacks onto the L, and then using the stack as a seat on the packed Red line flashed through my mind.

A normal person would have written that off as a funny thought, but I actually sat there and considered it for a minute. "I think I could do it," I thought out loud, tapping my chin with my index finger like it was a totally doable plan.

Then I thought maybe Reggie would let me borrow his car once a week. Then I thought, no.

He hadn't even let me sit in his car since I accidentally went the wrong way down Wabash's one-way street. To my credit, it was not one-way when I was walking on it and I didn't drive much. And we were fine.

I got disrupted from hypothetically arguing my point to Reggie when my computer pinged, alerting me of a new email.

That was quick.

Evie,

    It's good to hear from you!

    Congrats are in order for you too. I actually drop off at Loyola every Monday so I can stop by your place after–it's no trouble. I can give you a "Friends and Family" discount. As long as you're good to bag it yourself, you've got a deal. I can stop by next week after my drop at Loyola with the paperwork - sound good?

Take care,

Dean

A "Friends and Family" discount?

Considering I wasn't a friend or family, that deal seemed pretty sweet. Pretty sure it was a "Guilt Discount."

I felt a small tug inside that had me second-guessing if it was a good idea. I didn't want Dean doing me favors because he felt guilty. But I was poor and living off a box of rice and mushroom soup, so I didn't really have another option.

I made a promise right there and then that as soon as I was profitable, I'd have him remove the discount and I'd pay the same as all his other retailers.

I wrote him back and simply said: "Deal!"

Dean comes back inside and hands me the invoice. I take it over to my desk to sign it, noticing the thirty percent discount is still applied. I've tried so many times to keep that promise to myself and revoke the kick-back Dean gave me when I first opened but he always reapplies it.

I give him back the top copy and my eyes nervously float up to meet his. "Pour over?"

"Do I look *that* tired?" He laughs, scratching at his beard.

Truthfully, he does look a little worn out. His chestnut brown eyes look muted and his short, copper colored beard is a little scraggly. But mostly, I'm determined to pay him back for the discount he refuses to take off. I figure after about a thousand drinks, we'll be square.

Dean follows me through the swinging door and lingers just outside the office.

"Guatemalan or Ethiopian?" I ask him.

"Guatemalan," he answers, glancing around the café.

I swear I see a glint of pride any time he comes in here and some tension leaves my body when I notice it.

My hand circles the kettle of hot water over the grinds at the pick-up counter when I catch Otis furrowing his brow behind his laptop screen, making me snort a laugh.

He must be working on a story for the paper. I can usually tell when he's writing an article, and when he's working on his book. His whole demeanor changes.

He's got a real gift for writing. He can take really mundane subjects and make them interesting and always finds a unique perspective. I have no doubt that he'll be a published success as soon as he finishes his damn book.

Just then, Reggie emerges from the office, stretching his arms and cracking his neck like he just completed the hammer throw event at the Olympics, then he slumps his upper body over the counter. Mary pats his back and gently rubs his shoulders.

Oh, the dramatics.

"You okay there, Popeye?" My tone wreaks of condescension as I finish pouring Dean's drink.

Reggie gives me an exasperated stare before he collects himself off the counter and gracefully breezes past me, catching the attention of Abby, one of my baristas.

Wrong team, honey.

He walks to the space behind the register and bends down to open the fridge.

"Where's the cold brew?" he sing-songs into the fridge.

chapter four

otis

The woman was trying to save the alligator from her boyfriend who was going to try to flush it down the damn toilet.

Jesus.

Maybe Evelyn has whiskey behind the espresso bar. It's only ten in the morning, but a drinking problem seems like an appropriate quality for a writer to have. I've only finished a quarter of the article when I peer over the counter, desperate for a distraction and I see my brother talking with Evelyn as she prepares a snooty drink that I'm sure he loves.

Dean leans against the counter and Evelyn seems ... mostly relaxed. I know she still feels tense around Dean but she puts up a good front.

Reggie takes lazy steps toward my table, chewing on the straw to his drink.

Setting his cup down, he dramatically slinks into the chair across from me.

"How do you get out of sack-slinging?" he signs.

I wince. *Sack-slinging* might be the worst combination of words ever created.

"I pretend I'm working." I gesture to my laptop and Reggie's eyes squint as he nods.

"Smart," he signs. "Heard you had a hot date last night." He raises an eyebrow suggestively as he sucks every last drop of his drink, then shakes his cup around like it will magically produce more.

I snort a laugh, shaking my head. "I'm not sure a kiss on the cheek counts as a *hot date*," I sign. "But it was nice—she's cool."

Something pulls Reggie's attention back behind the counter and my eyes follow.

I see Evelyn laughing at Dean as he continues to lean against the counter, talking animatedly.

Reggie turns back toward me, rolling his eyes.

"Remind me to avoid Mondays," he signs, standing up.

My lips quirk at the corner. I'm not sure if he wants to avoid Mondays because he doesn't want to unload the order or because he wants to avoid Dean, but I'm leaning toward the latter.

I know Reggie still harbors a lot of anger toward him for what he did to Evelyn. Honestly, I still resent him for it too. It's tough, though. Dean and I were best friends before everything went to shit.

Hell, Evelyn and I were such fast friends that there was a time when all three of us were inseparable.

Dean, Evelyn and I were having lunch together in the cafeteria at Northwestern. The two of them really seemed to hit off. They started dating shortly after Dean and I met her at the Arts House about two months ago.

I instantly liked her. She was smart and funny and she genuinely seemed like she wanted to get to know me.

I'd learned that she took ASL for her language requirement in high school so she knew some basic signs and phrases, but she had asked if I'd help her get better.

"What's the sign for 'Chicago'?" she signed, but fingerspelled the city name.

I made a 'C' hand shape with my right hand and drew the number seven with it.

Evelyn repeated it back to me, and I nodded.

"I go to school in Chicago," she signed.

Her signs were all correct but her sentence structure was wrong. The grammar is always a hard concept for people. ASL also has no written form, so it can be pretty confusing.

I took the notebook we kept on the table and scribbled a note.

> Signs were all good but remember ASL has its own syntax. If it's not in the present tense, you need to establish the time, followed by the subject, then the verb, then the object.

She nodded and I demonstrated the way to sign it: SCHOOL I GO CHICAGO.

She smirked, glancing over at Dean, then back to me.

"No, you go to school in Evanston," she signed and Dean jerked forward, laughing.

I chuckled and rolled my eyes. I liked that she was feeling comfortable enough to tease me—but what the hell?!

"You can get here from the L. I stand by my statement," I signed slowly, giving her a take that look.

She breathed another laugh, nodding and jokingly put her hands up in surrender, then took the notebook and wrote something.

> Okay, I think I get it. So, if I were to say, "Otis is a good teacher," I would sign: Teacher good O-T-I-S.

I nodded, then wrote:

> Yes. But you can use my name sign so you don't
> have to fingerspell my name every time.

Then I showed her my name sign: "O. Book."

She smiled and repeated it back to me.

She had a really pretty smile. It was natural and warm. Infectious.

"I love that!" she signed, then looked at Dean. "Do you have a name sign?"

His arm was draped around her shoulders and his head dropped down as he let out a small laugh, which was really more of a sigh, I imagined.

He nodded, and looked back up at me with annoyed embarrassment, still smirking.

I shrugged my shoulders back at him.

Tough shit! I had given him the name when we were little and he was stuck with it.

"What is it?" she signed, furrowing her brow; her eyes filled with curiosity.

He signed: "D. Fart."

"Oh my God!" Evelyn laughed so hard she cried and hit the table with her hand repeatedly.

When her laughter subsided, she looked up at Dean adoringly.

"My boyfriend, D. Fart," she signed, giving him a small peck on his cheek.

He smiled and turned so his forehead pressed against hers, then whispered something in her ear and her cheeks flushed.

I averted my eyes down at my tray and pushed around my food, but saw Evelyn pull the notebook to her once again before she pushed it back in front of me so I could read:

Okay. Teach me all the swear words.

I'm staring at the blinking cursor of my document when a small, low wave catches my attention.

Dean.

A chuckle escapes, signing, "I see you, asshole."

Dean lingers beside the table but continues standing. His drink is in a paper cup, so I assume he's not staying long.

"How about those Cubbies?" he signs, disappointment marring his features.

My mouth tenses into a straight line. "Don't even get me started. Thirteen innings and only *one* run?!"

"I know, man. Fucking brutal." He shakes his head, taking a sip of his drink.

We've been loyal Cubs fans for pretty much our entire lives. We never missed a game and always tracked the offseason when we were kids. In fact, the first thing we did when I moved to Chicago was go to Wrigley Field for a game.

Dean's gaze is on the floor as he shifts his weight nervously, then peeks back up at me. "How was the date with your land lady?"

Goddamn. Did Evelyn put out an ad in the paper or something? I didn't tell him I had a date with Lexi, so I'm assuming she did.

"Good. Just went to dinner," I sign. "How's Marnie?"

"Good," he signs back.

Wow, this is the worst.

This is why I avoid Dean's visits at the café. We were able to move past his hasty exit from Chicago, but our bond never recovered. We see each other on some holidays and text each other periodically about baseball but otherwise, our interactions just remind me that we're not as close as we used to be.

His eyes drift to my open laptop. "How's the book coming?"

I groan, giving him an irritated look. He knows you never ask a writer, "How's the book?"

He laughs, shrugging his shoulders. His eyes stare down into his cup and there's a contemplative look on his face that seems like he has something else he wants to say, but he scratches the back of his head nervously instead.

"I've got to get going. I've got a tasting in Northalsted in twenty minutes," he signs.

I give him a quick wave, then pretend to busy myself on my laptop. It's ironic that I was looking for a distraction from writing, only to pretend to write to get rid of my distraction. This might be the Universe's way of telling me to get to work.

Yet, after the coast is clear and Dean has left, I walk over to the mixing station and pour myself some water from the jug.

My eyes drift over to Evelyn, caught in a conversation with Chatty Maddy. Serves her right for telling Dean about my date with Lexi. She meets my eyes for just a moment and I silently let her know.

We are fighting.

I see her stifle a small laugh and then shift her focus back to Maddy as I walk back to my station.

Goddamnit.

I'm determined to get this article done today. Once I finish the article, I can dive back into my book.

Okay. Lady. Alligator. Toilet. Go.

chapter five

evelyn

It's just after noon and I'm back in the office packaging up this morning's delivery when Mary peeks her head through the swinging door, stepping in.

"I'm heading out, love! Do you need anything before I go?"

She's hoping I ask for food. She loves to feed me and I *love* to eat her cooking. It wouldn't surprise me at all if her cooking was part of the reason Jim married her. Then again, his cooking is awesome too.

Some people really have this adulting thing *down*.

But I currently have my squashed granola bar hanging out of my mouth. "No, all good. I'll see ya tomorrow."

I toss the last half of my bar in my mouth all at once and give her a puffy cheeked smile.

"Okay, well, I have this soup in my bag..." She starts to dig through her *Mary Poppin's* tote.

"Mary—I'm *fine*," I promise her, but she hands me the Tupperware anyway. "Thank you." I stand, pulling her in for a hug.

God, she gives the best hugs.

"All right, love." She cups my cheek, shrugs into Fiona and heads out the swinging door.

I feel my phone buzz in my pocket and pull it out.

Mom: Hi Pumpkin! Just wanted to say hi and
I miss you. I know you're busy but please call soon!

I suck.

I don't make enough time to call my parents and I *never* visit. And I do miss them. They still live back in Pennsylvania so I have the distance as an excuse, but *I* know it's more than that.

It's just . . . too hard being back there.

I clamp my eyes shut, believing they're a steel door I can close to keep the shitty memories from creeping in like a home intruder.

After a few deep breaths, my eyes hesitantly reopen and my shaky thumbs tap out a response on my phone.

Me: Hi Mom—Miss you too. I'll call this weekend.
Love to you and Dad.

I shake my head hoping to rattle the guilt with it and start pouring the excess beans from the order into air-tight containers.

After the last container is filled, I pick up my mug, noticing I'm due for a refill. Pushing out of the office, behind the counter, I notice an unfamiliar face at the abandoned register.

My eyes skim the café, looking for both of my baristas but I don't see Abby or Greg anywhere.

"Hi there! Can I help you?" I ask, approaching the register. My fingers tap the screen, getting ready to ring him up.

"Small drip," he mumbles.

His order, coupled with his visible neck tattoos tell me he might be the silent brooding type.

Thank God Reggie's gone. He'd have a field day with this guy. And this guy does not look like he's in the mood to hear Reggie brag about his nipple ring.

I grab the sharpie I leave by the register to mark his cup.

"Name?" I ask.

"Mike."

As I turn and slide his cup across the pick-up counter, I notice that he's actually kind of hot. Mike seems like too much of a mainstream name for him, though. He strikes me more as a Dante or Demogorgon.

"I'm Evelyn," I say, giving him a closed-mouth smile.

He half grins. "Hi."

Is Demogorgon flirting with me?

He raises his paper cup in a silent thank you and starts toward the door.

"Damn . . ." I sigh, appreciating the fine man butt sauntering out of my café.

A few people have cleared out, so I grab a dish tub and walk over to the table that looks like a spool, collecting the empty mugs, then wiping it down.

The tables and chairs in the seating area are all mismatched. I'd love to say it was an intentional, vintage decor choice, but it's not. Some of the items were donated, some I bought at different estate sales, and I actually *found* my favorite chair.

It's bright purple, with a tall back and brushed gold embellishments on the corners. The chair was sitting next to a bench in a park.

Strangely poetic. I waited on the bench for an hour, making sure I wasn't stealing someone else's magical chair and then claimed it.

Otis is still at his table, working on his eyebrow wrinkle and my eyes shift to the ugly-ass mug sitting next to his laptop. A small, victorious smile tugs at my lips.

Early slug gets the mug!

After dropping the dishes in the sink, I see that Otis's face looks less like a grumpy puppet, so it's probably a good time to bug him.

His eyes peer up as he sees me approaching. "Want more?" I sign, casting my eyes down at the mug.

He shakes his head. His eyes refocus on his laptop, then meet mine again with pinched brows.

"What would you do if you saw an alligator on the L?" he signs.

Huh. Didn't see that coming.

He doesn't react to the confusion on my face. He just looks back at his laptop screen and scratches under his jaw at his reddish scruff.

Good God, I love that sound.

It's precarious timing, though. The sound is only right when the hair has grown back to be more than stubble, but less than beard.

Otis looks back up at me and now he looks confused as to what's happening.

What *is* happening?

"Why does your face look like that?" he signs.

My nose scrunches, annoyed. "What?"

We stare back and forth at each other for a few blinks, then he raises his eyebrows at me like he's waiting for an answer to something.

Oh, right. He asked me a question.

"I guess I'd ask what the alligator's name is?" I sign, tossing an arm up.

Why is he asking me this?

He slowly nods his head, turning his attention back to his computer.

Weirdo.

I head back behind the counter to leave him with . . . whatever the hell he's doing over there.

Pouring some oat milk into a stainless-steel pitcher, I insert the tip of the steam wand into the milk. The airy whistle sound starts as I pull the lever for the wand down and hold the bottom of the pitcher waiting until it's too hot to touch.

Just then, I see Abby walking through the seating area, seemingly from the bathroom.

Has she been in there the whole time?

"Abby, can you bring the retail bags up here and stock them?" I ask, my milk starting to rumble low.

My hand jerks the wand back up, then I tap and swirl the pitcher, pouring it on top of the espresso in my mug.

"Yeah, of course, Evelyn," she says quickly, then ducks her head as she walks in hurried steps to the back room.

I wonder if she's okay.

Before I have time to worry too much, Greg, my other barista, strides out of the bathroom and walks back behind the counter.

Wearing Abby's lipstick on his neck.

Gross.

God, if twenty-year-old me could see me now—scoffing at the teenagers having a little fun.

I was at the student center, late.

I had been monopolizing one of the practice rooms for hours, alternating between practicing for Cabaret that weekend, and my jury performance the following week.

Sitting at the piano, I plunked out the melody I was having trouble with, when my phone buzzed from on top of the piano.

Dean: *Open up!*

I pushed the bench back, causing a loud screeching sound on the linoleum floor. Peeking out the small rectangle window on the door, I saw Dean leaning against the wall just beside the practice room.

I opened the door, narrowing my eyes at him. "What are you doing here?" I whispered even though no one else was around.

It was after ten on a Thursday. Most of the campus was partying, of course.

Dean slipped past me and into the practice room. I glanced to the left and right of the hallway one more time before I closed the door, but as soon as the door latched, the lights in the room went out.

"Dean! I really need to practice—what are you doing?"

The room was dark, but the small window cast a bit of light in and I saw his silhouette leaning against the piano,

"I've heard you in here for the last half hour." His voice was low as he started to walk toward me, "You sound perfect, babe."

He closed in on me until my back was flush with the wall.

My breath hitched as he gently pinched my chin between his thumb and index finger, then leaned down and pressed his lips to mine. His tongue pushed through my mouth, moving against mine slowly.

He tasted like Irish cream coffee and cigarettes.

A small whimper ached in my throat as he settled his other hand at the nape of my neck, deepening our kiss.

His lips left mine and found the soft spot right below my ear as my hand threaded through the back of his thick hair, pulling him closer.

"Kind of," he murmured, his lips dragging down my neck. "Had me wondering." He pressed a kiss to my collar bone and raised my shirt up, pulling it over my head. "What other sounds," he whispered, his lips grazing the crown of my breast. "I can get out of you."

His mouth trailed down my stomach, dropping to his knees directly in front of me, pulling down my pants and panties at the same time, his eyes locked with mine. Once my bottoms were around my ankles, I stepped out of them and Dean's dark smile peered up at me as he hooked one of my legs over his shoulder.

He kissed me there *and I whimpered before he buried his face between my legs. Quiet, needy noises spilled from me as I jerked, knocking my head against the wall. My fingers raked through his hair, my nails scraping his scalp.*

"Oh God, Dean . . ." I moaned.

He chuckled softly, still pressed against me, a masculine "Mmm" sound escaping before his raspy voice said, "Now that's music."

The loud release of hot air shooting from the tip of the steam wand jolts me back to now, making me gasp. I quickly push the lever back up, exhaling hard.

I feel ya, steam wand.

Nervously patting my warm cheeks, I try to collect myself. But my wandering erotic memory only proves that I was too quick to judge the horny teens getting it on in my bathroom. They're not so bad, they're just horny teens.

"Hey, Evelyn?" Greg's looking at me like he broke something.

I take one more steadying breath and look over at him. "What's up?"

"I think I'm sick. Can I go home?"

Fucking teenagers.

chapter six

otis

I walk my mug to the sink behind the counter and scrub it with the sponge then dry it with a dish towel.

Yep, still hideous.

After hanging it back on the mug wall, I collect my notes and laptop, shoving it all in my bag.

The article took me a little longer today. I was distracted with Dean here and my sources took a while to confirm all the facts I wanted to include.

My stomach grumbles so hard I imagine it's audible and I quickly glance around to see if anyone's noticed but the seating area is empty.

Return a book at the library and then, I will eat all the food.

I start to play the game in my head where I think of all my possible food options. Do I make the responsible choice and eat my leftovers? Or do I make the delicious decision and get a sandwich from Bobby's on my way back from the library?

Shrugging into my coat, I sling my laptop bag over my shoulder when I notice Evelyn wrestling with the espresso machine. She's trying to clean it, but she looks more like a mad scientist trying to defuse a bomb.

I approach the bar to see that she's now squatting down, below the counter. She's trying to twist a small screwdriver underneath one of the filters where the espresso pours.

I peek over and look down at her. "Need help?"

Her eyes flick to me, then redirect to the screw. Suddenly, some pieces drop from the machine and onto the tray.

Still squatting, she slumps her head forward with small exhaustion, then pops up.

"I still got it!" she signs, then blows on her knuckles and brushes them over her shoulder, clearly impressed with herself.

Dork.

I snort and shake my head. "I'm going."

She's putting the pieces to the espresso machine in the cleaning solution. "Okay, have a good night!" she signs, smiling as I push through the door.

Christ, this wind.

I adjust the collar of my coat, popping it up so it blocks my neck.

And they say Chicago isn't called the "Windy City" because of the wind.

My ass!

It's kind of true, though. People assume that the nickname was given because of the wind but the origins aren't entirely clear. Some believed it was coined the "Windy City" because Chicagoans were known for being "full of hot air."

These are the useless facts you acquire when you love your city and spend a lot of time in libraries.

My steps are brisk and I keep my head down as the wind pushes a few fallen leaves around me on the sidewalk.

It's nearly four o'clock when I arrive at the brick building and I quickly approach the desk. The librarian is an older woman with a tight gray bun and small narrow glasses that hang around her collar like a necklace. I hand her my book and she simply takes it and stamps the index card without even looking up at me.

I love this place.

But I can't stay today—hunger calls!

As if on cue, my stomach growls again as I push back through the door and start toward my apartment. The wind has calmed enough that my pace slows. At a more leisurely stride, I can't help but appreciate the familiarity of this route.

I like knowing that there's more scenic blocks than others. It's nice to know shortcuts, especially when we're in the thick of winter. I have an understanding with the homeless guy on my block who uses the resident's unwanted furniture as his own.

Fast food invasion be damned. No way in hell I'm leaving this neighborhood.

Graduating Northwestern meant goodbye to Evanston. I wanted to live somewhere within walking distance to the L because I sold my car and got a job with a local paper that was a short walk from the Belmont stop.

The rent was a little cheaper up in Edgewater so it seemed like a perfect fit.

Evelyn was still pursuing her acting career and she was living in a small place with a girl she worked with at the theater—just a ten-minute walk away.

She turned to face me, walking backward as we approached my new building.

"We should count the steps it takes to walk from your place to mine!" she signed.

I laughed. "Yeah, you get on that."

It was early summer, and we were going to get the keys from the landlord.

I pushed the apartment door open and Evelyn walked the perimeter of the empty living room, gliding her fingers against the wall. Her smile was serene and slightly whimsical. It was almost like she was saying, "Yeah, we can eat food and play games here."

The thought made me laugh as I continued watching her.

She looked over at me curiously. "What?"

"Nothing. Do you approve?" I signed back, then took a look around myself.

She nodded. "Going minimalist with the furniture, huh?"

"My parents are coming later with some stuff."

Her smile faded and I knew she was thinking about how the last time my parents came with furniture was when she moved in with Dean just a little over a year ago.

She quickly shook her melancholy shifting to mischievous.

"You know what this moment needs?" she signed.

I already knew, I didn't want to do it.

She grabbed my hands and started swinging them back and forth, then swayed her hips. Swaying turned into head banging, and head banging turned to jumping.

It was like watching the evolution of dance, but only if dance had never evolved past an uninhibited six-year-old's abilities. She pulled on my hands, trying to get me to join her.

I slipped my hands from hers and stepped back. "I don't dance, woman!" I signed, giving her my "old fart face."

Her words—not mine.

"We're not dancing—we're jumping!" she signed.

She took both of my hands, again, and pulled them back and forth, then swung them up and over us, forcing us to turn underneath ourselves. She laughed and her smile was real. It started to look the way it used to. Before she was sad. Before Dean left. I wanted her to keep smiling so I found myself starting to match her wild movements.

She twirled me, I twirled her, we both banged our heads. We must have looked bat-shit crazy, but I'd be lying if I said it wasn't fun.

We plopped to the floor after our rock out, laughing while simultaneously trying to catch our breath. She leaned her back against the wall with her legs stretched out and I sat facing her with my elbows draped over my bent knees.

"You're a good jumper," she signed, still smiling.

Oh, shit!

A biker nearly runs into me while crossing the street. He speeds away, flicking me off and I exhale hard, sending a small breath cloud into the air.

Asshole.

As I reach my unit at the end of the hall, I notice there's a sticky note stuck to my door. I peel it off and see a drawing of a cartoon egg with a mustache holding hands with an avocado with curly hair.

The egg has a talk bubble above it that says: "Avocado tell you, last night was fun."

I'm already smiling. My eyes slide to the avocado's talk bubble which reads: "Next time, let's grab an eggs-presso!"

I know it's nerdy, but this is actually really cute. I hold on to the sticky note and unlock my door, then cross the living room and stick the note to my desk. Heading to the kitchen to preheat the oven, I slip my coat off and walk to my bedroom, grabbing my phone out of my pocket to text Lexi.

> **Me:** Your drawing is eggs-ellent! Thank you :)
> I'd love to grab a coffee. How's Friday afternoon?

Jesus, I have no game. I pull off my jeans and exchange them for sweatpants, slipping on a white t-shirt. The light blinks from my phone, lying on my bed, and I grab it as I head back toward the kitchen.

Lexi: Sounds great :) Bohemia around three?

Damnit.

It makes sense that she'd suggest Evelyn's place. It's the closest coffee shop to the building and obviously it's the best in the neighborhood. But Evelyn is going to do something—*so many things*—to embarrass me.

They're going to spend time together eventually if we continue dating, so maybe it's best if it's sooner rather than later.

Who am I kidding? I'm a dead man.

Me: It's a date!

chapter seven

evelyn

Jab—cross—uppercut!

I kick the ever-loving shit out of the boxing bag, and damn, does it feel good!

I'm not really an athletic person. When I was in fifth grade, I joined field hockey for one day to collect my free stick and never went back. I ended up sticking it in the ground and using it to prop up a scarecrow I made, so I think it was worth it.

But boxing has a purpose. It offers a skill set to defend yourself and it gets my heart rate up like no other.

I started doing it the year Dean left. My paranoia and anxiety were skyrocketing, and my "therapist" Reggie suggested I start boxing to regain some control.

Plus, punching shit is fun.

After one more half-hearted swing, I drag my shaky legs toward the bench situated at the perimeter of the studio and wipe the sweat from my forehead with the back of my arm. I'm breathing like a rabid cow as I rip the Velcro seal of my gloves, then toss them in the sanitation bin.

"Girl, we're getting old," Reggie huffs.

All I can manage is a groan in response. Yes, I think that's what old people do when they realize they're getting old. I'm only thirty but sometimes I feel like I'm pushing sixty.

I sluggishly shuffle to the cubbies where we put our personal belongings and grab my water bottle, gulping half of it down immediately. My hands sloth, grabbing the rest of my shit, then I turn to give Reggie a sweaty hug.

"We're gonna make it, Reginald," I mimic an old woman's voice, cupping his face with my palm.

"I'll see ya at the pearly gates, Evelyn," he replies, in jest.

We're both too tired to laugh, but the corner of my mouth pulls up. "Text me when you get home!" I say over my shoulder, heading toward the door.

I slowly pull up the zipper of my hoodie and a chill runs through me as I slip my jean jacket over top. With one earbud secured, I tap my music app, hearing the epic, acapella beginning of "Fat Bottomed Girls" by Queen start to play.

Stepping out of the studio, the brisk air hits me hard. My face is still sweaty and my muscles feel tight—I should really stretch.

I have this thought nearly every time I leave boxing and I never do it. I don't eat enough leafy greens either. *Maybe one day.*

My walk back to my studio consists of contemplating my life choices and matching my stride to Queen's song. I pass by the Thai place below my old apartment building and the smell makes my mouth water. But I have food at home. And Thai is not a leafy green.

I arrive at my storefront in record time and unlock the door, stepping inside and disarming the alarm. I quickly secure the place again, and head toward the back room where the light always remains on.

After locking the door that leads to the dark staircase, my pulse quickens and I muster up the energy to run up the stairs, quickly entering my studio.

My heart rate evens and I toss my keys on the small table by my door, dropping my bag in the process. I pull off my jean jacket and drape it on my love seat as I pass, then wiggle one shoe off, then the other, leaving them in the middle of the floor.

I'm like Hansel and Gretel leaving breadcrumbs on their path so they don't lose their way. Except in my case, it's dirty clothes and stinky shoes.

What a slob.

I grab the soup from Mary out of the fridge and tap the buttons on the microwave to heat it up. While I wait, I pull my phone out of my pocket, seeing a message from Otis.

Otis: Lexi and I are grabbing coffee Friday afternoon. Don't be weird.

Hah. Does this man know me at all?

Me: I'm saving all my weird for that exact hour on that exact day.

The microwave beeps and I immediately grab the bowl. Years of burning myself behind the coffee bar have gifted me lumberjack hands so the heat doesn't bother me. I blow on the soup as I shuffle over to the love seat and scarf it down. I eat it so quickly that I barely taste it, but I think there was kale in there.

The leafiest of greens.

As I drop the bowl in the sink, my phone pings and I pick it up to check the text.

Otis: I'm serious, Evelyn!! This girl actually
likes me for some reason—be cool!!

I honk out a laugh. It's too easy to work him up. My heart pinches at his self-deprecation, though. Why *wouldn't* she be into him?

Me: Best behavior. Scout's honor!

I end the message with a sunglass face emoji and head for the shower. My hand cranks the knob, and I let the water heat to just below scalding while I peel off my sweaty clothes. When I step into the stream, my body winces before adjusting to the temperature before my muscles quickly relax.

"This girl actually likes me for some reason" is itching at my brain.

Otis is a total catch. He's sweet and smart and *tidy*. Annoyingly so, actually.

My small bathroom starts to fill with steam and the water cascades down my face, allowing my mind to float.

Dean left six months ago and I finally found a room to rent with a girl who worked at the theater with me. I couldn't afford the rent of mine and Dean's place by myself. Plus, I was basically being haunted by the ghosts of our epically failed relationship.

My new roommate spent most nights at her boyfriend's place, so I had the apartment to myself most of the time. Things could have been worse.

Otis had come over about an hour ago with beer and playing cards. He had the brilliant idea to turn the wholesome game "Go Fish" into a drinking game. We were sitting on the floor, playing our third round and had already polished off a few beers each.

"Any kings?" I signed.

He swayed his head back and forth and groaned, as he handed me the card.

Two sips for him!

His eyes bulged when he saw me drop all four kings down.

Make that four!

He shook his head and then took his drinks.

"Let's take a break," I signed.

He nodded and I stood to go to get us some food. I got a head rush and felt instantly buzzed as I walked to the kitchen, clipping the corner of the doorway.

"Oops," I giggled.

I walked back into the living room where Otis was laying on his back and saw me returning with some chips.

"Food!" he signed, throwing one lazy fist pump in the air.

I laughed, flipping on the gooseneck lamp that sat on the desk since it was starting to get dark. I moved the flexible arm so the light was shining toward us in the living room, then plopped down next to Otis and settled the chips between us.

I grabbed a handful and shoved them all in my mouth at once. I was wearing a V-neck t-shirt and some of the crumbs fell between my cleavage. My bra caught them like a champ, and I picked them out, popping them into my mouth, too.

Otis's crunching slowed so I peeked down at him and saw him staring up at me with an amused smile. "Charming," he signed.

I shrugged my shoulders, smirking, then redirected my eyes toward the far wall of the apartment where the lamp's light shined like a spotlight.

I raised my hands, placing my flat right palm over the back of my left hand and linked my thumbs, then started rolling my fingers from the tips to the base in slow, rippling movements.

Otis raised his head, looking at the wall, while the rest of his body still laid flat on the floor and a slow smile crept up his face.

It was the sign for butterfly.

He sat up fully and positioned his hands in a way that cast a shadow to look like a dog.

We went back and forth making all sorts of shapes and laughing at our failed attempts. The biggest failure was definitely when I tried to make a cactus that looked like a misshapen penis.

I grabbed my beer taking a swig, and Otis did the same. I leaned my head on his shoulder and we just sat there.

I got lost in the silhouette of our bodies leaning into each other on the wall. It felt like I was watching two lovers admire a sunset.

Still pleasantly buzzed, I took a deep inhale and drank in the smell of him. He smelled like the woods; pine and clean, with just a hint of the beer we were drinking.

I turned my head so that my chin was resting on his shoulder.

Peaceful. Safe. Warm.

I kept my eyes closed, savoring the feeling.

When I opened my eyes and peered up toward his face, he was looking down at me with the same calm expression. There was a hint of something else in his gaze, but I couldn't quite place it.

We stared at each other for what felt like hours but was probably only a minute. His throat slowly bobbed when I suddenly heard the keys jingle in the lock to the front door.

My roommate entered the dark apartment and eyed us with heightened curiosity as we sat on the floor.

"Whatcha guys doing?" She dragged her words out with insinuation then looked between us.

"Are those my chips?"

"Shit!"

I fumble to turn the knob as the water quickly becomes cold. Grabbing the towel from the hook right outside the shower, I wrap myself up as shivers pass through me, and I think it's only partially from the shower.

I haven't thought about that moment with Otis in a long time.

Goosebumps rise over my arms and I rub them up and down with my hands trying to warm myself.

It feels like my whole body is vibrating. My left hand holds my towel around me while my right hand starts to spell with shaky fingers.

Towel, soap, toothbrush . . .

Deep breath.

God, this has been a long fucking day.

chapter eight

otis

seven years ago

I was in the middle of studying for my last final of my junior year at Northwestern when I saw the light on my phone blink.

I sighed, shoving the phone into my back pocket. Dean had insisted we grab a beer but I really didn't have time. I still had to study for this final and I was starting a summer internship with a publishing house in a few days—but I just couldn't say no.

Lack of time aside, I needed some time with my brother. The only time I'd seen him in the last month was for his graduation a few days ago, and that didn't really count because we didn't actually get to talk. And we had some shit to talk about.

I shut my laptop and grabbed my wallet, then went down the stairs. When I pushed through the door, I saw Dean over by the designated smoking area and nodded in his direction.

His chin lifted back at me and he put the cigarette out on the bottom of his boot, flicking it into the dispenser.

I was worried about him. I was also fucking furious with him, but worried, nonetheless. He looked paler than usual, his brown eyes sunken, and his usually clean-shaven face was sporting a five o'clock shadow.

We quickly made our way to a sports bar not far from campus and ordered two beers, and some wings. Dean gulped down half of his beer almost immediately and I pinched my eyebrows as my concern heightened.

"You should be excited, man. You never have to do homework again," I signed. "Not that you did it a whole lot when you were in school, anyway."

I was trying to break the ice but his tired eyes met mine before he nodded and his eyebrows shrugged.

"Yeah, now I just need to figure out what to do with my life. No big," he signed.

I watched him nervously wipe the condensation dripping down his glass and take another sip.

My eyes drifted up to the TV replaying highlights from yesterday's game.

Ordinarily, Dean and I would have been speculating about their season, planning what games we were going to go to, but I couldn't bring myself to slip into that familiar territory. Not when things felt anything but normal between us.

"Did you talk to Evelyn?" I signed, hesitantly.

He closed his eyes, shaking his head.

I groaned. "Dean . . . come on!"

"What good will it do her to know?" he signed with pleading eyes. "Seriously. I'm actually asking."

"It's not going to do her any good at all, but that's not the point," I signed.

He took another sip of his beer and looked up at me. I didn't recognize the expression on his face. I barely recognized *him*. He looked like the ghost of my brother.

I eyed him cautiously, signing, "What's going on?" You've been off all semester . . . and now all this . . ."

Dean stared at me for a long minute. His eyes looked painfully torn as he blew a frustrated breath through puffed cheeks. I had never seen Dean cry, not once in our whole lives, but he looked like he was fighting back tears.

"I don't want to talk about this right now. I just wanted to see you," he signed.

Cryptic. "Why?"

Our last interaction had been anything but pleasant and if he didn't want to clear the air about that, I didn't really understand why he wanted to meet up so badly.

"I just did, okay?" he signed, clearly agitated. "You're going to be starting that internship soon—hopefully I'll find a job . . . it might be a while before we get to hang out."

The waitress came by with our wings, dropping them on the table with a stack of napkins. I quickly grabbed one, biting into it, then immediately dropped it on my plate.

"Holy hot!" I signed, trying to blow the heat from my mouth.

Dean chuckled at me from across the table, shaking his head. "You never fucking learn. They literally just came out."

I took a sip of my beer, trying to cool my mouth.

We eventually finished the wings and polished off our beers, then got the check, and walked back toward campus.

"Sucks that Sweet Lou is gone, huh?" Dean signed.

I guess it was impossible to not talk about the Cubs.

I nodded. "They could just hire a sock puppet at this point—just need to rebuild," I sign.

Don't we all, I thought.

It was kind of weird that he walked me back to my dorm but I was still thinking he might want to actually tell me what was going on with him.

When we got to my building, his eyes met the ground and he scratched the back of his head, nervously.

"Well, not that you need it—but good luck on your final tomorrow," he signed.

I looked at him skeptically. *Was this really why he walked me back?*

"Thanks," I signed, still confused.

Dean pulled me into a hug. I was so taken aback that I actually laughed, but gave him a quick pat on the back.

He stepped back, pulling his cigarettes out of his pocket, still looking at the ground.

"See ya, Otis," he signed before turning to leave.

But I grabbed his arm. "Talk to Evelyn. Please," I signed. "If you don't tell her, I will . . . but it should come from you."

His face paled further, and he swallowed hard before he nodded. When his eyes met mine again, they looked cavernous—dark and empty.

He stuck a cigarette between his teeth and gave me a parting nod, then turned around and walked away.

I actually started to worry that he might be on drugs. It would explain the erratic behavior and sunken appearance.

God, I really hoped that wasn't the case.

I went back up to my room and tried to get in a couple more hours of studying, but I felt this gnawing feeling in the back of my brain about Dean all night.

The next day, I was leaving my last final, when I saw Evelyn sitting on the bench right outside the building.

A smile pulled across my face as I walked toward her. But as I got closer, I noticed her splotchy cheeks and her hazel eyes were bright green with tears.

Her gaze caught mine and she slowly stood. When I was finally right in front of her, she stared up at me and her bottom lip started to quiver as she tried to hold back her tears.

I dropped my books on the bench and pulled her against my chest. Holding her tight, I felt her body convulse against mine with sobs and her hands grabbed the fabric on my sleeves as she hugged me back.

Actually, it felt more like she was trying to hold herself up rather than returning a hug.

Slowly, she pulled back, wiping her eyes with the heels of her hands, then took a stuttered breath in and released a hard exhale.

"He told you," I signed.

Evelyn hugged her arms around herself as her eyebrows slowly inched together.

She looked back and forth between my eyes like they were two guilty kids, and she was trying to figure out which one of them shit in the pool.

"Told me what?" she signed, her eyes widening. "Told me what, Otis?!"

"Dean . . ." I couldn't find the next words.

Her stare was accusatory, and I sighed, preparing to break my best friend's heart.

"I caught him with his ex, Haley," I signed. "They were . . ." I couldn't bring myself to finish. "It happened a few weeks ago. I'm so sorry. I thought . . ."

My eyes nervously met hers and the moment they did, I knew I would never forget the look on her face.

I'd never seen someone's spirit break, but I saw Evelyn's shatter right in front of me that day.

She had already seemed out of sorts through most of spring semester, but this . . .

She pulled her hands through her already wild, wavy hair, holding her head tight. Her face turned red and her nostrils flared as she bent her knees, digging her fingers into her roots.

Just a second later, she shot back up and locked angry eyes on me.

"What the fuck, Otis?! Why wouldn't you tell me that?!"

Her signing was hard and emphatic, and her chest rose and fell heavily.

She was glaring at me, waiting for me to answer her, but I didn't know what to say. She stood there a few moments more and her rage-filled glare slowly cracked, filling her eyes with tears.

Looking up toward the sky, she cried. "Why?"

Her eyes closed with a heavy blink as her hands slid down her face.

She wasn't asking for an answer, it was a lament and it pinched in my chest. I had never seen her so upset and I didn't know what to do.

Her stare narrowed at me, her anger returning. "And you tell me now? After he's fucking *gone?*"

God, she looked so heartbroken.

Wait—gone?

"What do you mean gone?" I signed.

Her eyes turned greener the longer she kept the tears in them. She was working hard to not let them fall and somehow that made me feel worse. But her icy exterior melted for just a moment, thawing to something resembling sympathy.

"You don't know?" she signed, searching my face. A bitter expression pulled at her features, avoiding eye contact with me. "Dean left. He moved to Colorado."

"What?!" I stepped toward her and ducked my head, trying to meet her eyes. But she wasn't having any of it.

A tear trickled down her cheek before she quickly swiped it away. "He left this morning. He called me from the airport."

There was no way he left. I just saw him the night before; he would have told me he was moving halfway across the goddamn country.

But then I thought about him needing to see me, walking me back to my dorm, the strange-as-fuck hug he gave me before he left. Suddenly, it made sense.

My heart started to race and I looked back up at Evelyn. She cradled her cheeks in her hands, then rubbed them up and down like she was trying to scrub the heartbreak from seeping into her pores. But my insides sank, and I swallowed the rising emotion creeping up my throat.

Dean left.

My brother—my best fucking friend—moved to a completely different state and didn't even tell me. He didn't say goodbye and he let me do his dirty work as a parting gift.

As my anger rose, I saw Evelyn's disappear. She was staring off into space just past my shoulder.

She looked . . . empty.

Glancing back up at me, the pain returned to her eyes for just a moment when they made contact with mine, then hollowed back out as she brushed past me and walked away.

I wanted to tell her to stay, I wanted to be there for her but she didn't want anything to do with me. I should have told her when I found out, but I wanted to believe Dean would do the right thing.

But he didn't. He left fucking Chicago.

In a matter of ten minutes, I lost the two people I cared about more than anything.

I sank down onto the bench, replacing Evelyn's heartbroken body with my own and sat there for hours in a shaken haze.

I was shocked to see a message from Evelyn, later that night.

Evelyn: Can you ride me home?

I wish I could have laughed at her typo but it killed me to think of her drunk and crying on a bar stool.

Me: Where are you?

Evelyn: Pump Dump.

Me: Be there in 15.

I pulled up to our favorite dive bar, texting her to let her know I was outside.

A minute later, Evelyn stumbled out the door and I flicked my flashers on to help her into the passenger's seat. After she was in the car, I closed the door and rounded the front to get back into the driver's seat.

She cried through the whole ride back to the apartment she shared with Dean. I maneuvered her up the stairs like a sad puppet and got her to bed.

I took off her shoes before I got her a glass of water from the kitchen and placed it on her bedside table. She limply grabbed my wrist and rolled onto her back.

"Stay," she signed. "Please." Then she rolled back on her side as her body still shook from sobbing.

She always signed.

Even wasted, heartbroken, and falling apart, she signed. It was probably the wrong thing to focus on, but it touched me just the same.

Of course, I stayed.

I made myself a bed on the couch and didn't sleep for one fucking minute that night.

How would I ever forgive my brother for this?

I had always counted on Dean and he had never let me down before.

I was so fucking mad at him when I found him with Haley. There was no excuse he could give me that would make me understand why he did it but I still believed that something bigger was going on. My brother was loyal to a fault, so I really thought there were bigger things at play.

But he left—like a fucking coward. He cheated on the best girl I'd ever met, didn't tell her about it and then left us both.

When morning poked through the window, I went to the kitchen to grab my phone off the charger, ready to send Dean a myriad of angry messages but saw that I already had one from him.

Dean: I'm so sorry, Otis. I promise I'll come back.

chapter nine

otis

Thursday morning rolls around and I'm *wiped*. I roll over on my pillow and face the other wall, like it's a different time on this side of the room and I don't have to get up yet.

I've spent most of the past two days at the library gathering source material for my book and creating some outlines. It's crucial to have an organized outline with short stories.

I'm happy with the progress I've made but when I'm on a roll with the book, I almost forget how to be a person. I forget to eat, shower . . . *sleep*.

Fuck, I really need to get up.

Whining through the whole damn process, I brush my teeth and splash some cold water on my face, then wipe it dry with my towel hanging by my shower. My eyes will barely open as I stare back at myself in the mirror and groan.

I need to shave.

I promise myself to do it later, then throw a thermal shirt on, swap my sweats for jeans, and shove my bedhead under a beanie.

There's a staff meeting at the office in about an hour and I desperately need caffeine. I'll stop by Evelyn's on my way to the L. She'll fix me.

As I exit my building and start toward the café, everything is *of-fensive.* The sun is shining, I'm sure birds are chirping, and I *don't like it.* When I step through the door at Bohemia, there's a small line at the register.

Fuck. My. Life.

Evelyn is behind the espresso bar and Mary is ringing in orders. When Evelyn spots me, she smiles and . . . *laughs?*

Why is she laughing? There is no joy this morning. *None.*

I'm waiting patiently while the woman in front of me orders the whole goddamn menu, apparently. Coffee orders require too many questions.

"What size? What milk? Do you need room for cream?"

I. Don't. Know. I haven't had my coffee yet. It's a sick game that the whole world plays.

When I finally step up to order, Mary smiles at me like a mom trying to cheer up her fussy toddler.

"Hello, love. Americano?" she asks.

I nod, trying to smile back but I think I only manage my old fart face. I pay for my drink, then walk over to the pick-up counter. Evelyn is moving behind the bar effortlessly, handing off a drink to the woman in front of me, then presses a button on the espresso machine.

"You look like shit," she signs, giggling.

I deadpan. "I'm dying."

Her eyebrows lift as she pours the shots into a paper cup.

"And you say I'm dramatic," she signs, then slides the drink toward me on the counter.

My eyes pinch, noticing it smells different than usual. I'm not equipped for surprises today, and she knows it.

"What is this?"

"Red eye," she signs with a smile. "Americano with an extra boost."

She starts to make another drink and I take a sip before grabbing a lid.

Damn. She's good.

"Thank you," I sign.

Giving her and Mary a departing wave, I head back toward the door, already excited for bed tonight.

I've never done crack, but I think the drink Evelyn made me had crack in it. The staff meeting passes by quickly and my mood lightens.

Before I know it, I'm back on the Northbound red line. The L has always reminded me of a dull rollercoaster but I really love watching the city from up here.

We reach my stop and I'm practically jogging down the stairs and onto the street, heading toward my apartment to get in a workout and grab a shower.

I have to go back to Bohemia and lock up for Evelyn later, so I figure I'll just post up there when I'm done at home. I've got a free-lance article to write so I figure I can just do that while I wait for the baristas to close the shop.

As I reach my door and put in the key, I feel a tap on my shoulder.

Turning around, I see a smiling Lexi. Her tight blonde curls are piled in a ponytail on top of her head and she's wearing thick, dark rimmed glasses with what appear to be pajamas.

"Hi," she says.

I smile and sign, "How are you?"

"Good," she says, wiggling her nose and pushing the bridge of her glasses up.

I take my phone out of my pocket because she only knows some basic signs and lip-reading has the potential of going horribly wrong.

There's a message from Evelyn, but I'll check it later and I open my notepad app to type:

You look so cute! I didn't know you wore glasses.

I turn my phone around so she can see what I wrote. She squints her eyes to read and her cheeks turn the slightest shade of pink.

I guess I can thank Evelyn's crack for my sudden charm.

She hesitantly reaches her hand out to take my phone, silently asking for permission and I nod, letting her take it.

I only need them for reading or drawing on an iPad. I was just coming back from the laundry room and saw you and thought I'd say hi.

I smile and quickly write back.

Well, they suit you. All done with work for the day?

And the crack has worn off, I guess. I seriously can't believe this girl likes me—*they suit you?*

Ugh.

But I've already turned the phone around to face her. She reads it and then nods, taking the phone back. She quickly types something and her neck muscles tense as she shudders, handing my phone back to me.

Almost. Mr. Adler has roaches upstairs and I have to supervise the exterminators.

My lips pull back and hiss, giving her a sympathetic look.

"But I'll see you tomorrow?" she says.

I nod and she gives me a small wave. I smile back at her as she heads across the hall into her apartment, then I push through my door and flick on the light. As I pull my coat off and toss my wallet on the coffee table, I check my message from Evelyn.

Evelyn: Change of plans. Reggie found a hot guy
to help him move his shit, so you're off the hook for lock up.

Me: Sounds good. Want to do something tonight?
Your drink has me wired.

Tossing my phone on my desk, I head to my bedroom to change into gym shorts. I take my shirt off and start with sit ups then grab my jump rope.

Sorry, downstairs neighbors.

I usually jog the neighborhood for cardio but I got a late start, so hopefully they're still at work or something.

Twenty minutes later, I drop from the lifting bar, panting, and head to the kitchen to grab a water bottle. On my way back to my bedroom, I check my phone.

Evelyn: HELL yes. This has been the longest week ever.
Bobby's has trivia and thirsty Thursday specials?

Me: Done! I'll meet you at your place at 7?

Evelyn: No, you're closer! I'll be at your place by 7.

She ends it with a party face emoji.

Okay, now I know she's just doing it to piss me off.

chapter ten

evelyn

Well, the entire neighborhood also decided to go to Bobby's tonight.

Otis and I take three steps inside and see there are no seats at the bar, no seats in any of the booths, and no room to breathe. One glance toward each other, and we immediately push our way back outside.

Bobbing in place, I quickly try to think of Plan B when an idea blooms.

I jerk my head indicating that he should follow me, and he warily falls in step.

He's right to hesitate. My last-minute ideas usually involve a lot of patience on his part, but I know he'll like this one.

We make the short walk quickly and he pauses when we reach the block of the old bar.

"The Pump Dump," he signs, chuckling.

It's actually called Pumping Tap House, but we nicknamed it the

Pump Dump years ago when we used to come here because—well, it's kind of a dump.

Upon entering the bar, I'm immediately hit with the familiar smell of stale smoke and musk. It smells like fermented nostalgia and "MMMBop" by Hanson blasts at an obnoxious level.

I chuckle, quickly noticing that our old booth is free and point for Otis to look too. He smiles and we head over, shrugging out of our coats and wiggling into our seats.

"Did it always smell like this?" Otis signs with disgust.

I laugh, nodding. "I'm pretty sure it used to smell worse."

A waitress approaches our table and I notice her making eyes at Otis. She reaches our booth, placing a couple of small napkins down.

"Hi, I'm Katrina, I'll be helping you guys out." She directs her entire introduction to Otis, who is fiddling with his watch.

"Do you guys need menus, or are we just drinkin' tonight?" She throws a glance my way but looks back to Otis for his response.

This chick has balls.

We could be on a date, little Miss Push-Up Bra!

I smile, despite my sudden, irrational possessiveness of my best friend.

"Hi, we'll take some menus, but I'll take a beer and a shot of tequila."

My eyes fall back to Otis, still taping his watch. I lightly nudge his foot under the table. "What do you want to drink?"

"Same as you," he signs back.

"Two of those, please," I tell Katrina, whose eyes are bouncing back and forth between us now. She nods once, handing us two menus out of her apron, then saunters away.

"You have an admirer," I sign, trying to wiggle my eyebrows.

He picks up his menu, pinching his eyebrows. He thinks I'm messing with him, which is fair. It's my favorite pastime.

I look over the menu, noticing they have typical bar food so that definitely means I'm getting grilled cheese. I'm pretty sure my life became infinitely better when I discovered that you can melt cheese on anything, if you want to.

Katrina returns with our drinks, placing them on the table in front of us, and Otis's eyes widen then shoot me a narrowed stare.

"Sorry, not sorry," I sign to him and he chuckles.

"What can I get for you guys?" Katrina asks, looking to me.

"I'll take a grilled cheese and fries, please," I say, like a real grown-up.

She scribbles it down on her small pad and then nervously looks over to Otis. He turns the menu on the table so she's able to read it and points to the Cowboy Burger.

His burger comes with onion rings. I will be taking one.

"Just wave me down if you guys need anything," she says, then heads back toward the server's station.

Otis gestures toward the drinks in front of us. "Why?"

I smirk, shrugging my shoulders. "It's been a long week."

Lifting my shot glass, he begrudgingly does the same and we take our shots, followed by immediate hacking.

An embarrassing amount of hacking.

Ugh. Why are shots so much more fun in your early twenties? We each take a long sip of our beers, trying to chase away the burning sensation from the shot.

"Gross," he signs, quickly taking another sip of beer.

I nod. "I know. Bad idea."

He chuckles through a residual cough, glancing around the bar with distant familiarity. "When was the last time we came here?"

I can't place the last time we all came here together, but I remember the last time *I* was here and Otis picked me up drunk as a skunk.

I see his expression shift and I know he's reading my thoughts.

Our superpower.

We don't really talk about that day. Otis always gets this sad, guilty look on his face on the rare occasion that we even acknowledge mine and Dean's relationship. But he has absolutely nothing to feel bad about. He was my lifeline when Dean left.

He helped me find someone to sublet the apartment I shared with Dean, and he helped me move *twice* in the six months following.

His brother abandoned me at a very dark time in my life and Otis helped bring in some light.

He was my biggest cheerleader when I told him my idea for opening Bohemia. He wrote my fundraising blurb and tracked my donations. He went to countless spaces with me when I was finally ready to look, and those are just the *things* he helped me with in the process. It doesn't hold a candle to the emotional support he provided. He's *still* my lifeline. I don't know what I'd do without him.

An appreciative sigh escapes me as I stare across the table at my best friend, who is looking at me like I might be high.

"What happened to you?" he signs. "Can't handle the big kid drinks anymore?" He gives me a small, teasing grin and takes the last few sips of his beer.

Oh, it's on.

I toss a small smirk back at him and chug the second half of my beer, flagging Katrina down while I still have the bottle to my lips.

She makes her way to our table, and I forcefully place the empty bottle down.

"We'll take two more of the same, please," I say, but also sign, so the funny guy across from me understands.

His eyes widen and I give him a challenging grin.

Fucking tequila.

The grilled cheese did nothing to soak up the alcohol and I am *feeling* it.

Why do I do the things that I do?

We've been playing Hangman in his small notebook for the last hour and our sentences have gone from silly to fully moronic. When I finally guess the last of his sentence, I'm on the final leg.

NEVER WEAR UNDERWEAR WHEN YOU DON'T HAVE PANTS.

And we're done. I find Push-Up Bra and ask for the check. She places the bill on the table and I hand her my card right away.

I need water and bed as soon as possible, if not sooner.

"I'll pay you back," Otis signs, moving for his coat pocket.

"You can get it next time."

He makes a face like he wants to argue but has forgotten how, and it makes me giggle. He's picked up the tab plenty of times we've gone out, so I really don't mind.

It was a fun night, and it was cool to come back here. Maybe we'll stop back before another seven years pass.

Katrina returns my card with the check. I leave her a good tip, then grab my coat and purse, exchanging a lazy smile with Otis as we wobble to stand.

The wind billows around us as we step outside. I can't even tell which way it's blowing.

Every year, I think I'll be more prepared for Chicago's brutal winters but I'm not ready yet. October just started, for God's sake.

"I'll walk you home," Otis signs.

It's useless to argue with him about it, and honestly, I hate walking alone at night.

We start in the direction toward my apartment. I keep my head down to shield my face from the wind but it doesn't really help and my body is buzzing with tequila, so watching my feet is making me dizzy.

It's not until we round the corner of the block, just passing the back alley to the bar that I finally look up.

chapter eleven

otis

I 'm already dreading the inevitable hangover I'll face tomorrow morning. My feet stagger and my head angles down, concentrating on putting one foot in front of the other when I'm stopped by Evelyn's hand on my forearm. My gaze floats to hers but she's staring straight ahead.

Her hazel eyes are wide, and the color has drained from her face as her fingers tighten and curl on my sleeve. My face finally follows her sight line to see what she's looking at.

Two men are standing directly in front of us. Their heads are tilted down with black hoods shadowing their eyes and I can only see the bottom half of their pale faces. The man in front of me has some kind of burn mark along his lips and the other one has cuts or acne littering his cheeks.

My eyes scan the dimly lit street, trying to gauge if there's anyone else around us. But the block is empty and uneasiness sobers me. A prickly tension creeps up my spine, but I try to appear calm as I give the guys a tight stare. My arm moves to take Evelyn's hand, when one of the guys charges us, grabbing Evelyn and pulling her into the alleyway.

Shock paralyzes me for just a moment before I lunge toward the guy taking her when the other guy's fist immediately connects with my jaw.

The unexpected hit stuns me backward, stumbling as I try to gather my footing. I'm still struggling to regain my balance, when I feel a tugging on my coat, pulling me into the alleyway that Evelyn just disappeared into.

It's so dark I can barely see anything, but my eyes still desperately search the area, looking for her, when suddenly, my back meets the brick wall behind me.

I'm pressed hard and heavy. The rough surface digs into the back of my scalp as my fists curl at my sides. I'm breathing almost entirely through my nose, trying to steady my heartbeat.

Is this really happening?

My panic rises and adrenaline pulses through me when I suddenly feel Evelyn's hand cover my tight fist.

I blink hard, trying to get my eyes to adjust to the black darkness surrounding us. Evelyn's hand squeezes around mine and my head jerks in her direction. The light from the street to my left is barely visible but my eyes are able to make out the shadowy figures.

The guy who grabbed Evelyn slowly snakes his hand around her neck. His face is only inches away from hers, then invades closer, moving his lips over her ear.

He's a dead man.

I jerk toward him but the guy in front of me backhands my face, hard, and that's when I feel it. Cold metal.

These assholes are armed?!

My head whips in the opposite direction of Evelyn, toward the street.

Pain pulses and throbs through my cheek as I look at the empty fucking sidewalk.

Someone. Anyone. Please.

But the street remains lifeless as the metallic taste of blood fills my mouth. I spit it out and wipe the back of my hand across my mouth, dragging in deep breaths. I weakly straighten myself up and stand back against the building.

My legs wobble but I use the back of the wall to help keep me upright as my eyes drift to Evelyn again. Tears stream down her cheeks, as she slowly takes her phone out of her pocket, handing it to the piece of shit holding her neck.

My body instinctively moves toward her but then I feel the heavy weight from the guy in front of me shoving me further into the wall. He has me by my coat collar and his hood has fallen. My stomach rolls as I catch the smell of tobacco and bile rises in my throat. I swallow hard, trying to breathe through my mouth.

The guy's face is so close to mine that I manage to see a large birthmark at the corner of his receding hairline. His hollow, beady eyes are penetrating as he pushes me further into the wall, his forearm pressing up against my neck.

It's hard to breathe but I don't want to risk making him trigger happy by trying to move his arm. I'm taller than him so I straighten my legs in an attempt to relieve some of the pressure crushing my windpipe.

His mouth moves directly in front of my face and I can see that he's missing some teeth but my eyes strain to read his lips. Still, I fumble to grab my wallet from my coat pocket, handing it to him.

He pushes off my neck and I cough from the pressure as he holds the barrel of the gun to my chest. My breath catches as I lean into the wall in a feeble attempt to put some distance between myself and the weapon as the guy barks something else at me, but I don't know what.

I squint, but that seems to agitate him more as his head juts down to my side. My eyes drift to my right, still unsure of what he wants.

I feel Evelyn's hand erratically grab my wrist, tugging on my watch. My breath quickens as he presses the gun harder against me and I quickly unlatch the wristband and hand it over to him.

My head stays facing the guy holding the gun in front of me but my eyes drift over to Evelyn.

The guy holding her has loosened his hand from her neck, but it's still pressed hard against her chest, rising and falling heavily with what I'm sure is panicked breathing. Even in the dark, I see her terrified eyes, wide and glistening with unshed tears.

Her lips tremble as she says something and I feel the gun pressing into me so hard it feels like it's branding me. My head jolts toward the man in front of me and he nods.

What?

My eyes move back to Evelyn, straining them to see as she raises her shaky hand, extending her thumb and pinky, and curling her other fingers into a fist as she lifts it toward her ear.

Phone.

The guy holding Evelyn shoves her hard into the brick building and I'm able to see the back of her head smack the wall.

My hand digs into my pocket, grabbing my phone and shoving it toward the guy, then I lift my arms up in surrender.

Please, God, just make this stop.

The guy holding me turns his head toward the other one and says something but my mind races in the distracted moment.

I can't take them both *and* grab Evelyn. They have at least one weapon, and they've already knocked me around. Any sort of attack seems futile.

I feel around for Evelyn's hand, again, and find her fingers moving frantically down by her side. Her anxious tick—she's fingerspelling. I lace her fingers with mine, turning my head slightly to lock eyes with her.

I'm with you.

I'm. With. You.

She squeezes my hand hard in return, giving me a small nod.

Suddenly, her eyes move back to the men and the muscles in her neck strain. Her face turns from terror to furious horror as her mouth begins to open wide. The man that was holding her down, swiftly covers her mouth with his hand, pulling her tightly to him, yanking her hand from mine. Her back is flush to his chest as she thrashes, but his grip holds firm over her mouth.

Why was she about to scream? Did she just notice the gun?

All reasonable thought falls away and I plow toward her when the guy in front of me punches me in the stomach. I heave forward, gasping for air. I can feel my diaphragm spasming as I struggle to take long, jagged breaths and peer up to see Evelyn still fighting against the guy holding her.

I still haven't caught my breath, but I start toward her again and I'm immediately struck in the back of the head by something hard.

The gun.

My body meets the ground, feeling like my brain is vibrating inside my skull. I'm rolling from my side to my back, trying to catch a full breath, trying to regain some control. As I roll again from my back, to my side, a heavy boot drives into my stomach.

Over and over and over.

Each blow knocks more air from me as I choke and curl, trying to block myself, wheezing through my nausea on the ground.

Is he going to kill me?

I can't let Evelyn watch me die.

I can't.

I fist the gravel beneath me, grabbing it so hard I feel it puncture my palms.

The guy moves behind me and I jerk forward from a sudden kick to my back, tasting copper as blood spills from the corner of my mouth.

My body can't catch up with the push and pull of his attacks. He yanks my shoulder so I'm lying on my back then situates himself on top of me. His dirty hands curl around my coat, lifting me slightly, putting us nearly face to face. My eyes meet his and his soulless face tilts.

He punches, again, knocking my head back but he keeps a firm grip on my coat so my head lolls forward again, glaring back at him through heavy eyelids.

The sadistic fuck *laughs.*

Rage ignites me; it races through me, quaking my beaten body. With every bit of strength I have, I draw my neck back and spit my blood in his face.

Our eyes lock, my breathing heavy and painful but I hold his menacing stare before his lips curl up, wiping his face and dropping me back to the ground.

I feel his hand move down toward the top of my collar and I helplessly bat him away, but he easily shoves my hands back and starts to unzip my coat.

What the fuck?

I can't breathe deep enough; my vision is spotty. He pulls something out of his pocket, but it's not until it catches the light from the street behind us that I see what it is.

A knife.

He flicks it open and holds it between his teeth as he unfastens the top few buttons of my shirt.

My eyes are struggling to stay open when something causes him to jerk his head back toward Evelyn and his partner. He removes the knife from his mouth and I see the muscles in his neck strain as he yells something back at them.

My eyes drift to the side, just past the inhumane fuck on top of me to look at Evelyn.

If these are going to be my last moments, I want to see her face—even if it looks devastated right now.

I feel a sharp drag on my chest and my eyes slam shut. My body tenses, shooting sharp pain through my abdomen but I fight to inch my eyes back open.

Evelyn.

I feel my heartbeat in my temples before my eyes pull shut, again.

I force them open, seeing Evelyn maneuver the man's hand down just a bit.

My eyes flutter closed again, and I lift my head slightly then drop it to the ground, trying to keep myself conscious. Peering through hooded eyes, I see Evelyn screaming. The light behind us illuminates her face, tight and terrified with tears pouring down her cheeks.

My eyelids start to close again, but I feel the weight on top of me lift. I weakly grab at the gravel, trying to stay awake as soft hands cradle the back of my neck.

My head is resting on something, but my eyelids feel too heavy to open. The familiar smell of wildflowers and coffee wafts through me and I strain my eyes open.

Evelyn leans over me, my head resting on her lap as she pushes some of my hair from my forehead. Her hands hold my face as her big eyes stare down, tears streaming from the corners of her eyes and onto my forehead.

"Otis . . . oh my God, Otis," she cries, tightening her grip.

She's . . . really beautiful.

chapter twelve

evelyn

My roommate in college claimed she could read palms. When she took my palm in her hand, she found it interesting that my heart line and my head line were connected by a line that she couldn't decipher from any of the principles of palmistry.

I'm sitting in an uncomfortable chair, staring down at my unreadable palm, the lines of which are outlined with my best friend's blood.

Otis is in my head line, he's in my heart line, *he's in my skin.*

The urgent movement and sounds of the ER waiting room all slosh around me, like I'm underwater. My unblinking eyes just stare down at my messy, illegible palm.

I curl my hand slightly, making the indents of the lines darker and deeper.

Bend, straighten. Bend, straighten.

I have no idea how long I do this, but it's long enough that I'm finally aware that I'm the weird woman watching her hand open and close.

There's a chance I'm in shock.

My arrival here starts to replay in my mind and my fist curls as the adrenaline starts to find me again.

They insisted on checking me for a concussion but I told them I'm fucking fine. I'm not the one who just got the life beat out of me. The cops took my statement and I begged them to contact Dean since I don't have my phone and I don't know anyone's number.

My heart begins to pound against my chest, making my fist clench tighter when I hear a heavy push from the door. My head shoots up and I see Dean rushing through . . . with Marnie.

Perfect.

"Evie!" Dean rushes toward me.

My balance wobbles as I stand and Dean pulls me into a tight hug. I barely return the embrace, but lightly wrap one arm around him.

I step back and he rests his hands on both of my shoulders urging me to look at him, but I keep my head down.

I was *useless* through that whole fucking nightmare. I watched in horror as a psychopath beat the shit out of my best friend—his brother—and couldn't do a goddamn thing.

My nails dig into my palms, keeping my eyes cast down as Dean speaks.

"Evie, talk to me. What the fuck happened?"

My eyes float up, but they repel Dean's face, sliding to Marnie instead.

She's really pretty. Strawberry blonde hair, pale blue eyes, porcelain skin—like Cinderella.

"Evie," Dean says, his voice quiet but desperate.

My eyes blink, and my gaze crawls to meet his.

Yep. Big mistake.

He and Otis both have brown eyes. Dean's always reminded me of chestnuts, and Otis's have a soft, amber glow to them. But they're the same Roberts' eyes—round, sweet, warm.

My knees buckle and Dean clumsily catches me before I fully collide with the hard tile floor. I can't catch my breath and tears bite the back of my eyes.

It's like my whole body stops working all at once.

Marnie books it. *Smart woman.*

But she returns a few moments later with a small cup of water and cautiously hands it to me like I'm a gremlin. Maybe I am.

Dean sits on the floor next to me, gently rubbing my back. "Just breathe, Evie. You're safe."

I'm *safe?* He thinks I'm having a breakdown because I'm worried about my safety? His brother could have *died!*

He doesn't know any of that, dumbass. You need to tell him what happened.

I push out a shaky exhale, taking another sip of water.

"I . . . we . . ."

Oh my God, Evelyn, spit it out!

I take a deep breath. "We were leaving the Pump Dump and two guys jumped us. We gave them all of our shit, but one of the guys was a twisted fuck and decided to beat the shit out of Otis anyway."

Finishing my water, I crush the cup in my hand as my knee starts bouncing. My brain is a bully and my body is the victim. I feel like I need to move, but I can't and my heart is having a fucking dance party between the war. Then, I hear Marnie's voice, "Oh my God."

I look up at Dean's wife. Her hand rests on his shoulder but her pretty features are tight, her eyes wide with concern as she stares down at me. I'm not sure if I see empathy or pity, but it's genuine.

I look back down at my bouncing knee and my fingers start to spell but I quickly run my palms up and down my thighs, trying to release my bubbling anxiety.

"Have you talked to the cops?" Dean asks.

My mouth flattens to a tight line, sucking as much air as I can through my nose.

I have to remember it's my anxiety and trauma that are making me want to punch Dean right now.

OF COURSE I TALKED TO THE COPS, YOU FUCKING DIPSHIT!

My voice is tight. "Yes. They've already taken my statement and I asked them to call you since I don't have my phone."

I don't know why Dean's presence isn't providing any sort of comfort right now, but he doesn't deserve my anger.

"Right, of course," he nods. "Have the doctors told you anything?"

"They took him in for surgery to stop the internal bleeding. He has broken ribs, a concussion that they're monitoring and they gave him stitches in his cheek, lower lip and ch—"

A lump rises in my throat and I swallow hard. I already had to tell the cops the full story, and I thought they were going to have to sedate me after. Otis probably doesn't even know how the whole thing escalated and why the bastard carved into his chest.

I catch a break when I see the doctor I spoke to—well, cried *at*—appear and I stand abruptly, rushing toward him.

"How is he?"

"The surgery went well. We're going to have to administer fluids and keep an eye on his blood pressure as he recovers," the doctor says, then gives us a closed-mouth smile. "But he's stable."

I let out a strangled sob.

He's okay.

"Can we see him?" I blurt out.

"Unfortunately, visiting hours don't start until six," he informs us, regretfully. "Are you immediate family?"

I shake my head. Not on paper, no. But he *is* my family. *He's in my skin.*

I look back down at my blood-stained palm, slowly blurring behind my tears.

"I'm his brother." Dean's voice is hoarse as he steps forward, his hand linked with Marnie's hand.

He's lost his fucking mind if he thinks Marnie is going back to see Otis before me.

"Follow me," the doctor says to Dean.

My tears fall and my heart deflates. Dean pulls Marnie into a side hug, kissing her temple but then releases her.

There's the smallest bit of relief that comes from Marnie staying behind, too.

But not enough.

Dean lingers in front of me, but my gaze remains on the floor. I feel the rise from the bottom of my stomach. It feels like someone lit a trail of gasoline from my intestines up to my throat.

In what inhumane fucking world does *Dean* get to go see him right now? Otis wouldn't even want him there! My hand shakes and my fingers move down by my side, trying to extinguish the burning in my chest.

Doctor, clock, desk . . .

I don't even register that Dean is still lingering in front of me until he lightly takes my hand in his, but I quickly jerk it away.

I need that hand.

He's just trying to help—he's worried too. This realization finally pulls my eyes up. He stares down at me sympathetically; his Cubs hat shadows his eyes but I can still see distress.

He sighs. "He's okay, Evie. I'll go see him. I'll tell him you're here, and then we can all go see him in a few hours. Okay?"

Hat, chestnuts, flannel . . .

My eyes are wide, trying to keep more tears from falling as they drift back down to the floor with a weak nod before Dean leaves with the doctor.

Dean's demeanor is unnervingly quiet when he comes back from Otis's room. He seems worse than when he got here. I'm dying to see Otis, but Dean's blank stare has me fearing the worst.

I need to do something. I'm going crazy.

My stained palm catches my attention again. I can't bring myself to wash it off. Standing from my chair, I walk the small distance to Dean, his eyes drifting up to mine as Marnie rests her head on his shoulder.

I swallow, my voice cracking as I ask him, "Can I borrow your phone?"

He shifts his weight toward Marnie, pulling his phone out of his back pocket. His thumb taps the screen a few times, putting in his passcode and as he hands it to me, I see his eyes widen.

My eyes dart down to my hand and I see he's noticed my palm. I quickly extend my other hand—the one that doesn't have his brother's blood on it—and take the phone.

My stomach tightens as I realize I still don't know anyone's number when Dean clears his throat, saying, "Reggie's number is still in there."

My heart lifts, just a little bit. It lifts at the idea of actually being able to talk to someone I love but also from the fact that Dean couldn't bring himself to get rid of Reggie's number.

The corner of my lips quirk as Dean looks up at me before I push through the door, quickly typing in Reggie's name.

Every ring back accelerates my heart rate, finally dropping when I hear the call connect.

"Well, I know this isn't a booty call," Reggie's sleepy voice drawls through the receiver and my chest starts to shake.

A cry squeaks from my throat, suddenly feeling tight.

"Evelyn?!"

I nod but then remember that he can't see me. "Y-Yeah. It's me, I . . ." I choke.

I suck in deep breaths between my sobs. For some reason, the comfort of Reggie's voice tightened my lungs.

"Breathe, baby girl. Breathe," he soothes.

It takes me a minute, and several more reminders from Reggie but eventually my chest expands. I stutter my way through the footnotes of the horror show and ask him to go meet Mary to open the shop for me.

"Anything you need," he says, tenderly.

My voice shakes as I respond, "Thanks, Reg." I swallow another sob. "Love you."

"Love you too."

At six on the dot, I sign in and stick my stupid visitor's tag on, then barrel my way to Otis's room.

I just need to see him. I'll feel better when I see him.

I push through the door a little too hard, stumbling a bit as I enter the room.

Beep. Beep. Beep.

My eyes blink to match the beeping of his machines. Something, *anything*, to let him know I'm here with him.

Otis . . .

I can't move. *I need to move.*

My fingers wiggle, releasing some tension. I move one heavy leg, then the other and slowly find the chair next to his bed. My body slumps down and I just stare.

So. Many. Bruises.

I scan my eyes over all the injuries, feeling a sharp pain as I notice each one.

Those monsters gave me a front row seat to this, and it will haunt me forever. I'm sure of it.

I stand up to get closer, brushing his wavy, brown hair off his forehead but cringe immediately, remembering the last time I did it was right after I screamed at someone to call for help.

His jaw and cheek are bruised, and there's some stitching in his lower lip, but otherwise, he looks like him.

Calm, sweet . . . handsome.

I lower the bed bumper down, pulling the seat closer to the bed and then gently wiggle my fingers under his palm; the one that held mine in the dark.

A painful sigh slips through my lips before I place my other hand over his, creating a little hand-cocoon.

I don't say anything. That's not how we communicate. I keep my hands in place, lay my head on the bed next to him, crying until my eyes finally close.

chapter thirteen

evelyn

seven years ago

I was convinced that baseball was a sport of prehistoric proportions. It was a hot September day, and we went to Wrigley to watch the Cubs for Otis's twenty-first birthday.

He was lucky I loved him so much.

Any baseball game I watched was doomed to go into extra innings. And not just one or two. My presence had the uncanny ability to stretch the game into a fucking series, like one of those film franchises where they split the last movie into two parts, usually resulting in a pointless part-one.

It was the bottom of the seventh and I had just polished off my beer. Wrigley Field was the only place that I ate hot dogs and drank watery beer.

Looking up at the scoreboard, I saw that we were down 0-1 when, of-fucking-course, the batter for the Cubs knocked a ball straight up into the stands.

Dean and Otis jumped up, hollering and clapping at the home run while I cursed the sports Gods.

Why do you hate me?

The boys fell victoriously back into their seats and I shook my empty beer can. I remembered Dean telling me that they stopped selling alcohol at the end of the eighth inning and I was not about to sit through extra innings without alcohol.

"I'm gonna go grab another," I told Dean.

He kept his eyes on the field. "I'll go with you," he said, making no attempt to move.

I snorted a laugh. "It's okay, babe. I'll be right back."

As I stood, Otis looked over at me. I pointed to my can and raised my eyebrows, asking him if he wanted another.

His boyish grin made my own smile stretch. He was having a blast, which made the hot misery of watching the dinosaur sport worth it.

"Thanks!" he signed.

"Well, if everyone's having another . . ." Dean said and looked up, squinting from the sun with the tilted smirk that made my heart melt.

I leaned down, so my lips hovered right over his. "You owe me big," I whispered against his mouth.

He pressed his lips to mine, rubbing the fleshy part of my thigh. "Anything for a hot woman who brings me beer at the ballpark," his voice was low and husky and it gave me chills despite the sweat dripping down my back.

I giggled, then straightened back up, noticing that Otis was laser focused on the field and I breathed a small laugh.

The Roberts boys loved their baseball.

I climbed the stairs to the covered area where the concession stands of overpriced popcorn and beer stood, noticing a long-ass line.

I groaned. Apparently, everyone knew about the eighth inning booze cut off. I saw a small bar with a few people sitting on stools, watching the game on the screen.

Why come at all if you're just going to watch it on TV?

Sports bars offered the same environment and the beer was half the price. Still, it looked like I could probably grab three beers a little quicker over there.

The bartender was busy with another patron so I leaned against the counter and waited. I could feel eyes on me from the stool just beside me but kept my gaze forward.

My peripherals were fully activated as I saw the man shift his body to face me. Continuing to ignore his leering eyes, I watched the bartender like she was one of the holes in a whack-a-mole game.

I kept my hand slightly raised so I could quickly flag her down when she finally turned around but the man to my right cleared his throat and the noise shifted my eyes involuntarily.

"Hey," he said.

I casually leaned away from him and gave him a polite, leave-me-the-fuck-alone, smile.

He was at least forty and reeked of beer and onions. He took another sip from his pint glass when the bartender finally came over.

"Sorry to keep you waiting. What can I get ya?" she asked.

I straightened my posture, saying, "No problem. Three house brews, please." I grabbed my card and handed it to the bartender. "You can close it out."

"No way a cute little thing like you can finish all of those," the man said as his eyes scanned up and down my body.

My face scrunched in disgust. The man moved closer and I was two seconds away from shoving him when I felt strong arms hug my waist. Jumping at the unexpected contact, I craned my neck to see who I was pressed up against.

Otis.

My body relaxed, a relieved breath passing through me. I nervously smiled up at him, but his eyes narrowed on the man next to us.

Throwing up a defensive hand, the guy leaned back on his stool, redirecting his attention toward the screen above the bar.

Sure, my obvious disinterest wasn't enough for him to back off, but the well-built guy staring him down did the trick.

What a pig.

Otis kept one protective arm around my waist as I turned to face him. "You're missing the game," I signed.

He smirked down at me. "I had to go to the bathroom and saw your 'don't fuck with me face' when I was coming back."

"My hero," I signed, batting my eyelashes dramatically.

He chuckled, signing, "You don't need a hero, just a shield," then let go of my waist and leaned on the counter space between me and the creep, sufficiently blocking the man from my view.

The corner of my mouth pulled up. Otis was such a good guy. I couldn't believe some girl hadn't scooped him up.

The bartender returned with our beers. I grabbed two of them and started to walk back toward the stadium, but stopped when I noticed Otis wasn't right behind me.

I turned around and saw him still standing near the bar, wearing an expression I couldn't quite place.

Guilty? Sad?

I wasn't sure. I closed the small distance between us and he lifted his gaze from the ground up to me.

My hands were full, so I just stared at him, silently asking if he was okay. A beat passed before his mouth finally tilted, nodding, and a sweet feeling swelled in my chest. It was like we had just read each other's minds.

His smile brightened before he turned around and grabbed the last beer, throwing one more glare at the bar fly who bugged me.

Another small laugh escaped me as I shook my head. It was cute that he was protective of me. And I was honestly relieved that it was him and not Dean.

Dean was . . . fiercely protective. When it came to people he loved, he let his anger get the best of him sometimes. Otis told me he used to get in a lot of fights when they were in high school.

He was quick to add that the altercations were usually in Otis's defense. Dean had zero tolerance for assholes. I admired the honor in that quality, but I also loathed violence in every way.

Otis and I walked back down the steps and took our seats. I handed Dean his beer, sitting down next to him and his eyes shifted to Otis, who still seemed conflicted about something.

Dean glanced back to me, asking, "Everything okay?"

I nodded, raising my beer and taking three big gulps.

"Just preparing for part two."

The Cubs won!

And it only took eleven innings . . .

Otis came back to our apartment to cap off his birthday with some Mario Kart. I usually cozied up with a book or worked on homework when they slipped into video games, but Otis wanted me to play.

He wanted me to play because I was fucking terrible and it provided unbridled amusement for the two of them. I fell off of every surface possible!

I pulled the plug after the Sherbet Land course. I ran into about ten bouncy penguins that knocked my poor Yoshi into the freezing cold water.

Dean stared at the TV, almost impressed. "Wow baby, I've never seen someone so bad at this game," he laughed.

Otis laughed too. "It's okay, you're good at other things," he signed.

I narrowed my eyes at him which only made him laugh more. His laughter slowed and settled into a sympathetic smile as he stood up from the floor.

"I'm going to head out," he signed.

"Wait!" I popped up from the couch and scurried to our bedroom, quickly returning with a small package and held it out to Otis.

His eyes widened and a surprised grin crept up his cheeks. He timidly reached his hand out to take the gift before his eyes drifted back up to mine.

"Happy birthday," I signed.

He took a minute to inspect the wrapping. I had wrapped it in Northwestern's student newspaper. Truthfully, I didn't have any actual wrapping paper and we always picked it up when we were at Northwestern because Otis occasionally wrote articles for it.

"It's silly, but I hope you like it," I signed, then looked at the package, urging him to unwrap it.

He peeled back the paper and his head nodded appreciatively when he saw what it was.

A copy of Shel Silverstein's *Where the Sidewalk Ends.*

He had told me about a month ago that he was trying to exclusively read Chicago authors and I was shocked to find out that he had never read the sweet childhood poetry of Shel Silverstein.

He turned to the dog-eared page I had folded down with my favorite poem: "Ickle Me, Pickle Me, Tickle Me Too."

He chuckled, his eyes glued to the book, then he slowly lifted his chin. A truly touched expression lit on his face and the warm feeling had my own smile pulling at my cheeks.

His arms wrapped around me and I hugged him back.

A moment later, his arms loosened signing, "Thank you, Evelyn. This is awesome."

Dean draped an arm around my shoulders, pressing a kiss to my temple. "So sweet, baby."

Otis looked back down at the book and Dean slipped his arm off of me to give his brother a hug, then walked him to the door.

Otis's expression seemed slightly sullen as he was leaving but evened out again as he turned around to face Dean. He tucked the book under his arm and signed, "Dude, you need to work with her on Mario Kart . . . she's really bad."

Dean laughed and clapped Otis's shoulder. "I know, man. I'll try, but she might be a lost cause."

I waved my arms wildly from a few feet away and they looked over. "Hey assholes, I can see you," I signed, giving them a *what the fuck* look.

They laughed again and Otis lifted the book in thanks toward me once more.

I flipped him off, blew him a kiss, and the three of us erupted into more laughter.

chapter fourteen

otis

My eyes flutter open and I instantly slam them shut again.
What the fuck?
I groan, feeling like the piñata at a kid's birthday party.
Everything hurts.

I swear to God, even my hair hurts. A flash of Evelyn looking down at me with bright green eyes and tear-stained cheeks snaps into my mind. I squirm but halt the movement immediately.

Fucking hell, that hurt.

My heart rate jumps as I try to keep still but notice my hand feels warm. I slide my eyes down to see a sleeping Evelyn hunched over the side of the bed, both of her small hands cupped around mine.

My eyes flinch and squint from the fluorescent light so I close them again, trying to piece together what happened.

We were at the Pump Dump ... we had some drinks, then we left ...

I suck in a sharp breath and wince.

Fuck! Ow!

We were mugged.

Not just mugged, but . . . I squeeze Evelyn's hand and close my eyes again. Her terrorized face flashes before me and I try to sit up, wanting to hug her—make sure she's okay—but before I even raise my head my body writhes, which only hurts more.

Holy fuck, I need drugs.

Evelyn stirs but her eyes remain closed as she rubs her thumb back and forth over the back of my hand, then she jolts up and her eyes bulge as she closes in on me.

"Oh my God, oh my God, oh my God . . ." she says over and over, getting as close as possible to my face. Her hands latch to the sides of my head and she gently presses her forehead to mine. My eyes close but open again when I feel her body shuddering and her breath staggering as she holds me to her, face to face.

Pulling her head back just a little, she keeps her hands in place as she examines me, like she's not entirely sure this is actually happening.

She looks exhausted. Her hair is piled in a mess on top of her head and she looks paler than usual, with dark circles under eyes. Her eyes are bright green and bloodshot, evidence of her sobbing. They well up even further directly in front of me as she drops her chin.

She cries so hard; I feel it deep inside me. She sucks in huge breaths only to cough them back out again, but she keeps her hands planted on the sides of my head. She's holding gently but her fingertips grip like she's holding onto the edge of a cliff.

I want to lift my arm and hold her back but my limbs feel like they weigh a goddamn ton and moving hasn't gone well so far.

Through her tears, she pulls away from me, grabbing a small pitcher and pouring some water into a plastic cup, then offers it to me as she wipes some loose tears.

I carefully nod, trying to lift my arm with no success. All I manage to do is shrug my shoulder which still fucking hurts.

Seriously. Drugs. Now.

Evelyn places her hand on my shoulder and shakes her head, encouraging me not to move. She pops a straw in the cup, slowly lowering to my lips and I chug it down quickly. She immediately pours another, then another until she signs, "Good?"

Oh my God, her hand.

I grab her hand, and flinch from the abrupt movement, tightening my grip. I breathe through the pain and Evelyn's other hand rests on my shoulder. I loosen my hold on her hand, then turn it over, looking for a wound. But I don't see one.

She gently pulls her hand from mine. "I'm okay. It's not . . ." she signs, hesitating before adding, "It's not mine."

Jesus—she has my blood on her hand?

My face softens as the pain subsides and I realize she's not hurt. She sits back down, gently taking my hand in hers again, continuing with her small, aimless rubbing. I rub my thumb back and forth over her hand too. It's the only movement I can manage right now.

Her mouth twitches ever-so-slightly at my small comfort but frowns as her eyes drag along my body, like she's memorizing my injuries. She shakes her head, closing her eyes and breathes deep before her hand squeezes mine, then releases.

"Dean was here," she signs, standing. "And Marnie."

My eyes widen.

Cool. That doesn't hurt.

But man, that sucks. I feel a different ache when I think about how lonely and scared she must have felt after what happened. It's one thing to deal with Dean at the café, but to be stuck in a waiting room with him and his wife immediately following a traumatic night surely only added to her hysteria.

"I should call him. He took Marnie home and I told him I'd let him know when you woke up," she signs, but lingers beside the bed.

She doesn't want to leave.

I gather every bit of strength I have to curl my fingers into an 'E' hand shape and slowly lift it toward my mouth. I tap the 'E' by my mouth and then take my index finger and thumb, pulling them from the center of my lips out to my cheek.

"*E. Smile.*" Her name sign.

Her mouth slowly pulls up through her tears, before she gives a gentle nod and leaves.

It's dark. I'm pressed up against a brick wall by a man in a black hood as a hand holds mine tightly at my side.

My head slowly turns to see Evelyn's wide eyes staring ahead at a man in front of her. I move to hold her—comfort her—but the weight holding me against the wall is too heavy.

I shift my eyes back to the hooded man in front of me, but I feel Evelyn's hand pulled from mine. My head snaps back in her direction, her mouth is covered and she's being hauled away, disappearing slowly into darker darkness.

I writhe under the weight holding me down, but it won't budge and my eyes shift forward again.

Hollow eyes stare back at me and a sinister smile inches up the hooded man's face . . .

My breath catches in my throat and I jerk awake, staring up at the ceiling tiles while pain radiates through my whole body.

Goddamnit.

Waking up is heavy pain and sleeping is dark terror. This has been the cycle all day and it's starting to wear on me.

Last time I woke up, I was informed that they'd be keeping me here another night for observation, which is bullshit. They're just racking up my bill and ensuring they don't get sued if I die because they let me leave before they *watch me not die* for another twenty-four hours.

My head drops to the side and I see my brother sleeping in the chair next to my bed. Evelyn ran to my apartment to grab a few things. She made sure to mention she was bringing back my body wash, too—not-so-subtly hinting that I smelled like shit.

I open and close my fists and that doesn't hurt. I raise my arms slowly, bending them at the elbows; still good. I straighten my arms and start to lift but immediately drop them back down.

Well, that fucking hurt.

I groan and suddenly notice Dean shift in his seat, his eyes blinking rapidly as he straightens out in the chair.

"You okay?" he signs.

I tightly nod, huffing out a heavy exhale.

"The doctor stopped by while you were sleeping. He said a full recovery could take up to six weeks. You'll need to rest and move as little as possible," he signs.

Fan-fucking-tastic.

He slowly stretches his neck, then stands, pointing down to the remote that controls my bed, asking if I want to sit up. I barely nod but he understands and hits the button that lifts my upper body so that I'm sitting upright.

I raise my arms so that they're hovering just over my lap and it still hurts, but it's manageable. I drop them down, still feeling defeated and wince again.

Dean's eyes shift nervously. "Do you want to come stay with us till you're able to get around?"

Nope. Not even a little bit.

I shake my head but luckily my inability to move quickly masks my strong objection to that idea.

"Do you want me to call Mom and Dad?"

Holy Christ, which one of us got a concussion last night?

I *do* shake my head hard at that, then wince again.

"Easy," Dean signs, and I try to swallow my irritation.

I know he's just trying to help, but I don't want his help. I don't want help at all. I hesitantly look up at him and he runs his palm down his beard, exhaling hard.

"What are you going to do, Otis? You're going to need help getting around . . ." he signs then lowers his chin, massaging the back of his neck. "At least for a little while."

I really don't know what I'm going to do. But I can't stay with Dean, and my Mom will drag my limp body back to Rockford by my feet if she hears about this. She already hates that we live in the city.

The doctor comes in with a small woman trailing behind him. He gives me a small wave, but I can only manage my old fart face in return.

"How's the pain?" he asks, and the woman beside him signs it.

"Painful," I sign.

The corner of his mouth draws back as he looks over the chart at the foot of my bed.

"I'm going to have one of the nurses administer more morphine soon. But I just wanted to stop in and give you some referrals for some therapists that I think you should consider contacting." The doctor waits for the woman next to him to finish signing, giving a small nod.

"Post-traumatic stress tends to sneak up on us. It can manifest in all kinds of unpleasant ways. I highly recommend you talk to some-one," he says, leaving a piece of paper on the table.

He parts with another small nod and the woman follows behind him like a tail.

I lean my head back, looking up at the ceiling.

Therapy?

I look down at my body that I can't move and a humorless laugh escapes me. Between the unrelenting pain, the nightmares, the likes of which don't provide any real clarity of what actually happened last night, I feel my resolve holding on by a thread.

Dean shakes his hand low, getting my attention. "Do you want me to stay here tonight?"

Snap.

"I don't need a babysitter, Dean! Just go home. I'm fucking fine!"

The movement coupled with the anger tensing my body sends ripples of sharp pain through my abdomen and I breathe heavily as my fists ball the fabric of the sheets down by my side.

Dean stares at me but he doesn't look angry. He's looking at me like someone might look at an old photograph that got caught in a house fire or something.

My breathing evens and my fists release, trying to reel myself back in. This isn't his fault, but his presence doesn't seem to be helping either.

"I'm sorry," I sign. "But really, just go. I'm just going to email the paper and try to get some more sleep."

He looks unconvinced but still nods and starts toward the door.

"I'll be back tomorrow," he signs.

A nurse opens the door and passes by him and he leaves.

The nurse comes over to my bedside and pushes some liquid into my IV. She's my new best friend so I smile up at her.

"Ten minutes," she says clearly, and smiles back down at me before leaving the room.

Five minutes later, I'm willing time to speed up, as Evelyn creeps through the door wearing a backpack, holding a plastic bag on one arm and carrying a book in her other hand that she drops as she enters the room.

Why does this woman never use her bag to carry her shit?

Still, seeing her clumsy ass lightens my mood. I chuckle as I watch her gracelessly bend to grab her book and her focus shoots to me. She gives an apologetic smile as she straightens back up and walks to the chair, plopping her stuff onto the seat.

"I thought you might be sleeping; I didn't want to wake you," she signs.

"Loud noises suck when you're trying to sleep, huh?" I sign back to her, waiting for her to realize the ridiculousness of what she said.

She does, and immediately falls forward with laughter, shaking her head before she digs through her backpack.

"Mary made chili," she signs, grabbing a thermos out of her bag and placing it on the side table.

So she does keep things in there.

"Thanks," I sign.

She smiles and I feel my own mouth inch up. Her smile is the stuff of magic, like a Mary hug.

She turns on her heel, going back to the chair to get something out of the plastic bag she brought with her. She pulls out a box the size of a brick and hands it to me.

My eyebrows hitch when I see it's a new phone.

I lift the box appreciatively, thanking her, and her chin dips in a small nod.

"The guy at the store said we should be able to recover anything that's stored on our clouds," she signs, shrugging.

Our clouds. The way she refers to "our clouds" has me cracking up for some reason. I'm imagining her cloud and my cloud are just up there floating next to each other, holding all our data, sharing secrets, playing cards.

The drugs must be kicking in.

The laughing hurts my stomach, but I can't stop.

She's giving me a confused smile. "What?"

"Do you think our clouds are friends?" I sign, still laughing.

Her eyebrows pinch but she can't seem to help but laugh, too. "I want some of whatever they gave you."

She moves the bed bumper, as she calls it, then sits next to me on the mattress. Our laughter settles and I start to get lost in her big hazel eyes. They've looked so sad all day, but there's some light back in them and it's giving me a fuzzy feeling.

She rests her cheek on the top of my head and I lean my head into her, trying to savor this small comfort on an otherwise hellish day.

Eventually, she folds forward, starting to take the phone out of the box.

"I'll pay you back," I sign.

Her face drops and my eyes search hers. She stares back at me with sadness she can't seem to shake and I remember then—it's the last thing I said to her before we left the bar.

My hand laces with hers, resting my forehead on her shoulder, wishing I'd never said it, wishing so badly that none of this ever happened.

chapter fifteen

evelyn

I leave the hospital when the staff makes me leave. "Visiting Hours end at nine, ma'am."

Fuck you, nurse! Do I look like a ma'am to you?

No, Evelyn, she was being nice. You look like something that gets caught in the drain right about now.

Otis is sleeping when I leave, thankfully.

The trek home feels like a dream. My latest read, *Verity* by Colleen Hoover, sits closed on my lap as I stare at the CTA map on the side of the L car. The multicolor transit lines all swirl and blur together in the Loop and it feels like a diagram of my mental state.

Somehow, I end up back in my studio and linger in the doorway, feeling like I teleported here when my phone buzzes.

Mom: Hi honey! How's tomorrow for a catch up?
I miss you so much!!

My insides drop and I follow. I slam the door shut with the back of my body, sliding down as guttural heavy cries bellow out of me. I cry so hard that my fingertips claw at the floor and my body heaves.

I can't breathe. I can't fucking breathe!

I force my mouth closed, sucking in a deep breath through my nose, trying to calm myself down. My fingers shake . . .

Lamp, loveseat, floor . . .

Deep breath.

Book, bowl, blanket . . .

I sit and spell for long minutes and my cries soften slowly, my breathing evens—but I stay put on the floor until I can be sure the moment has passed.

Never have I ached to hear my mom's voice so badly. I want to call her, crying and falling apart, and let her wrap me in a warm blanket of comforting words.

"It'll be okay, sweetheart."

My thumb trembles over my phone, imagining her voice. But if I call her, I'm not sure I'll be able to stop talking.

My shaky knees push me off the floor and stagger toward my bed.

> **Me:** So sorry, Mom—emergency with the café.
> I'll call next week. I promise. Love you.

I immediately fall, passing out on my bed before even taking my coat off.

"How's our boy?" Reggie asks as I scrub the shit out of the morning rush dishes.

"They're discharging him in a few hours. I asked Mary to come back and close up so I can go meet him at the hospital."

Mary deserves a raise. Actually, Mary deserves a monument, but a raise will have to do. She came in this morning with a lasagna tray and endless hugs.

I finish the dishes, wiping my hands dry with a small towel then grip the edge of the sink, suddenly overwhelmed. Reggie comes up behind me and rubs between my shoulders as I feel tears emerging in the back of my eyes and shut them tight.

I'm *so sick* of crying. At this point, I don't even know what these tears are for. Are they aftershock; are they because it's Saturday? *Who the fuck knows?*

"What do you need, Evie?" Reggie asks softly.

My throat tightens and my voice cracks as I tell him, "I don't know."

I really don't know. My emotions feel out of control and I don't know what to do. I hope I'll feel better when Otis is home, when he's moving toward actual recovery.

I turn to Reggie, pulling him into a long hug. He holds me tight, almost like he's trying to transfer some strength into me. We pull apart and he tilts my chin up to look at him.

"You are Evelyn Fucking Gray. You've got this," he nods, decidedly.

His confidence helps. Reggie has seen me through a lot and he's always believed in my ability to overcome. And so far, I have . . . kind of.

I take a deep breath, trying to match his resolve.

I am Evelyn Fucking Gray. I'm going to pick up Otis from the hospital, he's going to agree to let me stay with him while he gets his strength back, and I am going to learn to cook.

My manifestation is persuasive. I believe everything but the cooking part.

The ride from the hospital to Otis's apartment is . . . awkward. We're in Dean's truck and I'm seated between the two brothers like a sandwich made with Roberts bread. I can't even remember the last time the three of us were together like this. It seems like a different life.

We pull up to Otis's building and Dean flips his hazard lights on, then hops out of the truck and rounds to the passenger's side door.

Otis tenses, staring up at the roof of the car, bracing himself. I gently take his hand in mine and squeeze it. He looks over, giving me a wary smile.

Dean opens the door and holds out his arm for his brother to hold on to, and I sit there.

God, woman, do something!

I reach behind the passenger seat to grab Otis's laptop bag but manage to spill some papers out. Gathering them up, my body twists into the back seat like a pretzel and by the time I've actually retrieved the bag and sit back up, Dean has gotten Otis out of the truck. Otis moves slowly, holding onto Dean for support, but I can see he's hating every minute of it.

He punches in his code to the front door and as we enter, I'm hit with a shitty realization.

The stairs.

I silently curse the old building I once loved for it's charm and now resent because it doesn't have a fucking elevator.

Otis shakes Dean's arm from his side then grimaces from the sudden movement. My fingers timidly touch his shoulder as I step in front of him at the foot of the staircase. "Let him help you. It's three flights," I sign.

He darts his eyes to the railing and holds it hard.

I stand still, unsure of how much I should press him. His eyes drift back to mine and I hold his stare for just a moment before glancing nervously over to Dean right behind him.

Dean's head shakes, ever-so-slightly, and I sigh, looking back to Otis. "Slow," I caution, and he nods.

Dean's mouth straightens into a tight line. He takes a deep inhale as his eyes drift up the staircase, stepping back slightly but staying close behind Otis. I situate the laptop bag across my torso and follow Otis slowly up the stairs.

Every time he raises his leg onto a new step his face scrunches in anguish. As we reach the first landing, his breathing becomes shallow and the veins in his neck begin to bulge.

"We should take a break," I sign.

Sweat pools at his temples as both of his hands grip the railing. I reach into his laptop bag and pull out the prescription we picked up on our way here, and plop myself down a couple steps ahead of him, noticing his knuckles turning white as he fights through the agony.

His head slowly lifts to look at me and I wiggle the prescription bag like a prize. "You get the goods as soon as we get up there," I sign.

It earns me a tight smile from Otis while Dean stands behind him, basically as a spotter.

"Ready?" I sign, after a few seconds more.

We continue our painful pace up the next two flights.

After giving Otis his pills and helping him into bed, I fill up a bag of ice from the kitchen and wrap it in a small towel for his ribs.

He settles the bag across his abdomen, and I take a minute to glance around his room. It occurs to me now that I haven't spent much time in here.

He has a *ton* of books. In addition to the large bookcase in his living room, he has another small one in here. My eyes land on the other bedside table, and I see a framed photograph. Taking a few steps, I pick up the frame to get a better look.

It's us.

We're in front of the Bean, both wearing cheesy grins and his arm is hooked around my waist. I'm on my tip toes, trying to hug his neck, with one leg lifted and bent back, while my other arm is up in the air.

My smile stretches wide. *I want a copy of this picture.*

As I set the frame back on the table, I look over at my best friend. He's watching me with a dopey look on his face, while he adjusts the ice pack across his belly.

"Good to be home?" I sign.

He responds with a lazy nod.

"I'm staying here tonight," I sign, my eyes cautiously ready for an argument.

"Okay," he signs back

Huh. Thank you, painkillers.

His eyes drift close and I leave. I keep the door cracked and walk back into the living room, but I'm surprised to see Dean lingering in the small entryway.

"Aren't you double parked?" I ask.

"Yeah. I just . . ." He exhales hard and stares at the floor. "It just feels wrong to leave him like this."

I feel a tug in my chest and my Dean walls lower just a little. I haven't seen the vulnerable side of him in a long time and to be a witness to it now has my heart on a seesaw.

"I'm staying with him." I clear my throat, adding, "He won't be alone."

Dean's eyes float from the floor to meet mine and something about the eye contact feels surreal. This is such a strange situation to be in with someone you once knew so intimately but who is now basically a professional acquaintance.

"You don't have to stay here, Evie. I can figure something out," he offers.

"It's only five minutes from the shop. It's no trouble." I shuffle my feet. "I *want* to stay here."

He looks down at me with conflicted eyes and still seems hesitant to leave.

I don't know *this* Dean, but the Dean I knew all those years ago would be gutted about what's happened to Otis. He'd probably be canvassing the neighborhood—pounding the pavement—trying to find the assholes and take out his own form of justice.

I have a feeling *this* Dean wants to do that too. He just no longer feels entitled to protecting his brother and the thought alone makes my heart ache.

"He's okay, Dean," I say for both of us.

He moves suddenly, startling me, and pulling me tightly to his chest. My body tenses and my arms don't react right away, but slowly, eventually, they wrap around him too.

"I'm so glad you're okay, Evie," he says quietly, still holding me.

A strange emotion crawls up my throat, but I swallow it back, giving him a pat on the back and then pulling away from the embrace.

He looks toward Otis's bedroom, then back at me. "You'll call if you need anything, right?"

I nod, still not really sure what's passing between us right now. He glances back at me once more, then opens the door and leaves.

My hand starts...

Couch, coffee table, carpet . . .

chapter sixteen

otis

E velyn has lost her damn mind. She's always been insane, but I think something has finally snapped. She's in the kitchen, and she's cooking.

Like, actual food.

It's been five days since I left the hospital and it's the first day I haven't slipped in and out of consciousness every hour. Part of me is grateful since my nightmares have only gotten more intense. But I'm not sure they're worse than being stuck with my thoughts all day.

Evelyn helped me move to the living room before she left for the shop this morning so I could watch some TV. She gave me strict instructions to not move until she stopped back here for lunch.

I believe her exact words were: "Don't. Fucking. Move. Or else."

She came back to my apartment after work with a bunch of grocery bags. I figured they had another sale on the giant tubs of cheese puffs but five minutes later she came out and asked me if I had a colander.

She's been in the kitchen for nearly twenty minutes now, so I know it's something more involved than a microwave dinner. I can smell garlic and oregano and occasionally, I see her tasting something she's stirring from the cut out in the wall that overlooks the living room.

I just hope she doesn't start a fire; getting me out of here in any sort of timely fashion would be damn near impossible.

The pain in my ribs is the worst of it, but as long as I lay down and don't move too suddenly, the discomfort is bearable. Aside from getting up to go to the bathroom, I'm pretty much always resting, and it's pretty fucking miserable.

I nearly lost my shit earlier when I thought Evelyn was going to try and help me change my clothes. I wasn't mad at *her*—just the unbearably aggravating reality of not being able to take care of myself. But I'll throw myself through the goddamn window before I have Evelyn changing or bathing me.

Every ache feels personal. If I move just a little too quickly, if I allow my brain to shut off from all of this for just a second—I get a shooting, painful reminder somewhere in my body.

My chest expands from a heavy inhale before I release it with a huff. I can only hope that if I take it easy now, the recovery time will shorten, and things can start to go back to normal sooner rather than later.

Evelyn emerges from the kitchen with two bowls in her hands, carrying them slightly higher than normal like she's presenting a masterpiece.

She places the bowls on the coffee table then scurries back to the kitchen. When she returns, she places a plate with garlic bread down between the two bowls.

"Ta dah!" She wiggles her fingers over the dishes.

Somehow, it makes me chuckle, despite the tension building inside me.

My back is propped up on some pillows against the arm of the couch and I slowly move to put my feet on the floor and face her, but my body contracts, flinching from the small movement.

Goddamnit.

"Don't move!" Evelyn signs. She takes a piece of the bread, plopping it in my bowl and I take some shallow breaths as the pain still ripples through my abdomen.

Wow . . . This actually looks really good. And it smells fucking incredible.

But tension still holds my body, irritated that I can't move to sit with her properly.

"What's wrong?" she signs.

Damnit, of course she noticed.

"Nothing," I lie.

Her mouth tilts sympathetically and her eyes move back and forth like she's trying to devise a plan. After a moment, her eyebrows lift and she tosses a piece of bread into her bowl, then slides it on the coffee table, closer to the couch.

She rounds the side of the table and nervously looks at my outstretched legs. She bends and gently lifts them, just barely, so they're hovering slightly above the couch. It hurts but it's tolerable.

I'm thinking she's going to move me like a rag doll until I'm in a seated position and *that* thought truly makes me want to crawl into a hole—not that I fucking could right now—but she carefully wiggles herself just underneath my calves so that my legs are resting on the top of her thighs.

This is new.

She glances over at me, signing, "Better?"

I nod, feeling a genuine smile pull at my lips; the soft feeling almost feels foreign given how defeated and irritable I've felt all day. My fork plows into my bowl and Evelyn slowly leans over my legs to pick hers up.

Holy shit, this is delicious. I start to pile the pasta into my mouth faster, only taking a break for the garlic bread.

The only reason I slow down is because my mouth is full, but my eyes close, savoring the flavor of the rich, homemade sauce. When I open my eyes, Evelyn is facing me with a wide grin. She adjusts her bowl so she's only holding it with her left hand.

"You like it?" she signs.

I nod emphatically but keep the lower half of my body as still as possible. Evelyn finally takes a bite, wiggling beneath my legs, as a small smile inches up her cheeks.

Watching her enjoy warms me more than the hot, homemade food coating my stomach.

She's still running the café, hauling back and forth between her place and mine, and now she's cooking us meals.

I've been caught in the bullshit of my bitterness all day, but things could be worse. *I need to remember that.* I could be going through this alone.

But I'm not.

Evelyn's the most loving person I know, and I've never been so grateful to be someone she cares about.

She was so pretty.

It probably wasn't cool to be thinking that about my brother's new girlfriend, but I couldn't help it. I thought she was pretty when I met her at the Arts House too, before she even met Dean, so I couldn't feel too guilty about it, right?

Evelyn was a theater major at UIC, which is where Dean went to school and he was all too excited to get her number and "meet up on campus."

He asked me to meet them at a coffee shop in Edgewater. Evelyn could sign and knew a decent amount of vocabulary but she couldn't carry on a full conversation.

She took my notebook and wrote something, then handed it back to me.

I took ASL in high school but I really want to get
better. Will you teach me?

I looked up at her and smiled. Dean had his arm draped over her shoulder, sipping his mug as she shyly smiled back at me.

Dean had dated Haley for two years in high school and she never cared to learn sign language, even though Dean and I were pretty much always together. I really didn't like her. There were a few times I'd caught her staring at a reflective surface, watching herself while she pretended to listen in a conversation with someone.

Evelyn was the complete opposite. She was lively and present and pretty in an effortless sort of way. Dean had only been seeing her for a few weeks, but he was completely smitten. I thought it was cool that she saw how close Dean and I were and wanted to be able to communicate with me when we inevitably all hung out.

There was a small, illogical thrill I got from her asking me to teach her. Dean was just as fluent—he learned it with me, basically, so he easily could have taught her.

My eyes drifted to my brother, but he was whispering something in Evelyn's ear then pressed a kiss to her temple. I darted my eyes back down to the notebook, trying to distract myself from the strange bit of jealousy.

I'd love to!

I slid the notebook back, across the table between us, trying to avoid witnessing more PDA. She leaned forward and picked it up, then wrote a quick response:

Thanks Otis! Let's do lessons here. Coffee on me!

The moment felt oddly prophetic and I didn't know why. Maybe it was because I could see that Dean was crazy about her or maybe it was because I was making a new friend, which didn't happen often. But something about the moment felt like it was already a cherished memory, like she was someone I already knew—someone important. For the first time in my life, I had an instant connection with someone.

Evelyn carefully wiggles out from under my legs, pulling me back to now and my body shifts as I clear my throat.

The memory of how pretty she looked that night wasn't something I let myself think about in a long time.

Why am I thinking about it now?

Evelyn takes my bowl, signing, "Want some more?"

I shake my head and her expression turns guilty.

"What'd you do?" I sign, with light accusation.

Her mouth gapes but a smile pinches the corners. "The kitchen . . . *may* look like a war zone," she signs. "But don't worry, I'm going to clean it!"

I chuckle and barely start to move when Evelyn's finger shoots out toward me. "Stay!"

A groan vibrates in my throat. I never thought I'd be jealous of clean up duty but *holy hell*, this sucks.

Why did this happen?

It's been ticking through me all day.

I just don't fucking get it. We gave them our shit. If they wanted to kill us, they could have so what was the point of beating me senseless?

An image of Evelyn being torn from my hand, on the brink of screaming flashes through my mind.

That's when it turned. But I don't know why.

It's possible that there's no reason at all for why the guy did this to me. I'm thankful that Evelyn wasn't physically harmed the way I was, but the fact that she wasn't only furthers my confusion.

Why me?

Evelyn comes back into the living room with a mug of tea and her laptop. She plops on the floor in front of the coffee table and I feel a pang of jealousy at her ability to easily drop to the floor, then immediately feel guilty for feeling jealous.

These emotions are fun.

She must have better insight—at least she could hear them.

My hand waves low, getting her attention and her eyes meet mine but her face quickly falls.

When you're deaf, you communicate a lot with body language and facial expressions. Evelyn and I have known each other so long and have become so close that we say a lot without saying anything. She's called it our superpower, but right now I think she feels like it's a curse.

I don't want to talk about that night either, but I just need to know if I'm missing something. Their attack didn't seem like it was planned or I imagine they would have beaten us first, possibly even killed us, and then taken our stuff.

It seemed . . . *personal.*

I see Evelyn's hand fingerspelling down by her side and a heavy sigh escapes me. I hate making her relive that night, but maybe it will help. My anger is simmering constantly, ready to boil over at any given moment and it's becoming too much to manage.

"Evelyn, why did they do this to me?"

chapter seventeen

evelyn

My hand is moving and he notices.

Goddamnit.

I just want to go back to watching him eat. It was the first time since this whole fucking mess that I've actually seen him enjoy himself. I was already searching for some recipes online, trying to decide what I would make tomorrow when he got my attention.

I can't explain it, but I knew the second I looked at him that he was going to ask me. Partially because I've always known we'd have to talk about it but also because I swear, we can read each other's minds sometimes.

I sigh. "You sure you're up for talking about this?"

I'm hoping he changes his mind and decides to save it for another night.

Or never, his choice.

He nods, signing, "I know it sucks, but I just want to know what you know."

Well, that breaks my heart. *He's* the one that got the shit beat out of him and he doesn't even know the full story.

It's the first day he's been awake for more than an hour at a time, so I haven't really been able to have a conversation with him, but I'd be lying if I said I didn't want to put it off as long as possible.

I need to ease into this. Rising from the floor, I start slowly toward the couch. My eyes fall on his legs, stretched across the length of the seat before I glance at his face, silently asking for permission to resume my earlier spot under his legs.

It was nice to sit that way through dinner.

He nods, letting me know that it's okay and I repeat my movements from earlier, scooting beneath his calves. Except this time, I make sure that the side of my torso is pressing into the back of the couch cushions so I can face him and he can see my hands.

I notice then that I'm holding my breath and my lips whistle out a shaky exhale. I don't want to make him talk about this either, but I need to know what he remembers. Plus, I'm a coward still trying to buy some time.

"What do you remember?" I sign.

He stares at me a minute, then lifts his shoulder.

"Just that we were mugged. We gave them what they wanted. I thought they might let us go, and then I saw you start to scream," he signs, but stops abruptly.

His fists start to curl on his lap and his eyes fall to look at them, like he's crushing the memory in his hands. I lay my hand on his leg, trying to ease his tension, attempting to keep him *here.*

His fists eventually release and the tightness he's holding in the rest of his body loosens.

"The guy grabbed you and held you back while the other guy . . ." He trails off and his eyes squint.

Nearly killed him.

119

His eyes clamp shut and he shakes his head, releasing a heavy exhale and then looks back up at me.

"That's all," he signs, his shoulders slumping.

I mean, he did get the gist of it. I can see him fighting a war to keep his body still while he's surging with anger.

I'm honestly in awe of him right now. It was obviously difficult for him to revisit the memory. But he muscled his way through it, and now he wants to confront the things he doesn't know.

Not like me, who falls into a black pit of despair remembering dark things. My palm holds his leg a little tighter, hoping to absorb some of his strength.

I remember learning about the Greek goddess Antaeus in school, who renewed her strength whenever she touched the Earth. Maybe Otis's leg can renew mine.

I am Evelyn Fucking Gray.

I hold his leg, trying to steady my heart, giving myself an internal pep talk.

I can do this. *I can do this.*

My hand is stuck to his leg.

Fucking hell. I am *not* a Greek goddess and Evelyn Fucking Gray is a wuss. Attempting to delay the inevitable, again, I start my recollection from the beginning, but Otis stops me.

"I know all of that, already," he signs, urging me forward.

I fill him in on a few details he might have missed because they were things the men spoke about. I'm pretty sure they were addicts. There may or may not have been a third accomplice waiting for us if we ran.

But my heart begins to race, knowing the next part is where I blew it and tears begin to fill my eyes.

"When you didn't hand over your phone, I told them you were deaf, and that's when I signed 'phone' to you . . ."

My signing becomes slow and rigid. "The guy holding me was ready to knock us out and leave, but the other guy . . ."

I want to die right now. I really want to die, but he deserves to know the truth.

He's honest with you, even when it's hard.

"He asked me if you spoke at all. When I told him no, he said . . ." A sharp inhale inflates my chest as I picture the creep's disgusting grin. His evil laugh as said, *"Just the right hit and I'll make this mother-fucker scream."*

Swallowing hard, I sign, "He said that he bet he could make you say something . . ."

My eyes clamp shut and my tears arrive, trickling down my cheek.

It feels like I'm there again. I swear I can feel the same roll through my stomach as I did when it was happening.

My eyes are cast down, across from Otis. I can't look at him.

"I lost it and the sidekick grabbed me. I could barely breathe; he was holding my face so tight. The guy beating you had no fucking mercy."

I'm shaking, but I need to get through this. It feels like I'm about to melt or explode, I'm not sure which one. My hands open and close a couple times, trying to steady themselves so I can finish the hideous memory.

"The guy holding me was trying to get your guy to stop and get out of there. He was on top of you but when he turned around, I saw he had a knife."

My eyes float up to his chest, where the guy cut him and more tears fall. I shake my head back and forth like maybe it will loosen the vivid-ness of that night.

It doesn't.

"My guy must have lost his nerve, because his grip loosened just enough that I was able to bite his hand and scream. Someone from the street heard me and called out into the alley and the guys ran."

I finish the end of the story in quick emphatic movements, like it would exorcize the pain if I did it really fast.

Like ripping off a band-aid. Or duct tape.

But I feel no relief. *None.*

"I'm so sorry, Otis," I sign through my tears, finally looking up at him.

Oh my God, his face.

He looks like someone revisiting wreckage as they take in all the damage. His jaw ticks before he clears his throat suddenly. My body jerks in surprise at the unexpected noise when I see his expression turn to something I've never seen on him.

Rage.

He swings his legs off of me, planting them on the floor in front of us. His torso doubles over while a hiss escapes through his teeth as he tries to breathe through the pain, which only seems to anger him more and he slams his fist into the coffee table.

I'm not scared of Otis; I'm *not.* But I've also never seen him this angry. I want to bring him back to me. I timidly reach my hand out to touch his shoulder but before I reach him, he abruptly stands up, recoiling for a second and then takes slow, deliberate steps toward the bathroom.

I pathetically follow behind him, desperate to help, but he continues on without looking back before he opens the door and immediately clicks it shut.

The shower has been running for half an hour when I finally hear the water turn off. I've already decided that I can't push him to talk to me right now. I'm only here because I wanted to help him until he's more mobile. But if he needs time alone, he's entitled to it.

This *is* his apartment. Maybe I'll go stay at my place tonight. But I also don't want him to feel like I'm abandoning him.

Jesus Christ, one conflicting issue at a time, please.

The couch is situated in a way where I can't see the bathroom door, but I hear it open followed by his slow footsteps. Pushing off the couch, I go to see if he wants help but as I reach the archway, I stop.

Nothing prepares me for the sight of him half naked with a towel tied around his waist. His biceps are toned, bulging as he uses the wall for support, and even though he has harsh bruising along his abdomen, the muscles are lean and cut.

Oh my God. You are gawking at your best friend, you perv.

The unabashed staring continues as I notice his damp, tousled hair with some loose pieces falling over his forehead. *What would it be like to sift my fingers through it and grab hold?*

Whoa. What the actual fuck?

He stops walking when he notices me standing there like a fucking weirdo. His facial expression is that of confusion and irritation, which is fair.

For the love of God, Evelyn, get your shit together!

My eyes drift to the large bandage on his chest and that seems to slightly knock me back to reality.

"Need help?" I sign. Pretty sure my mouth is hanging open.

He shakes his head and continues, but I open the bedroom door for him anyway.

As he passes me to get into his room, I drink in his clean scent. He smells like the woods took a bath.

He smells like the woods took a bath?!

He pauses in the entryway, staring down at me and I tilt my head up to meet his gaze from a foot below. My back is against the open door while his arm is situated on the molding for support and we stand in this strangely charged moment.

Bitch, you need to leave.

And that's what I do. I finally move out of the doorway and Otis continues into his bedroom. I scurry back to the living room, grab my shit and haul ass out of there.

> **Me:** I'm gonna give you some space, I know tonight was a lot . . . I'll be back in the morning before I open the shop. Let me know if you need anything before then.

He doesn't respond. *Why would he?*

Oh my God, I can't believe I basically eye fucked him right after I recounted the worst night of his life.

I can't believe I eye fucked him, *period.*

He's Otis.

He's Otis.

chapter eighteen

otis

I need to chill the fuck out and stay put. I've resumed my *resting position* on the couch but there is nothing restful about my clenched body right now.

It seems that Evelyn, in her hasty departure, threw an ice pack, my painkillers, and a water bottle on the couch before she ran out of here.

I popped the painkillers immediately before I situated myself back on the couch and now—I'm just trying to get my body to relax.

It's an endless cycle of pain. Learning *why* the twisted son-of-a-bitch did this was so much fucking worse than I could have imagined. My entire body is pulsing with anger and it's leaving me in excruciating pain, which makes me squirm, only making it worse.

Sadistic dominos.

But for as much pain as I'm in, I still find my mind drifting to Evelyn . . .

What was that?

I've never seen that look on her face. *I could have sworn she was looking at me like . . .*

I shake the ridiculous thought from my head. She was probably horrified at the sight of me stubbornly suffering through unnecessary movement.

Get a grip, dumbass.

A frustrated growl erupts as I slowly reach to flick off the light. I'm sleeping on the couch tonight since I've already moved around too much.

My eyes stare at the ceiling, burning in this special slice of hell. I can't move and I've just learned that the reason I can't move is totally fucked. Plus, I think I freaked out Evelyn.

The drowsiness slowly kicks in as I remember that she texted me. I grab my phone but drift to sleep before I can respond.

I'm on the ground. I can't move.

A vile looking man is on top of me with a knife, laughing. He dangles the blade over my chest and then cuts into me.

I weakly thrash, trying to pull back from the sharp drag, but it's useless. My eyes drift just behind the man, just over his shoulder.

Evelyn is being held by an equally horrifying piece of shit, as the man on top of me continues to carve into me, but I keep my eyes on her.

Her eyes are wide and full of terror. The man holding her has his hand clamped over her mouth, but she bites it hard, letting out a tear-filled scream.

The man on top of me quickly moves off and charges at Evelyn. Any bit of strength I can find is trying to move, trying to stop him.

But I can't move. All I can do is watch.

He grabs her by the neck, pinning her against the wall. Evelyn cries as she stares back at the man, but then her eyes drift to mine. My fingers stretch down by side, but the rest of my body lies limp. I hold Evelyn's stare with mine.

I'm with you.

I'm. With. You.

The man glances back at me and his disgusting smile widens. He draws his knife back, plunging it into Evelyn's stomach.

"No!" I scream.

"No, no, no, no!"

My eyes bulge open and I helplessly gasp for air. Small, warm hands hold my face and the smell of wildflowers and coffee hits my nose.

Evelyn.

She helps me sit up on the couch, grabbing the extra pillow from the floor to prop me up against the arm rest. My breathing is erratic and a film of cold sweat lines my forehead as she hands me some water, keeping one hand firmly on my shoulder.

It's so dark in here, I can barely see her.

As if reading my mind, she leans over me to flick the light on, putting me face to face with her cleavage peeking through the top of her shirt.

This helps.

She settles on the sliver of couch to my side and looks at me in a way that makes my heart ache.

That *fucking* dream . . .

"I'm having them too," she signs.

Pulling her tightly to my chest, she gently wraps her arms around my torso. It hurts but I need to feel her right now. That nightmare was so vivid. It feels like *that* might be real life, and *this* is the dream.

Please, God, I hope this isn't the dream.

I pull back, but keep my face close to hers, running my thumb along her jaw and staring deep into her eyes.

This is real, right?

I'm a man possessed. My hands clutch each side of her face, pulling her mouth to mine—just a gentle brush to each other's lips before I swallow hard, my grip tightens, and I crash my lips against hers. Her fingers immediately dig through the sides of my hair, grabbing the unruly strands for leverage, deepening the contact.

My tongue slides to the seam of her lips and she opens for me, pulling me closer, our tongues tangling desperately.

A low groan rumbles through my chest, working my mouth against hers just as the vibration of a small whimper escapes her mouth and flows into mine.

And *holy fucking God,* it's my undoing.

Losing control, one of my hands slides to the small of her back pulling her closer—I *need* her closer. But the pull shoots a sharp pain through me, forcing me to jerk and break our fused lips.

We pull apart, foreheads pressed, our heavy breathing mixing between us. Her hands remain in my hair, while one of mine cups her face, and the other one balls the fabric on the back of her shirt, like we're both holding on for dear life. Finally, opening my eyes, I see that hers are still closed.

Another second passes before her big hazel eyes flutter open and immediately widen. She pulls her hands from my hair, and I drop my hands as we stare at each other.

Holy shit.

We just sit and stare.

Now that I know I'm not dreaming, my heart starts to race. We've been friends for almost a decade and never navigated through anything like this. I never thought anything like this would ever happen between us.

I'm trying to reason with myself: It's late, I just dreamt a reimagined version of our attack where she was murdered, and then she shoved her beautiful boobs in my face. *That's it.* I just got carried away.

But she kissed me back.

"We should get some sleep," she signs after another long minute then readjusts her shirt.

Good. She blames her boobs, too.

"What time is it?"

"A little after midnight," she signs, starting to stand.

"You came back," I sign, realizing she only left for a couple hours.

"I'm sorry I left." The corner of her mouth turns up, apologetically. "I'll help you get to bed."

I should definitely *not* stand up right now. My dick is rock hard, and I've embarrassed myself enough tonight.

"You take the bed," I sign.

Her face pinches. "Why?"

Great question. Why, Otis?

"I think I overdid it earlier," I sign back.

The dual interpretation of the excuse is not lost on me.

Her teeth tug her bottom lip into her mouth. She looks concerned but I can't seem to focus on anything other than the fact that that lip was just in *my* mouth. I readjust under my blanket, hoping she doesn't notice.

Thankfully, if she does, she doesn't make it known. She quickly goes to the kitchen, returning with a new ice pack.

"Goodnight," she signs, flicking the light off behind my head, then disappears behind my bedroom door.

Back in my *resting position,* I fidget slightly, then wince.

Goddamn.

I'm on the couch with a raging hard on and Evelyn is in my bed.

What is happening?

chapter nineteen

evelyn

The café is slammed this morning. There's something going on at the school this weekend and it's bringing in a bunch of newcomers. I usually *live* for this.

The busy morning *has* provided a decent distraction, I suppose. It's given me no time to think, and to be honest, I'm so exhausted that it's taking most of my energy to just pretend I'm an actual human being right now.

When the rush finally dies down, I'm able to clear some mugs off one of the tables. My tired eyes zone in on the mug wall, landing on Otis's ugly-ass mug, which has hung unused since the attack.

My mind floods with memories from last night; hearing his distressed moans while his body writhed, his terrified eyes when he woke up, the relief they found when he saw me—followed by delirious need before he kissed the life out of me.

I flinch, smacking my forehead like it will knock the memory from my brain.

It doesn't. And ow.

Otis and I *kissed*. And not just *any* kiss . . . it was a, *saw through space and fucking time* kind of kiss. I shake my head, redirecting my attention to the dish collection. My sluggish legs drag from the seating area to the back room when Mary stops me.

"Love, don't take this the wrong way, but you look completely knackered."

I don't know what *knackered* means but I can only assume it's a nicer word for shit.

"Just didn't get enough sleep. I'm good," I say with a shrug.

It's true, but the reasoning for why is *not* something I'm ready to talk about. Giving her a strained smile, my feet stagger back through the swinging door.

I crank the faucet and then load the mugs into the sink. As it fills, my hand digs through my pocket to fish out my phone.

Almost time to go back.

In all the years I've known Otis, I can't ever remember a time when I felt like I needed to avoid him. I've never felt nervous or worried about what he was thinking because our connection is so strong that his thoughts and feelings have become my sixth sense.

I drag my hands down my face then slide them to the sides of my head, feeling like it could use the extra support right now.

How did this happen?

Honestly, I blame my addiction to romance novels for the whole thing. They sensationalize stupid lapses in judgment like this, embellishing them into earth shattering, romantic grandeur. It was just a kiss for God's sake.

Don't forget about your shameless ogling in the hallway!

I groan turning off the sink, then twist and lean against the edge of it. Frustrated hands pull at the roots of my hair and my eyes clamp shut. When I reopen them, I catch a glimpse of my reflection in the small window above my desk and inhale sharply.

131

Christ. I look like Doc Brown's exhausted stunt double.

I try to tame the frizzy mess, and head back out behind the counter. Grabbing a to-go cup, I fill it with coffee to bring to Otis. If he's feeling okay, he might be working and would probably appreciate the caffeine.

Mary catches me again on my way out. "Give that boy a hug around the neck for me!" she says, smiling, and I don't tell her that I can't hug him right now because I ate his face last night.

"I'll be back in an hour so you can get out of here, Mary. Thank you!" My mouth tilts sheepishly.

I don't deserve this woman. She's been pulling extra hours and handling things that are most definitely *not* part of her job description. I have to figure out a way to manage this new routine in a way that doesn't inconvenience other people.

Despite the wind whipping around me as I make the short walk to Otis's apartment, my feet drag. My right hand starts to spell but then my fingers absentmindedly float up to my lips, tracing them.

His mouth on mine, his hands on my face, his tongue . . . he's a really good kisser.

A growl erupts from deep in my throat as I approach his building. I punch in the code and then slowly climb the stairs. Outside Otis's door, just like I've been countless other times, my heart flutters as I push the key in and linger another moment before pushing the door open.

Breathe. It's just Otis.

As I enter, his back is to me, leaning against the arm of the couch while he taps on his laptop. I move to flick the light switch that controls the overhead light, just to let him know I'm here, when he lifts his hand in a lazy wave.

See, nothing's changed. He knew you were here before you even made it known.

I push out a shaky exhale as I walk into the living room. Rounding the couch, I offer him the coffee and his eyes widen.

He nods appreciatively, carefully reaching out to take it, signing, "Thank you!"

Our fingers brush as I hand him the cup and it feels like an electric shock. I jerk, then stand there awkwardly as my eyes meet the floor. When I glance back up, Otis is smiling, but his eyebrows pinch slightly as he takes a sip of his coffee.

You're being weird.

Good God, I'm so tired and the flip-flop cadence of my anxiety is only exhausting me more.

I walk to the other side of the couch, pulling my coat off. "Are you working on an article?" I sign.

"No, they haven't sent me my assignment yet. I'm trying to get some work done on the book."

Flip.

Now *that* makes me smile, and there's nothing forced about it. It's hard to keep creative passions alive even under regular circumstances. I was worried that the trauma from the attack might delay the project altogether.

A relieved exhale pushes through my lips. "Hungry?"

"Starving," he signs, then takes another sip of his coffee and sets it down on the table.

He seems . . . totally fine. Maybe I'm making too big of a deal out of this.

I nod then go to the kitchen and make us some sandwiches. When I come back to the living room, he closes his laptop, giving me a tilted smile.

I hand him his plate, my eyes drifting to my new spot on the couch, under his legs. I take the less confusing seat on the floor in front of the coffee table and he settles his plate on his laptop. He pauses before taking a bite, like he noticed my absence on the couch as well, but he doesn't say anything.

Flop.

Why is he so okay? I know I'm the eccentric one of the two of us, but he seems so normal. He actually seems *better* than normal and I'm over here with the cast of *Inside Out* running rampant through my brain—like all of the emotions met in the middle of my head and all shrugged their shoulders, simultaneously.

Someone needs to do something!

"Want to watch a movie tonight? I can pick up some wine on the way home!" I sign.

Apparently, *someone* was fear, and *something* was stupid. I immediately regret the suggestion. Wine always carries these romantic undertones, but I don't really know why. I've displayed some of my least charming behavior whilst wine drunk.

Ugh. I can't take over-analyzing my thoughts. Not with him.

"Sounds good," he signs, flashing a boyish grin at me, giving my heart a small flutter.

Friends don't flutter for each other, dipshit.

I have *got* to calm down. One mind-blowing kiss will not derail Otis and me. Ten years of steady, dependable friendship will not be taken down by *one* moment.

I've given up on lunch. I wasn't even hungry to begin with, but Otis has finished his sandwich already.

Plate, table, laptop . . .

I see him notice my hand, but he doesn't say anything about it. He never says anything about it.

Flip.

This is Otis. He knows me better than anyone. I take his plate and my sandwich to the kitchen. I wrap my sandwich and save it for later then wash both of the plates.

In the quiet moment alone in the kitchen, I feel my heart start to race for no obvious reason. Struggling to breathe deep enough, my hands grip the counter, trying to ward off the climbing panic coming out of fucking nowhere.

Flop.

The more I try to calm myself down, the more unstable I begin to feel.

What the fuck?

I pull the fridge door open and grab a bottle of water, shutting the door with more force than I meant to. After I've gulped down most of the bottle, my head leans against the freezer door.

The cool surface feels good on my clammy forehead and I stay there for another second while my heart rate evens, slightly. I twist and lean against the fridge and my eyes drift up, landing on a loose flake of paint on the trim of the kitchen doorway.

Gloria and Paul Roberts were the quintessential parents. Gloria was in the kitchen cooking food for Otis to freeze and Paul was putting a bed frame together with Otis in his bedroom while I chipped away at some loose paint around the molding of the doorway to the kitchen, trying not to be awkward.

I had only seen Gloria and Paul once since Dean and I broke up, and it was at Otis's graduation. They had only ever been sweet to me, but I just felt out of place. I didn't know how to interact with them since I wasn't Dean's girlfriend anymore.

"Can I help with anything?" I asked Gloria.

She peeked over her shoulder as she shoved some sort of casserole in the oven.

She had kind brown eyes and stood a little taller than me, which wasn't hard to do since I was five-foot-three on a good day. Her long dark hair had silver streaks pulled through at the roots and sat on top of her head in a ponytail with a colorful bandeau decorating her hairline.

Her bohemian style was always something I admired, and it was a funny contrast to Paul's simple white t-shirt and jeans uniform.

"Oh, honey," she said with the faintest Midwestern accent.

She closed the distance between us and pulled me into a hug. It felt motherly in every sense of the word: comforting, warm, safe.

It felt good. So good and so distant from anything I'd felt in a long time, that I found myself swallowing down the tightness in my throat.

"We need to put some meat back on these bones," she said, squeezing a bit tighter.

I breathed a laugh, releasing our hug. "I'm on the 'poor diet' right now—trying to live up to the starving artist stereotype."

It was the same line I gave anyone when they made a comment about my weight.

She held my arms a moment longer, her hands decorated with a different ring on every finger, and she smiled down at me affectionately.

"I know this has been a tough year. It's been hard for us too." She looked over toward the bedroom and sighed. "But honey, thank you for being so good to our other boy. He just thinks the world of you, and you've always been such a good friend to him. He's lucky to have you," she said, then opened the fridge and pulled out some orange juice.

Lucky to have me? *I was pretty sure that if it weren't for Otis, I'd be homeless and curled up in a box somewhere.*

Still, it warmed me to know that she didn't only think of me as Dean's ex-girlfriend, but as Otis's dear friend. It was my most honored title.

"I'm the lucky one. It's easy to be good to Otis," I said and she smiled.

My alarm goes off on my phone, reminding me that I need to get back and relieve Mary. The memory of Gloria acknowledging our special friendship soothes me for the moment.

When I go back into the living room, Otis is back on his laptop, brow furrowed, sipping his coffee and my mouth curls up.

Flip.

He looks like my friend Otis.

His eyes drift up to me, giving me a warm smile in return, signing, "Thanks for lunch."

"Need anything while I'm here?"

He nods. "Can you grab my notes and a pen? They're on the desk."

His desk is pristine. It's so organized that it makes me wonder if he's actually a robot. As I pick up his things, I notice a small sticky note with a drawing on it.

At first, the picture has me curiously smiling and then my stomach sinks. I pick up the cute drawing of an avocado and an egg having a pun-filled conversation.

Flop.

Lexi.

chapter twenty

otis

I see it.

I see her realize what she's looking at and she deflates in front of me.

It seems like another lifetime that I came home to that drawing. I know it makes me an asshole, but I honestly forgot about Lexi until this moment. But I know Evelyn, and her mind is running away with her right now.

She sticks the note back to the desk and stares down at it like it's a bomb threat. She can tear it—burn the damn thing—I don't care.

I could see her fighting an anxious spell from the moment she got here. I've been struggling with how to confront what happened last night, too, but I tried to act as nonchalant as I could just to try and give her some relief.

She seemed to have settled into something resembling normalcy when she came back from the kitchen, just now. Until she saw the drawing, that is.

I just want her to know that we're okay.

We'll always be okay.

She hands me my notebook, but her eyes dart back and forth on the floor, like they're a magnet repelling my eyes.

"I have to go," she signs.

Her worn face is riddled with dejection, and it's killing me. I don't want her to regret last night. I don't want to be any source of pain for her.

I take the notebook and place it on the keys of my laptop, then gently take her hand in mine.

"Evelyn . . ." I sign with my other hand and stare up at her, begging her to look at me.

She finally does; her big earthy eyes are filled with uncertainty and something else I can't quite place.

"I have to go," she signs. "Mary is waiting for me."

Slipping her hand from mine, she takes long, heavy steps toward the door. I turn my head over my shoulder, even though it hurts, and I see her give me one more glance from underneath her lashes before she opens the door and leaves.

Fuck.

I run my hands down my face. *I feel like such an asshole.*

Evelyn and I have been on the same, familiar road together for nearly ten years. I've never had to wonder where she's going to turn because I'm turning too. But our moment last night side swiped us, and now I don't know where we're going.

I don't know what to do.

I'm not sure I even understand why she's upset.

This is obviously new territory for us, so I expect some of her anxiety stems from that simple fact.

But . . . there's also a chance she still carries around some insecurities that my dumbass brother left in his wake.

He cheated on her.

Is that how she sees this? That I cheated on Lexi with her last night?

I would never do that.

A queasy feeling twists in my stomach. Lexi and I had only gone out once but still, I would never pursue two women at the same time. Hell, the fact that I've had romantic encounters with two women in a week's time is fucking bizarre.

I'm not absolving myself from being a douchebag who stood up a perfectly nice girl. I mean, I was in the hospital, but I'm still an ass for not contacting her until *this* point.

I immediately open my email and begin writing Lexi a message:

> Lexi,
>   I don't know what to say. I'm sorry I didn't show last Friday, and I'm sorry it's taken a week for me to write to you. My life is really complicated right now and I need some time to get my shit together. I hope you can understand.
>
> Otis

Send.

Well, I'm still an asshole, but what else can I do? I don't want to tell her about everything and have *another* person feeling sorry for me.

But really, the shitty truth is I haven't thought about Lexi one time since all of this happened. *And after last night . . .*

Evelyn and I need to talk. I can usually tell what's going on inside her head, but something got lost in our kiss. It was a delirious and desperate moment, but I can't deny that it meant something to me.

It meant a lot to me.

Our situation is complicated for a plethora of reasons. My temples pulse as I consider all the things that make our moment last night a messy one.

But every bit of me believes it's worth the mess.

Time is standing still as I wait for five o'clock. Bohemia closes at four and Evelyn usually finishes her closing list within a half hour. She'll probably stop at her studio and grab a couple things . . . she said she was stopping for wine too, so maybe it will be more like 5:15.

Wow, I sound like a stalker.

I need to relax. She left so quickly earlier; I don't even know for sure how big of a deal this is. She could have forgotten about it already.

Yeah, because that sounds like her.

I've situated myself on the couch so that I'm in a seated position. That way I can skip the part where it takes me an eternity to move. She walks into the apartment at 5:10 which confirms that if writing doesn't work out, stalking is a viable career option.

Evelyn wiggles her way inside, wearing her backpack and carrying two shopping bags on each forearm. Of course, she's *carrying* her phone and keys—it would just be absurd to use one of the three bags.

I snort a laugh at her clumsy entrance when she closes the door and starts to walk toward the living room but is suddenly yanked back. A loop on her backpack must have gotten caught on the door and she flails wildly.

I shoot to a standing position but then immediately keel over in pain. Evelyn falls to the floor, landing against the wall, holding one of the shopping bags in her hand like she just scored a touchdown.

I'm still standing, but my torso's bent with my hands resting on my thighs, looking down at her on the floor as she blinks up at me.

We burst into laughter, which hurts even more, but I can't stop. I clutch my midsection, trying to breathe and ease the pain.

This feels like us.

She places the bag on the floor next to her, triumphantly signing, "I saved the wine!"

"Thank God!" I sign back to her, breathing a few residual laughs.

My hand extends to help her up, despite the pain because . . . well, she saved the wine, and she looks so ridiculous in a pile on the floor that I just can't help myself.

Once she's standing, she becomes all business. "No more moving. Sit," she commands me back to the couch.

"Yes, ma'am."

She hurries to the kitchen and I return to my pal, the couch. It takes me the entirety of her time in the kitchen to situate myself. She emerges with two wine glasses I didn't know I had, then hurries back to the kitchen, bringing out two plates with burritos on them.

She tries and fails to wiggle her eyebrows. "Fresh from the microwave."

I laugh and shake my head.

Adorable.

This night took a surprising turn. Evelyn hands me my burrito and wine, then sits on the floor across from me. I put my plate on my lap, wedging the wine between my hip and the couch cushion.

"You don't want to watch a movie?" I sign.

"I do," she signs. "I got popcorn!" She smiles and digs into her burrito.

Her smile. The real one. It feels so good to see it.

She seems lighter, almost like nothing happened. And while I'm grateful to see her in better spirits, I'm not entirely sure why. I don't want to ruin another night, but I also feel like I need to explain myself. At least tell her that I ended things with Lexi. Truthfully, Lexi and I had barely started.

I look over to her, ready to clear the air and see her burrito is *gone.*

She ate it so fast it has me second guessing if she had one at all. I remember now that she barely ate her lunch earlier so she must have been starving.

"Want mine?" I offer her my plate.

She laughs with a closed mouth and puffy cheeks, her mouth still full of the burrito I'm convinced she ate whole. She shakes her head, chewing vigorously.

"No, thank you. Popcorn, remember?"

She finally swallows her food, then disappears back into the kitchen but I'm still trying to figure out what changed between when she left and came back that lifted her mood.

I've watched Evelyn slip into emotional sinkholes before. She always claws her way back out and she fights vulnerability like a disease. I've always respected the fact that her emotional management is hers to decide, but her coping mechanisms . . . well, I'm not certain she *actually* copes. She turns and slides past her problems.

I can't let her turn and slide past me.

She comes back to the living room with a bowl of popcorn and the wine, setting down the bottle and scooping up the remote.

"Let's watch *The Conjuring*," she signs, then shivers as a giddy grin stretches across her face.

Goddamnit. I want to clear the air, but she seems so relaxed I can't bring myself to ruin the first easy night we've had since the attack.

I snort a laugh, sliding on my delusional mask, signing, "We've seen that!"

"Yeah, but it's so good! And we already know all the scary parts!"

I chuckle, taking a sip of wine and immediately smack my tongue against the roof of my mouth. I've never been much of a wine person, but Evelyn loves it. I'm not going to drink much anyway—painkillers and all.

She gets the movie set up, turning on the subtitles, then twists around and the air thickens. She's looking at my legs the same way she looks at my plate when she wants a bite of my food.

Asking, without asking.

I sweep my arm out in the direction of my legs, inviting her to take her new spot.

She edges toward the half of the couch with my legs on it, situating herself underneath my calves. As the movie starts, she reaches over my legs to get the bottle of wine, pouring more into her glass before raising the bottle in my direction.

"I'm good," I sign, watching her take a sip and wiggle into the cushions.

Seeing her cozy up on my couch in our new position makes me *so* goddamn happy. I know this denial can't last forever but I want to keep it going for as long as she looks like this.

As we're watching the horror movie we've seen already, Evelyn still jumps at all the scary parts.

She's watching the movie, but I'm mostly watching her.

Her hair is in a ponytail on top of her head. She's wearing a tight maroon thermal shirt that hugs her small curves and oversized gray sweatpants. Her face is clean of any makeup, but her cheeks are just a little rosy—probably from the wine.

But it's her smile that gets me. It's the most beautiful thing about her. She has a few smiles, but there's one that's my favorite. It's almost like a light turns on inside her, making her glow as the warmth spreads across her face.

Watch the movie before you do something stupid.

She's inched closer to me since the movie started because she's *not scared.* Staring wide-eyed at the screen, she tosses another piece of popcorn into her mouth but her head turns slightly, eyeing me in her peripherals.

Caught.

Kind of hard to miss when you're less than a foot away and openly staring at her, you fucking weirdo.

chapter twenty-one

evelyn

So, this is bad.

I can't look away. He's studying me; I can feel it, and it's making me fidget. His shiny amber gaze is like a pool of caramel—thick and heavy and impossible to escape.

Suddenly, the alert light on his phone blinks, breaking our collective spell. *Thank God.*

The wine needs to start doing its job and knock me out already.

He slowly picks up his phone and his eyebrows raise slightly, then furrow.

"What's wrong?" I sign.

"Nothing." He's not looking at the phone, but his eyes are slanted down and shifting back and forth.

"Liar! Who is it?" I glance down toward the phone.

He looks nervous, but it's not like him to keep secrets from me and it's making *me* nervous.

He sighs, finally signing, "Lexi."

And there it is.

We both knew this was coming. When I tumbled my way into his apartment earlier, the tension fell with me and I left it on the floor.

Truth be told, I would have left it there for as long as Otis would allow, stepping over it like dirty laundry that I procrastinate throwing in the wash. It's kind of my thing, literally and figuratively.

I probably should have sought Lexi out when we first got back to tell her what happened, but I didn't even think about it. And I'm sure as hell not going to have that conversation *now*. Not after last night.

I swallow my unease and pause the movie. "Otis, you don't need to feel guilty about talking to Lexi," I sign, suffocating the small stab of jealousy.

When I first saw the note, I wanted to rip it up into tiny pieces and blow it around the room like a confetti cannon. I spent a good hour in the back office at Bohemia in a seething fit.

I thought Otis had made me *the other woman*. I knew what the receiving end of that kind of betrayal felt like and I was furious that I'd allowed myself *and* Otis to do something like that to someone else. And if that didn't make me shitty enough, I was *jealous* of the woman we did the shitty thing to.

Eventually, I reasoned with my unhinged alter-ego, whom I've named Greta. I put her back in her crazy cave, assuring her that I'd get to the bottom of it later. But now that it's happening and I *still* don't know where his head is, I feel a prickly panic crawling up my neck.

Otis's eyebrows pinch as he stares back at me. "I'm not seeing Lexi anymore," he signs.

A sharp inhale nearly chokes me and my body goes stiff. My earlier emotions resurface for just a moment before they quickly evolve and mutate into panic, lying low and heavy in the bottom of my stomach.

I swear to God, that kiss blindfolded me, spun me around, and left me on a different goddamn planet. Up could be down, green could be red, lima beans could be good!

If Otis ended things with Lexi because he believes there's a possibility of *us* . . .

My breathing becomes shallow and my hands start to tremor as I try to sift through my own feelings while still trying to gauge his. My head shakes, trying to force a concrete feeling to fall free, but my hands start to move before anything mindful makes itself known.

"You can't stop seeing Lexi because of last night!" I sign, desperately. "It was just a kiss, Otis. I can't . . ."

Lose you. Survive you hurting me. I'm broken.

I've been obsessing over this kiss, but the kiss doesn't matter. It doesn't fucking matter because I *can't* lose my connection with Otis. Nothing has even actually happened yet, and I'm already losing touch with him.

I can't put us into a position where he could potentially leave me. *I need him.* He's a part of me.

My eyes meet his, suddenly aware that I just assumed he broke things off with Lexi for me and my fingers start to spell on my lap as my eyes strain to read him.

Why is our superpower not fucking working?

His gaze slides down to my hand then back up to meet my eyes. He isn't looking at me like I'm crazy, but there's a tender sadness in his expression. We sit there for a few long moments, staring at each other, unsure and uneasy, and then he finally shakes his head, puffing out an exhale.

"I forgot about Lexi until you saw the drawing earlier. She hadn't even crossed my mind, so I ended it with her because . . . I think if I really had something with her, I would have thought of her . . . at least once, right?"

Oh. Well, I feel like an idiot. Otis is honorable. He wouldn't have kissed me if he was still pursuing Lexi. *I knew that* and I freaked out anyway.

What is wrong with me?

"Of course," I nod. "That makes sense."

I *should* feel relief knowing he didn't end things with Lexi because of me but there's this tinge of disappointment tugging at me. I imagine Greta, in her cave, sitting in an ornate armchair. She looks up from her romance novel, lowering her reading glasses while slowly shaking her head in disapproval. *"You wanted him to choose you,"* she sneers, raising one eyebrow.

I'm losing my mind.

This is the right thing to do.

You were in a serious relationship with his brother, for God's sake!

My eyes slam shut, trying to block it out—wishing I could take it all out of my brain and throw it into the lake. As I reopen my eyes, my unfocused gaze stares down at his hand laying on his lap.

That hand cupping my face, pulling it close. His fingers . . .

Fucking hell.

I see my forgotten wine glass on the coffee table and take a few big gulps.

Turns out, it's *not* a chugging beverage and a few coughs, a burp and a hiccup erupt as I drop the glass back down on the table.

Otis's expression still seems despondent, but his lips quirk at the corner. "You okay?" he signs.

I'm not sure if he's referring to my charming display just now, or my manic behavior *just before* now but I nod, starting to ease back into the couch, trying to trick my brain by relaxing my body. Neither one is actually calm.

I go to pick up the remote when I feel Otis's hand on my forearm and my eyes meet his again. He almost looks like he's about to *say* something, but he doesn't. He runs his tongue along the seam of his lips and I swallow hard, the potent memory of how his full, warm lips felt against mine.

Earth to Evelyn! Focus on something else—literally anything else!

"You know I'd never hurt you, right?" he signs, looking back up at me with wounded eyes.

The look on his face digs nails into my heart and I wince, then nod emphatically. "I know."

I drop my hands, but suddenly realize that I didn't say anything that would suggest I was worried about him hurting me. I didn't say much of anything at all.

Our superpower still works.

My lips pull up, realizing our connection is safe and another hiccup escapes.

Goddamnit.

Otis chuckles, but his smile doesn't reach his eyes. My eyebrows pinch, studying his sadness. Is he hurt that I believed him to be capable of kissing me while still leading another woman on?

Is he . . . disappointed?

"I'm sorry," I sign, not even able to pinpoint exactly which part of my frenzied behavior I'm apologizing for.

I glance at him from under my lashes, but his eyes still look down between us. His hand gently covers mine, sending warmth under my skin. His eyes drift to mine and hold me still. The power of his stare and the warmth from his hand is like a solar charge to my body.

I inhale deep, overwhelmed by the energy and another hiccup jerks my chest.

Fuck.

My involuntary spasm sufficiently breaks the tension. Otis slowly leans back against the arm of the couch and I sink back into the cushion, pressing play on the remote. Our eyes are on the screen, but neither one of us are watching the movie anymore.

It's still dark when I wake up on the couch. I don't even remember falling asleep. It seems that drinking nearly a whole bottle of wine *did* finally knock me out and now I have to pee.

I shuffle to the bathroom, groaning at the headache that's already starting but I hear a noise in Otis's room as I walk back down the hallway.

I slowly push his door open, hearing pained whimpers—him writhing on his bed.

Another nightmare.

I jog to the bathroom and dampen a washcloth, then hurry back to his bedroom, sitting down next to him on his bed and gently touch the washcloth to his neck.

The gesture sparks a memory of Dean doing this for me years ago when my nightmares were so intense that I had to start taking sleeping pills.

God, I hope it doesn't get to that point for Otis.

I continue dabbing his neck while my other hand cups his face, trying to coax him awake without shaking him. My thumb travels to his forehead and smooths over the crease between his eyebrows, moving the washcloth across his chest to the other side of his neck. His body settles a bit, but his eyes shoot open and dart around the room frantically.

"It's okay, it's okay . . ." I say over and over, keeping both hands firmly on him, trying to ease him into reality.

His eyes are round and dark, and his chest heaves with breath so heavy I feel my own lungs seize.

A sad squeak scratches my throat as it tightens from the sight of him like this, but I fight back my tears and continue holding him until his breathing is a little less erratic. I start to stand, but he grabs my arm, hard, shaking his head desperately and slams his eyes shut.

That's when I see tears trickle from the corners of his eyes.

Otis . . .

I sit back on the bed, running my fingers through his thick, wavy hair—damp at the roots from sweat. When his eyes finally reopen, they're red with tears and exhaustion and his breathing is stuttered, trying to hold back sobs.

I don't know what to do.

What would have helped you?

My shoulders slump. Nothing helped me. I place the towel on the side table, still without a plan, but hold his hand in mine. His chest continues rising and falling and his hand tightens in my grasp. Pulling his hand toward my chest, I gently pry it from mine to hold it over my heart. I take a deep inhale, then a long exhale. He looks at me, his breath still staggering, but I do it again.

In and out. In and out.

He starts to match my movements. His chest flutters a bit to begin with but eventually he's in sync with me. We sit and breathe until I see the panic fall from his eyes and fatigue take its place.

I'm still holding his hand against my chest, rubbing the back of it with my thumb. When I feel the tension fall from his fingers. I gently place his hand down next to him, then push a stray curl off of his forehead.

"I'm just going to get you some water. I'll be right back," I sign.

He continues his practiced breathing, nodding once. I hurry to the kitchen, grab a bottle of water and an ice pack and go right back to his room.

He's laying on his back, staring at the ceiling, so I sit next to him.

My arm cradles his lower back, helping him sit up to drink some water. I imagine it hurts his stomach when his muscles are so tense, so I show him the ice pack, then lightly place it across his belly.

He flinches at the cold contact but then I see the muscles relax.

"Want to talk about it?" I sign.

He shakes his head, letting out a heavy exhale. His eyes close, shaking his head again, and I know he's trying to rid himself of whatever hell he was just in—unfortunately, I know it well.

"Can you stay here tonight?" he signs.

"I stay here every night, goofball." I smile, holding his forearm.

"Here?" He extends his arm to the unoccupied side of the bed.

His eyes are pleading and of course, I can't say no to him. I know that there can at least be a small comfort with a body next to you in this situation. But it still makes me nervous, given what's happened between us recently.

I nod, sliding over to the other side of the bed. Otis is staring down at the space between us in an exhausted haze.

Leaning my head forward, I try to meet his eyes and when he looks up at me, his face softens.

"Just so you know, I snore," I sign, smirking. "Loud."

A small smile slowly pulls at the corner of his lips before he shrugs one of his shoulders. "That's okay. I'm deaf."

Touché.

chapter twenty-two

otis

D ean is coming today.

Ugh.

He texted me yesterday, letting me know he was stopping by after he drops off Evelyn's order at Bohemia. You'd think for a guy who's only company is the wall for the majority of the day, I'd be a little more excited.

I should be. It's actually really cool of Dean to stop by, especially since I was less than appreciative of everything he did for me while I was in the hospital. But it doesn't change the fact that there's always this heavy air when we're together.

I also can't lie for shit and I'm worried he'll be able to read the *I kissed your ex-girlfriend and she sleeps in my bed every night* expression on my face.

It's been a week of innocently sleeping next to each other since our not-so-innocent tonsil hockey and even though there's some lingering awkwardness, things have mostly gone back to normal.

My nightmares have calmed and my pain level has marginally decreased. My movement while I'm sitting or laying down is better, but walking around is still pretty brutal—which blows because I'm going absolutely stir-crazy.

Evelyn is hosting an open-mic at the café with a friend of hers from college on Halloween. She said she's determined to have me go.

Live music has never really been something I enjoy for obvious reasons, but I'd sit through an hour-long concert of that guy who plays spoons on the corner if it meant leaving this fucking apartment.

Even so, Halloween is still nearly two weeks away. I might not make it till then.

I've blown through most of my current book and I'm already done with my article for this week. My eyes scan the living room, looking for a way to kill time until Dean gets here. Except, I've already murdered time in a slow, gruesome fashion at this point.

I see Evelyn's book on the side table by the couch and decide to read that until Dean gets here, turning to the dog-eared page.

"He takes her wrists in his hands and pins them above her head with one hand, while his other hand slowly finds the wetness pooling between her legs. 'Yes,' she whimpers."

Nope.

Not gonna read Evelyn's porn book. Not moments before my brother gets here, not ever. I close it, gingerly placing it back on the table like it might bite me.

I snort a laugh. I didn't know she read smut. A small tinge of excitement pinches inside me, knowing I've learned something new about her. My eyes curiously glance back at the book when the alert light on my phone blinks.

Dean: Hey - I'm in the hall.

Me: Door's open.

Dean walks through the door holding a small white bag with grease stains on it. After shutting the door behind him, he raises the bag up and I nod appreciatively.

He tosses the sack onto the table, taking his jacket off while he aimlessly scans the living room.

"Burgers and fries!" he signs. "I figured you could use some man food."

Hell yes.

"Thanks, man. I'm starving." I reach for the bag, digging out both burgers and the pockets of fries.

Men don't use plates. *No time, need food.*

I start in on the burger as Dean plops down next to me on the couch and does the same.

We sit in delicious oblivion for the first few minutes before Dean drops his burger on the wrapper, turning to face me. I slowly turn toward him while popping a fry in my mouth.

"Marnie's pregnant," he signs.

I cough, nearly choking on the fry. I didn't know what our lunch conversation was going to involve, but that was *not* it. I finish chewing and nod. "Wow! Congratulations!"

I actually have no idea how to respond to this. I'm staring at him, trying to gauge whether he's excited or terrified, and it seems like he might be both.

"Thanks, man. I've wanted to tell you for a while but . . ." he trails off and his lips twitch nervously.

But you were attacked by a sick psychopath.

It's interesting—when people go through something shitty in life—we think that mentioning it will suddenly make them remember and fall into the darkness. But any person that's lived through a traumatic event knows that it's not forgotten. Your world just kind of becomes . . . less light.

Dean runs his tongue against the roof of his mouth, like he doesn't know if he should keep going now that the attack has been alluded to.

Quickly reverting, I sign, "When is the baby due?"

"April 3rd," he signs and the hint of recognition in his eyes tells me that he's aware of the strange coincidence, too. *Evelyn's birthday.*

A few beats pass and I need to somehow shift the focus off of Evelyn before he notices my *I kissed your ex-girlfriend and she sleeps in my bed every night* face.

Pushing myself off the couch, I flinch with each step toward the kitchen to get us a couple of beers from the fridge. I grab two bottles and hobble back to the living room as Dean grins, shaking his head.

"I've still got three more drops to do," he signs, but twists the cap off anyway. We clink them together, each taking a sip.

I stay standing, looking at my brother while he inspects the label on his bottle.

He's going to be a dad. I really can't believe it. The thought causes a flood of memories to pass through me like a time warp.

I see us in our treehouse, spying on our neighbor. We called him One-Eyed-Willy, but he had both eyes, and his name was Wayne.

I see us playing man hunt with the neighborhood kids; Dean letting me hide with him, so he could tell me when to run.

A flash of him sneaking out of the house in high school to go meet his girlfriend at the park propels me into a memory I wish I could forget.

I had gotten all the way to the L station before I realized I left my laptop at Dean and Evelyn's place. I used the key they had given me to let myself in and saw that the apartment was dark. But my eyes burned when I almost immediately noticed Dean's bare ass on the couch.

Scoffing, I jerked my head back toward the door.

156

I really could have gone my entire life without ever seeing my brother's thrusting, pasty ass and have been just fine.

But that's when I remembered that Evelyn and I left at the same time. She had a rehearsal and I had a study group so we walked out together.

Dean tumbled off the couch, revealing his ex, Haley, underneath him. He grabbed a pillow from the couch to cover himself while he frantically searched the floor. Haley hugged her body to cover her breasts while yelling something at Dean and I clumsily stumbled back into the hall, rubbing my eyes until they hurt.

I blinked down at the hallway carpet that looked like an ugly sweater pattern, trying to convince myself that I was misinterpreting what was happening on the other side of that door. I had to be misunderstanding, because there was no fucking way that Dean would cheat on Evelyn. My brother wouldn't do that to her.

Honestly, I just wanted to get the hell out of there, but I still needed my laptop.

Suddenly, the door swung open and Haley's annoyed glare met mine. The feeling was mutual, I guess. She adjusted her purse over her shoulder and then hurried past me, urgently walking toward the stairwell.

What the fuck was Dean thinking?!

I lingered in the hall, stalling. I couldn't believe what was happening. In his couple years with Haley in high school, I had never seen Dean give her even an ounce of the adoration he gave Evelyn; he worshiped her, and he should. Evelyn was fucking perfect. She was warm and sweet and she deserved so much better than this.

My fists curled and I inhaled deep through my nose, looking at the door before I opened it, shutting it hard behind me.

Dean stood in the living room, right in front of me, his eyes only meeting mine for a millisecond at time before they sunk to the floor again.

I seethed staring at him.

Who was this guy?

I didn't even feel like I was looking at my brother—just some dirtbag that was cheating on my best friend.

His eyes finally locked with mine, filling with guilt, and it only confirmed what I already knew to be true. My whole body tingled with fury; fury that pulled my arm back and swung at Dean.

He clutched the bridge of his nose and I held my throbbing knuckles with my other hand as I bent over trying to fight off the pain. I had never punched anyone before, and never in a million fucking lifetimes did I think the only punch I'd ever throw would be at him.

Still, my anger pushed me forward and he held his hand up, warding me off.

"Wait! Let's talk. Please," he signed, breathing heavily, then rubbed his nose again. He gestured toward the couch but there was no way in hell I was sitting on that thing.

I eyed the couch then stared back at him, signing, "I'll stand."

Dean took a few deep breaths as he rubbed his nose again, shaking his head. He sat down on the couch, but immediately stood back up and ran his hand through his hair, massaging the back of his neck.

"Otis, I know I suck for this. I do. Evelyn and I . . ." He stopped, dropping his hands. His eyebrows pinched and he stared at me. It was weird—almost like he was pleading with me for something.

There was no way I was helping him cover this up. He was damn lucky to have a girl like Evelyn. I was sure he knew that, and it only confused me more. My eyes grew impatient, waiting for him to start making sense, though I was already convinced there was nothing he could say that would make me understand.

"Evelyn is slipping away from me and there's nothing I can do about it. She's been really distant for months and I can't help her. I can't fucking help her," he signed, then dragged his palm down his face.

He looked destroyed. His eyes were dark, his skin pale and creased with distressed lines like a crumpled piece of paper, but I couldn't bring myself to feel bad for him.

If they were going through a rough patch, he needed to talk it out with her. Hell, if he really didn't think they could fix it, he should have broken up with her.

Anything but this.

"Why does she need help?" I signed.

Admittedly, I'd noticed a few changes in Evelyn in the last few months. She had lost some weight and she'd seemed a little more on edge. But the biggest difference I'd noticed was her smile that almost never reached her eyes anymore.

Dean's ghostly face had somehow become more discolored, almost gray, as he just stood and stared at me. He finally shook his head, puffing a labored breath between his cheeks.

"She's just different, man. She doesn't want me and I don't know what to do. I had a moment of weakness," he signed. "It's not a good excuse, but it's all I can say."

The way he looked at me, something in his expression told me he wasn't telling me everything. But it didn't matter.

"You need to tell her. Man up and tell her what you did. She deserves to know the truth," I signed, the tension holding my limbs like a tightrope.

His head dropped and shook once, but then nodded as he kept his head down.

"I'll tell her. Just give me some time, and I'll tell her," he signed, deflating completely.

The memory causes me to chug half of my beer while Dean eyes me from the couch.

"Where'd you go?" he signs.

I clear my throat, snapping back to reality. I really don't want to get into it right now. Dean and I are actually having a genuine moment and I don't want to ruin it by trudging up the past.

Plus, I need to keep Evelyn's presence in our conversation to a bare minimum. I shake my head as I limp back to the couch.

"I was just wondering if your kid was going to be as big of a shit as you were," I sign.

His eyebrow cocks, smirking. *"Were?"*

I chuckle, but my mind is still partially stuck.

I'll never understand why he did what he did back then.

I had never worried about Dean's loyalty until that moment with Haley. He had never let me down and I wanted to believe so badly that that part of him still existed somewhere.

He seems to be a good husband to Marnie. He's attentive and loving—but he was that way with Evelyn too.

My body fidgets, feeling guilt poke my insides. It's kind of hypocritical to be lamenting about Dean's lack of loyalty when I'm omitting my own little indiscretion with Evelyn a week ago.

No Evelyn thoughts! Your face will give you away, dumbass!

I lean back, sipping my beer on the couch and suffocate my nerves with the rest of my greasy food. I ball up the wrapper, tossing it in the bag on the table.

"How's recovery?" Dean signs.

I roll my eyes. "Fucking slow."

If that isn't the understatement of the year.

"I know. Just try to be patient." He takes a sip of his own beer. "My kid is going to need an uncle they can kick the shit out of properly."

We laugh and an ease settles between us.

This feels good.

There's even a hint of how we used to be dangling in the air. We finish our beers and Dean takes the bottles to the trash. He comes back to the living room and shrugs on his coat.

"Do you need anything before I head out? Evelyn threatened to stick my hand in the coffee grinder if I let you move too much," he signs, pulling his mouth back tightly.

I laugh. "Can you grab my book for me—it's in my room on the nightstand."

Dean nods, heading to my room.

I slowly readjust myself on the couch so that my back is up against the arm rest and my eyes catch Evelyn's porn book again.

No.

Dean returns with my book but his face looks uneasy and I think he feels bad for leaving.

"Don't worry, I'm really into this book," I sign. "And Evelyn wouldn't pulverize your hand. That grinder is expensive." I laugh but Dean only manages to tilt the corner of his mouth.

I really look forward to the day when I'm able to spend time with people without constant concern. Dean's expression eventually evens out and he gives me a lazy wave as he walks toward the door. I give him a small jerk of my hand in return and then check the time on my phone.

It's 1:30—which means it'll be at least another four hours until Evelyn is back here. So, I open my book, and wait for my next visitor.

I feel like an exhibit at the zoo. But not even a cool one like the lion's den. I feel like that container of bugs they put in the dark, air-conditioned room that you really only go into to cool off.

I groan and lean forward, grabbing Evelyn's book. *Just a peek.*

chapter twenty-three

evelyn

Social media is psychological warfare disguised as entertainment.

I hate it.

I'm sitting on the floor, staring at the event page I've been trying to create for a half hour. I invited all my "friends," I wrote a dumb blurb about it, and I added a picture to the profile but it *won't let me publish it.*

Why?

My only solution to fixing technical issues is to unplug it and then re-plug it, or turn it off and back on, but after that—I'm out of moves! And I can't unplug, re-plug an event page!

Can I?

I make a noise similar to what I imagine a pterodactyl sounded like and drag my hands down my cheeks. My eyes peer over my laptop screen to see Otis's amused face from the couch, making me laugh.

"It's not funny!" I sign, still laughing.

"It is. But do you want some help?" He extends his arm, inviting me to give him my laptop.

"It won't let me publish!" I pout, handing it to him.

Otis moves quick fingers around the keyboard, quickly handing it back to me. It's like when you can't get the lid off a jar. I put in the sweat and *totally* loosened it for him, and he just pops it off like it's nothing.

"Thank you," I sign, begrudgingly and he laughs again.

I scroll through the page, skimming the pictures Wes sent me.

"How do you know him?" Otis signs.

"I met him in a show I was in at UIC," I sign back. "He played guitar in the pit, but he was also in a band. I went to a few of their shows around the city and we ended up at a few parties together."

Wes always had rockstar energy. Even in college, he had groupies and now he has a pretty big following. I'm surprised he agreed to play at Bohemia on Halloween. A few locals have played there before, but none with as much notoriety as Wes.

My hand starts to spell, nervously hovering over the keyboard. Now that the open-mic is official, my anxiety is starting to climb.

I'll need Wes to keep the show more low-key than he's used to since his popularity will bring in a bigger crowd. I made the event page because it's a good way for me to get an idea of how many people will attend.

RSVP . . . so not rock 'n' roll.

Whatever. No one's ever accused me of being cool and I need to make sure I'm ready for a crowd.

"It's going to be great," Otis signs, smiling.

Telepathic superpower intact. I smile back at him, then take the last sip of my tea when I see a notification pop up on my laptop.

Ten people are already attending and I *just* published it. Well, *Otis,* just published it. My breath catches in my throat and I swallow hard.

It's fine. This is why you created the page. Calm down.

Otis slowly starts to stand, signing, "I'm heading to bed."

"Me too."

I glance back down at the laptop screen.

Thirteen attendees. Closing the laptop, I walk it over to Otis's desk to charge, noticing that Lexi's note is no longer there. A satisfied smile curls my lips and I want to slap it off my own face.

It's not fair to take joy in the fact that he's not seeing Lexi anymore. I'm the one who panicked and basically reduced our kiss to a desperate moment of weakness.

I wince and head to the kitchen, hoping to leave my crazy-ass, whirlwind emotions with my computer on the desk. Grabbing a bottle of water, I walk to the bedroom and place it on the nightstand— next to our picture.

It always makes me smile. I can't place the memory from that day but I'm glad he has a picture of it. Otis walks in and even though my eyes slide to him, he still caught me staring at the picture.

He walks to his side of the bed with careful, slow steps then lowers himself to the mattress and I go to the bathroom to brush my teeth and wash my face.

When I get back, he's propped up against the headboard, reading.

"New one, huh?" I sign, eyeing the book, and he nods before refocusing on the page.

I wiggle under the covers on my side of the bed and lay down, seeing Otis give me a small, low wave in my peripherals.

"Will the light bother you?" he signs.

I shake my head, hugging my pillow to get comfortable.

The light really won't bother me but there's a small unease that swirls in my belly. Reading in bed while I sleep next to him seems like such a couples routine, like reading the paper at the breakfast table or picking unwanted items off your plate and giving them to your partner.

I roll my eyes, realizing I've done some variation of both of those things with Otis already.

Get a grip, Evelyn.

"Goodnight," I sign, giving him a closed-mouth smile, then flip over to at least turn away from the soft light. But my eyes stare wide at the wall. I'm not even tired.

Why did I go to bed?

I'm hyper-aware that Otis is awake and next to me. I hear a page turn every few minutes and his relaxed breathing. It's calming but it also has my heart picking up speed and it seems like those two things shouldn't be happening at the same time.

I jerk, suddenly, feeling his hand on my shoulder and turn to face him with my cheek still resting on my pillow.

"You okay?" he signs. "You're fidgeting."

I nod, rising up. "I guess I'm not tired yet."

My back leans against the headboard and a heavy exhale pushes past my lips. I don't really have anything to do, so I feel a little awkward.

"You could read your book," he suggests, the hint of a smile pinching his cheek.

Why is he smiling like that?

My body leans, slightly encroaching. "Did you read my book?!"

He shrugs, signing, "I skimmed it," as he suppresses a laugh.

Well, isn't this just great! I smother my face into my pillow trying to suffocate my embarrassment. He clearly "skimmed" something steamy because he's laughing and trying to coax me from self-asphyxiation.

He gets me to loosen my grip and I look up at him. His smile is amused but there's no trace of judgment on his face.

"Why are you embarrassed?" he signs with curious eyes.

I don't really know why I'm squirming so much. I openly admit my appreciation for the romance genre, but there's something about Otis reading the actual words that has me feeling itchy.

I guess this is how men feel when their wife or girlfriend finds their porn stash.

Does Otis have a porn stash?

My eyes shut, shaking that thought from my head. *Why the fuck am I wondering about Otis's porn?*

I need to go to sleep—shut this conversation down.

"I'm not. It's just funny," I lie, and he definitely doesn't buy it, but he takes pity on me and lets it go.

Thank God.

I'm still not tired but tell him I'm going to try to get some sleep.

"Me too," he signs, folding the corner of the page he's reading down, marking his place in his book and then flicking off the light before gingerly lowering himself flat on his back. I see the shadowy silhouette of his hands sign, "Goodnight."

Flipping back over to face the other wall, I lie there for a long while—stupidly wondering what kind of porn my best friend watches—when finally, I drift to sleep.

Bohemia just closed, but I haven't locked the door yet.

I'm clearing the long rectangle table of a mug and some napkins when I hear the bell above the door ring.

"Sorry, we're cl—" I stop when I see Otis walking through the door.

"What are you—" my sign is cut short when his mouth takes mine. One of his strong hands grips my waist as the other one locks around the back of my neck, holding me in place. I drop the mug and napkins, balling the fabric of his shirt in my hands—pulling him closer.

His tongue slides along my lower lip, instantly opening my mouth for him. A small moan escapes me as his hand trails up my waist, then slowly palms my breast.

He lifts me onto the table, continuing his greedy invasion of my mouth, then pulls away for just a moment while running the pad of his thumb across my lips.

Taking that same hand, he raises it up, so that the palm is open and facing me, gently moving it toward my body.

"Yours."

My lips twitch nervously, and I slowly nod. His fingers curl around the hem of my shirt, pulling it over my head and he urges me back until I'm flat on the table. My chest rises and falls heavily, my body is aching.

His amber eyes shine down at me as he hovers above, kissing me again. This time, his hands cup each side of my throat and I whimper at the contact, but he pulls away, smiling mischievously.

He swiftly removes my bottoms and I close my eyes, simmering with anticipation. My eyes open a moment later to find him staring down at me, again. One hand lies flat, high on my chest with his thumb resting on the base of my throat while his other hand travels down between my thighs.

A needy moan pushes past my lips, heat swirling low in my belly, gasping when his finger quickly finds my spot.

He removes his finger, just for a moment and a sexy, challenging smirk pulls at the corner of his mouth. "Louder," he signs.

Placing one hand back at my neck, his other hand moves expertly between my legs, slowly pushing his finger back into me and I suck my bottom lip into my mouth. He adds another finger, and a moan vibrates through my throat as my hands grip the edge of the table. My eyes flutter to him above me, his eyes burning with desire as he slowly nods.

Louder, I understand.

His fingers continue their delicious movement in and out when his thumb begins to circle my core and my breathing becomes desperate. His hand slides from my neck, splaying flat across my chest as his mouth moves down my neck, each kiss feeling like a sparked match lighting me up from the inside, out.

His full, soft lips press against the crown of my breast, then continue to my belly button. He hooks my legs over his shoulders, removing his hand from my chest for just a moment.

He glances up the landscape of my body from between my legs.

"Louder, Evelyn," he signs.

His smile is dark and promising, his hand resumes its place on my chest and he lowers his face between my thighs . . .

I'm woken up by Otis hovering over me and something between a yelp and moan escapes. The visual is too reminiscent of my dream so I carefully move him away and sit up, but potent arousal is still pulsing through me and his proximity is making me dizzy.

My breathing calms, finally braving a look at him.

"Nightmare?" he signs, searching my eyes.

I nod because it's the less embarrassing admission. "I'm going to get some water. I'm fine, go back to sleep."

I try to give him a smile but I'm sure it looks like a hot-and-bothered mess.

Shuffling my way to the kitchen, I turn on the sink and splash some cold water on my face, then grab a water bottle and chug nearly the whole thing. I slam the bottle down on the counter and take a deep breath.

What the fuck?!

chapter twenty-four

otis

My grip is tight on the wall as I step out of the shower, gingerly drying myself off. I inspect my injuries, noticing that the bruising on my abdomen is lighter, then pat the curved cut on my chest with my towel. After making sure it's completely dry, I apply some ointment then replace the bandage.

It's healing but it will definitely leave a scar, permanently branding me from the night those assholes decided that robbing us at gunpoint just wasn't exciting enough. My mouth moves to a hard line and my hands tighten around my towel.

Any nightmare, any pain, anything that reminds me of that night feels fucking personal. It feels like the Universe is just waiting for me to relax just so it can beat me over the head, reminding me of what happened.

I take a deep breath and close my eyes, trying to calm the abrupt burst of anger.

My fuse has become shorter and it takes me longer to calm down these days. I've never felt this way before and I don't have any coping mechanisms. All I can do is breathe through it and try to focus on something else.

My feet take slow, careful steps toward my bedroom, feeling a small bit of gratitude that at least walking isn't excruciating anymore. And I actually have a reason to put on normal pants, so I do.

Mary and Jim are coming over tonight. Evelyn texted earlier asking if I would mind if they brought dinner over. Apparently, Mary has been bugging Evelyn about it since she found out I could move around again.

Not that I mind. I texted Evelyn telling her I'd love to see them. I would never say no to Mary's cooking or spending time with her and Jim.

It's impossible not to love Mary. I've already considered writing a compilation of short stories about her. She has such a complicated past—from alcoholic parents, to foster care in Ireland, to traveling to America where she swore she would never marry an American man. She's an inspiring woman.

I pull on a black thermal shirt and I even run some of Reggie's product through my hair to tame the wild curls that have gotten used to roaming free.

Looking in the mirror, a relieved sigh pushes between my lips; I look more like myself than I have in a while . . . and it feels good.

When I open the door, I'm surprised to see Evelyn standing right outside.

"Sorry!" she signs, her mouth pulling back apologetically.

Wow . . .

I swallow and my heart rate picks up. "You look beautiful," I sign, without even thinking about it.

She's wearing an evergreen sweater and black skinny jeans while her thick, wavy brown hair sits perfectly tousled, hanging just a couple inches past her shoulders. Rose gold earrings peek out from under her hair with a twisty leaf pattern dangling, and her cheeks have the slightest rosy tint, hugging her smile.

"Thank you," she signs, looking up at me from under her eyelashes before quickly sneaking past me to get into the bedroom.

She searches the floor, picking up her wool socks and slipping them over the pair she's already wearing.

Always, with the cold feet.

I smile and shake my head, stepping out of the bedroom and toward my high-top table that sits in the small space right off the kitchen. I barely ever use it, but Evelyn seems to have used it for everything she doesn't know what to do with. I pick up some old receipts, a couple of partially full water bottles, and . . . one sock.

One sock? Where's the other one? Why is this *one on the table?*

I chuckle, throwing away the trash, then take the single sock to the bathroom and toss it in the hamper—hopeful we'll find its partner at some point. As I walk back to the living room, Evelyn catches me in the hallway.

"They're here," she signs.

She scurries to the door and opens it. Mary quickly hugs Evelyn then cautiously charges me like I'm a small bunny in her garden that she wants to hold but doesn't want to scare.

Her smile is beaming as she reaches me, wrapping her arms tightly around my neck. She's such a tiny woman; I have to bend over to hold her back. It hurts, but it's worth it. Mary's hugs are the best—small but mighty. She holds me for a long minute then finally steps back and cups my cheek.

"It's so good to see you, love," she says clearly, and I smile.

I pull her to my side for another half hug when I see Jim walking toward us. He pulls me into an equally warm hold, stealing me from Mary. Stepping back a few beats later, he carefully claps my shoulder.

171

"Looking good, son." He also enunciates so I'm able to understand and I nod, appreciatively.

He and Mary immediately busy themselves in the kitchen with the food they brought and my eyes drift over to Evelyn. She's watching them with magic in her eyes, like she's witnessing a fairytale come to life. It's captivating, watching her watch them. I can't look away. Her head starts to turn toward me before her eyes follow, meeting my gaze.

A shy smile tilts her lips but before I have time to analyze it, Mary emerges from the kitchen with four wine glasses, placing them on the table, then hurries back to the kitchen and brings out a bottle of wine.

"After dinner, we're switching to the hard stuff!" she says, and Evelyn interprets for me. I laugh as we collectively clink our glasses before settling into seats. I sit next to Mary and Evelyn sits across from me, beside Jim, so she can sign anything I can't catch.

It's hard to read lips with a group of people. It seems that the art of conversation can involve talking quickly and interrupting each other sometimes, so it's comforting to know she'll be a safety net.

After dinner, I'm drying the last of the dishes when Mary taps me on the shoulder. She pulls a bottle of Irish whiskey out from behind her back and dances it in front of me like it's a children's book. The gesture, coupled with her wide-open mouth makes me laugh. I grab four rocks glasses from the cabinet and walk out to the table where Evelyn and Jim are laughing.

Setting the glasses down, I sign, "What's so funny?"

Evelyn wipes a tear from her eye, signing, "Jim was just starting to tell me how he proposed."

"Oh, I need to know this story!" I sign, sitting back down and Evelyn verbalizes for me.

"Do you want the foot notes version or the full story?" Jim asks.

Evelyn and I unanimously agree we want the full story. Jim laughs, giving one loving look across the table to Mary who is rolling her eyes, but still wearing a smirk.

"Well, I had been on a mission trip with my brother when Mary first came to the states. While I was over there, she found a job working for my parent's company. They loved her instantly—so much so that my Dad actually wrote me a letter telling me all about her."

He takes a sip and his mouth pulls back slightly from the bite of the liquor, then raises his eyebrows. "But I never got the letter," he adds.

Evelyn is signing the story but she's also listening to it for the first time, so her puppy dog eyes are fully puppy-ing.

"My dad picked me up from the airport when I came back and *on the ride home* asked me if I had gotten his letter about Mary. When I said no, he groaned and said that he'd met my wife."

Jim chuckles before his mouth settles into an affectionate smile. "My dad was a bit of a romantic, so I wrote it off as him just . . . being him," he says, shrugging a shoulder.

"Anyway, I started working for my parents, too. I was on the first floor and Mary was on the third, but . . . she was a whirlwind. She ended up on every floor at some point throughout the day," he says through a chuckle, looking at Evelyn.

Evelyn giggles, sweeping her eyes to Mary. It's a knowing look but full of pure adoration and it tightens my chest.

She is so pretty.

Goddamnit. I need to focus on something else. My eyes drift to Mary, next to me, but her smirk indicates that she caught whatever doe-eyed look I was just giving Evelyn.

I clear my throat and refocus on Jim, paying close attention in an attempt to read his lips and avoid looking at Evelyn.

"We started dating and my Dad was right. She was my wife, my life, before I'd even proposed," Jim says, taking Mary's hand.

Mary's other hand cups my shoulder. "Tell 'em how you almost fecked it all up," she says with a smile still aimed at Jim.

He chuckles, explaining, "Mary's visa had run out and she had to go back to Ireland, and I still hadn't proposed. I had the ring, but I thought it would be fun to make her sweat so I waited until she was at the airport and about to board the plane . . ." He pauses and I almost spit my fancy whiskey out.

"At the airport?!" I sign and Evelyn verbalizes, but her wide eyes stay fixed on Jim, completely invested in the story.

"I threw the ring back in his face! Told him he was too late and I got on the plane." Mary nods decisively and takes a sip of her drink.

I gape at her and then sneak a peek at Jim, who is laughing and shaking his head.

"She came back a few months later. I was at the airport waiting for her with the ring in my pocket and a bullet proof vest on," he laughs, adding, "Not really, but I was a little scared of her."

"She marched up to me and said . . ." he trails off, holding his hand out toward Mary, inviting her to finish.

She says something but I don't understand. My eyebrows pinch, glancing at Evelyn.

"No idea. It's another language," she signs.

Mary finds a piece of paper on the desk and writes:

Tá mo chroí istigh ionat.

My eyes squint down at the paper but then peek back up at her, still not understanding.

"It's Gaelic for 'My heart is in you,'" she says, then smiles.

A surprised grin tilts up my cheek as I stare back down at the words. It's such a romantic concept for Mary. She's always poked fun at Jim for his romantic notions so it seems even more poignant that *she* said it to *him*.

I smile at Mary and she grabs my wrist, gently wiggling it in her hand with a surreptitious smirk.

As we finish our drinks, Mary looks at her watch and slumps over.

"We should get going. Can't have everyone scared of the banshee servin' em drinks in the mornin'," she pats my arm and we stand.

Evelyn rounds the table, signing, "Belligerent babble has begun," with a laugh but then darts her eyes away from me again.

Pulling on her coat, Mary walks back over to me.

"Thank you," I sign, before she pulls me into another hug. She holds me so long that Jim has to peel her off of me and then hugs me himself.

Evelyn closes the door behind them, turning the deadbolt, then twists and leans against the door. Her eyes slowly drift from the floor and then lock with mine before her cheeks flush and her chest inflates with a sharp inhale.

In an instant, she closes the distance between us, grabs my shirt and pulls me to her mouth.

chapter twenty-five

evelyn

The ancient buzz of desire awakens in me with a vengeance. I kiss him like I'm starving. I *am* starving—I'm ravenous. His body tenses at my unexpected advance but he quickly recovers and grabs my face, stroking my cheeks with his thumbs as my hands twist the fabric of his shirt.

This. I want this.

Our tongues explore and tease while we move toward the couch. I gently nudge him back and he drops to the cushions, our lips still fused together as I plant one leg on each side of his lap, raking my fingers through his hair—pulling him closer.

More. I need more.

His hands grip my waist tight but loosen when he feels me inch back. Staring down at him, I'm met with hungry, amber eyes. He starts to lift the hem of my sweater but then looks back up at me, asking permission. I nod and he continues to slowly lift it over my head, tossing it to the floor as his fingers dig back into my side.

Oh my God, the look on his face . . .

It's overwhelming. My heart begins to beat fast and wild against my chest; a complete contrast to the savoring slowness that's taken over.

Otis's eyes are worshiping as he slowly runs his hand up my stomach and over the mound of my breast. His fingers lightly trace the top of my black lace bra, sending waves crashing low in my belly.

It's been so long, my body is aching.

My hands tremble from the mind-blowing arousal—and maybe some nerves—as my arms move to unclasp my bra. He catches my hand behind my back and gently shakes his head. I run the back of my knuckles over his cheek, searching his face, then smirk with understanding.

Otis is a bra guy.

The hint of a shy smile peeks up at me as his hands tighten around my back, lowering me onto the couch.

He settles on top, holding his weight on his forearm, resting beside my head. His mouth finds mine again, groaning as his tongue parts my lips.

My hand lifts to his cheek, scratching at his scruff with my fingernails, and my lips curl up against his. He breaks apart from me and looks down curiously.

"I like that sound," I manage to sign, small and close to my chest and his smile widens.

Our initial need has slowed to a sensual study—my body pulling with need but pushing to prolong. His hand settles with his palm splayed flat on my chest and he begins to trail his mouth down my neck.

The soft brush of his lips gives me goosebumps and he pauses—his eyes dancing around my body—taking in his effect on me before he kisses me again. I moan and he catches the sound in his mouth as I feel his fingers curl on my chest.

He's listening to me.

He moves his hand slowly up to the base of my throat, sweeping more soft kisses and licks down my chest. He continues down, pressing his lips right below my bra, then my belly button.

A needy whimper escapes as my eyes drift down to look at him. His hooded eyes gleam and his mouth grins appreciatively as he reaches the button of my pants, glancing up at me, again.

I want him. So much.

I slowly nod and he starts on my buttons, then my zipper.

The aroused excitement of my heartbeat quickly turns frantic and my body goes stiff. The crashing waves in my stomach turn violent and I gasp as the air gets stuck in my throat.

Otis stops immediately and looks at me. I feel my eyes widen, unable to recover as I fight desperately to get the sweet, floating feeling from a few seconds ago back. My eyes slam closed but my head starts to spin as Otis pulls me up to a sitting position.

My head sways and my eyes squeeze further shut, feeling his hands cup my face and his warm breath against my cheek. As his hands slide to my jaw, I grab his wrists; it feels like he's the only thing keeping my head upright.

I hesitantly release my eyelids and meet his eyes, which are darting back and forth between mine. I stare back, searching for comfort in the familiarity of his stare as a shaky exhale pushes its way through my lips.

He nods slowly, as if to say *keep breathing.* I unsteadily nod back in a feeble attempt to reassure him that I'm okay.

I'm okay, right?

Swallowing hard, the emotion rises up my throat like a violent river. My body is rigid, and it feels like any movement might break the dam.

Otis grabs the blanket draped over the arm of the couch and wraps it around my shoulders, covering me, then pulls me into him. I hug the blanket around my chest and settle my face into his neck.

We sit locked together for long minutes. I stay pressed into his neck and his chin sits on top of my head as he intermittently runs his fingers through my hair and rubs my back. My fingers move frantically below the blanket.

Otis, Otis, Otis . . .

My eyes are closed but he's all I see. I smell pine and sweat and comfort and the tension holding my body slowly starts to fall. I keep breathing him in and eventually my lungs contract and expand, allowing me to get enough air.

Jesus Christ.

My body shakes from the adrenaline rush. I wiggle my mouth, trying to relieve my aching jaw and I finally lean forward but then turn my head back to look at him, despite my embarrassment.

His expression is concerned but tender. He reaches his hand out, tucking my hair behind my ear and my mouth quirks into a sheepish smile. He tries to return it but then frowns.

"I'm sorry. I thought . . ." he signs, his eyes filling with guilt.

I quickly shake my head and turn to fully face him. My hands latch to his face and I lean my forehead to rest against his, wishing I could just transfer everything racing through my mind into his head from this position.

I lean back and wait for his eyes to meet mine. "You did nothing wrong. *Nothing.*"

He doesn't look convinced. I run my hand through the side of his rustled, wavy hair and swallow another lump in my throat.

"It's just . . . been a really long time . . ." I sign, my eyes falling.

It's true, it has been a really long time, but that had only fueled me.

I wanted him. I still want him.

I fidget and glance up to see he's still staring at me—probably wondering whether he should have me committed or hug me again, but the corner of his mouth quirks up and he takes my hand in his, placing it over his heart. It's beating hard against his chest.

He was nervous too.

He's being so sweet and a relieved exhale drops my shoulders. I lean in, kissing the corner of his mouth and he smiles, but he continues to scan my face, looking for clues.

My eyes suddenly feel heavy and I wobble with exhaustion.

"You should get some sleep," he signs

I nod even though I still feel like I owe him more of an explanation, but the sudden and intense fluctuations of my emotions have me feeling spent.

He nods and slowly stands.

Noticing the bulge in his pants only adds to my guilt. He finds my sweater on the floor and I stand with the blanket still wrapped around me as I shuffle pathetically to the bedroom.

Otis leaves and I take the opportunity to put on my oversized t-shirt and sleep shorts. He returns as I pull my bra out through my sleeve.

He smiles, signing, "I always thought that was a cool trick."

I breathe a laugh, pulling back the covers. My body sinks into the mattress and Otis slowly rounds the bed and sits on the side, looking down at me. He runs the back of his knuckles along my jaw.

"So beautiful," he signs with a soft smile and my heart swells.

Can I wave the white flag for Otis?

He's staring down at me with adoring eyes, calling me beautiful, minutes after I completely fell apart for reasons he hasn't asked me to explain.

I was convinced that adding romance to our relationship was too risky but right now it feels like it could be my greatest reward.

He leans down, pressing a sweet kiss to my lips, then signs, "Sleep well."

He stands up and I roll to my side, watching him leave. I'm not surprised he's not ready for bed, seeing as I riled him up and then left him hanging.

"You are such a fuckin' tease, Evelyn."

I flinch and my hands clutch the sides of my head, trying to slow my racing mind, but tears trickle out anyway. My eyes clamp shut, breathing deep. I see Otis's warm eyes staring at me. I drink in his woodsy scent on my pillow. I fall asleep to the memory of his hands touching me.

I'm fucking late! Racing around the shop, I hurry to get through my morning checklist before we open. Mary has finished her routine already and has pulled a stool behind the counter to sip her coffee and watch me run around like a lunatic.

"Did you kids have fun after we left?" she asks, her eyes peeking over her mug like a nosey groundhog.

Her insinuating tone and faux casualness cause me to stop and look at her.

What does the devil woman know?

"Uhh . . ." I stutter. "We just went to bed," I lie. Kind of. Some other stuff happened in between there that I can't even think about right now.

"We went to bed last night too, ya know," she says with a wink.

My body twists with a sharp turn. "Mary!" I scold but laugh nervously.

How does she know?

She shrugs, taking a sip from her mug, still watching me.

I'm not at all ready to talk about this. I sigh, moving the morning roasts to their place behind the register. When I turn back around, Mary is standing in front of me.

Looking at her knowing eyes, I feel my face sink.

I felt so safe in Otis's bed last night—so sure that everything would be okay. But with a new day comes new fears. I can feel how big this shift in us is, and I won't be able to keep things from him.

I don't *want* to keep things from him, but I'm also scared.

Mary's playfulness disappears and she places her mug down on the counter. She holds my arm, then pulls me in tight and rubs my back.

"Keep calm, love," she says and releases me. "He may be on the first floor, and you may be on the third, but ya know what that means?"

I recognize the reference from her story with Jim last night but it's about as helpful as a fortune cookie, so I shake my head.

"It's time to visit the second floor." She shrugs, smiling, and goes to move her stool back to the seating area.

Damnit Mary.

chapter twenty-six

otis

Twenty steps.

It's only twenty steps from one side of my apartment to the other, and it's not enough. I'm pacing the length of it again, something I've done countless times already today, and I just feel like there should be more space.

More room to move, more air to breathe.

I've never struggled with anxiety before and I've got to say, I'm not a fan. I've always felt empathetic for Evelyn when I see her fighting off an anxious spell, but she deserves a fucking medal for managing this feeling regularly.

The unpredictability of when or why it strikes is the thing that freaks me out the most. That, and the fact that once I've noticed it, the feeling escalates and I don't know how to calm myself down.

It's like trying to convince yourself you're safe while you're sitting at the bottom of a well. You can see the light peeking out from the top, but you have no idea how to get up there or how you ended up in a well in the first place.

I close my eyes, breathing deeply, remembering the feeling of Evelyn nuzzling between my shoulders before she got up for work this morning and some of my tension falls.

My heart steadies but I still don't feel quite calm enough to sit, so I walk to the kitchen and grab a water bottle from the fridge.

Turning around, I stare at my couch through the cut out in the kitchen wall. My mind wanders to Evelyn's sparkling eyes staring down at me, full of want. My tongue runs along my bottom lip remembering the feel of her soft skin against my mouth and a smile tugs up my cheek.

But it quickly falls as a flash of her stiffened body and haunted stare passes through me. My palm swipes my forehead, trying to wipe the image away—but still, it stays.

I noticed the change immediately. It's like her whole body was hit with electroshock. It scared the shit out of me.

I missed something.

She's been at Bohemia all day, so we haven't had a chance to talk about it all, but I know it's not something she's eager to discuss. I thought my bouts of anxiety might be residual unease from last night, but the truth is, thoughts of Evelyn have only calmed my nerves today.

When she came back from Bohemia just an hour ago, her face held an affectionate smile when she saw me, and it quite literally pulled me toward her. I held her against my chest for a few minutes, slowly feeling our bodies melt and mold against each other.

I run a hand through my hair and rub the back of my neck, feeling the last of the tension release.

It's probably just jitters about going to this open-mic tonight. Even before the attack, I was never particularly social, but I've only seen a handful of people in the last month so I'm probably just a little amped up from the anticipation of a crowd.

Just then, Evelyn gracelessly stumbles out of the bathroom door and clips her shoulder on the doorway leading from the hall to the living room.

"Ow!" she whines and rubs her shoulder, scrunching her face as she slaps the molding. I laugh as I walk out of the kitchen and stand by the table, stealing a minute to take her in.

She really is the most beautiful woman I've ever seen. She's wearing a short gray dress with sleeves that fall right above her elbows with thick black tights and her wavy hair hangs wild and free.

She notices me looking at her and laughs, rolling her eyes.

"Can you believe the nerve of that wall?" she signs, walking toward me.

"Asshole," I sign back, chuckling.

She gathers her bag off the table, then wraps a scarf big enough to be a blanket around her neck. After slipping on some black slouchy boots, she straightens, smiling up at me.

"Ready?"

That smile. I can't help myself. I brush some of her hair out of her eyes. tucking it behind her ear. My fingers linger, noticing she's wearing the same earrings from last night.

I smile, signing, "I like these," my fingers still toying with the earring.

She tugs her bottom lip between her teeth, then timidly runs her thumb over my bottom lip.

"I like these," she says, her eyes dropping shyly to the floor.

Could she be any cuter?

I take her hand and press a small kiss to the corner of her wrist.

God, this feels right. And so good.

We linger a minute more and then head for the door.

There are a lot of fucking people here. I've never seen this place so full. Some of the patrons are dressed in costumes but most of them are wearing normal clothes.

My usual table was taken but I snagged another one closer to the counter. Reggie is pushing toward me, dressed like a caveman, pulling a tall guy with dark hair and a leather jacket behind him.

"OTIS!" he yells.

I laugh and stand to hug him. He squeezes me tight and I wince but hold on to him anyway. I've missed his crazy ass.

"Sorry," he signs, ducking his head with an apologetic smile.

The guy he was holding hands with stands just behind him and I can see some kind of tattoo on his neck. I raise my eyebrows in his direction, urging Reggie to introduce us.

"This is Mike," Reggie says. "My boyfriend. He just doesn't know it yet," he signs, winking.

I chuckle, shaking Mike's hand. Part of me believes Reggie only learned sign language to talk shit and gossip, but it means a lot that he took the time to learn it at all.

Sitting back down, I find Evelyn behind the bar, preparing and handing out drinks like a machine. Her eyes find mine for just a second and her head dips, smiling at me from beneath her lashes.

The shy smiles are too fucking much.

I don't know what it is; I guess it's because I've never known her to be bashful in the slightest. It's a *new* smile and it feels like it's reserved for only me.

Her eyes shift to the door and her smile falls, replaced by a nervous expression. I follow her gaze to see what she's looking at—actually, *who* she's looking at . . .

Dean is here.

I fidget in my seat, trying to suffocate my blip of nerves. Evelyn and I haven't even had a chance to talk about everything that's happened between us with each other, so I hadn't even thought about Dean yet.

Evelyn plasters a fake smile on her face, talking to Dean. She nods her head in my direction and his head turns toward our table. I try my best to give him a casual wave and he throws a hand up before he continues his conversation with Evelyn.

It feels like my face forgot how to be a face. I wiggle my jaw, trying to relieve some tension as my eyes drift back to Reggie across the table.

"How's it going? Has Evelyn trashed your place yet?" he signs.

I snort a laugh, relieved that Reggie doesn't seem to suspect anything is off.

I nod, signing, "Her entire sock collection is shoved between my couch cushions," and Reggie laughs.

I pick up Evelyn's ugly-ass mug and take a sip of my drink while Mike taps his thumbs on his phone next to Reggie.

"So, when did this start?" I sign, tilting my head in Mike's direction.

Reggie's smile turns devilish. "A couple weeks ago," he signs, then adds, "He has a tongue piercing." His mouth opens wide, fanning himself dramatically.

I laugh and clink my mug with his but notice the crowd becoming restless. People are looking around, cheering aimlessly. I don't really know what's going on and my body starts to hum again.

Reggie leans into Mike and I see their lips moving close to one another's face.

Feeling like I'm intruding on a private moment, my eyes sweep the room. Everyone starts to look in the direction of the small space they've cleared out for Wes to perform and I notice a few rowdy people clapping.

Evelyn stands at the microphone, starting to speak, but she also signs.

She always signs.

"Hey, guys! Happy Halloween! I just wanted to take a minute and introduce myself. I'm Evelyn and I own this place, so please treat it well."

She smiles and laughs but she looks nervous. It makes me wish we could sneak away and hold each other, give each other the same comfort we did earlier.

"And without further delay, I'd like to introduce a man that needs no introduction; give it up for my old friend, Wes Barrow!" She extends her arm toward the counter and claps.

The crowd joins her with the clapping and a few eager women jump around. I see a guy with shaggy hair emerge from back near the counter, striding up to the performance space.

Once he reaches Evelyn, he pulls her in for a hug. She wraps her arms around his neck, and he lifts her slightly off the floor, then lowers her back down and whispers something in her ear.

I've never been a jealous guy. Not ever. *Why does this bother me?*
Get a grip, man.

Evelyn walks back through the crowd and Wes takes the microphone. He says something and then turns his face toward the jumping women, who seem to be yelling. He winks in their direction, then turns back toward the rest of the audience and strums his guitar, just once, looking back up at the crowd with a grin.

Ugh.

He sits on the stool, starting to strum and I watch as everyone's feet start to tap, heads bob, bodies sway.

There are a lot of fucking people here. I noticed it earlier but now that everyone's attention is on the show, I'm starting to feel a little uncomfortable. I shift in my seat, looking down at my mug on the table, finding an odd comfort in the familiarity of its ugliness.

Reggie ducks his head to meet my eyes. "You good?" he signs.

Shit. He can tell I'm anxious.

I nod quickly, straining to manage a casual smile, then take another sip of my drink. Except I definitely don't need more caffeine amping me up right now.

My eyes drift around the room, trying to find a distraction. I find my usual table and take in the intruders. There's a girl wearing cat ears with whiskers and a nose drawn on her face. She's hanging on the shoulder of a guy whose head is buried under the hood of his black sweatshirt and my heart starts to race as the hair on the back of my neck stands up.

Men in black hoods.

My breath catches in my throat—I need some air. Giving Reggie a low wave, I point toward the door. Walking quickly, I try not to bring any unwanted attention to myself as I pull on my coat and push through the door.

The cold air hits my face and fills my lungs. My exhale pushes a billowy breath cloud from my mouth and I watch as it floats and evaporates. I continue my breathing efforts and lean against the building but then immediately jerk forward.

The feeling of the brick against the back of my head digs into my memory—seeing a dead-eyed man only inches from my face. I turn, pressing my palms against the wall, my fingers curling into the mortar between the black bricks. My head hangs, inhaling deep, and I catch the pungent smell of smoke.

My neck jerks in the other direction to see where it's coming from when I see Dean with a cigarette hanging from his mouth.

His *oh shit* face actually pushes a nervous laugh through my lips.

"I thought you quit," I sign.

"So many times," he signs back, rolling his eyes, but then stares at me, cautiously. "You okay?"

He obviously saw me struggling just now, but I'm desperate to change the subject so I just nod.

189

"Why'd you come to this?" he signs.

It's a fair question. I've never been one for concerts and given my teetering mental state, I probably should have sat this one out.

But Evelyn really seemed to want me here. And truthfully, I want to be wherever she is. But I can't say any of that to Dean so I give him the only truth I can.

"I had to get out of my apartment," I sign.

I'm a terrible liar. I've never been good at it, and I've never been compelled to do it before, *especially* to Dean.

He nods at my bullshit anyway and that somehow makes me feel worse.

"How'd you know about it?" I sign, unable to meet his eyes.

"Wes texted me. I had a tasting in Rogers Park so I told him I'd swing by after."

He knows Wes, too. The reminder of Dean and Evelyn's history adds a jealous current to the anxiety already charging my body.

Flicking some loose ash off his cigarette, he signs, "How're things with your landlord?" then leans against the wall on the opposite side of the door.

My eyes nervously drift to the window on the door, catching a glimpse of Evelyn.

She bends down to Reggie and he lifts his chin toward the door. She turns, locking eyes with me through the glass and smiles.

She smiles, I smile.

Dean cranes his neck around the wall, curiously looking through the glass and Evelyn's face falls. She didn't know he was out here. She abruptly starts to busy herself with the customers and my eyes slowly shift back to Dean.

He's staring at me through squinted eyes, taking a long drag. He flicks his cigarette into the street but holds his eyes on me.

"I've gotta go," he signs.

Turning on his heel, he walks away so quickly that I don't have a chance to respond.

What the fuck was that?

I'm thrown by his abrupt exit but also by the strange exchange that just passed between us. There's no way he knows anything from witnessing one look, right?

Of course not.

Jesus Christ, I feel even more wound up than before I came out here.

My body is starting to ache from my tightening muscles, partially from this building anxiety and partially because it's fucking cold. I suck in one last deep breath, then pull the door to the café.

The drastic change from the cold temperatures outside to the heat causes my body to twitch as I shut the door behind me.

I find Evelyn behind the bar and start to walk toward her, feeling desperate for something that will stop the freight train barreling through me. Her eyes snag on me and she rounds the pick-up counter, but suddenly stops.

I notice the crowd is collectively shifting their heads, looking around. I start to do the same and see Wes looking at Evelyn.

She's shaking her head, saying "No" through nervous laughter but the crowd is cheering and Wes is now walking toward her.

I'm already on edge and I have no idea what the hell is going on. He takes her hand, trying to pull her toward the performance space and my adrenaline peaks. My fists curl, starting to move, wanting to tell him to back the fuck off, like the macho weirdo that I am *not*.

Why can't I calm down?

Evelyn quickly moves to hold my arm, sticking her index finger in Wes's direction and he heads back through the crowd.

"Are you okay?" she signs, but her eyes distractedly dart toward the stage.

I swallow hard and nod, keeping my eyes on the floor. Every person

I've talked to tonight has asked me if I'm okay, so I guess I'm not. I shuffle my feet, feeling nervous, but feeling dumb for feeling nervous.

She ducks her head to meet my eyes, which are still searching the floor for some dignity.

"Wes wants me to sing with him. But I'll be right back, okay?" she signs.

My head lifts and her eyes search my face. I nod quickly, aware that people are waiting on her and therefore probably looking at us.

She hesitates a moment longer, so I try to manage an encouraging smile, but it feels tight and I'm pretty sure she notices. She gives my hand a small squeeze, then walks to the performance space, standing behind the microphone.

She glances toward me as Wes starts to strum. A moment later, her shoulders pull back slightly, and her mouth starts to move as she scans the audience. Her smile is modest, her cheeks dusted pink.

She's not dramatic when she sings. It almost looks like she could just be talking, but her eyes close every once in a while, and it does something to ease my tension.

I start to watch the crowd, watching Evelyn.

A few people's eyes are glued to her, leaning in and whispering to each other. I watch some couples hold each other, swaying. My eyes find Reggie, who is staring up at her with shining pride.

My presence here feels contradictory, like a tidal wave in a desert. My anxiety is crashing through me, pulling me down in the undertow and the rest of the café is basking in the sun.

Enjoying the music.

My heart begins to pick up speed. The crowded room, Dean's face before he left, the flashbacks . . . it's all stacking inside me like a block tower starting to wobble from the weight.

I look back to Evelyn, who is still looking at me and I try to soak in the warmth and comfort of her eyes, but then her head shifts, looking over to Wes and the tower tumbles.

chapter twenty-seven

evelyn

A loud screech jerks my head up. I see Otis dragging the stool Wes used during the show back toward one of the tables and my eyebrows pinch with worry. He's been urgently moving tables and chairs back into place since everyone cleared out about ten minutes ago and I can't help but keep a watchful eye on him.

I had no idea Dean was coming tonight and I definitely didn't know he was outside with Otis so I'm curious to find out what happened while they were out there.

My attention refocuses on getting the place ready for tomorrow. Mary told me she'd open the café with Abby since I knew tonight would go late. It should be a relatively slow morning since the city parties pretty hard on Halloween, but I still want to make sure it's as easy as possible for them.

I tuck the filters full of ground coffee into the baskets, then slide them into the brewer, noticing Reggie openly checking out Demogorgon's ass as he bends down, grabbing the last of the trash bags.

Needless to say, he was definitely *not* hitting on me when he came here a few weeks ago.

Bohemia is mostly empty with the exception of my handful of helpers. Well, helpers and Wes—who is schmoozing with two women that I'm sure can't wait to *help* him.

Stocking the last of the cups, I see Otis hang his mug on the wall. His body looks exhausted and tightly wound all at once and it feels like an elbow jabbing me in the heart.

I walk over to him and he slowly turns.

His tired face stares down at me and I resist my urge to run a hand through his tousled hair. Too many eyes on us here.

"Do you have your key?" I sign. "You can go upstairs if you want. I'm almost done."

I jump as a loud giggle erupts from one of Wes's lady friends and I peek over at them before glancing back at Otis, noticing his eyes dart over to Wes, then back to me as he shakes his head.

My eyes squint, not sure exactly what has him so bothered, when suddenly Wes is at my side, slinging his arm around my shoulder.

"Evie! That was a great show! Thanks for the song." He stares down at me, smiling and my head slowly turns but my eyes are slower to move from Otis.

"You've always had such a pretty voice," Wes says, then looks over at Otis. "Didn't she sound great?"

I open my mouth but no words come out because my eyes drift back to Otis and he looks . . . *pissed?*

My mouth finally starts working. "He's—" I'm cut off by Otis blowing past us, clipping Wes's shoulder as he passes.

What the hell?

"Woah, man!" Wes says, throwing his free arm up in surprise, then turning to watch Otis as he walks back through the swinging door.

I'm stunned. I have no idea what just happened. I turn to Wes, who doesn't look angry, necessarily, but tautly surprised.

"I-I'm so sorry." I shake my head. "That was . . . very unlike him."

I've never had to apologize for Otis's behavior before. *He's* the steady one. If anything, these roles are usually reversed so I don't really know what to do.

"I kind of dragged him here tonight and he's deaf so he's probably just . . . had enough," I explain awkwardly, keeping my gaze at the swinging door.

"Oh . . . that's Dean's brother?" he asks, but it's more of a realization.

"Yeah. That's Otis." I swallow hard not wanting him to start asking questions about Dean *or* Otis.

Wes nods and I shuffle to the register, pulling out the stack of cash from cover charges. I clear my throat nervously, managing a sheepish smile, waving the stack of cash.

"Seems you have some fans, Barrow." I hand the stack toward him.

"You can keep it, Evie," he says, not making any move to take the money.

"No, no. I insist. You brought me a lot of business tonight and I appreciate it." My eyebrows raise, wiggling the stack again, urging him to take it.

He finally does, nodding modestly as he says, "Thanks," raising the cash appreciatively. "Hey, tell . . . Otis?" he asks, and I nod. "Tell him . . . you know . . ."

I quickly say, "Yeah, of course."

My nerves settle a bit. Wes doesn't seem pissed about the tense encounter and *of course* he didn't mean to offend Otis.

I peer over his shoulder, seeing his *helpers* idly waiting.

"Thanks again, Wes. Don't forget about us when you're playing the big shows." I round the counter, pulling him in for a parting hug.

Reggie and Mike disappeared somewhere in the middle of all of that, so I lock the door behind Wes and set the alarm. Once I reach the back room, I take a steadying breath, not really sure what I'm walking into upstairs.

I open the door and lock it quickly behind me, then run up the stairs and down the hall toward my studio, but stop abruptly when I see Otis right outside my door.

He looks behind me, just over my shoulder, and then closes the distance between us as his eyes scan my face.

"Why were you running?" he signs.

I let out an exhale, not realizing I was holding my breath before I shake my head and breathe a laugh.

"I always run. The stairwell is dark," I sign, shrugging.

His eyebrows furrow in confusion before he nods once, as if to say *okay, crazy.* I'm caught in his attentive stare for an extra second, then slide past him to unlock my door.

Once we're inside, I toss my keys on the small table, flicking on the lamp that sits on top. It doesn't provide much light, but it gives the room a soft, warm glow.

My studio is an even bigger disaster than usual, but it's mostly just been a place to make a quick stop between work and Otis's apartment for the past month.

Otis walks past me and leans against the back of the loveseat. He's looking around the small space with a soft expression and a slightly more relaxed posture, like his mind and body finally exhaled. Eventually his eyes land on me and I sigh, walking over to him.

He shifts his weight, just barely sitting on the back of the loveseat. Even with him sitting, he's still got an inch or two on me, so I stare up at him, meeting his tired eyes.

My hand gently rubs the back of his jaw, feeling the tension fall under my fingers as he leans into my palm, holding the back of it with his hand.

His eyes shut, but reopen a second later, and I tilt my head, silently encouraging him to tell me what's wrong.

He finally lets go of my hand, dropping his head, then looks back up at me. "I'm sorry," he signs.

My eyebrows pinch, still searching his eyes. I've never seen Otis be anything but kind, so his behavior downstairs confused me.

I'm grateful that Wes didn't seem too bothered by it since I'd like to maintain a good working relationship, but I'm more focused on *why* Otis reacted that way in the first place.

"What's going on?" I sign but try lightening the mood with a playful smirk. "Why the chest puffing?"

He doesn't laugh, or even smile. He just drops his head, pulling his palms down his face. When he finally looks back up at me, a heavy sigh sinks his shoulders.

"I'm sorry about that," he signs. "I've been stuck in my head all day."

My chin dips in a half nod before he pulls his hand behind his neck, rubbing it nervously,

"I ended up having some flashes from the attack," he signs, his eyes falling to the floor. "I wasn't expecting to see Dean tonight and I think he might have suspected something." He shakes his head before adding, "Or not. I don't really know. I've just been stuck in anxiety hell and I can't tell what's real or if my mind is fucking with me."

His eyes finally meet mine again. "And I really wish I could have heard you sing," he signs.

My face falls, my throat suddenly feeling swollen.

God, I feel terrible. *What was I thinking?*

I'm no stranger to anxiety. I should have known. I should have recognized the signs and tried to help.

My arms wrap around his neck, pressing a kiss into his temple and then dragging my lips over his ear. "I'm sorry," I whisper, articulating so he can feel the breath from my words, placing a small kiss on his earlobe.

His posture straightens as his fingers latch to my waist, digging into my sides. He rests his head on my shoulder, breathing me in and my hands move from his neck.

Running my fingers through his rustled waves, I press a kiss to his forehead, then lean back, meeting deep amber eyes, burning with want.

His head dips, sweetly taking my lips while his hands slide from my waist to the small of my back, pulling me closer, continuing to move his mouth against mine. I run my tongue along his bottom lip and then pull it inside my mouth.

He tastes like coffee and I hum against his mouth.

His tongue parts my lips, forcing a barely audible groan to tickle down my throat, all the way to my belly. One strong hand slides up my waist, cupping the side of my breast, massaging it over my dress.

His kiss deepens before he releases, pulling me toward the bed and guiding me down to the edge, kneeling in front of me on the floor and slipping off my boots. His hands start to pull on my tights but he pauses, his eyes drifting up to meet mine. I don't stop him, so he inches them down my legs.

Leaning forward, I start to unbutton his shirt and he sucks in a sharp breath. My eyes lock with his, but my fingers continue to open up the rest of his shirt, sliding it down his shoulders. His breathing is heavy and I finally let my eyes wander down his chest.

The bandage that covered his cut is gone, but there's a large crescent-shaped scar on his chest. The bruising from his injuries is still visible but now has a yellow tinge.

He's healing.

A small smile pulls my lips, my gaze drifting back to his. Unease stares back and I feel it too. But I take his hand just before my lips press into the base of his neck, then over his heart. My mouth moves to kiss his scar and he flinches, gripping my hair, before his fingers soften and sift.

His hands cradle my face and his mouth swallows mine, again. It's deep and slow and *so fucking good.* Gasping from the intensity, I pull away to catch my breath.

My body is on fire staring back at him, panting and overwhelmed in the best possible way.

Lost in his eyes, drunk on my lust, I lift my dress over my head and drop it to the floor.

Otis takes my hand and pulls, prompting me to stand as he remains kneeling on the floor. I'm left only in my bra and underwear and his hungry eyes feast on me from below.

He inches toward me on his knees, his head coming to just above my waist. His hands run up both of my legs, squeezing my thighs, then he hooks his thumbs through the side fabric of my panties. His eyes drift up to me and I swallow my nerves, nodding.

His thumbs stay in the thin material but he presses his lips *there*, over the fabric and I whimper. He lets out a small chuckle, staring up at me as he pulls my panties down.

My heart begins to beat faster once I'm totally bare but I try to focus on his face, which is still staring up at me in awe.

He pulls me back to the bed and lays me down as he hovers above me. His tender lips touch mine as he brushes my cheek with the back of his knuckles. Fingertips feather down my body as he reaches between my legs and I tense.

I want this so much. Just breathe.

He pushes up on his elbow, searching my eyes—his eyebrows pinch, trying to gauge if this is okay. I nod frantically and swallow, trying to steady my nerves. I manage a timid smile as I run my hand through the side of his hair and hold it there, anchoring myself.

He cups me with his hand, then gently slides one finger into me. I tug on his hair still threaded through my fingers, then find his eyes. Pools of sparkling amber—warm and reverent stare down at me and my body melts into his touch.

Another finger and I moan, pulling harder on his hair as his hand moves slow and deep. My hips start to rock into his hand as the pleasure builds, feeling his breath on my neck as he watches from above. His mouth pinches at the corner, enjoying the sight of what he's doing to me.

His thumb begins to circle my core and my eyes slam shut, my legs starting to quake. My hand falls from his hair and lazily falls over my mouth, stifling a moan. Otis's free hand uncovers my mouth, gently shaking his head.

He lowers his ear to my chest and his movement between my legs picks up speed. Sounds I didn't even know I could make erupt from the deepest part of my throat while he works his magical fucking fingers with steady and relentless pressure. My insides tighten and the rippling tickle deep in my belly makes me cry out and squirm beneath him.

Good thing I don't have neighbors. Hell, Otis's neighbors probably heard me a few blocks away. Peering down, I see his head still resting on my chest, rising and falling with my heavy panting.

He lifts his head, looking at me with an adorable, smug grin. My breathing mixes with a few tired laughs from the aftershock of my climax and I sift my fingers back through his hair, pulling his lips to mine.

His hands move between us to unbutton his pants, pulling his zipper, and all the air leaves my body. My hands tighten in his hair and my mouth falls from his, wincing through my gasp.

No, no, no, no . . .

I'm trying with everything I have to get my body to calm the fuck down, but it only makes me panic more.

Otis stops and pulls me up.

Déjà-fucking-vu.

"What's wrong, Evelyn?" he signs desperately.

Tears bite the back of my eyes as he cups my cheek, searching my face for any clue it might give as to why I would be freaking out when *ten fucking seconds ago* I was in euphoria.

One freak out can be written off as a *moment.* Two, right in a row, is a fucking *pattern.*

I can't do this.

I grab his hand at my cheek and use it to cover my face. My humiliation is already devouring me, chewing me up and spitting me back out to be gawked at like some distasteful exhibit. I inhale a deep breath and exhale a shaky one, then let go of his hand.

It's Otis. Talk to him.

"I'm sorry." I sign, covering my eyes with my hand as a few tears fall before he pries my hand from my face.

"You don't have to be sorry. Just talk to me," he signs, then pulls the blanket over my lap and rubs my knee.

His eyes are so tender but wide with worry and it's only breaking me more. My fingers start to twitch and spell in rapid fire down by the side of my leg.

Otis moves his hand from my knee and gently places it over my anxious hand, rubbing his thumb back and forth.

"It's me, Evelyn. You can talk to me," he signs, staring deep into my eyes.

I swear it feels so deep, I almost wonder if he can see what I'm trying to tell him.

I wish. So badly.

I release a jagged breath. "I haven't had sex in a really long time."

He nods, signing, "You said that. How long has it been?"

Deep breath—in and out.

My eyes refill with tears as heat creeps up my neck, spreading across my cheeks. "Seven years," I sign.

His eyes widen a bit, but then furrow slightly. "Why?"

Part of me kind of thought he might already know—that maybe Dean told him, and he just always had the decency to never say anything about it. Just like he notices my hand when I'm anxious and never mentions it. I always hoped he didn't, but at this moment I wish so badly that he did. I wish he did, so I didn't have to tell him.

Pressing the heels of my palms into my eyes, my shame is swallowing me and I want to hide any way I can. But I need my hands to tell him. A roll of nausea passes through me, but I try to breathe through it.

Finally, I drop my hands but my eyes stay tightly shut. I feel Otis's hand take mine and his lips lightly graze over my knuckles.

Be brave, Evelyn.

I open my eyes and tears pour down like they've been locked behind a watertight door. It takes a long time for my eyes to drift up to his, but I want to look at him one more time before he looks at me differently, forever.

He's sitting, patiently, looking at me with affectionate concern and a squeaky sob pushes through my lips as I shake my head.

I don't even know how to sign it, so I fingerspell the ugly word, keeping my head down, unable to watch his face turn.

chapter twenty-eight

otis

My mouth is dry. My throat feels like it's made of sandpaper. *My heart is breaking.*

Evelyn was *raped?*

I finally swallow but wince at the scraping feeling trailing down my throat. My unblinking eyes stare down at the medallion designs on Evelyn's duvet, trying to collect myself. My head slowly lifts to meet her eyes. Even in the soft light of the room, I can see they're bright green from her tears; her face looks...

Shattered.

I quickly pull her into me and hold her tight against my chest. Her body shakes and I feel my own eyes sting with tears but blink them back, holding her tighter. I hold her for all the time that's passed. All the years I *haven't* held her through this.

Seven years? Some piece of shit took what he wanted one night and Evelyn has carried it for seven fucking years . . . she'll carry it forever.

Did she ever tell anyone?

She was my closest friend when this happened to her and she only just told me about it. And she only told me because she felt like she had to. The sadness tightens in my throat but I swallow it down, squeezing her so hard I'm worried I might be hurting her.

I loosen my grip and Evelyn leans back but keeps her head down, threading her fingers through her hair, gripping the roots.

I'm suddenly brought back to that day outside at Northwestern, the day Dean left. The day I saw her spirit shatter right in front of me.

My eyes fill and spill down my cheeks and I don't even try to stop them. Sadness I've never known crackles through me, and I croak.

"Evelyn . . ." I say, through my sob.

Her eyes shoot up at the sound of my voice. Her shallow and shaky breaths steady. Tears still fall but her eyes widen and the corner of her mouth twitches up for just a second.

"Your voice . . ." she signs.

She makes a fist and kisses the back of her hand then lazily moves it toward me. *Kiss fist—"I love it."*

I can't even find it in me to smile back at her. I didn't even intentionally speak. It was like a hiccup or a cough. An involuntary sound that my body made; but it was *her name.* A stubborn tear falls from the corner of my eye and she leans forward, wiping it away with her thumb.

She shakes her head, rubbing her face with her palms but her chest convulses with more sobs.

"I'm sorry," she signs, her eyes falling down. "I think I'm . . . broken."

She wipes under her eyes, puffing her cheeks out with a jagged exhale and her bottom lip trembles.

No. Fuck no.

My body snaps to attention. I move closer to her, cupping her face in my hands. I swallow hard and take a deep breath, keeping my hands planted.

"You are . . . *not* broken. You're *not.* You're perfect."

My speech is slow and I'm not even sure it's coherent. I haven't used my voice in fifteen years, but she *needs* to hear this. She needs to know that she is not broken. Fragile, maybe, like a dandelion in the wind, but not fucking broken.

Seven years.

My hands finally drop from her jaw and I shake my head then rub my palm down my face, trying to process.

"When did this happen?" I sign.

She exhales a stuttered sigh. "Senior year. Winter break."

My fists curl at my sides and I breathe deep trying to feed my anger some oxygen.

It happened when she was with Dean.

"Did you ever talk to anyone?" I sign.

She shakes her head. "Not a therapist. I told Reggie . . ." she signs, her eyes becoming nervous. "And Dean . . ."

My jaw ticks as my anger runs through me like a stampede. The edges of my vision blur and pure rage starts to blind me when I'm suddenly brought back to the night I caught Dean with Haley.

"I can't help her."

My palms run down my face, trying to relax the building tension in my body.

I unclench my jaw, wiggling it back and forth, then breathe deep. I look over at Evelyn who is now eyeing me carefully and it makes my heart sink. She's never seen me like this before. I've never experienced this kind of anger and I can see the worry on her face.

It won't help her.

I need to be here, with her. Now that she's told me, maybe I can help, somehow.

"When does it change?" I sign.

Her face is a little thrown. "What?"

"You're—" I pause, dropping my hands.

God, I can't ask her this without sounding like I'm reaching for pleasure praise. But maybe if we can pinpoint where she starts to panic, we can work from there.

Shifting uncomfortably, I sign, "You're into it for a little bit, right?"

She nods, but her eyes flinch. The hint of a blush kisses her cheeks as she tucks her hair nervously behind her ear.

My mouth flattens into a tight line. The injustice of all of this is fucked. It's impossibly unfair that she even has to have this conversation, but maybe she can turn into the slide here.

When your car skids off the road, you're supposed to turn into it, even though every instinct you have tells you to turn away. If she can lean into the trauma, just a little bit, maybe she can get some control back.

"So, when does it stop?" I sign, trying to keep my expression even and calm.

She stares unblinking for a few seconds and I have to wonder if she's ever actually talked this out before. She said she told Reggie and Dean but that doesn't mean she worked through anything with them.

"I don't know," she signs.

She really may not know. She's gone to extensive lengths to avoid thinking about this, that much is clear. But I need to delicately push her to dig a little deeper.

"Is it a smell? A look?" I sign.

She shakes her head, her eyes squinting. "It seems like it's when I feel like I've reached the point of no return. Like as soon as the pants—" she halts, her eyes widening, before she signs, "The zipper . . ."

She swallows and signs again, "The zipper—the sound of his zipper was the last thing I heard before . . ."

She shudders and I feel the tension take hold of my body again. *Breathe. Try to help.*

I mask my anger, trying to keep calm. "Okay, no zippers," I sign, attempting to give her an encouraging smile.

Her mouth tilts and her posture straightens a bit, but her eyes slide back down to the bed and her brow furrows. "But there's also this sudden panic that happens, like . . . once the pants are off, I *can't* say no," she signs, then her eyes dart up to mine. "Not that I want to say no to *you!*"

She flinches, rubbing her forehead with her palm nervously and my heart deflates.

I sigh. "You can always say no, Evelyn . . . and you can say no to me, too," I sign, letting my eyes sink into hers.

She pulls her bottom lip into her mouth and then abruptly crawls toward me, placing a leg on each side of mine and lying against my chest, like she's a koala and I'm the tree. It's so sweet and surprising that a small chuckle escapes as I rub her back.

It's hurting my ribs but it's absolutely fucking worth it to have her wrapped around me. I feel the tension fall from her body the longer she lays against me, nuzzling her face into my chest.

We sit, just like that for a few long minutes and I feel her start to hum against me. The vibration of her voice, her wildflower scent, her body melting into mine—it sedates me.

She slowly sits up and leans back, signing, "I feel bad . . ."

She looks down and I pull her chin up with my thumb. "Why?"

"I gave you blue balls two nights in a row," she signs.

I snort a laugh. "Do you know how many times I've given *myself* blue balls?" I sign back at her and she giggles. And goddamn, I wish I could hear her laugh. I don't often wonder about sounds since I have no frame of reference, but I'd give just about anything to hear *her*.

She leans back into me and we sit in our koala in the tree position until I feel her breathing even.

She's asleep. I carefully lower her back on the bed, pushing some fallen hair off her face. The studio is kind of cold, so I grab her fuzzy blanket from the loveseat and drape it on top of the duvet, taking in her peaceful face.

Beautiful.

You would never know that she was a pile of tears and devastation just a little bit ago.

My heart aches and I feel my eyes well again.

That's just it. She hid this so well and for *so long*. I claim to know everything about her. She's been my best friend for nearly a decade and I had no idea.

My mind starts to search for any memory from around that time . . .

She was so thin. I'd noticed a steady weight loss through spring semester, but I hadn't seen much of her in the last three weeks—since I caught Dean with Haley. Evelyn was always a petite girl, but her clothes were practically falling off of her.

She had texted me earlier to see if I wanted to grab dinner and I missed her, so I met her at a small café off the Howard stop. She was sitting across from me, mostly just pushing food around her plate.

"You ready for graduation?" I signed.

She gave me a half-hearted smile and shrugged. "I guess so."

I wanted to ask her if everything was okay, but her eyes looked like they were wearing armor. The sparkle they usually held had a shield in front of them. I wondered if Dean had told her about Haley and she just didn't want to tell me. I could see her keeping it to herself for fear of me thinking less of him.

Too late.

"How's everything with Dean?" I tried.

She looked at me strangely, which was fair. I didn't really ask her about things with my brother.

"Fine?" she signed, her eyebrows pinching.

I nodded but continued to study her as I cleared my throat, taking a sip of water.

Her curiosity faded and she looked like she was about to cry. I immediately regretted bringing up Dean. If she wanted to talk about it, she would have.

Her eyes met mine, widening with panic, and quickly shifted to accusatory.
"What did he tell you?" she signed, looking more upset as the seconds passed.

"Nothing! I was just asking!"

Her eyes were penetrating. She was staring at me so hard I thought she
might actually be reading my mind.

She knew I was full of shit.

Evelyn shook her head as she dug through her bag, taking out some cash.

"What's wrong?" I signed, searching her eyes but she closed them tight,
taking a deep breath. When she opened them, she looked ready for war.

My head pulled back—I had never seen her like this.

She didn't say anything else. Her eyes filled with tears but she didn't let
them fall and her face remained guarded as she quickly walked out the door.

I shudder at the memory.

She still had no idea about Dean and Haley. I got the pleasure of
telling her about that a week later.

Heat prickles my neck remembering that Dean left a little over a
week after that dinner, a few days after they graduated.

A few months after it happened.

I feel the rise again. It feels like my body is full of dynamite. My
fists open and close, trying to relieve some tension and my eyes fall to
Evelyn sleeping on her bed.

Her pretty face is serene with slumber and the longer I stare at her,
I feel the burning anger slowly flicker out.

She's stronger than she thinks she is. She's not damaged or ruined
or fucking *broken*.

She's Evelyn.

I'm more calm but still too amped up to sleep so I do the only
thing I can think of: I grab my laptop and start to do some research.

chapter twenty-nine

evelyn

Do I smell bacon?

I roll over, peeking across the small length of my studio, rubbing the sleep from my eyes to see Otis's backside at the stove. A sleepy smile inches up my cheeks as I sit up, taking the opportunity to check out his ass in those pajama pants.

Fine man butt.

I shuffle over, gently wrapping my arms around his waist from behind and press a kiss to his shoulder blade. He twists around, still in my arms, and smiles down at me.

"I'm cooking!" he signs, and I giggle as my arms tighten around him and he winces.

"Sorry!" I say, my eyebrows flinching.

He kisses the top of the head. "This is supposed to be breakfast in bed," he signs, raising his eyebrows, eyeing the bed.

"You're bossy in the morning," I sign and he laughs.

Traipsing back to the bed, I snuggle under the covers. It's been so long since I've had a lazy morning. Usually, I wake up and run down-stairs. But a morning with Otis, like this, I could get used to.

Warmth tickles me with how normal this feels. *How good it feels.*

I pull my legs toward my chest, hugging my arms around them as I let the contentment wrap around me. My eyes sweep the room, wanting to take it all in.

So much laundry.

In my memory, the studio will be clean and my clothes will be put away.

My stomach contracts when I notice my dress from last night on the floor and a cold shiver creeps up my spine.

He knows now.

The smell of bacon and the sight of Otis cooking feels like a dream and my discarded dress on the floor is an ice-cold bucket of water, waking me up.

I bury my face in my arms, trying to become as small as possible. I close my eyes and his heartbroken face flashes through me, catching my breath in my throat.

Stop.

I told him, he was devastated, but then he told me I was perfect.

His voice. The thought of his voice instantly soothes me. It's so different than I'd ever imagined it would be. It's raspy, and deeper than his laugh. Dean had told me that he used to speak but stopped when they were teenagers.

I suddenly feel his hand on my arm and slowly lift my head to meet his eyes. He puts a plate on my bedside table then tucks my hair behind my ear.

"What are you thinking about?" he signs.

"Your voice," I sign with a tight smile, still trying to shake the tension holding my body.

His eyes pinch. "That bad, huh?"

I shake my head immediately. "No! No . . . I love your voice. It just saved me from a panic attack, actually." My quirks at the corner.

Otis doesn't smile, a grimace tilts his lips before he drops his head.

I stretch my legs out, inch-worming my way toward him and tilt my head, giving him a playful smirk. He lifts his eyes and my eyebrows hitch.

"I'm in bed . . . I was promised breakfast." I hold my hands out in front of me, awaiting my plate and his adorable grin slowly stretches.

He grabs the plate from the bedside table and hands it to me, bowing his head, slightly. I give him two condescending taps on his tousled hair, and he laughs.

I sigh, feeling an ease—a lightness filling me. The moment feels familiar and wonderfully new at the same time and it pushes all the darkness from last night to the side.

We haven't actually discussed our evolving relationship yet, but we've always communicated so much without words. I don't feel like I've found a new boyfriend with Otis. It feels like I found a lost family heirloom. Something that was always mine to keep but couldn't find. I smile at him, feeling like I found treasure.

I take a big bite of my eggs and *holy yum!* Otis laughs at my yummy wiggles and digs into his plate. We finish our breakfast quickly and I take our plates to the sink.

Strong arms hug my waist while soft lips press against my neck. My hand lifts to his cheek, giving his scruff a small scratch and I feel him smile against my jaw. I stop scratching but we stay locked together.

This feels so good.

As much as I want to stay in this world, I know we have realities to face. I can tell Otis is thinking it too, because his arms tighten around me.

Let's stay, just a little longer.

I twist in his arms, his gaze contemplative as he stares down at me.

"Can I take you somewhere today?" he signs.

I smile. *Somewhere else with Otis today sounds perfect.*

"I have to check on the things downstairs . . ." I sign and he looks disappointed. "Give me an hour?"

I'd do just about anything for the smile he gives me.

Okay. Maybe not anything.

We're approaching a large brick building with a light green, ornamental roof and some kind of statues on the corners.

Are they gargoyles? I squint my eyes. *No, they're owls.*

I give Otis a confused but amused smirk as he pulls me toward the building.

"The library?" I sign, laughing.

"My *favorite* library," he corrects me.

It's the Harold Washington Library Center. I've heard of it, but I never made the walk over here when I was at UIC.

We're both bundled up, still in sweatpants. He assured me that I didn't need to dress up and I guess he was right.

We enter the building and it looks . . . well, like a library. But Otis has an excitement in his eyes that makes my heart flutter. Still, I can't help but tease him.

"If I'm good, can we get lunch after?" I sign.

He deadpans, pointing to the *Quiet Please* sign they have right past the front desk.

"The beauty of sign language," I sign, wiggling my head.

Take that, library!

He chuckles leading me through the large open space with some books and tables. There's a section of movies off to the corner but Otis pulls me toward one of the elevators. Once inside, he hits the button for the ninth floor.

"Ten floors?! This place has *ten floors?*" I sign.

"It has over a million books, and the tenth floor is just offices," he signs, defending the library's honor. "The ninth floor is the best, though."

The best, what? Books? Air? I laugh, shaking my head but we quickly arrive at the ninth floor.

Wow . . .

It's not at all what I was expecting. We emerge into a large court-yard-like space. The roof is made of glass, showering the room with natural light. I can see views of the city from the large windows around the perimeter of the room and there's live greenery decorating the walls. I notice a few people set up at the tables spread around the room.

"Quite the study environment," I sign to Otis with an impressed nod.

His expression holds a nostalgic smile. He almost looks boyish as he takes in the space and I sigh. I used to tease him for his love of libraries, but I'd never seen him at *this* one before.

His eyes finally make their way back to me and he holds out his hand. I take it and he pulls me into a sweet embrace. My face rests against his chest, breathing him in, watching the sunlight bounce off various parts of the room.

I like it here.

I pull back. "It's so quiet. It's hard to believe that the noisy city is right outside," I sign, looking toward one of the windows.

He smiles softly, and I wonder if that's part of the reason he likes libraries so much. He's an avid reader, of course, but I think part of him likes being somewhere where talking is not only limited but dis-couraged.

I pick up his hand, holding his palm to my face. I soak in the quiet and the feel of his big hand holding me, then press a kiss to his palm.

His smile stretches, keeping my hand linked with his as he leads me toward the stairs.

We only travel down one floor and I hear the faint sound of a piano. We walk through the space and I notice that there are practice rooms lining the hall.

This place has a little bit of everything.

"What's your favorite book?" he signs.

My eyes squint, staring up at him—it's kind of funny that he's never asked me that before. The corner of my mouth pulls back, sucking air through my teeth.

It's a tough question. My book and music tastes have always been pretty eclectic. But when I really think about it, only one title comes to mind.

I smile, signing, *"The Alchemist."*

His eyebrows hitch; he looks surprised and it makes me giggle. The last book he saw me reading was a smutty romance—which I will defend until I die. They're fucking great. But *The Alchemist* is my desert island book.

He nods before we walk down to the seventh floor.

So this is where they keep the books.

Ironically, I don't see any other people on this floor, but a large wooden sculpture captures my attention and I walk over to inspect it.

The sculpture has two large, rounded pillars creating a base. The pillars almost resemble human bodies but at the top, where the heads would be, is a series of smoothly swirled wood. The arms and heads of the sculptures are so entwined, you don't know where one ends and the other begins. I look at the plaque beneath it.

Together 2: Jerzy Kenar.

Otis comes up behind me, kissing the top of my head and then takes my hand again, leaning his head in the direction of the books. He quickly navigates through the stacks and finds Paulo Coelho's *The Alchemist.*

I take the plastic covered book, flipping through it, inhaling deep. Old or new, it doesn't matter; the smell of books is always good.

I hand him the book and he smiles, doing the same, then slips the book under his arm.

"I already have that one," I sign.

"Yeah, but I don't," he signs. "I want to read your favorite book."

I stand on my tip toes, pulling on his coat and press my mouth to his. The magic of this place, the smell of the books, the sight of him, his words—I'm high in this moment.

He's surprised but melts against my mouth quickly. He must put the book down because his hands slide to my jaw as we move to the back of the stacks.

My tongue licks the seam of his mouth and he opens, letting me in. Pressing my back against the wall, his body leans into mine as we kiss each other deeply. I nip at his bottom lip then pull my mouth from his. I look up into his eyes, feeling his hardness press against my hip.

Something takes over me.

There's something about the idea of watching him come apart in his favorite place that has me feeling devious. I peek over his shoulder and don't see a soul in sight. His arms have caged me in against the wall and a playful smirk tilts my lips.

"Can you be quiet?" My hands dance over the waist of his pants.

His eyes widen, hesitating for just a second before he nods.

I pull the elastic of his sweatpants toward me and slowly sink my hand through the front of his pants, starting to stroke the thick, long length of him. His arms are still firm against the wall but his head drops with a sharp inhale.

I tug his chin up so that he's looking at me and his hooded eyes burn as my hand moves faster. He pulls his bottom lip into his mouth, stifling a moan and I pull his lips to mine. My fist makes long pulls up and down him while my mouth catches a small deep sound he makes as he bends his arms, bringing him closer to me. He starts to thrust into my hand and I can tell he's close.

The sight of his handsome features losing control sends a deep flutter inside me, but I want this to be all about him. A gasp escapes me as I pump him harder and faster, his hips bucking into my hand and just as he comes, I grab the back of his neck, swallowing his strangled groan.

Our lips stay pressed as my hand slows and he breathes heavily through his nose. I pull my hand from his pants, finally breaking our kiss and smile up at him—feeling victorious.

My dexterity with my left hand is weak as I sign, "Is this the kind of place with bathrooms?"

chapter thirty

otis

Well . . . this day turned out to be pretty fucking great. I don't even remember much of lunch or the ride back to Edgewater; it's all just a hazy sequel to our time at the library.

Evelyn's rub down in the stacks is probably the single best moment of my life thus far. The look she got in her eyes, the way her hand felt wrapped around me . . .

I need to stop. We went back to her place so she could check on things at the café before she decided to take a shower. And I'm trying not to think about her wet and naked body.

Grabbing my laptop from the floor next to the bed, I lean against the headboard. Working on this week's article seems like a decent distraction from a beautiful, naked woman in the room next to me.

I open the screen but immediately cringe. I didn't close out of my browser last night and my research stares back at me.

"Rape is a power crime. Sex is the method."

My mouth flattens into a hard line looking at the words. It seems too clinical of a statement for such a violating act.

All violent crimes are manipulated by *some* imbalance of power, whether it's a difference in physical size, threatening words . . . *A weapon.*

My insides sink remembering how powerless I felt in that alley. The fact that I couldn't hear anything they were saying and couldn't see much because of how dark it was took away any small chance I had of getting us out of there—*and* they were armed.

A flash of Evelyn's tear-filled eyes locking with mine passes through me, stiffening my body. Even though we were terrified, there was a small comfort in knowing we had each other. But the tension only stacks inside me, knowing that our attack was the second time Evelyn has stared evil in the face.

She was alone the first time.

The telltale signs of my anger taking hold are starting to become familiar and it's freaking me out.

Is this how I am now?

I've never been a hot head—I've never even had a violent thought whatsoever. But when I think about what was done to Evelyn, I want to hurt someone.

I want to hurt him.

Evelyn suddenly walks out of the bathroom and I'm breathing like a damn bull. Anger won't help her, and that's the only thing that matters. I clear my throat, tapping my mouse pad a little too hard then peer up at her.

"What's wrong?" she signs.

My shoulders release, taking her in.

She is . . . fucking pretty. Her damp hair is curly and she's wearing a small white t-shirt that rides up her stomach, just enough to see her belly button with cozy gray sweatpants.

A relaxed exhale pushes past my lips, enjoying the view. "Absolutely nothing," I sign back.

"Your flaring nostrils beg to differ," she signs, raising her eyebrows.
Damnit. I really can't hide anything from her.

I place my laptop to the side as she sits on the bed across from me, searching my eyes.

I sigh. "Truth?"

"Always," she signs back, making a face mirroring exactly how I feel.
Denial day is over.

"There's been a few times since the attack where I've felt like my anger is beyond my control and I don't know how to deal with it. And after what you told me last night . . ." My fingers start to curl, feeling the rise. I wiggle them, trying to release some tension. "I just want to help—but I feel like I can't push past this anger."

She looks at me with tender sympathy, taking my hand in hers. Her forehead leans against mine and she kisses me between my eyebrows, then leans back but keeps her eyes downcast.

"You *are* helping me. I haven't been with anyone or even *tried* to be with anyone since it happened."

Her eyes stay down but fill with nerves while she aimlessly traces the design on her duvet before signing, "But I understand if it's too much . . ."

Oh my God, no.

I pull her into my lap, holding her tight—so tight—like I'm trying to squeeze the ridiculous thought out of her.

She thinks I wouldn't want to be with her because of this?

I keep holding her a long minute more, then stare up at her. "Why would you ever think that?" I sign.

She shrugs but I can see a distant sorrow in her eyes. Rubbing my thumbs along her cheeks, I kiss her like she's my life source.

Isn't she?

Her mouth releases mine, our heavy breaths mixing with each other's between our lips.

It's not easy learning what was done to her; I may not have a good handle on how angry it makes me, and I may not know exactly how to help. But none of that has any bearing on how crazy I am about her. How happy I am that in all this mess, all of this ugliness, we've managed to sink deeper into each other.

I hold her beautiful, earthy eyes like they're my whole world.

"Perfect," I say, tracing her bottom lip with my thumb.

Her body melts and her lips curl up as she pushes my hair away from my forehead then curiously tilts her head.

"You used to talk. Why did you stop?" she signs, and I flinch. "Sorry, did I hurt you?" She glances down between us, but I shake my head.

She didn't hurt me but the idea of telling her why I stopped using my voice is pretty fucking humiliating.

I sigh. "Can we save that for another night? I just want to hold you."

A soft smile pinches her cheeks and she nods, pressing a small kiss to the corner of my mouth. Laying down, she snuggles into my side, her head fitting perfectly between my neck and shoulder. One of her leg curls around mine, rooting us together and I slowly drift to sleep.

Darkness surrounds me but I feel fingers thread through mine. Rolling my head to the side, I see Evelyn laying beside me.

She looks so scared.

I try to lift my other arm to touch her face but I can't; it feels so heavy.

Suddenly, my hand is pulled from hers, my body dragging across the gravel. There's a tug on my coat and my upper body is leaned against a brick wall by a man in a black hood. Another man with beady eyes and a large birthmark on his forehead starts to creep up to Evelyn.

I need to move!

The man has no soul, I know this somehow, staring at me with a menacing smile. His head jerks to Evelyn—her neck veins bulging as she screams, tears rolling from the corners of her eyes. The man hovers over her with a knife and uses it to rip her shirt.

Oh my God! No!

Sitting there, motionless, unable to do anything as the man defiles her. She's crying but her head drops to the side, locking eyes with me. Her face is full of anguish as her tears pour from her bright green eyes.

"Don't look!" she signs, desperately.

Oh my God, I need to stop him!

My shoulder jerks, trying to move, but I can't. I can't fucking move!

"Don't look, Otis!"

My eyes bulge open and my throat vibrates. *I think I'm screaming.*

Evelyn sits next to me on the bed patting my face. My lungs are in a choke hold and I gracelessly push to sit up.

Panting, sweating, my eyes wide and blinking. I can't get a grip on reality. My fingers rake through my hair, pulling hard just to prove that I can move. Evelyn kneels down in front of me and grips the sides of my legs.

I lift my chin but my vision blurs, my eyes filling with tears.

"It's okay," Evelyn signs.

Not okay. Definitely not okay.

I shake my head, still struggling for air. I thought the nightmares had subsided, but that was the worst one yet.

My sobs push and stall in my chest and my fingers curl, clutching the edge of the bed. Evelyn runs her palm along my thigh, prying my hand from the bed and placing it over her heart, breathing deep—in and out.

I focus on the soft skin of her hand, the steady grip it holds around mine. She holds it there, over her heart, and I feel it beating. Erratically, but it's there. She places her hand over my heart too, which probably feels like a bug caught in a light fixture, but she keeps breathing, keeps holding.

My lungs finally find the air and she reaches for the glass of water on her bedside table, handing it to me. Draining it all, I drop the empty cup back on the table.

I pull her into me, tucking my face into her neck, breathing deep, inhaling her.

After a long minute my body and mind start returning to Evelyn's studio. She's in my arms, her heart is beating against mine as we're pressed together, the smell of wildflowers enveloping me.

She gives me a small squeeze, then leans back. "Do you want to talk about it?" she signs.

I really don't. I want to wipe my memory just so I never have to think about that fucking nightmare ever again.

A pained exhale escapes and I shake my head, combatting the aftershocks of my panic. I just want to have a normal fucking night with her.

I don't even know what normal is anymore.

My knees wobble as I stand, but I steady myself then look down at Evelyn still kneeling on the floor.

Her eyes are full of concern, but her mouth tilts up her cheek.

"I'm going to take a shower. Then maybe a movie?" I sign

She stands up from the floor, her smile evening. "Sure. Nothing scary this time," she signs.

"Deal," I sign back at her.

chapter thirty-one

evelyn

I'm staring. I'm someone who stares now. Well, someone who shamelessly stares at Otis while she should be working, at least. *He's just so . . .*

God, who am I? I might as well have giant pink hearts for eyes, but I just can't help it.

It's like I've been looking at a magic eye book for ten years and I've just now adjusted my eyes to see the hidden picture. Everything I've ever admired about him has a bonus feature I didn't know about and it makes my toes curl.

My phone buzzes in my back pocket and I begrudgingly stop gawking to pull it out.

Otis: I don't want to alarm you, but there's a beautiful woman staring at me . . . and I'm trying to write about a homeless man who stole a mannequin and made it his wife.

Caught. I twist away, shutting my eyes tight, but laughing. The things he has to write about for the paper are always amusing. He hates it, but I always read his articles and they're *so good*. I've even kept some of them. My bottom lip tugs between my teeth and I tap a message back.

Me: That bitch better back off!

I wait just a second . . .

Me: That homeless man is MINE!

I turn around, watching him read my messages and he chuckles. Just then, Reggie comes sauntering through, looking like a man on a mission.

"Bitch!" he announces, more than yells.

"The greetings are going downhill," I retort, busying myself with wiping down the countertop behind the bar.

"I texted you, inviting you to dinner at my new place tonight and you didn't respond. *Bitch* was the nicer word." He eyes me, then moves behind the counter, walking toward the fridge and pulling out the cold brew.

My nose scrunches, feeling guilty. I haven't made any time for Reggie lately. He's always taken care of me like a protective older brother while keeping it real with me like a bitchy big sister. He deserves more than ignored texts and our fleeting chats at Bohemia.

He leans against the counter, pouting. His hand waves in Otis's direction and my eyes linger on Otis—you know, because of my staring problem—and I practically feel Reggie gasp.

"Oh my God!" he shrieks.

My shoulders jump from the outburst and he charges me. "Back room. *Now*."

Pushing through the swinging door, I toss my arms up. "What the hell was that?!"

Reggie's pinching the bridge of his nose, dramatically. When he finally drops his hand, his gray eyes pierce me.

"You are having *sex* with *Otis!*" he says. "OTIS!" he squeals, splaying his palm over his chest.

My eyes widen, heat burning my cheeks.

"I am not! Stop clutching your damn pearls! We're just . . ."

What are we doing?

I sigh. "It's complicated."

He rolls his eyes, closing some distance between us. "Evie, the only complicated thing about you and Otis is the fact that it's taken *this fucking long* for you two to bump uglies."

I flinch. *Bump uglies? Gross.*

Wait—what does he mean *this long*?

"I was too dick-stracted at the open-mic to notice, but *holy shit*, you guys are finally doing the damn thing!" he muses.

Two things cannot be denied: one, "dick-stracted" is a great pun, and two, he's not entirely wrong about Otis and me. We haven't actually slept together, but things are . . . different. Though the thing that's throwing me most is that Reggie's not shocked, or even surprised that it's happening. He's . . . giddy.

"Reggie, Otis and I have been best friends for years. I dated his brother for three of those years, remember? What are you talking about?"

He sighs. "Baby girl, that boy looks at you like you hung the dang moon."

I shake my head, snorting a laugh.

Reggie plays the part of bitter cynic, but deep down he's a hopeless romantic. He cried huge, ridiculous tears when Buffy sent Angel back to Hell. He has a stash of Colleen Hoover books that he *doesn't* think I know about.

He's made up some narrative about Otis and me in his head and thinks he's finally seeing it come to fruition.

I can't say that my evolving feelings for Otis aren't big—they are—but they're also *new*.

Reggie's watchful gaze softens, pulling me into a hug.

"This is where it starts, Evie," he says, squeezing me tight.

I suppress an eye roll at his dramatic and confusing statement as he pulls back, firmly planting his hands on my shoulders.

"Dinner. Tonight. Bring the man," he demands, then pushes through the door.

Otis and I arrive at Reggie's apartment fifteen minutes late because I don't know how to be on time. We walk hand in hand as we approach the front door, simultaneously unlinking them as I knock.

I just can't take Reggie's knowing grin if he witnessed us showing up, holding hands. There's this strange need I feel to protect whatever is happening between Otis and me. It's inevitable that our small social circle will see what's happening at some point, but it feels too precious to share yet.

The door opens to Reggie wiggling in excitement. "Prepare to be jealous," he says emphatically.

Otis laughs, bringing Reggie in for a hug and my heart becomes pudding.

These two men are the reason I'm still upright and breathing today and seeing them love on each gives me all the warm-and-fuzzies.

"Miss Evelyn, you're a vision," Reggie signs, pressing a kiss to my cheek and I laugh.

"Did you start drinking without us?" I sign.

My eyes scan the industrial aesthetic of Reggie's new home.

There's exposed brick and pipe everywhere but the fixtures are all new. The updated kitchen sits to our right as we enter, and I see Mike opening the fridge.

My eyebrows hitch, glancing at Reggie. He mirrors my expression, and an understanding passes between us.

We'll both behave tonight.

Otis looks back and forth, signing, "What'd I miss?"

"Nothing!" Reggie says and I sign, at the same time.

Mike places a charcuterie board on the oversized coffee table. "Hey guys, good to see you again!" he says with a sincere smile.

"Nice to see you too, Mike," I say while signing.

Reggie prances to the kitchen to get us some drinks and Otis sinks onto the big orange armchair that I love while I settle on the floor, promptly eating all the cheese off the board.

Reggie returns with our drinks, huffing as he hands me my wine.

"Evie! What the fuck?" he scolds, then signs, "I even put out extra for you!"

Otis laughs so hard he nearly spits his beer out and so does Mike. I shrug, giving Reggie an ingenue *oops* face and he rolls his eyes, settling next to Mike on the couch.

"So, you guys all went to college together?" Mike asks.

I nod. "Well, Reggie and I did. Otis went to Northwestern."

Signing while talking is a little bit like patting your head while rubbing your belly. The sentence structure in ASL is different than English so I always feel a little disjointed.

My eyes find Otis smiling over at me and I give him one back.

"That's cool," Mike says. "How did you guys meet?" He nods toward Otis and me.

Well, this is awkward.

A long beat passes while I try to form an uncomplicated response, when Reggie leans forward and grabs his wine glass.

"Evie and I went to a party up at Northwestern our sophomore year and we met Otis there," Reggie says and my shoulders sag with relief.

I meet Reggie's eyes, silently thanking him for being quicker on his feet than me. He gives me a small smirk, then shifts his stare to Otis.

"You seem even better than a couple weeks ago," he signs, arching his eyebrow. "You getting in some good workouts?"

My hand pauses mid-sip to shoot a glare at Reggie.

First he saves, then he smites. He suppresses a laugh and I finish my sip, my eyes sliding to Otis.

He seems to have caught Reggie's insinuation too because he's stifling a smile.

"Definitely better," Otis signs, leaving it at that. *Thank God.*

I steal another look at Otis from under my lashes and my mouth curls up when I see him staring back at me.

Reggie stands. "How about some music?" he sing-songs.

I chuckle. "You bougie bitch! Any excuse to show off your turntable, huh?"

A wry smirk tilts his lips as he fiddles with the record player.

Suddenly, "River" by Leon Bridges starts to softly play.

"Ohh, good one," I sign, starting to quietly sing along.

One of my favorite songs.

"How do you sign 'you have a pretty voice'?" Mike asks.

Well, if that isn't just the sweetest thing.

I show him how to sign it and he repeats it back to me. Mike starts to ask about some other signs and Reggie eagerly gives him a hands-on lesson as my eyes drift back to Otis.

The longing of the song pulls me toward him. Reggie and Mike fall to the background, then disappear completely as Leon Bridges croons.

The chair Otis is sitting on is big, so I wiggle my way between his lap and the arm of the chair, closing my eyes, leaning into his chest. His heartbeat is strong and steady below my ear and his arm hugs around me, pulling me tighter. Between his hold and the music, it feels like the world's sweetest lullaby.

The song ends, but I don't move. I can't even bring myself to care that I'm breaking my own rule.

Another song starts to play, Reggie disappears back into the kitchen, returning a moment later with a few dips and crackers. I kind of love that we're having snacks for dinner.

The rest of the night passes as a comfortable double-date—confessing to Mike that I named him Demogorgon in my head when I first met him. He thought it was hilarious.

I find it pretty funny, too, after getting to know him a little better. His hard exterior with the leather jacket and neck tattoos are a complete contradiction to the big softy he seems to be.

He's from Cleveland, visiting whenever he can to see his Mom and sister. He volunteers regularly at Lakeview Pantry, which provides food distribution to residents all over Chicago. They also supply counseling, which is where Mike's real passion lies. He's currently completing his Masters in Psychology at Loyola.

Boy, did he find the right group of people.

Otis's apartment is starting to feel like home. I've always felt comfortable here, but now it feels strange to *not* be here—*to not be with him.* He sits against the headboard, book open, when I come back from brushing my teeth. I settle my legs on each side of him, lying against his chest; my new favorite spot.

Chuckling, he puts his book on the bedside table, running his fingers through my hair before I sit up and lightly press my lips to his.

230

Pulling apart, an adoring pulls up his cheeks. "Everyone loves your voice," he signs, brushing some fallen hair from my eyes.

"I love *your* voice," I sign back and his smile falls.

I don't want to pressure him to tell me why he stopped verbalizing and I don't want him to feel like he *has* to do it either. But the sound of his voice—it's like the steadiness he's always provided me with has an unlocked level of power.

A bonus feature.

Still, my gut tells me that the reason he stopped speaking is painful and I don't feel like I can ask him to talk if I don't understand why he stopped in the first place.

I brush his wavy hair from his forehead, kissing the space between his brows. I start to hum the song we listened to earlier and his hand moves up my neck, gently pressing at the base of my throat. I hum louder, locked with him until his lips collide with mine.

His mouth feels tight, pained, and his fingertips sprawl up my jaw.

As he pulls back, my hands hold his shoulders to steady myself. Sometimes his kiss leaves me breathless, but they *always* restore me. I've shared conversations, meals and drinks with this man for ten years and never knew the vitality of his lips.

Another bonus feature.

A peaceful sigh escapes as I open my eyes but he's staring up at me with a tight, saddened expression.

"I stopped talking when I was sixteen," he signs.

chapter thirty-two

otis

I swallow hard, shifting uncomfortably. "I was dating this girl, Jen. She was cute, kind of out of my league," I sign, peering back up at Evelyn sitting across from me.

Her mouth moves to a tight line, breathing deep, pulling her shoulders back just slightly and it gives me a quiet laugh.

Evelyn gets jealous.

There's a real gift in learning new things about someone you thought you knew everything about. Learning things that only a lover gets the privilege to know.

She shakes her head once, her face softening into an inquisitive gaze.

"We took some of the same classes and went to the movies a few times," I sign, trying to push down the cramped feeling even *that* memory gives.

The movies didn't have subtitles so between trying to figure out what was going on in the movie and trying to "make a move," I always left feeling a little defeated.

"She came over to my house after school. Dean was at Haley's and my parents were at work. We were making a snack in the kitchen when she wrote in her notebook that she wanted to have sex," I sign, trying to breathe some dignity in through my nose.

"I had never done it before, but I was sixteen and she was willing, so I thought—hell yeah," I sign, peeking up at Evelyn.

"Lucky girl," she signs.

I grimace and cast my eyes down. I'm so uncomfortable—this story is embarrassing, but it's another level of humiliation to recount it to a woman you're trying to have a relationship with.

Evelyn isn't just any woman.

Her big hazel eyes stare back at me and I borrow some of their strength—they're the same eyes that found the courage to look at me and tell me *her* secret.

"We had sex, and I thought it was great. I had nothing to compare it to, but I thought everything had gone the way it was supposed to," I sign. "She didn't think the same."

Evelyn's eyebrows pinch, her head tilting in confusion. I swallow hard and try to steady my nerves.

"She told her friends, who told a bunch of other kids that it was like screwing a farm animal," I sign, barely able to look at her. "Apparently, I had gotten pretty vocal . . . loud.

"Eventually, most of the school knew. Kids left pictures of pigs on my locker with crude drawings. I noticed girls whispering and laughing."

Evelyn's hand shoots up between us. "I'm sorry. I'm so sorry. I just need a minute," she signs then cradles her face in her hands.

Oddly enough, her reaction soothes me. I honestly never thought I would tell anyone the whole story—especially someone I hoped to sleep with—but I also never thought I'd be with Evelyn in this way. I was worried about how humiliated I would feel, but she's reacting exactly the way my *friend* Evelyn would—deeply compassionate but not an ounce of pity or disgust.

I slide my arms around her waist, pulling her closer to me. Her knees bend and box me in on the sides of my torso and I pull her hands from her face.

"It was a long time ago, Evelyn." I sign.

She breathes deep, shaking her head. "I'm sorry, please continue," she signs.

"That's it." I shrug. "I stopped talking after that. I stopped going to speech therapy, which was fine. I kind of hated it. I had to leave class to go and it just brought more attention."

Evelyn nods, wiping away a stray tear. "Your parents didn't talk to the school?"

"My parents don't know. I just told them I hated speech therapy and it was true. All it really did was remind me over and over again that I couldn't hear—that I sounded different.

"But mostly I thought that if I just stopped talking completely . . . I don't know. Maybe they'd forget faster? It seemed like the best way to disappear," I sign.

Her bottom lip quivers, trying to suffocate her sadness. She breathes deep, closing her eyes and puffs the air back out her mouth but reopens them a moment later.

"What's your favorite smell?" she signs.

My head juts back, slightly—it wasn't what I was expecting her to say.

"Burning leaves," I sign.

The smell is ingrained into the walls of our treehouse. Dean and I spent *hours* up there, especially in autumn before it got really cold. It's the smell of home.

A soft smile pulls on her face. "Your voice is burning leaves to me, Otis."

My heart flips, pinching a nervous smile up my cheek. I can't believe I'm nearly pressed together with Evelyn Gray and she's saying these things to me.

As a deaf kid, and sometimes even as an adult, life can be isolating in a hearing world. But Evelyn, since the day I met her, always finds a way to connect with me.

Her stare moves me. I literally fall back against the headboard in awe of her. We sit, staring for a few long moments.

Her hazel eyes—eyes I've seen for years but never allowed myself to stare into, worried I'd get lost in their beauty and risk ruining what we had. Her wild hair—hair I never thought I'd run my fingers through and kiss. My eyes slide to her chest.

Her heart. Nothing beats the heart I've known for years, but never let myself believe she'd share with me, that it would speed up in my presence and still me in moments of unease.

My eyes drift back up to meet hers and the words stutter out of me, like they too are trying to catch their breath.

"I love you."

Her pupils dilate and her breath hitches. My heart drops for a second before her lips crash with mine. Her hands latch to the sides of my hair, pulling me desperately against her mouth.

"I love you," she breathes against my lips and I unravel.

My tongue plunges inside her mouth then moves down her neck, lightly licking behind her ear, admiring the goosebumps that ripple down her arms.

She wiggles back just enough to pull her shirt over her head, and *holy shit.*

She isn't wearing a bra . . .

My eyes linger, taking her in like a masterpiece. Her lips twitch nervously, crossing her arms across her chest while I inch closer, pulling my own shirt over my head but keeping my eyes locked with hers.

I gently lower her arms so she's no longer covering herself but stay lost in her sparkling eyes. Her cheeks flush and her chin tilts down, her shyness making me weak.

Brushing the hair off her shoulder, I kiss down her neck again as my hand slides up to meet her breast. My arousal swells as I knead her, feeling her gasp as I start to circle her nipple with my thumb.

I trail from her neck down to her chest, drunk on her taste. My lips meet my thumb, still tracing small circles. The skin tightens under my touch and I slowly pull it into my mouth. My fingers move to her other breast, while my mouth continues to suck and tease, feeling her shake. I peer up, meeting fiery, lustful eyes.

I flick her one more time with my tongue then straighten up in front of her. She grabs the sides of my face, pulling my lips to hers again.

God, her face when she pulls away from me—hot, dizzy, wanting.

I swallow. "You can always say no, Evelyn. You can say no to me," I sign, reminding her.

She nods but slowly wiggles out of her panties, tossing them to the floor. *Holy fucking God, the sight of her completely bare is short-circuiting my brain.*

On her knees, breathing heavily, staring at me with *so much* desire. But I can see unease still holds her. I match her stance, running my knuckles gently over her cheek.

"So beautiful," I say as softly as I can.

Her shoulders melt as she sinks down on the bed, pulling me toward her. My mouth molds to hers again, her hands gripping my biceps, tight. I lower myself, holding my weight on my elbow just beside her head as my other hand cups her breast, earning me a whimper that I catch in my throat.

She takes my hand, guiding it between her legs. My fingers feel the evidence of her arousal immediately and push inside her, swallowing down a moan rumbling low in my throat.

My other hand splays across her chest, trailing my tongue down her stomach. I kiss her mound, settling my face between her thighs. I flick my tongue at her core and her hips buck as I start to circle her with my tongue, my fingers sliding in and out.

My other hand stays on her chest, feeling her heartbeat quicken, deep moans singing against my palm. I glance up, still working her with my mouth and fingers, picking up my pace.

This is officially the only fucking movie I want to watch from now on.

My fingers feel the tightening inside her when she suddenly tugs my face to hers, kissing me madly. She pulls the shit out of my hair and nothing has ever felt so fucking good. Mouth opening, teeth colliding, tongues tangling—we're desperate, hungry, and she frantically works to get my pants off.

My erection springs free, lowering myself on top of her, and *holy hell.*

Her naked body pressed up against mine is fucking nirvana. Wedging her hand between us, she takes me in her hand, slowly fisting me up and down. I push up on my arms, overwhelmed by the feeling of her wrapped around the length of me. Hovering above, a moan starts but I instinctively pull my lips into my mouth.

Evelyn releases her hand and I stare down at her before she pushes me onto my back, straddling me. I'm a little thrown by the power play but I'm also *totally fucking into it* before she sits up, smirking down at me.

"Let's wake the neighbors," she signs.

Her wavy hair billows around her face, perfectly sexed. Her mouth slightly open as she takes me in her hand again, beginning her torturous, slow movements—driving me toward insanity with every pump. My eyes close, as a low groan stirs in my chest.

My eyes flutter open again to see her nodding, her fist picking up speed.

My hand fumbles for the drawer on my bedside table, clumsily opening it, digging my hand around for a condom. My body contracts feeling her thumb circle my tip.

God, if she keeps doing that *we won't need one.*

I finally find the square package and grab her waist, flipping her back on the mattress. She's staring up at me with bright eyes and rosy cheeks. I give her the condom and she timidly tears it open, sliding it over me.

I've never been so turned on in my life, but the gravity of this moment isn't lost on me. She's trusting me with something she hasn't given to anyone since someone took it and I want her to know that she can say no, even now, and everything will be okay.

Like she can read my mind she looks up at me, panting wildly. "Please, I want you," she breathes, and I settle myself between her legs, tangling her fingers with mine then placing our hands over my heart.

I can't believe this is actually happening.

I slowly push into her.

Holy fucking God she feels so good.

A moan I couldn't stop if I wanted to rolls out of me, but her body tenses.

I stop, buried inside her. "I love you," I say, still pressing her hand against my chest, waiting for a sign that she wants me to keep moving.

She nods, releasing a shaky exhale. I thrust slow and steady, keeping my eyes on hers and her hips begin to meet mine. I lower myself to kiss her, dragging my lips to her ear.

"I love you, Evelyn," I say, again.

Her nails dig into my chest where I still hold her hand pressed to me, her breath hot and heavy on my face as she runs her tongue along my jaw.

Her legs wrap around me and I lose it. *I fucking lose it.* I thrust harder, deeper, feeling my chest rumble unapologetically.

So fucking good.

Evelyn tightens around me, and I rock into her a couple more times, feeling her cry out against my palm as I shudder my own release.

My head collapses on her chest, rising and falling with heavy breath as I feel her heartbeat thumping hard and fast under my ear. Suddenly, her chest shakes and I jerk my head up.

I see a tear running down her cheek and my heart drops, but as I lean over, her smile is euphoric.

She looks like love.

Beautiful, happy, warm.

I wipe the tear, kissing where it fell. She grabs the nape of my neck and her lips take mine tenderly, sighing against my mouth. I pull back, pushing some hair off her forehead as she stares up at me with a dreamy smile.

"Burning leaves," she signs.

chapter thirty-three

evelyn

I s it supposed to look like that?" I sign, staring at the dish.

Otis is rinsing out his coffee mug in the sink and peeks over my shoulder.

"Uhh," he stalls before signing, "I bet it tastes delicious."

Damnit.

Bake a pie, they said. It will be fun, they said.

I'm an amateur in the kitchen and I decided to try and make pumpkin pie from scratch to bring to Mary and Jim's for Thanksgiving tonight. And Mary's an *awesome* cook.

I'm screwed.

Maybe I'll run to the store and get a can of cranberry sauce. It's a cop out, but Mary probably won't expect anything more than that from me anyway. I stare contemptuously at my friend turned foe: the pie.

How could you? And on Thanksgiving!

Otis's arms hug my waist and my head turns to lean into his neck and whine.

I wish he was coming with me, but he always goes to Dean's for the holiday.

It's been two weeks since we admitted to loving each other. We've had two weeks of undisturbed bliss, ignoring a difficult reality we'll have to face eventually.

Dean.

Neither of us have seen him since Halloween, nearly a month ago. He's had another roaster dropping off the order at the café the last couple of weeks, and that's pretty much the only time I see him anyway.

I feel bad leaving Otis to deal with Dean on his own, but it's not like I was invited to go. And what will I really do to help in the unlikely event that they *do* end up talking about Otis and me?

Still, a shiver runs through me at the thought.

Otis chuckles. "Cold?" he asks, his lips hovering over my ear.

I'm not cold but his whisper gives me chills. I shake my head, pressing a kiss to his jaw.

He pulls me back across my studio, toward the bed, a smile pulling up my cheeks. He lets go of my hands and grabs the two books we have on my bedside table, weighing them back and forth. One is Paulo Coelho's *The Alchemist* and the other is Erik Larson's *Devil in the White City;* my favorite and his newest book. I point to his and he grins, placing the other one back on the table.

Otis sits on the bed, his back upright against the headboard and I snuggle between his legs, resting back against his chest. He holds the book with his arms wrapped around me and opens to where we left off.

We read and as I finish the page, I rub his leg.

A moment later, he turns the page. I read the next one and when I'm almost finished, he runs his hand down my arm.

I finish the page and turn it.

I've never loved reading *so fucking much.*

We continue through a few more pages, touching each other to let the other one know when we're ready to go on. But as this game usually goes, the reading ends, and the touching continues. He drops the book beside us on the bed and twists my neck to kiss him. His hand holds my jaw, slowly moving his lips against mine.

Scooting me over his leg, he moves in front of me, keeping our lips locked. My back is now against the headboard and he's all fours between my legs, kissing me with such passion it feels like a fire burning in my throat. I whimper, feeling his lips curl against my mouth before he finally releases them.

I squeal from a tug on my legs—my back staying slightly propped on some pillows—as he reaches under the bed, picking up the smut book he "skimmed" and handing it to me.

What?

He takes my lips once more, then pulls back and smirks.

"Read," he says.

Oh my God, the rasp in his voice—the dark, seductive tilt of his lips. The word *read* just made me flood my panties.

Rapid breaths spill out of me as I register *what* he said and my eyebrows pinch.

He wants me to *read? Now?!*

He waits as I eye him curiously before I hesitantly take the book and begrudgingly start to read. And by *start to read*, I mean stare at the page. In seconds, Otis's fingertips trail up my thighs. I peek over the book and he stops.

I fight a smile, reluctantly pulling my eyes back down to the words.

He's upping the ante.

My panties inch down, and heat sweeps across my cheeks, still hidden behind the book as soft lips trail up my inner thigh. A gasp escapes but I concentrate on the words, trying to play it cool.

Never been cool, Evelyn.

My legs hook over his shoulders, feeling his tongue glide slowly between my folds and I drop my arm with the book in my hand.

Otis stops, but stays put with his head between my legs. He eyes the book then shifts his gaze to me.

I scrunch my nose, slowly bringing the book back. The last thing I see is his mischievous smile before the book is back in front of my face.

His hungry groan vibrates against my core, tickling up my spine. *Oh. My. God.*

I arrive at Mary and Jim's home in Lakeview twenty minutes late. I stopped by the store and grabbed a can of cranberry sauce, but I still brought my ugly pie.

Maybe it will taste good.

I roll my eyes for even thinking it. Mary will have a great spread and everyone will be too full to eat my shitty pie. I'll get credit for bringing dessert and none of the blame for ruining it.

Go me!

Jim answers the door and quickly steps aside, welcoming me in. He takes my coat and hangs it, then brings me in for a Jim hug.

I'm convinced that his and Mary's hugs could open their own business and be wildly successful.

"Hey kid, you brought pie!" he says with a big smile.

"I brought pie's ugly step-sister," I crack, handing him the dish.

He leads me through the dining room, toward the kitchen, and I take in the homey ambiance.

They have the kind of house that's decorated in a way that mirrors the time of year, but also has their lifetime of memories sprinkled through it.

Their story through changing seasons.

We pass through the doorway from the dining room, into the kitchen, and witness Mary in all of her whirlwind glory. She's peeking in the oven, sipping a glass of wine while stirring something on the stove. Sometimes I truly believe she has a secret, extra set of arms that extend to assist in hugging and multitasking.

She closes the oven with her hip then spins around and approaches me like she's sneaking up on me, like I'm not looking right at her.

Pulling me in for a hug, she says, "Hello, love," while squeezing me tight.

"Evelyn made pie!" Jim announces behind me.

"Oh!" Mary exclaims, raising her eyebrows.

"Don't worry, you don't have to eat it. I also have a can of cranberry sauce in my bag."

"That's my girl," Mary says, tipping her wine glass.

She scurries to the fridge to get the bottle and pours me a glass, then refocuses on her cooking efforts.

"Can I help with anything?"

"No, love. I've got a fire going in the living room. Go enjoy and get on my level!" she orders over her shoulder.

Celtic holiday music plays lightly as I wander into the living room, sitting next to the fire, soaking up the heat.

The warmth is so inviting but I find myself missing Otis, which is ridiculous because it's only been two hours since I was wrapped around him in bed.

I just wish he could be here. I've spent Thanksgiving with him before, but that was a long time ago.

"Evelyn!" Gloria squealed as I shut the passenger door.

My smile widened as she hurried toward me, her turquoise jewelry bouncing with each step before she threw her arms around me in a bear hug. I returned her embrace, meeting Dean's eyes over her shoulder.

He laughed, mouthing, "I told you." My eyebrows raised as if to say, "you weren't kidding."

I was so nervous on our drive to Rockford, not to mention the month prior, knowing I'd be spending Thanksgiving with my new boyfriend and his family.

Dean and I had only met a few months ago so I was truly touched when he offered to let me go home with him and Otis for the holiday.

Gloria released her hold. "Oh honey, I'm so happy you came. The boys have told me so much about you, I feel like I already know you." She held my arm affectionately then swung around to greet her sons.

The boys?

Otis had told her about me too?

We had become fast friends despite the language barrier, but it still warmed me to know that he told his mom about me.

Gloria linked arms with Otis and I rounded the car to meet Dean.

He chuckled, shrugging. "She's a hugger."

"I like her," I smiled.

Dean slung his arm around me, nuzzling his face against my temple as we walked inside their cozy ranch-style home.

I met their dad, Paul, then we dropped our bags in Dean's room and quickly started making out on his childhood bed.

Later, I was in the kitchen, staring at the sweet potatoes like they were a rabid animal I was trying to keep calm. Gloria had asked me to peel and slice them and I pretended that I was the kind of girl who had totally done that before.

The house was quiet and warm. I could see from the window above the sink that Dean and Paul were on the screened-in patio attached to the back of the house—cleaning up so we could sit out there later. Gloria stood with them, barking orders and criticizing their inability to clean properly.

I giggled and nervously started peeling the potatoes, humming quietly to myself when I heard feet shuffling behind me. I turned and saw Otis in the archway leading to the kitchen. A shy smile inched up his cheeks and my own mouth curled up at him over my shoulder.

"Want help?" he signed.

I shrugged, pulling my mouth back through clenched teeth, feeling caught in my domestic ineptitude.

He blew out an amused breath and stood beside me, grabbing another peeler from the utensil drawer.

The woman had two peelers. I was doomed.

Peeling, I started to quietly sing again. Otis stopped and turned toward me, so I faced him. I had only just started to work on my signing, so I had to pay close attention.

"What are you singing?" he signed.

I swore he was a superhero. He noticed everything. He could tell you every detail about a stranger we'd see on the train and he read people like he could see into their souls, which is one of the reasons I felt so flattered that he seemed to like spending time with me.

My shoulders shrugged. "I don't know the sign," then I fingerspelled, "C-H-R-I-S-T-M-A-S music."

He smiled and made a 'C' hand shape, sweeping it from left to right, arching it like a rainbow. Or a wreath, I thought. I repeated the movement back and he nodded.

He went to the living room, just off the kitchen and rifled through some CDs, putting one in the stereo that sat on a shelf in their entertainment center.

Alvin and the Chipmunks' "Christmas Don't be Late" blasted through the speakers, making me jump and laugh. He quickly turned it down, giving me an apologetic expression and I laughed again.

He came back to the sink, I smiled up at him and we peeled potatoes.

It's like my memories are from a new angle, lately. Some of the background details have become the main attraction. I've thought about that Thanksgiving so many times, but that piece of the memory was always just a passing feature. But I see now, that even then, as his brother's new girlfriend, Otis cared for me. He wanted me to feel comfortable at their home, with their family.

And now I *really* miss him.

chapter thirty-four

otis

I only arrived at Dean and Marnie's house a little over an hour ago and I'm already preparing for a speedy departure after dinner. Marnie has provided a nice buffer for the awkward tension between Dean and me, so I'm thankful for that, at least.

I'm leaning against the counter in the kitchen, sipping my beer like its water when Dean comes in from the living room.

He goes right to the fridge, grabbing another beer and Marnie stops stirring at the stove, giving him a pointed look. I immediately slow down on my own drink.

Don't want to piss off the buffer.

He twists the top off anyway but walks up behind her and kisses the top of her head, giving her swollen belly a small rub. Her mouth straightens into a tight line as she resumes her stirring, watching the pot with a concentrated intensity.

Dean's eyes drift up to meet mine and I dart mine away. His stares haven't been exactly *friendly* since I got here.

We haven't mentioned the weird moment on Halloween so the energy has been ... uncomfortable. I almost bailed on coming at all, but then he definitely would have known I was avoiding him. We've spent every Thanksgiving together since he came back from Colorado.

Once we were grown, our parents decided to travel for the holiday.

"We love you guys. But drinking on the beach in November is fun!" Mom had said.

"Okay, I think we're all set!" Marnie says, walking to the kitchen table.

At least I think that's what she said. I'm still squinting from trying to read her lips when she hands me a casserole dish of corn pudding while Dean grabs a jar of jam for the rolls and a plate of breaded chicken.

Apparently, turkey isn't agreeing with Marnie through her pregnancy, so breaded chicken it is. Which sounds fucking amazing, actually.

I carry the dish to the dining room, watching Dean manhandle the jar of jam at the table. I offer my hand, seeing if he wants me to give it a try, but he stubbornly continues to struggle with the jar. A moment later he pops the lid off and places it victoriously on the table.

My phone buzzes, and I slip my hand into my pocket to grab it.

Evelyn: Can we spend Thanksgiving together next year? I won't make pie!!

She is so damn cute.

I can't help but smile, feeling totally fucking smitten.

> **Me:** I'd love to! And I can't wait to try some of your weird-looking pie :)

Sliding my phone back into my pocket, I pull out my chair, catching Dean's drawn-out stare on me from across the table. My eyes squint in his direction, determined to play dumb until I know for sure that I'm not just being paranoid.

The three of us pile food onto our plates—it all looks so good.

I feel bad that I didn't contribute anything, but Marnie insisted she had it covered.

She raises her water and Dean and I follow.

"To family!" she says simply, rubbing her belly.

Dean leans in to give her a kiss but she turns her head and he ends up planting it on her cheek.

Something's off with them.

The three of us clink our glasses while I try to manage a genuine smile. My eyes meet Dean's for just a second before shifting them back to my plate.

I quickly start shoveling food into my mouth, trying every combination possible—but I don't miss Marnie eyeing Dean as he sips his beer.

I wonder if the smell bothers her; I've heard your senses can heighten during pregnancy. My hand awkwardly moves my beer closer to me, further from her, but I don't take a sip.

Totally normal, jackass.

"This is so good, Marnie!" I sign.

I try to make my signing simple since she only knows the basics. And I'm definitely trying to suck up to the buffer, but it really is delicious.

She smiles, nodding. "Thanks, Otis. I'm glad you like it."

"How's Evelyn doing?" Dean signs, then picks up his fork, twirling it with his thumb while it leans against his index finger.

Uhh.

My eyes drift to Marnie but then back to Dean, clearing my throat. "Good," I sign back, casually.

He nods slowly, taking another swig of his beer and I direct my attention back to Marnie, searching for a subject that won't add to my nerves.

"Do you know if it's a boy or girl?" I sign, glancing at her belly.

Her eyes squint then look over to Dean.

"Boy or girl," he clarifies.

Marnie nods before looking back at me. "No. Dean wants to know, but I want it to be a surprise!" she says, small excitement lifting her shoulders.

Dean rubs her back, smiling at her before his gaze finds me, again, and his smile falls.

Fucking hell.

The rest of dinner is spent learning all about babies.

Not gonna lie, the little *casual fact* about the belly button nearly did me in.

I offer to help Marnie clean up, but she pats my shoulder. "That's Dean's job later," she says with a grin.

I breathe a laugh, continuing into the living room and sitting on the recliner while Dean and Marnie take the couch.

I'm leaving soon—I've already planted the seed by mentioning I have a deadline, but I feel like I need to hang around for a little bit just so it doesn't seem like I came to eat and run.

Dean puts a football game on, and I see Marnie cross her arms, shooting intermittent glares in his direction.

I'm trying to remember if she dislikes football. Not that I really care to watch it either, but it's as good of a distraction as any.

She's probably pissed about how much he's drinking. I've got to say, even for Dean, he really is throwing them back tonight.

Marnie only lasts about five minutes before excusing herself to go nap. I stand up to say goodbye since I don't intend on being here when she wakes back up.

"Thank you for dinner, Marnie. Everything was awesome," I sign.

She smiles, giving me a hug. "Bitch to see you, Otis," she signs.

I chuckle. *Bitch* and *good* are both chin signs, but I get the picture.

She continues toward the kitchen, but throws a disapproving glance at Dean's empty beer bottle as she passes the table and leaves the room.

The buffer is gone.

Dean goes to the fridge, cracking another beer and plops back down on the couch. My fingers tap the arm of the recliner as I start to sip my drink a little quicker, feeling my body buzz with nerves.

This is stupid.

Anxiety is fucking stupid; it's been messing with me all night. Dean's having some beers because it's a holiday, something he's done plenty of times before and it has absolutely nothing to do with him witnessing a look between Evelyn and me.

I sneak a side glance at Dean, noticing his eyes are on the ceiling, his palms rolling the bottle between them.

It's fine. Maybe he had a fight with Marnie.

She seemed pissed about *something*—that's probably it.

Dean suddenly puts the bottle down hard on the coffee table, leaning forward so that his elbows rest on his knees and his hands clasp. He keeps his head down for a couple seconds and then twists to look at me.

His stare is hard, but it doesn't necessarily seem angry. It's like he's *waiting* for me to respond, but he hasn't said anything. I nervously bring my bottle to my lips, taking another sip.

Keep calm.

"So, you're fucking Evelyn now?" he signs.

I choke on the beer and cough. A burning sensation tickles my nose, continuing to hack from his crude question.

I swallow hard, finally taking a full inhale. Once the coughing subsides, I shake my head, peering back up at Dean.

"No, I'm not *fucking* Evelyn," I sign, tightly.

His shoulders relax but he eyes me intuitively. "Sorry . . . I just . . . I don't know."

My expression stays even as I shrug at him, still not willing to admit to anything until I know what he's thinking.

"I don't know . . . when I got your book from your room a few weeks ago, I thought I saw—" he halts, shifting uncomfortably. "I thought I saw her bra on your floor."

My spine stiffens, tension rising at my immediate jealousy.

He's seen her bra before . . . among other things.

Evelyn and I weren't together at that point, but she *had* been sleeping in my bed. A small throb pulls across my forehead and the pads of my fingers rub over it, nervously.

"I saw that picture on your nightstand of the two of you, and the way you were staring at each other on Halloween . . ." he signs, his eyes pressing.

Shit.

I could avoid this all on technicalities. *I could.* But I'm a terrible liar—I'm probably even less convincing right now because I don't want to lie about this.

I don't want to lie to him.

My eyes search the floor, like maybe I'll find some courage down there.

I sigh and then look back at my brother. "We're in love, Dean."

Any small relief he may have just felt turns to anger in an instant and his face contorts into a look of disgust. He stands, suddenly, and I follow suit as his eyes darken, shaking his head.

"You're in love . . ." he trails off, his stare slowly turning to stunned outrage. "Fucking *Evelyn Gray*?!" he signs sharply.

His eyes scan the room like he's waiting for the punchline.

Dean and I have only fought one other time and I hit him, so I stand still, on high alert.

My head nods once while my eyes fill with sympathy.

Dean wasn't just my brother growing up, he was my best friend—

my only friend. Our relationship might not be what it once was, but I don't want to hurt him.

I'm a little taken aback by his reaction, though. It's not like I thought he'd be happy about Evelyn and me—but his anger seems so potent, like a fresh wound instead of one that's had seven years to scab and scar.

He squints his eyes at me, his expression turning smug as he sucks his teeth.

"That's fucking . . . ridiculous," he signs, laughing humorlessly. "She feels *bad* for you, Otis—she always has. And she's happy you didn't die in that alley. It's *pity,* not love."

I blink hard, feeling like a bat just hit a grand slam into my chest. My stare darts back and forth between one of his eyes, then the other—suddenly feeling like I'm looking at a complete stranger.

My mouth gapes at his nasty fucking words but my face fights to mask the blow, signing, "Are you serious?"

Pulling a frustrated hand down his beard, he signs, "I know the two of you are close now. And when we were together, I noticed you checking her out sometimes. She thought it was cute."

Holy shit.

He noticed . . . *She* noticed?

My knees wobble and a cold sweat starts to pool at my temple. I grab the side of the chair to steady myself as Dean stalks toward me.

"But she was *my* girlfriend. I *lived* with her. You were just her boyfriend's brother—I'm pretty sure she thought you were gay when we first met," he signs.

The air becomes thick. I feel like I'm being buried alive. My eyes slam shut, actually hoping it will make me disappear.

I breathe deep, reluctantly reopening my eyes to meet Dean's unforgiving, angry glare.

He was my hero growing up, he literally saved me countless times and right now it feels like he's trying to kill me.

My head shakes, at a complete loss. The bullying in school was awful, but it was fucking child's play compared to *this. Dean* saying these things, insisting they're how Evelyn feels . . .

"Your voice is burning leaves to me, Otis."

My heart lifts remembering her words, straightening my spine.

He doesn't know her. Not anymore.

I lock eyes with him, ready for fucking war.

If he thinks he can use their history as a weapon, then I will too. My feet close the distance between us so that I'm standing directly in front of him, inhaling deep through my nose.

"You wouldn't know a goddamn thing about her anymore, Dean! You lost that privilege when you fucking *left her!"*

His eyes bore into me and his jaw ticks. "You may think you know everything Otis, but you have no fucking clue what happened with us," he signs, pacing away but turns back quickly. "I'm so sick of you holding the fact that I left over my head. You're my fucking brother, and you never even asked why I *had* to leave!"

I feel the rise, my heart quickening, my breath becoming heavy.

"Okay. Tell me," I sign.

He looks at me with surprise, like he didn't actually expect me to want his explanation. His expression slowly turns defeated as he shakes his head.

"I can't," he signs. "Don't you think I would have told you by now, if I could?"

Well, what do you know—there is an honorable bone in his body.

We've never confronted him leaving Chicago. All of the resentment only grew while he was away and by the time he came back, it just felt like a mockery to try to recreate what we had before.

But if I knew then what I know now . . .

My eyes burn through him, finally signing, "She told me."

His gaze narrows, trying to gauge if we're talking about the same thing.

"I know, Dean," I confirm.

The color falls from his face, his eyes widening. I watch his body stiffen and a whole minute passes before he even blinks.

"She told you?" he signs, and I nod.

We're at a standstill. He seems to be expecting some kind of understanding but I'm still waiting for an explanation. Every moment he stalls only fuels the fury running hot through my veins.

Say something!

He lets out a pained sigh, massaging the back of his neck. "You don't understand . . ."

My fists clench. I swear to God, I'm shaking from the restraint it's taking to not throw him into the fucking wall right now. I bark out a humorless laugh, trying to get *some* kind of release.

My hands move sharp, aggressive. "I understand. I fully *understand* that you abandoned Evelyn a few months after she was fucking raped."

He winces, shutting his eyes tight.

Good. I hope it hurts, asshole.

They reopen a moment later, hard and dark. "Otis, you have no idea what it was like."

Please don't tell me he's looking for sympathy.

He steps closer, trying to get me to look at him and I begrudgingly do for some reason.

"She was *ruined* when it happened. I mean, the shit bag was a fucking *friend* of hers. She wouldn't tell me his name or I would have found—" he stops, running his tongue along the roof of his mouth.

A friend of hers?

Bile rises in my throat. I hate that we're talking about this at all and finding out a new detail from anyone other than her feels invasive, but Dean's hands start moving, again.

"She was having these awful nightmares. One night, it was so bad she . . ." he pauses before nervously scratching at his beard.

Is that why she loves that sound?

256

His eyes become haunted, welling with tears, but he blinks them back. "She was so disoriented she actually thought *I* did something to her . . ."

A chill runs down my spine. *Jesus Christ.*

"I begged her to go to therapy. I offered to go with her, but she refused," he signs. "I was *so fucking angry.* I know that nothing compares to what she went through, but something was taken from me too. *She* was taken from me."

His eyes glaze and his head drops. "I left because I couldn't help her. I was a kid, and I was in over my head. I wasn't perfect—I know that. But I'm not a fucking monster."

My head sways with heaviness, but it's a lightweight compared to my heart. I don't know what to make of everything Dean is saying.

He spewed pure venom when I told him about Evelyn and me, but he seems gutted recounting the aftermath of her assault and the end of their relationship.

I don't know what to believe. But there's one thing he said that I *know* to be untrue.

My throat feels swollen, tears bite at the back of my eyes but I swallow them down, zoning in on my brother.

"Evelyn wasn't *ruined.* Something awful happened to her by someone she thought she was safe with . . . it made her believe that trust was an unnecessary risk that could easily backfire. Even by people who claimed to care about her." A heavy sigh escapes me, signing, "Still, she trusted *you.*"

My anger resurfaces, rising with realization. "But you backfired. *You* fed that fear," I sign. "And for that, I fucking hate you."

257

chapter thirty-five

evelyn

Something's off.

I got back from Mary and Jim's late last night when Otis messaged me, telling me that he was crashing at Dean's.

Under normal circumstances, I would assume they had too much to drink and he didn't want to make the long trip back to Edgewater. But he wasn't exactly looking forward to spending time with Dean.

It's after noon and he hasn't come by the café and I just can't shake this feeling in the pit of my stomach that something is wrong. Pulling my phone out, I send him a text.

> **Me:** Hey handsome, your absence is forcing me to actually work. You coming in today?

Playful, casual. Nothing about it says I'm a nutcase who's stressing over not seeing her boyfriend for twenty-four hours.

Get it together, woman.

I start to restock some cups, then brush some stray grinds away when my phone rings. I anxiously pull it from my pocket, even though I know Otis wouldn't be calling me, and I see a Chicago number that I don't recognize.

I answer, "Hello, this is Evelyn," tucking my phone between my shoulder and chin, continuing to clean.

"Ms. Gray, this is Detective James from Chicago PD."

My heart stops, nearly dropping the phone. I clear my throat, mostly just to force myself to breathe, starting toward the back office.

"Hi, Detective. How are you?"

"Fine, Ms. Gray, thank you. I just wanted to let you know we believe we've caught the men who robbed you. They were attempting to do the same to another woman last night and luckily, we were able to intervene," he says, matter-of-factly.

Another woman?

My stomach turns. "You're sure it's the same guys?"

"We've collected DNA samples from the suspects. It matches the samples we gathered from you and Mr. Roberts," he explains.

"Wh-who are they?"

"Their names are Jacob Tesley and Charles Reiger. They were both high on methamphetamines when we arrested them."

I assumed they were drug addicts. They looked strung out—*and the violence . . .*

"Which one is responsible for assaulting Otis?" I ask urgently.

"We believe that to be Charles Reiger. He matches the description that both you and Mr. Roberts provided following the assault," he says. "I see here that Mr. Roberts is deaf? It may take me some time to get an officer with a qualified interpreter to go to his residence and inform him."

"Well, that's bullshit," I mumble, then wince. "I'm sorry. That won't be necessary, I'll tell him."

But really, that *is* bullshit. Otis could have *died* and the police can't pull their resources in a timely manner to update him?

"Okay. The state will be charging them with armed robbery. Once we conclude our investigation, we also intend to charge Mr. Reiger with assault and battery. Mr. Roberts, of course, has every right to file his own charges."

I nod, picking at some old tape on my desk. "Okay. Thank you, Detective," my voice cracks.

"You're welcome, Ms. Gray."

I hang up, seeing a message from Otis and my heart lifts, slightly.

Otis: Sorry—at the library. Trying to get some work done on the book.

His response doesn't exactly settle my nerves, but the fact that he responded at all assures me that he's safe, at least.

I decided to go to the store and grab supplies to make homemade macaroni and cheese. Otis loves it and I thought it'd be a nice surprise when he gets home from the library. I clumsily jiggle my key into the lock, trying to keep my forearm level so the shopping bag doesn't slip off.

Pushing through the door, I close it behind me and as soon as I turn around my heart drops to my feet, weighing me down, making it impossible to move. I blink hard trying to register what I'm looking at—actually *who* I'm looking at.

Lexi is sitting on the couch with wide eyes, smiling nervously and my jaw clenches.

What the fuck?

My eyes shoot to Otis, sitting next her, but my vision tunnels as I drop the shopping bag to the floor.

At the library—*my ass!* He probably didn't stay at Dean's last night either.

I'm suddenly hit with every shitty scenario for why Lexi is here. Sitting closely next to him. *Too close.*

My mind immediately lands on: he went to Dean's, ended up telling him and Dean reminded him what a basket case I am so now he's distancing himself.

Exploring his options.

I knew this was too good to be true.

I knew it, and I let myself get caught up in the bullshit whirlwind of it anyway.

Fuck.

My legs regain some control, backing up toward the door. I think Otis gets up off the couch, but I don't stay long enough to know for sure. I swing the door open, taking quick, angry steps down the hall, back toward the stairs.

Each step crushes my despair and charges my anger. Tears pool in my eyes but I swallow them down.

Don't cry.

Crying is for heartbreak. I need to start looking for cover from the apocalypse descending on me. I need to build a goddamn bomb shelter and never fucking leave it!

I've just reached the stairs when I feel a pull on my elbow, but I don't turn around. Jerking my arm free, I step down, but I'm stopped again when Otis maneuvers his way in front of me, blocking my path.

I won't look up. I won't.

I try to step around him, but he moves in front of me. My body shifts to the other side, but he follows like we're doing some sort of disjointed tango.

My pulse beats in my temple as my glare rises, just to tell him to get the hell out of my way, but I'm met with his wounded eyes.

"You know I'd never hurt you, right?"

My eyes clamp shut and my chin drops. It feels like I mentally just got smacked upside the head. When my eyes reopen, I keep them down, but they slowly lift.

I'm a couple steps higher than him, basically putting our eyes at the same level and the hard stone feeling in my chest melts like candle wax, trapping me in the thick, heavy drips.

He looks destroyed. The dark circles under his eyes are like shadows to his pain-filled stare.

I'm suddenly aware of my unhinged alter-ego from the first time Lexi resurfaced. I imagine Greta, dressed in lingerie, her smug grin meeting mine and she shrugs, as if to say, "Gotcha again."

My face softens and my bottom lip starts trembling as a pathetic squeak trickles from my mouth.

What is wrong with me?

Otis runs a hand through his hair, nervously scratching at the back of his head as he looks down at the steps.

We just stand and stare a few beats more before he takes my hand and leads me back down the hall to his apartment.

He's not sending me away?

Once we're back inside, Lexi has left, probably across the hall filing a restraining order against me and my shame wraps around me like a weighted blanket.

I turn around to face him but smack my palm over my eyes. After a few calming breaths, I finally drop my hand.

"I'm sorry . . . I don't know what came over me," I sign, feeling like an idiot.

Otis shakes his head, running a tense palm down his face. His eyes squeeze shut before he rubs his forehead back and forth, like even *preparing* to deal with me is exhausting.

I've never been on the receiving end of his anger before, and I officially hate it.

He sighs hard, looking at me desperately. "Why don't you *trust me*, Evelyn?" he signs.

"I-I do," I say meekly.

His eyes widen, looking at me like I'm deranged—which is fair.

"That?!" His eyebrows raise, gesturing toward the door. "What the hell was *that?*"

I shake my head, tears filling my eyes.

Jesus Christ, stop crying!

"I don't know . . . I've been worried about you today . . . I showed up here unannounced, I thought you were at the library and then I saw Lexi . . ." I sign, wondering if I look as pathetic as I feel.

Otis closes some distance between us, his expression serious, tight.

"Lexi and I ran into each other downstairs when I got home from the library. I haven't seen her since I blew her off and she asked if we could catch up."

I flinch. *Of course* he would talk to Lexi.

He's a nice guy who left her high and dry without much of an explanation.

He's not his brother.

"I'm sorry . . ." I sign, again.

He deserves more than sorry.

My eyes finally find the courage to look at his—the crease between his brow is deep, but I still see love in his gaze. I still *feel* it and I want to explain myself . . .

"I really don't have a good answer for you," I sign. "I know it sounds stupid and dramatic but some part of me really believes I'm . . . doomed. *Broken.*" I frown, trying to piece it together.

I trust Otis more than I've ever trusted anyone and still, it didn't stop me from believing the worst. I was able to snap out of it, but it doesn't change the reality of my reaction.

"I don't know . . ." I sign. "It's the reason I've avoided relationships . . . *this.*" I wave my arm between the two of us. "I never actually feel safe. There's a piece of me that's always ready for betrayal—expects it. It's happened before . . ."

I'm not even sure I'm making sense, but it's how I feel.

Otis's expression stays tense while his eyes spark new anger.

"Dean," he signs, tightly.

I nod, swallowing the lump in my throat. "Not *just* Dean," I sign. *"He* was a friend of mine. I'd known him since preschool."

Otis's expression softens, nodding solemnly as his eyes meet the floor. He doesn't look as surprised as I'd expect but I can also see that he's exhausted. His head lifts back up and the look on his face tightens my lungs.

I hesitantly inch toward him, staring up into his muted eyes. They're missing their amber hue and I feel like *I* stole it.

He's never done anything but love me. He's always been honest with me, even when it's hard. I've thrown all my baggage at him and he didn't shove it back in my face or leave me alone to pick it all up. He took my hand and brought me back.

He won't hurt you.

I lean my head into his chest, breathing him in. My palm presses over his heart for just a second when my eyes float up to his, again. "I'm so sorry. I *do* trust you," I sign, choking back my regret. "I love you."

He keeps his gaze down, releasing a heavy sigh. He looks back up at me, holding my eyes with his for another moment, then gently cradles my face, softly brushing his lips against mine. His mouth moves tenderly but timid and I ball the fabric of his shirt in my fists.

Our mouths pull apart, but I hold him a moment longer.

A silent promise.

I'll do better.

His body fully relaxes in my arms and my shoulders sag with relief. I lean back, taking in the tired lines on his face; the heavy bags under his eyes.

Did he sleep at all?

"You look beat."

He snorts, nodding.

"You and Dean had a little too much fun last night?" I sign with a playful smirk.

"Definitely not," he signs back.

My eyebrows pinch but between my outburst and how tired he looks, I don't have the heart to ask him about it right now.

"Why don't you go lay down?"

He hesitates but then slowly nods. Leading him to his bedroom, he pulls back the covers, sinking down to the bed and I tuck him in on all sides.

My mouth tilts up my cheek, signing, "That's one tasty burrito," before I lean down, pressing lightly against his lips with mine, then hold my hand to his jaw, giving his scruff a scratch.

He takes my hand from his face, kissing the corner of my wrist. A heavy sigh escapes him as he rolls over, falling asleep immediately.

I still feel uneasy leaving his room. He seemed to understand my deep-rooted neurosis, or at least seemed willing to tolerate it while I try and work through it, but something still feels off.

What happened last night?

He stayed at Dean's, so I can't imagine anything too dramatic occurred. It was probably just a late night and his exhaustion was only made more tiresome by dealing with his batty girlfriend.

Standing in the living room, an anxious groan rumbles my throat. The dark cloud of embarrassment hangs over my head, soaking me in an unexpected downpour.

Why is this so hard for me?

I used to be someone that jumped into relationships with both feet. I fell in love quickly, trusted easily.

But that was *before*.

The depressing thought slumps me to the couch. I mindlessly take my phone out, wanting a distraction but my hand moves on its own accord.

My thumb taps the screen, feeling more and more desperate for comfort with each ring back I hear. After three rings, the call connects.

"Pumpkin!" she squeals, and my throat tightens.

My eyes fill, but my shoulders fall before I say, "Hi, Mom."

chapter thirty-six

otis

My steps are slow, way slower than normal as I walk the hallway to Evelyn's studio. When I finally reach the entrance, I twist the knob, opening the door.

Soft morning light pools in through the small window and I see tiny dust particles circling in the sunlight. My head sweeps the space, finding Evelyn on her bed, propped up by her elbows. She's wearing a black crop top with lacy black panties and her hair is piled on her head with some loose pieces hanging around her face.

God, she's beautiful.

She peeks up with a seductive grin, but her eyes look just past me, just over my shoulder and a large figure brushes past.

He walks toward her and she lays back on the bed, stretching her arms above her head as she gently wiggles her hips.

The man stops, turning his head back over his shoulder to look at me . . .

Dean.

"Thanks for keeping her warm for me, brother," he says with a dark smile.

I reach my arm out, but it moves so slow that he easily steps away, meeting Evelyn on the bed.

She pushes back up on her elbows as Dean leans down and kisses her.

Evelyn . . . No . . .

Their lips stay pressed as she raises her hand to his cheek and scratches his beard lightly with her fingers. His mouth moves over her ear, whispering something and she giggles, her eyes slowly floating up to meet mine as Dean trails his mouth down her neck.

"That is so cute," she says.

She doesn't sign. Her face is mocking, her smile sneering, unlike any smile I've ever seen from her.

I'm unable to move, and unable to look away.

I jerk awake with a gasp and quickly rub my face with my palms.
Fuck.

My head twists to look at the clock on my bedside table: 6:10 p.m.
Jesus Christ, I need more sleep.

I lie there a moment more, closing my eyes, but I'm immediately hit with an image of Evelyn and Dean kissing and I groan, shoving the covers off and swinging my legs to the floor.

My knee bounces as the dream plays and repeats over and over again in my mind.

After taking a heavy inhale, I release it out.

Reality isn't much better at the moment, though.

Evelyn's face when she saw Lexi in my apartment killed me. It broke my heart that she thought I would do that to her.

She looked . . . *possessed* when I caught her on the stairs.

It was the strangest thing. It was like a light turned on in her eyes when she finally looked at me.

I'm grateful that she seems willing to try to work through things she's spent a long time burying.

It's understandable that the wires are crossed in her mind, and I just have to be patient while she untangles them.

My body tenses and my adrenaline starts to rise.

She shouldn't *have* to untangle and rewire.

Fucking Dean.

I breathe deep, trying to steady myself. I know this isn't all Dean's fault, Evelyn said as much herself, but I'm still so wound up from everything that's happened between him and me in the last twenty-four hours.

Another groan. *I guess more sleep is a lost fucking cause.*

Pushing off the bed, I start toward the kitchen when I notice that the TV is on.

My eyes drift the couch, seeing Evelyn curled up in a tight ball, sleeping.

How does she make herself so small?

Relief fills my chest. It's nice to see her—not half naked and kissing my brother right in front of me. I grab a water bottle from the fridge, chugging it down in a few gulps.

Through the cut out in the kitchen wall, I see Evelyn sit up with tired, blinking eyes. Her eyelids flutter until she eventually spots me, giving me a dopey smile.

"You're awake," she signs from the couch, her eyes still blinking.

I chuckle. "Are you?"

She blinks, one eye at a time. "I think so," she laughs.

Her hair sits on top of her head, reminding me of my severely fucked, voyeuristic dream from hell. I close my eyes and shake my head, trying to wipe the image from my brain as I go to the couch and sink in next to her.

She's yawning and stretching, making me yawn.

"I thought you'd be out all night," she signs, scooting a little closer.

"Bad dream," I sign back.

Her face wilts, tugging her bottom lip between her teeth as her brows furrow.

"Why are you making the angry puppet face?" I sign.

She releases her lip, moving to a nervous smile. "I need to tell you something."

She shifts so she's facing me head on, releasing a heavy exhale.

"They caught the guys, Otis." Her eyes shift back and forth between mine, watching me carefully.

My head juts back. Of all the things I thought she might need to tell me, *that* didn't even cross my mind.

Chicago has its fair share of crime, so I really didn't expect them to catch the creeps who attacked us, and certainly not so quickly.

"How?" I sign.

She shifts uncomfortably. "They tried to jump another woman last night."

Jesus.

I grab the top of my head with my hand. Sometimes I really wish I could pull the darkest shit from my brain and light it on fire.

Feeling Evelyn's eyes on me, I look over at her. Coincidentally, she's watching me like I may just burst into flames. I try to manage a small smile, reassuring her that I won't.

I don't think, anyway.

"What's wrong?" She pushes some unruly waves away from my forehead and kisses my temple. "I thought you'd be relieved."

A long, drawn out sigh pushes between my lips. I *am* relieved that the sick fucks are in jail.

But my injuries had healed and there was so much other shit going on, it was easy to not think about it too much. Thinking about it now, I'm all too aware of something.

"It's . . ." I pause, not really sure how to articulate it. "It's just some fucked up irony."

Evelyn tilts her head, waiting for me to elaborate.

"I stopped using my voice when I was a teenager so I'd stop being bullied, only to be nearly beaten to death for *not* using it as an adult," I sign.

I don't know if it's my exhaustion or if I've become a bit numb to the whole ordeal, but I don't feel the raging anger running through me at this realization for some reason.

I look to Evelyn for commiseration, but her gaze is down, eyebrows pinched. She stays like that for a few seconds before she tilts her chin up.

"Maybe it's the Universe's fucked up way of telling you that you've been silent long enough," she signs, tilting her lips.

She leans into me, kissing the corner of my mouth, then runs her thumb over my lips.

"She just feels bad for you, Otis."

I flinch and Evelyn's eyebrows pinch.

I can't talk to her about this. Not yet.

"Be right back," I sign suddenly, pushing off the couch.

I need a minute to shake off the queasiness turning in my stomach. Tension creeps up my spine as I make my way to the bathroom, quickening my steps.

Shutting the door, I turn the faucet and splash some water on my face. My eyes close and I grip the edges of the counter, breathing deep.

In. Out.

I'm not sure I should talk to Evelyn about the fight at all. Dean said . . . *a lot*. And I'm not even sure what was true. I grab the knob to turn off the sink a little harder than necessary, catching a glimpse of myself in the mirror.

Holy hell, I look rough.

I move to the shower and turn it on, waiting for the water to warm up. My eyes zone out on the heavy cascade pouring down and I absentmindedly run my hand through it, jerking away when the temperature is nearly scalding.

Perfect.

Undressing quickly, I step into the hot stream. My shoulders fall and my jaw drops, my mind starting to slow as I turn to let the water run down my face.

Small hands suddenly wrap around my waist while soft, gentle lips press between my shoulders. The rest of the tension holding my limbs falls with her touch.

I feel her cheek rest against my back, lacing my fingers through hers as they hold around my midsection, my back to her front.

I lift one of her hands, brushing her knuckles against my lips, kissing each one.

I know she's naked and wet behind me, so turning around is tempting, but this feels *so good.*

"I'm pretty sure she thought you were gay."

My hand squeezes hers tighter, remembering Dean's words.

Something takes over me.

Twisting around, I crush her mouth with mine. A surprised whimper squeaks from her mouth and it fuels me. My tongue plunges through her lips, stroking every inch inside her mouth.

I move us out of the flowing water, pinching her nipple, using my weight to pin her against the wall.

I feel savage . . . I feel like . . .

Like you have something to prove.

I break our fused lips, dropping to my knees. After hooking one of her legs over my shoulder, my other hand presses flat across her stomach and I dive between her thighs.

She jerks against the wall and I growl, licking and sucking, devouring. I grab her thighs to spread them further, tonguing her deeper, when she grabs my hair.

The tug pulls my gaze up to her face.

Panting heavily, eyes wide, she looks . . .

Oh my God.

I gently take her leg from my shoulder, lowering it to the floor. My knees wobble, standing back up and I cup her face with my hand, searching her eyes.

She doesn't look scared but there's apparent shock and I can't tell if it's good or bad.

What was I thinking?

She holds my forearm while my hand continues to cradle her cheek. I still can't read her and its only heightening my panic.

Why can't I read her?

I drop my head, shaking it. She pulls my chin back up to look at her. All the shock has worn off and now she looks . . . *worried*.

Fuck.

I drop my hand from her face. "I'm sorry."

I can't seem to make eye contact with her; any time I try, my shame spikes them back down to the floor. Evelyn ducks her head, trying to get my attention.

"Otis," she signs. "Look at me."

I force my eyes up from her hands, meeting her earthy eyes as she runs a hand through my damp hair.

"You just . . . surprised me," she signs. "It didn't even feel like you were here . . ."

I wasn't here. I was in my head, and she knows it. I may be having a hard time reading her right now, but she knows me like her favorite book.

The Alchemist.

I'm a fucking idiot.

She dips her head to meet my eyes which have returned to their proper place on the floor.

Planting her palms on each side of my face, she pulls it up to meet hers.

"You can go down on me anytime you want. But I want *you* there. Okay?" She gives me a timid smile and presses a soft kiss to my lips.

It's more than I deserve, but I take it because I *need* to feel her.

I need to feel her lips against mine, I need to feel her heart against my palm.

I need to feel like she wants me.

chapter thirty-seven

evelyn

ucking hell.

F I guess Mondays are harder if you've had a weekend off, but I spent most of the weekend catching up on all the work I've been slacking on the last few weeks.

The good news is, I think I'm all caught up. The bad news, I feel totally run down.

Before Otis and I got together, I *lived* to work—always at the shop—constantly trying to find ways to make it better and keep it running smoothly.

No one is going to care about Bohemia like I do.

But I'd be lying if I said Otis's larger piece of real estate in my heart didn't make it challenging to keep up with the place the way I did before.

The bell above the door jingles and Reggie walks in with sunglasses and a baseball cap on.

Shit.

He's either hung over, heartbroken or hangry. It's also his disguise when he's "not stalking" a hot new guy but I don't think that's the case.

Mary notices him too, arching her eyebrow as she helps a customer at the register.

"Evie. I'm dying," he says with all seriousness.

It still could be any one of the H's . . . I need more information.

"It's the holidays, Reg. I probably can't get Lady Gaga to sing your eulogy. Think you can make it till the new year?" I tease.

He deadpans, pulling his sunglasses off.

Woah. He looks . . . well, he looks how I probably look from putting in all that overtime this weekend. His usually vibrant skin has a gray tinge to it, his eyes worn and bloodshot.

"What's wrong?"

He sighs, twisting the legs of his sunglasses between his fingers. "Mike . . ."

Heartbroken.

"Oh Reggie." I walk over and hug him tight. "What happened?"

My sweet friend. He really does look so sad. It's been a while since Reggie was actually involved with someone. He's had flings here and there, but I had high hopes for Mike—he seemed special to him.

"I don't even know. He's busy with school, said he needs some time to think. Goddamnit, Evie. We're in our thirties. When does this shit end?"

I think he's actually asking me, but I don't have an answer for him.

It was easy to distract myself with work, but things were off with Otis and I this weekend, too. The shower incident was . . . intense.

I would have been totally fucking into it if I thought he was in the moment with me. It was like he was acting out a scene or something, like he wasn't him and I wasn't me. He felt so awful about the whole thing, he could barely look at me all weekend.

I can't help but feel like it had something to do with Dean. I still don't know what happened on Thanksgiving, but whatever it was, it seems to be getting to him.

I look at my best friend, now encased in a Mary hug. Opening the fridge, I find the cold brew, pouring him a cup. His eyes widen just a bit, taking the drink from me.

"Should we go kick the shit out of the bag tonight?" I ask, with a taunting smirk.

"Hell. Fucking. Yes."

A loud bang at the back door startles me.

Shit! That's Red Line with my order.

I scurry to the back room, pushing the heavy door open. Sharp wind hits my face, but the real blow is Dean standing in front of me.

I gasp but quickly try to fix my face, which I'm sure resembles something close to a zebra running into a hungry lion.

"H-Hey," I stutter.

Put that theater degree to good use and act better!

He seems annoyed already, which only adds to my nerves. I'm really wishing I had pressed Otis more about what happened so I felt prepared to deal with whatever this is.

He holds up the invoice, saying, "Got your order," practically shoving the papers at me.

I take the invoice, pushing the heavy crate by the door to hold it open.

"Haven't seen ya for a few weeks," I say over my shoulder as I drop the invoice on my desk. *Maybe the beast likes small talk.*

Back outside, Dean is standing in the bed of his truck as Reggie emerges, stopping suddenly like he just ran into the wall of tension.

"Hey, Helen," he says cautiously, giving me a side glance.

Dean looks up from his task, nodding in Reggie's direction. "Hey, Reg."

Great, the lion's cordial to the gazelle.

Dean hands me a heavy burlap sack and I wobble a bit from the weight, carrying it inside, taking the time to steady my heartbeat.

Did Otis tell him?

It seems highly improbable that they talked about us at all on Thanksgiving with Dean's pregnant wife as a bystander, but he seems . . . abrasive. Maybe I'm just paranoid because I know we have to tell him.

But I'm also having a hard time believing that Dean would even be that bothered by it all. Sure, it might be a little weird for him because we dated—*seven years ago.* And . . . he's the one who cheated on *me!*

I drop the bag to the floor, finding some new confidence from my internal pep talk. I go back out to get another and Dean drops it into my arms. Losing my balance, I stumble back, breaking the bag's fall as it lands on top of me.

"Evie! Are you okay?!" Reggie squawks, hauling the heavy bag off of my chest.

Coughing from the impact, I croak out, "I'm fine."

I lie there a minute, mostly because it fucking hurt, but also because I just need a minute. Dean stands over me, extending his hand. I hesitate for just a second before I take it, brushing imaginary dust off of myself while my eyes study him.

Does he know?

He clears his throat, his eyebrows pinching. "Sorry about that. You okay?"

His voice is soft, remorseful. Confusing.

I shrug, awkwardly. "I'm good. Just lost my footing, I guess."

I haven't taken the time to really look at him in a long while. He looks so different from the boy I met in college. Still handsome, but he's just . . . such a man, now. Another reminder of how much time has passed.

"The invoice?" he says, impatiently.

A grumpy man.

"Right!" I hurry back into the office, Dean following behind me, waiting by the door.

I grab a pen, signing the top copy when I notice . . .

The discount is gone.

I tear the white copy off, turning around to hand it back to him.

Our exchanged glance is quick, but heavy.

"Dean . . ." I start to say.

But the door is already closing.

Jab—cross—punch!

Oh yeah. Definitely needed this. Reggie did too. He's wailing on his bag like a maniac!

I hadn't come back here since the attack. Mostly because I was too busy between helping Otis and the café. But if I'm honest with myself, I know that's not why I kept my distance.

PTS: Post Traumatic Superstition. I worried that if I came back here again—if I did what I did before—the attack could happen all over again. Or *something* awful would happen. I probably would have avoided Bohemia if I could have, but life isn't free, unfortunately.

It's completely illogical. It's not even a real disorder, at least not according to my many internet searches. It's just a special slice of fucked up made for me.

I'm actually kind of proud of myself for braving it to come here for Reggie tonight. The avoidance happened after I was assaulted too, but even more so.

I've blocked out a lot from that time. Repression, my therapist Reggie informed me, is a pretty common response to trauma.

But the problem is, the memories are still there. They haven't been erased—they're just hiding.

Blood trickled from my mouth as I writhed, screaming. I couldn't get enough air in my lungs. My eyes felt like they had been fused shut but when I finally pried them open, a shadowy figure hovered above me.

My violent scream rattled my throat. "Get off of me!" I cried, thrashing.

I pushed him out of the way. My feet stumbled a couple steps before falling to the floor. I still couldn't catch my breath.

"Baby . . ." he said softly behind me, gently touching my shoulder.

"Fuck you! Don't touch me!" I screamed through my heavy sobs.

He took his hand off my shoulder immediately but shuffled around, sitting on the floor across from me. My head was down, still trying to catch my breath, still stuck in hell.

My fingers curled into the wood, choking out, "How could you?"

My body shook violently as I folded forward, my forehead pressing against the floor.

"What?" he hissed.

Something about the pained way he said it forced me to sit up.

Holding my weight on my hands in front of me, I slowly lifted my chin.

My boyfriend sat in front of me—destroyed. His own tears streamed down his face, looking at me like I was a wild animal.

My snarl softened with recognition, but my throat felt raw.

"Dean?" I rasped.

His head dropped and he lost it. I had never seen him cry before but he cried long, hysterical tears.

I'd had another nightmare. They were getting worse and the sleeping pills I was taking were making it harder to wake up.

Wiping the blood from my chin, I squeaked, "I-I'm sorry . . . I thought . . ."

I felt the gash on the inside of my cheek, realizing I bit it in my sleep.

"Dean . . . I . . ."

There was nothing I could say to him. Even though I wasn't thinking clearly, I had lumped him in with the piece of shit that made me this way.

"Evie . . . Baby . . ." *he choked, still crying. "What can I do? I'll do anything, but I don't know what to do."*

He leaned toward me, cautiously pulling me into him, as he had done every time since I told him. Every touch came with a warning light.

I felt weak and tired and in so much fucking pain that I actually thought I might die. And I was killing the boy who had his arms wrapped around me. The boy who was trying to love me through it.

But it didn't matter. I was never going to be okay again. I couldn't even bring myself to appreciate his comfort because shattered things can't be fixed. You can glue the pieces back together but even then, when you look closely, you'll see the cracks.

They're still broken.

"Fuck!"

My teeth clench feeling my knuckles tear. I shake my hand, still wrapped in the leather glove as I walk to the bench at the edge of the room. I drag in heavy breaths, pulling the strap on my right hand off with my teeth and then shaking the glove off.

Bloody knuckles.

I blink through the green spots in my vision, trying to shake off the blackout that tore up my hand. My torso folds forward, holding my weight on my elbows, trying to get my breathing under control.

God, of all the memories I wish I could actually block out—that one is top five.

I might need a top ten.

Reggie plops down next to me. "Baby girl!"

He grabs my hand and I wince, pulling it away, telling him, "I'm fine."

He huffs, waiting a second before he murmurs, "Dean?"

I shrug, taking my other glove off and grabbing my water bottle and bag from my cubby.

Right. I have *current* Dean problems to deal with right now.

I don't know why Otis wouldn't tell me that he told Dean about us. I would have understood—it had to happen. I just don't know why he didn't tell me.

I texted him earlier telling him I was hitting the gym with Reggie tonight and he told me he'd come to my place after.

Reggie and I toss our gloves into the dirty bin.

"Ready?" he asks.

chapter thirty-eight

otis

God, it's cold.

Evelyn should be back any minute and I figured I'd wait out here instead of having to disarm and reset the alarm twice, but goddamn.

My neck crouches further into the collar of my coat, turning my body in the opposite direction of the wind.

Evelyn rounds the corner of the block, practically running toward the black brick building. As she gets closer and sees me, she slows a little bit. I guess I shouldn't expect her to be running into my arms at this point.

I'm pretty sure in a typical relationship this is where both parties would agree to take some time apart, give ourselves a minute to collect and regroup. But honestly, time apart would just give Dean's garden of bullshit deeper roots—give it more room to grow.

Any time I think about mauling her in the shower, it feels like a red-hot poker to my brain. Only made worse by the fact that I can't get Dean's fucking words out of my head.

Evelyn finally meets me, quickly twisting the lock and pushing through the door and instant relief soothes my limbs from the heat.

She resets the alarm and I absentmindedly glance around Bohemia.

This was just an ordinary building and she made it *this*. Even now, in the dark, I feel immense love for it—like watching someone you love tucked into bed at night.

My eyes wander back to Evelyn but she's looking at the floor, shuffling her feet.

I feel terrible.

It's my fault that things are so weird between us right now. I walk over to her, gently pulling her into my chest. Her body still feels rigid, but she wraps her arms around my torso.

We pull apart and she fidgets with the collar of my coat then drops her hands.

"Let's go upstairs," she signs.

Following her lead through the back room, she slips her hand through mine as we walk up the dark stairwell and down the hallway to her studio.

She's afraid of the dark.

I've always known this, but I guess I never realized it was an actual phobia. I caught her running up the stairwell on Halloween, the light in the back room is always on . . .

She opens the door then closes it behind us. I flick on the small lamp by the door and when she turns around, her mouth is in a tight line.

She sighs, slinging her coat over the loveseat. "Dean dropped off the order today."

Oh my God.

I barely register what she's said because of the dried blood on her hand. I know she went to the boxing club but, *holy hell.*

I walk toward her, tenderly taking her hand, but she pulls it away.

"It's fine. It happens when you're punching shit sometimes," she signs.

I've never seen her hands torn up before . . .

"What happened with Dean?" I sign.

She sucks her teeth, looking down at the floor then back up at me. "Otis. Why didn't you tell me that you told Dean about us?"

I know I need to answer her, but I'm too fixated on what he could have said or done that would make her hit so hard that she bled. I force my gaze up to her eyes, seeing pure determination staring back at me and I sigh.

"I wasn't going to tell him, but he seemed to know already and I couldn't deny it. It went . . . poorly."

Her lips quirk up to the side, nodding. "I gathered that," she signs.

"What happened?"

She gives an annoyed exhale. "Nothing. He just seemed agitated, and he removed the discount from my order," she signs. "I've been trying to get him to take it off for months and he wouldn't, so it was fair to assume *something* changed his mind."

What a prick.

But I know her hand doesn't look like that because of the discount, she just said she wanted him to stop it, anyway.

"You don't know everything, Otis."

I clamp my eyes shut. *Goddamnit*—I need to get rid of Dean's bullshit. My desperate need to do just that has me signing before I think.

"Do you feel bad for me, Evelyn?"

Her head jerks back, eyebrows pinching.

"Why would I feel bad for *you*? You're the one withholding from me! What the hell are you talking about?" she signs.

She's angry and it's fair. I'm not making any fucking sense.

I take a deep breath, trying to suppress the pathetic feeling already crawling up my neck.

"When I told Dean . . . he seemed so sure that there was no way you'd want to be with me," I sign, my skin prickling. "He said you pitied me, that you've always . . ." I trail off, officially wanting to crawl into a hole.

Evelyn's face softens, her mouth opening slightly. She rubs her forehead with the pads of her fingers before leaning toward me.

Earthy eyes lock with mine as she signs, "Otis. *No*. Never."

My gaze drifts down to my hands, laying in my lap, and she grabs my wrists, gently shaking them. My eyes drift to hers, meeting a serious expression.

"Not. Ever," she enunciates.

She leans back a little, tucking some loose hair behind her ear.

"Do you remember the night we met?" she signs.

I nod, *of course* I remember.

She laughs, signing, "Do you remember me making an ass of myself trying to sign to you?"

"I thought it was sweet," I sign back to her.

"I noticed you the minute you walked in the room. I thought you were handsome, but that wasn't what initially got my attention. It was the way you *saw everything*," she signs. "Watching you take in the room; I could just see you were paying attention—noticing things that others overlooked or ignored. I can't explain it, but I felt like I *had* to know you."

Rose tints her cheeks but I'm in a trance, hanging on her every word.

"Reggie practically had to push me over to the couch to talk to you," she signs. "And after Dean told me you were deaf, I only found myself wanting to impress you more. I wanted the guy who noticed everything to notice me."

She rolls her eyes, judging herself, but her admission swells in my chest. For someone she thought noticed everything, I seemed to miss a lot that night.

"You didn't make me feel dumb for trying to communicate with you. You were kind and patient and I remember it reigniting my interest in sign language. I actually went home that night and pulled out my ASL dictionary, hoping that by the next time I saw you—and I did believe I would see you again—that I'd be better."

She laughs again. "We know that didn't happen," she signs. "*You* helped me. And I fell in love with the language. You barely knew me. I was just your brother's girlfriend and I felt so honored that you cared enough about me to want to communicate with me—teaching me something I didn't even realize meant so much to me."

I had no idea. I always thought it was the other way around. It never even crossed my mind that she actually liked signing. *Loves it.*

"I know you've noticed my hand . . ." she signs, then fidgets her fingers nervously. "You gave me a *gift*, Otis. Something that grounds me when I can't hold on to reality.

"You brought me into this beautiful world. And it was *never* pity. It was always love."

She leans forward, kissing me lightly, then runs her thumb along my chin and my shoulders drop, releasing a heavy exhale.

There was always this bit of resentment I carried for Dean when he asked her out. Obviously, the fact that I just happened to meet her first didn't give me any sort of claim on her, and I was still so scarred from the whole Jen ordeal that I didn't really have an interest in even trying to ask a girl out.

But I'm still a guy. I still saw how beautiful she was and my interest only piqued when she signed to me.

Learning that she was watching me—that she found me intriguing—it feels like my soul just grew wings.

"I love you," I say, lost in my wonderment.

"I love you too, Otis. But I need you to tell me everything." She inches closer to me on the love seat. "Tell me what else Dean said."

I grimace, not ready to leave the oasis of my cloud. But the honesty she just gifted me deserves a matching response. My face falls staring back up at her. Running my thumb along her hair line, I pause at her ear, wiggling the soft skin between my thumb and index finger before dropping my hand.

"You never thought I was gay, did you?"

She snorts a small laugh, giving her head a shake like someone just sprayed her with water and stares at me, utterly confused. Her expression quickly melts, shaking her head.

"No, Otis. I didn't think you were gay." She thinks for a second, adding, "I *did* ask him on a number of occasions why you didn't have a girlfriend." Her cheeks flush. "I always thought you were a catch."

"Wait, really?" I sign.

She laughs, giving me an adoring smile. "You're so cute."

Taking my hand, she holds it in hers and I stare at the gashes on her knuckles, again. She notices my staring and gives me a tilted smile.

"Don't worry. It still works just fine," she signs.

Her leg swings over me, settling on my lap and my hands find her waist like a magnet. My body aches for her even though I'm still worried about why her hand looks like that.

She lowers her hands between us, unbuttoning my pants, keeping our eye contact as she pulls my zipper down. Her breath hitches and I press my lips to hers, lightly trailing my fingertips down her arms.

You have the control, Evelyn.

She melts against my mouth. Her tongue brushes with mine, nibbling on my lip as her hand sinks into my pants. An involuntary groan erupts and my muscles contract feeling her hand tightly wrap around my length, slowly fisting me up and down.

When she leans back there's a fierceness sparkling in her eyes, knowing she's unraveling me with every pump of her hand.

I want to rip her fucking clothes off but something in her eyes is telling me she needs to feel this power, so I keep my clenched fists at my sides.

Taking her hand off me, she tugs her shirt off, like she was reading my goddamn mind and my head falls back at the sight.

She's wearing the same black lace bra she wore the first night we did this. My hand drags up her body but just as I reach her breast, she catches it.

"No touching," she says, kissing my palm, laying it back at my side. *Holy shit.*

She wiggles her way off my lap and walks to her bedside table. A second later, she comes back with a condom and tosses it on the loveseat next to me.

"We only use that if you follow the rules," she signs, giving me the sexiest smile, I've ever seen.

A new Evelyn smile.

My eyes must look mystified right now—for as much as I love her shyness in the bedroom, *this* is driving me fucking insane. Her fingers hook the sides of her sweats, pulling them down, and my breath becomes heavy—practically drooling.

She drops the bad girl act for just a second, blushing as she stands in front of me in just her bra and underwear, but quickly regains it when she kneels in front of me, slowly dragging my pants and boxers down to my ankles.

It's torture not to touch her. I think my hands are actually shaking from the restraint but I keep them at my sides, determined to follow her rules.

She stays kneeling on the floor, restarting her torturous movement up and down.

Staring up at me, her smile darkens before lowering her lips and taking me in her mouth.

Holy fucking hell.

My eyes slam shut, grabbing whatever part of the cushion I can. Her movement pulls moans from deep in my chest and my hands tighten on the loveseat—doing everything I can to not rake my fingers through her hair as she works me with her soft, warm mouth.

My hips start to buck as she takes me deeper, a moment away from exploding when she suddenly releases me. Standing, she slips off her panties, but keeps her bra on and resumes her place on my lap—one leg on each side of me.

My hands move to grab her thighs but she eyes them, reminding me, *no touching.*

A frustrated groan rumbles my throat, fidgeting underneath her as she pulls her bottom lip between her teeth, smiling down at me.

Threading her fingers through my hair, she sits in a high kneel above me, putting me face to face with her breasts. I can't resist—I lean forward, licking the crown and she glances down at me in warning, but keeps a closed-mouth smile.

She kisses me deep and as she sits further down on my lap, my thumb meets her upper thigh, gently rubbing it back and forth.

She pulls back from my lips and untangles her fingers from my hair.

"That's two," she signs, her lips quirking with amusement.

Damnit.

Her hands ball the hem of my shirt, pulling it up and over my head, before she trails her soft lips across my chest, lightly running her tongue from the base of my neck up to my jaw.

"You can touch one thing," she signs, some shyness returning.

One?! Only one?

My eyes scan every inch of her body, knowing exactly where I want to touch her.

I place my hand on her chest right over her heart, beating hard and fast under my palm.

She sucks in a sharp breath and smiles, placing her hand over mine. Leaning over to grab the condom, she tears it open and slides it over me, then teases me at her entrance.

My fingers curl against her chest as she settles on top of me, slowly sinking down until I'm buried deep.

She takes a second to adjust to me inside of her then places one of her hands on the back of the loveseat and starts to slowly rock against me.

So. Fucking. Good.

My hips thrust up to meet hers, feeling her moan against my hand. Our pace quickens and her lips devour mine. My other hand starts to move to her hip but I drop it back down and basically sit on it.

No touching.

She rides me faster, harder, digging her fingers into my shoulder. I push myself further into her and she tightens around me before crying out against my palm still weakly splayed over her chest. My hips pump a few more times, growling out my own release into the curve of her neck.

She sits limp over my shoulder, both of us panting, feeling her rapid heartbeat flutter under my hand. As we come down, she leans back, her lips curling with dazed satisfaction.

"I love you," I say between pants.

"I love you too," she says, then signs, "Definitely not gay."

Her smile widens and she giggles, pressing her lips to mine, again and I laugh against her smile, still inside her.

chapter thirty-nine

evelyn

A n insatiable, sex-crazed beast has been unleashed, and she is me. *I can't get enough of him.*
It all started last week when my loveseat lived up to her namesake. I don't even know how it turned into what it did. I wanted him, but I really wanted his focus off my hand and out of his head.

After he enlightened me about what Dean said to him, the likes of which are still hard to swallow, I wanted to do anything I could to squash the insecurities he put there.

But something *changed.*

I made it past the sound of the zipper and I felt . . . strong. It was the first time in so long that I felt in complete control. And he let me have it.

That was the sexiest part of the whole thing—his restraint. I thought he was going to combust, but he played along. He did what I asked and *that* . . .

Oh my God, I need to stop.

I'm practically drooling on the pick-up counter. Heat spreads across my cheeks and I hurry to the water jug. It's all I can do to keep from fanning myself like some hot-and-bothered woman.

Aren't you though?

Otis sits in his usual spot with a knowing smile, but his eyes are on his laptop.

Goddamnit.

I walk back behind the counter, starting to take inventory of the products I have in the fridges, knowing they can't judge me. I open the door, letting the cold air cool my flushed face when I see a tiny frame in my peripherals.

"Oh love, you're in trouble," Mary says.

I look up at her from my crouched position, still partially in the fridge. My cheeks heat again, and I squish my face with my hands.

Jesus Christ, they have me surrounded.

Letting the fridge door fall shut, I twist against the counter, still squishing my face, trying to hide from watchful eyes.

I have new sympathy for men trying to hide the bulge in their pants. In less than a minute, two people have caught my face boner.

I stop squishing but keep my hands clasped around my neck, just below my chin as an overwhelmed sigh escapes me. Mary's hand finds my shoulder and my eyes float to meet hers.

Leaning toward me, she smiles. "Nothing more beautiful than love, love."

The bell above the door jingles and I surprisingly see Sal.

As far as landlords go, Sal is pretty much the shit. As long as I send him his checks, he doesn't really come around. I usually only see him for city inspections or if there's a maintenance issue with the building.

"Sal, hi! What a nice surprise."

"Evelyn! How ya doin', kid?"

I smile, saying, "Everything's great!" not missing the agreeable sound Mary makes next to me.

I eye her once, reminding her to behave. We're in the presence of a real adult, here.

"Can I get you something to drink?" I ask,

"No, I'm good. I've gotta cut back on the caffeine," he chuckles. "Listen, can we talk in the back real quick?"

Suddenly, I'm nervous. I'm trying to remember if I've missed a check or something important due to my new status as a woman in love/sex fiend, but I can't think of anything.

"Yeah, of course." I sweep my arm toward the back room, letting him take the lead.

Otis peeks over his laptop as we walk and I shoot him a wary glance before pushing through the swinging door.

I lean against the sink, trying to appear nonchalant. "What's up?"

He grabs the back of his neck, rubbing it nervously which only worries me more.

"Did you hear about all the shit they're building around the neighborhood?" he asks.

No, my newspaper got pushed to the floor before Otis and I had an afternoon delight on his kitchen table. Also, it wasn't a newspaper—it was a utility bill. Also, I'm blushing again.

Goddamnit.

I clear my throat. "Um . . . I heard they're building some fast food place over on Pratt?"

He laughs half-heartedly. "Yeah, I think it's done, actually. But that's not what I'm talking about." He shifts his weight, adding, "There's a bunch of developers in the area buying old buildings. Some are trying to restore them, some are tearing them down—trying to revitalize the neighborhood."

"Fuckers," I commiserate.

Sal is an old school Chicagoan. His parents came here from Italy and worked on the railroads until they were able to open their own restaurant, which is what this place once was until they outgrew it and got a new location in Near West Side.

"Yeah . . . I know. But there's a builder who offered me a small fortune for this place, Evelyn. I mean, we're talkin' *I can retire early and put the kids through school* kind of money. My ma isn't doing so good so I need to be at the restaurant more . . . I'm really sorry to do this kid, but I'm gonna take the offer."

My heart sinks. "W-What?"

"Aw, kid. I feel terrible. I know this place means a lot to you—it means a lot to me too. It wasn't an easy decision. And I'm gonna see what I can do as far as letting you stay upstairs until you can find somethin' else."

Something else?

This *was* my "something else." I went to theater school. And the thing they don't tell you about the starving artist lifestyle is that even *that* requires some privilege. I wasn't good enough *or* rich enough to make it as an actor, so I found *something else*.

I want to rip my hair out and have a full-blown temper tantrum in my back office. I want to pee around the perimeter of the building and mark it as *mine!* Instead, I look at Sal, fighting the narrowing tightness in my throat.

"Sal—this place . . . it's all I have," I squeak.

He looks down at the floor, shuffling his feet. "Evelyn, I know that's not true. You're special, kid. You *will* find something else. I'll make sure you get some money from selling the business and I know you'll do something great." He places his hand on my shoulder and I want to bite it.

I should be more understanding. Sal gave me a break when I wanted to open this place, and I'm sure it's not a financial gain for him to rent my studio out for as little as he has, but this *fucking sucks*.

I clear my throat, trying to choke back my tears. "When?"

"Sale goes through the first of the year," he says.

FIRST OF THE YEAR?! That's three and a half weeks away!

My eyes bulge, and my chest caves in. Sal ducks his head, trying to meet my eyes which are desperately searching the floor for a solution.

"I'm serious, Evelyn. I'm gonna see what I can do about you staying in the studio until you can figure something out. It's gonna be okay."

He gives my arm a firm hold then turns and pushes through the swinging door.

Why? Why life, do you have to capsize when the waves were just becoming manageable? Not even smooth, just fucking *steady.*

Otis pushes through the door a moment later, but my eyes are staring at a cracked floor tile from when I dropped an urn on it after I took it to the farmers market for the first time. It was the first day I sold anything for Bohemia. It's where I met Mary and Jim.

And now the tears are falling.

Otis pulls me in for a hug. He runs his hands over my back, letting me cry—another thing he's gotten used to. I suck in some shaky breaths, trying to calm myself down.

After squeezing and crying into his chest for a minute, I finally pull away, wiping the wet spot on his shirt from my tears.

"What happened?" he asks.

I feel a small flutter in my stomach at the sound of his voice. The sound wraps around me like a hug. It's not even just the *sound* of his voice—it's what it means for him to use it that fills something inside me.

"Sal is selling the building. Bohemia is done January 1st," I sign, wiping a rogue tear.

His eyes widen, shaking his head in disbelief. "No . . . baby. I'm so sorry," he says softly, pulling me against his chest again.

And goddamn, if that doesn't light a small match in the dark hole forming inside me where this place lives. He called me baby and I can't help but smile.

But *fuck. What am I going to do?*

I take a deep breath, deciding to take the mature route. I pull back, still encased in Otis's arms and stare up at him with wide eyes.

"Can we get very drunk tonight?" I sign.

He laughs, kissing my forehead, then nods. "But no tequila," he signs.

"Deal."

"EVIE!" Reggie squeals.

"Red foot blue!" I sign and yell.

"I think she means *right* foot blue," Otis signs at Reggie, still bent over.

I'm pretty sure when I suggested drunk Twister, Otis assumed I'd be playing too and we'd end up tangled up together. And while it's tempting, my drunk ass is finding it hilarious watching my two favorite men roll their eyes at my belligerency while tangled up on the mat together.

I flick the spinner to give them their next move and then glance up toward the mat.

Otis straightens for a second to regain his balance and *damn*, he looks good. He's only in gray sweats and a white t-shirt but his wavy hair bounces around perfectly when he needs to adjust his position, his amber eyes sparkling with amusement as he laughs at Reggie bitching on the floor.

"Hey, what do we get if we win this shit?" Reggie barks.

"A kiss from me!" I giggle then hiccup and Otis laughs.

Reggie falls to the floor dramatically. "Okay. I'm out," he signs, belly up on the mat.

He pushes himself up and grabs his coat from the loveseat before walking over to me and pulling me up off the floor.

"I love you, you beautiful hot mess. It'll all be okay," he says, kissing me on the cheek.

I wobble on my feet, giving him a dopey grin. The alcohol is buzzing through me, so the sad feelings get pushed down by the drunk ones and I hug him goodbye.

Reggie strides out of my studio with such ease, it makes me wonder if he was drinking at all.

Maybe I drank everything.

Otis plops on the floor next to me with a carefree smile that makes my heart flip.

"What now?" he signs.

A playful smirk pulls the corner of my mouth as I hold the spinner board up, wiggling it at him.

He laughs, signing, "I'm going to make another drink if there's more Twister."

He walks to the fridge and I check out his ass, per usual.

Still, a fine man butt.

My eyes float around my small home and my sad feelings start trying to cozy up to the drunk ones. I can't believe I have to leave. It's the first place that's felt like home to me since . . . well, since I moved in with Dean all those years ago.

The apartment was sparsely furnished.

Gloria and Paul had dropped off a small couch, an old beat-up chair from Dean's room and the spare bed they had in their garage. We bought a small coffee table and a desk and we were set!

Otis and Dean were holding up a tapestry I wanted to hang on the wall behind the couch while I checked to make sure it was straight.

"It's good!" I signed.

Dean hammered his end into the wall, then handed the hammer to me. I walked it over to Otis so he could secure the other side and I smiled wide, feeling on top of the world.

I had a live-in boyfriend who I was crazy about. I just secured the lead in the theater department's first musical of the season, and I was finally able to sign fluently. It was going to be the best year ever.

The boys hopped down from the arms of the couch, stepping back to look at the tapestry and Dean quickly groaned.

"Baby, it's crooked."

"Is it?" I signed, giving Otis a side glance.

His eyes met mine, laughing under his breath.

"Yeah, my side is way lower than Otis's—don't you see?" He pointed and looked back at me.

I laughed because I really didn't see. But it amused me that it bothered him.

"Crooked just makes it feel more like home, like we've been here long enough for dust to collect and pictures to tilt." I walked up to him, lacing my arms around his neck.

Dean planted a kiss on my lips, squeezing me as he lifted me off the floor and I squealed.

He put me back down and whispered in my ear, "We've gotta christen the place, then it will really feel like home."

"Dean!" I playfully smacked his arm, darting my eyes to the side—reminding him that his brother was still here.

He looked over at Otis and took his hands off my waist.

"You want a beer, man? I can fire up some video games," he signed.

Otis shook his head, signing, "I've got to go. I've got a newspaper meeting in an hour."

Dean hugged him and my chest tightened. I never had a sibling, but I thought it was so cool that they were best friends.

I walked over to Otis, giving him my own hug. "Thanks for all your help today," I signed.

"For you, of course. You!" He pointed at Dean. "You owe me food. Good food," he signed on his way out the door.

I laughed, giving him a small wave, then looked over at Dean, feeling giddy.

"Well, look at that . . . I get free favors. You have to pay in food," I teased.

"It's called 'pretty privilege,' babe. And don't gloat, it's very unbecoming." He picked me up under my thighs, saying, "Now . . . where to have you first?" He peeked around the apartment but carried me to our room as I laughed, hugging around him.

I clamp my eyes shut feeling like I opened a trap door. Memories of Dean—things I haven't thought about in a long time—stuff I thought I had blocked out are resurfacing and it's freaking me out. Even in my drunken state, I can't help but feel guilty thinking about him at all when Otis is walking toward me, looking *so damn good.*

I sigh, deciding to let Sober Evelyn deal with that. Drunk Evelyn has plans. My finger flicks the needle, reading the command.

"Left hand green."

Pushing off the floor, I go to the mat, planting my hand on one of the green dots. Otis spins, his eyes already hungry as he walks over to the mat, putting his right hand on a yellow dot, right next to mine.

His eyes gleam with a promising smile as he slowly leans over me.

We play the game that ties you up in knots.

chapter forty

otis

oly hell, I'm out of shape!

Rounding the corner of my block, my muscles ache and my lungs struggle to suck in the cold winter air.

My jogging route didn't used to take it out of me like this. But I guess it's to be expected with the abundant couch time I had while recovering.

But the last hundred feet to my building are spent walking, holding my hips and gasping. As I reach my building, Lexi walks out the front door.

Awesome. This wasn't embarrassing enough.

She spots me, holding up a hand, and I do the same.

"Hi Otis, how are you?"

Still breathing like a pack-a-day smoker, I sign, "Good, how are you?"

"Good," she says.

We stand there for a minute, awkwardly. I'm trying to mask my extreme fatigue as I pull my phone out of my pocket and tap out a message for her.

> **I knocked on your door last week. I just wanted to apologize . . .**

Lexi takes my phone, reading the message, then looks up at me with a tilted smile. She types, then turns the phone around to show me the message.

> **It's okay. That was Evelyn, right?**

I nod, and my breathing finally evens out. She cradles the phone in her hand, typing something else, and then twists it around again.

> **Well, for what it's worth, I'm happy for you. The way you talked about her kind of made me think there might be something more between you guys.**

I can't help but smile. Lexi is really cool. Even though we had only gone out once, I didn't handle our ending the way I would have liked. But she was understanding and didn't even pressure me for a more detailed explanation—something she definitely deserved.

She types one more thing, then hands me my phone.

> **And I saw the article, by the way. I'm glad you're both okay.**

She gives me a timid smile, then walks down the block.
But it's suddenly hard to breathe again.
Article?

TWO MEN ARRESTED FOR VIOLENT ATTACK ON A LOCAL MAN. CHARGED WITH ARMED ROBBERY IN MULTIPLE CRIMES.

The article doesn't mention our names, but it's easy enough to put two and two together. Evelyn, the local coffee shop owner and me, the local writer who couldn't be reached for comment.

I don't recall anyone *trying* to reach me for a comment. Not that I would have given one, but still.

The article concludes that Charles Reiger is responsible for the "violent attack."

Learning his name doesn't really give me much relief but knowing *something* about him does settle me, somehow. The less unknown he is, the less of a shadow he becomes and that is strangely comforting.

But it feels fucked up to find out with the rest of the city.

I close my laptop, exhaling a shaky breath. My stomach turns but surprisingly, the anger that usually accompanies thoughts about the attack is absent.

Still, an unease prickles through me, like I'm waiting for a violent gust of wind to blow, but it never comes.

Jesus Christ. What level of screwed up are you when you feel anxious because you don't feel enraged?

I start toward the bathroom. Between my pathetic excuse for a workout and my edging anxiety, a sheen of sweat coats my skin. Cranking the knob to turn on the water, I don't even wait for it to heat up before stepping in.

An hour later, Bohemia is buzzing with life. Evelyn wrote a long message on her website, informing all the customers about the closure to happen in the new year. All of the regulars have been spending even more time here, trying to soak up their last couple weeks of Evelyn's beloved shop.

I can't believe it's actually happening. My insides sink when I think about it for too long. Evelyn's doing her best to put on a brave face, but I know she's devastated.

My eyes catch her behind the counter, talking with Mary, and I give her a quick wave. She smiles and Mary turns around, immediately scurrying over to me, throwing her arms around my neck and squeezing tight.

She grins, saying, "Hello, love. How are you?"

My heart feels lighter with Mary. She has the kind of presence that just soothes, instantly. I love her because she's her, but I cherish her because of how good she's always been to Evelyn.

My head gently tilts from side to side and my mouth flattens. She grimaces with a nod for just a moment before her smile returns. "Americano?" she asks.

The familiarity of our exchange curls my lips, dropping my head in a grateful nod. She laughs, cupping my cheek, then goes over to the mug wall and gets my ugly-ass mug. She stops to talk to a family at the spool table when Evelyn walks up and laces her arms around me.

I hold her tight in return, kissing her hair. She tightens her arms, like an exclamation point to the embrace, then leans back and stares up at me.

"Good morning, handsome," she signs between us.

I smile, sneaking a quick peck but notice that my table opens up. My feet move quickly to my corner, claiming it, catching Evelyn giggle. She walks to the table and leans against it.

"Lots of work to do?" she signs.

I nod. "I picked up some freelance work and there was an extra article up for grabs at the paper so it'll be a full day." I scoot in on the bench, opening my laptop.

She nods slowly, getting lost in a thought and my eyebrows pinch, wondering.

"Did you see that article?" I sign.

She looks at me like I've asked her what moon juice tastes like and it makes me chuckle.

"You know I don't read the paper. Just select articles written by the hot guy that frequents my shop." Her smile fades referring to *her shop*.

I take her hand, running my thumb over her knuckles.

I just wish she could see how capable she is. She made this place from *nothing*. It'll be hard, but I know she'll do something else great. I just wish she knew it too.

She squeezes my hand once then slips it away.

"What was the article?" she signs.

My mouth makes a hard line. I feel bad for bringing it up, now.

"It was about the attack. It doesn't use our names, but it mentions us in the incidents. It did report *their* names."

She frowns. "I know their names, Otis. The detective told me when he called," she signs, sitting down in the chair across from me. "I'm really sorry I didn't mention them to you."

Her eyes fall, tracing an imaginary pattern on the table and I lean back against the bench with a frustrated sigh.

It's not her fault. It's not like I asked her about it. To be honest, when she told me about the arrest, I was lost in my head about other shit.

It shouldn't have been her responsibility to begin with, but it just irritates me in general that no one contacted me.

My heart rate quickens, anticipating the anger I've come to know is finally going to start to rise and take hold but it surprises me, again. Other than some irritation at the lack of notice, I feel fine.

Glancing back at Evelyn, still staring down at the table, I take her hand in mine, giving it a quick squeeze.

"It's okay," I sign. "I'm okay."

Still, the corner of her lips pull before she signs, "I know. It just isn't right. *Someone* should have told you."

Mary approaches our table, putting the abominable mug down next to my laptop. I pick it up immediately, desperately in need of caffeine. *So good.*

Evelyn's sentimental smile stares back at me, sighing before she quickly becomes all business.

"All right, get that cute butt to work, mister," she signs.

Saluting back to her, I sign, "Yes, ma'am."

Evelyn found a slightly dead, three-foot Christmas tree and decided she needed to have it, so we're sitting on the floor of her studio, decorating. Mostly, I'm watching her decorate it.

Tucking some of her hair behind her ear, I notice she's singing.

"What are you singing?" I sign.

She smiles up at me. "Christmas music."

My own lips inch up, recognizing the familiar exchange we had years ago when she came to spend Thanksgiving at our house for the first time.

"I used to love Christmas," she signs, wistfully staring at the tree.

"Used to?" I sign back.

She simply nods, sucking her lip into her mouth and I remember now that her assault happened when we were all home for the holiday.

I wander back through years past, recalling how Evelyn always seemed to enjoy Christmas from afar, like a kid just outside the fence at a playground.

She never goes back to her parent's house. In more recent years, she's always said she was too busy with the café but before that she always said money was too tight. Whenever I offered to stay back to spend the day with her, she always refused.

My parents were ecstatic to hear that Evelyn and I are together.

It actually surprised me a bit. They've always loved her, but given how Dean reacted to the news, I figured there would be some conflicting reactions.

"You boys will work it out, honey," Mom said.

I didn't have the heart to tell her that there was pretty much no chance of Dean and I working it out. Evelyn was quick to deny the things Dean put in my head, and I believe her.

There's not a doubt in my mind that he said what he said just to be an asshole and to get into my head, which is why I don't see us getting past it.

But, unfortunately, we still share parents, so I'll have to deal with his moody ass at Christmas.

I'd just say fuck it and skip it this year if I didn't miss my mom and dad so much. I haven't seen them since summer—since before the attack that they still don't know about. I'm determined to take it to my grave as far as they're concerned.

My eyes slide down to the box of ornaments, noticing a small wooden "I love you" hand sign. A smile pulls up my cheeks while picking it up.

Evelyn sees me holding it and frowns. "Dean gave me that," she signs. "Sorry."

My smile falls immediately and the familiar buzz of anger I've been anxiously awaiting all day starts to tighten my body. And it's not even remotely related to what happened in that alley.

Dean.

Why does she still have this? Why did he give it to her at all? He's not the one who's actually deaf. My fingers curl around the ornament, wanting to crush it because apparently, I'm a caveman when it comes to thoughts about my brother now. Rather, thoughts about him and Evelyn.

Evelyn cups my fist, prying my fingers open. She takes the small wooden ornament out of my palm, replacing it with her own hand, then threads her fingers through my hair with her other hand.

Her big hazel eyes aren't scolding or irritated—they're full of compassion as she shakes her head, releasing my hair.

"Otis, I love *you*. I didn't keep this because Dean gave it to me."

Superpower intact.

"He gave it to me before our last Christmas together. The last one before I went home for winter break that year," she explains.

What is wrong with me? I've replaced one source of anger with another. It's not gone, just redirected.

At *Dean*.

My brother, who I'll never be able to avoid completely, triggered by the history that he and Evelyn share.

I clear my throat, just trying to release some tension. Evelyn scoots closer to me, rubbing her hands up and down my legs, trying to give me some ease.

"I only kept it because it was the last gift I got *before*," she signs. "I kept it because I used to love Christmas, and I held on to it hoping that one day I would love it again."

I'm an asshole.

I've only had a couple months battling my own trauma from what happened in that alley and it's been absolute hell at times. I don't know how I would go through something like this—face it alone.

But she did.

I could never fault her for keeping something that gave her hope. She's already sacrificed so much by taking on her trauma alone.

A sharp inhale inflates my chest, suddenly realizing—*she never told her parents.*

I understand wholeheartedly not wanting to tell people, especially loved ones, but it physically pains me to know that that's why she's become so distant from her parents. *That's* why she never goes home.

My face falls looking down at her small box of ornaments. They've gone unused for years, just sitting and collecting dust, hoping one day Evelyn would want to use them again.

I pick the wooden "I love you" ornament back up, hanging it on our sad, dead tree, watching the branch droop from the weight as it hangs.

But it doesn't snap. Despite the odds, it holds on, and a smile slowly pulls at my lips. I turn to look at Evelyn, my remaining despair falling completely.

I cup her cheek in my hand, rubbing my thumb back and forth over the back of her jaw. She leans into my hand, holding my forearm, placing a small kiss to the inside of my palm.

God, I love her.

She's strong. She didn't break and she won't. This year, she bought a tree and dusted off her ornaments. Maybe next year, she'll want to go back to her parent's house. But this year . . .

"Will you spend Christmas with me?" I sign.

She smiles. My *favorite* Evelyn smile. The one that lights up her whole face and my heart.

chapter forty-one

evelyn

seven years ago

December 23rd. It was my favorite day of the year.

I woke up early and went downstairs before the sun came up. Hearing the erratic bubbling of the coffee brewing, I saw my dad at the kitchen island and hugged him around the neck from behind his stool.

"Are you ready for our business meeting?" I joked.

He clasped my linked arms with his hand, squeezing them.

"I'm fully prepared," he said, playing along as he nodded toward the coffee.

I laughed, walking over to the pot, then poured us each a cup. Dad drank his black, but I added some oat milk and honey to mine, then sat at the stool next to him.

My dad and I didn't talk much—I swear we saved it all for this one day a year—but my love for him ran deep. We didn't require a lot of words.

"All right Evie Bear, you're running this meeting. Where should we start?" he asked, taking a sip from his mug.

My head tilted, sifting through everything that had happened during the first half of my senior year. A smile inched its way up my cheeks—I had a lot to feel good about. It was a great feeling to have on your favorite day.

"Well, we finished *The Last Five Years*. It was great! There were some big wigs in the audience so maybe an agent or a job offer might come of it." I played with the thumb rest on my mug. "But I just love the show . . . I wish you guys could have been there."

My dad's face shadowed, nodding and I instantly felt bad.

"Daddy, I didn't mean it like that. I know you would have come if you could. I just meant I missed you," I said, rubbing his shoulder. "I think the director filmed it for some festivals. Maybe I can get a copy so you and Mom can watch?"

He perked up, and his lightened face warmed me inside and out. My dad was a sports guy, but he went to every performance I had in high school. He sat through long-ass dance recitals and tortuous show choir concerts. He showed up when he could, and I always loved him for that.

"I would love to see it. So would your mom, you know that." He cleared his throat, before adding, "Is it a sad one, though? I need to know if I should drink before—you know, depending on the level of weeping from your mom."

I laughed at how true that statement was. It never failed—Mom always cried. I couldn't poke too much fun though, I was a crier myself.

"It's sad enough for wine but not sad enough for whiskey," I advised.

He laughed, nodding. "How's Dean? He's being good to you?"

"Daddy . . ." I rolled my eyes.

My dad played the part of protective father, but he never actually tried to intimidate any of my boyfriends. He trusted my judgment and if he didn't, he let me make my own mistakes and helped me through the heartbreaks in his own way.

I saved a note he gave me after my high school boyfriend dumped me. I had been moping around the house for days and he left it on my nightstand one morning before he left for work.

> You've always been someone who loves deeply, Evie. You give it so freely, but it's a gift that comes at a high price because unfortunately, not everyone will treasure it the way they should. Some people will take what they need and leave. But please, always remember, even if they do: It's still a gift. It's invaluable. It's my favorite thing about you, baby girl. And no matter what, I'll always treasure it. And you. Love, Dad.

I smiled as I thought about it. My dad had always been a man of few words, but he always managed to find a few good ones when he really needed to.

I looked back over at him, breathing a laugh. "Dean is great, and our apartment is awesome! It's so nice to live off campus." I took a sip of my coffee, adding, "I think we'll keep the place, even after we graduate."

Dad sighed contently. "That's great, Evie-Bear. I can see how happy you are, and it does my heart good. And from everything your mom tells me, it sounds like Dean loves you hard right back."

"He does," I agreed. "And I've become pretty good friends with his brother, Otis. I've told you about him, right?"

He nodded. "He goes to school in Chicago too, right?"

"No, he goes to school in Evanston," I giggled to myself and my dad stared at me, confused.

"It's an inside joke," I explained. "But yeah, he's out there too. I'm finally fluent enough in ASL to keep up conversation with him, so that's cool."

"Very cool," Dad mocked, and I playfully elbowed his arm.

"So . . . Otis?" He looked at me for confirmation and I nodded. "He's deaf?"

"Yep," I said. "He's great. And it was so nice of him to work with me on ASL. I really love it."

And Otis.

My lips pulled up at the realization. Our friendship developed so naturally that I hadn't even really noticed when Otis transitioned from my boyfriend's brother to one of my dearest friends—perhaps my best friend.

My dad looked at me curiously and I took the remaining sip of my coffee.

Clearing my throat, I said, "He and Dean are pretty much joined at the hip, so it's nice that we get along so well."

Dad nodded. "It sounds like things are pretty good in your world," he said, raising his mug appreciatively, taking his last sip.

He hooked his finger through my mug handle and carried both of our cups to the sink and rinsed them. Turning around, he leaned back against the sink, then glanced at the clock on the microwave.

"Should we get breakfast?" he asked, like it wasn't what we did every year.

"Yeah!" I smiled, like it was the first time he ever suggested it.

"Evie! I need that for the pastitsio! There's more cheese in the fridge!" Mom swatted my hand away and I laughed.

It was my contribution to dinner. My mom made my favorite dish and I ate cheese at the counter while she cooked. It was better that way—I was much better at eating than cooking.

It was actually dinner for tomorrow night, but Mom always made it on Christmas *Eve* Eve, knowing how much I loved it and that I would inevitably sneak a piece later that night.

My phone buzzed in my pocket as I opened the fridge, not about to slack on my duties. I placed the deli package on the island before pulling my phone out.

Jessica: EVELYN GRAY I BETTER SEE YOU TONIGHT! XOXO

An involuntary groan slid out as I closed the fridge door.

I forgot that my old friend Trevor was having a party at his house tonight. Jessica was one of my best friends in high school and she and Trevor had started dating a few months ago.

I felt a pang of guilt. I hadn't seen Jessica since last summer and I hadn't seen Trevor since . . . I couldn't even remember.

I had known him since we were in diapers, basically. Our moms became friends and still kept in touch, so I felt bad for letting so much time pass.

But I really just wanted to be home. Dad was on the couch watching *It's a Wonderful Life* even though Mom and I were playing Christmas music in the kitchen, only a few feet away.

Me: I don't know. My parents are commandeering my time this visit. I'll let ya know!

Blame the needy parents, when in reality a night at home with said parents just sounded more appealing than a house party with Trevor's gross Jungle Juice as the signature drink. I slipped my phone back into my pocket, watching my mom in amused horror.

She was stirring the sauce for the topping of the dish, singing horribly off-key but loving fucking life.

I laughed and shook my head. It instantly brought me back to all the car rides where she would basically speak-sing to Shania Twain, jiving her head, glancing back at me in the rearview mirror, copying her.

She looked up at me, starting to add some shakes and shimmies and I folded on top of the counter, unable to handle the sight.

Dad moves were embarrassing, but *Mom moves* were *mortifying.*

Her hair was pulled up in a messy bun, bobbing whenever her head moved and her jingle bell earrings pinged lightly with each wiggle, still singing along.

"Hey, you didn't get your voice from me . . . or your dad for that matter," she mused.

"That's for damn sure!" My dad yelled from the living room. "And Liv, I love you, but angels are trying to get their wings out here and you're scaring them!"

I howled with laughter, my mom gasping in faux offense, marching closer to the living room.

"IT'S BEGINNING TO LOOK A LOT LIKE CHRIIIISSST," she sang louder, and worse somehow, and my dad ran into the kitchen like he was going to chase her.

She stood still, spoon in hand, ready to whack if needed, but my dad leaned down, giving her a small peck.

"Aw, Dan. That was sweet." She gave him a loving tap on the shoulder.

"Mistletoe." He grinned, pointing up. "Now, please, Liv. My love. Please, stop singing." He smiled sweetly and I barked out a laugh, sufficiently ruining their moment.

My dad moseyed back into the living room and my mom suppressed her own laugh. She cleared her throat walking back toward the stove.

"You!" she commanded. "Either help or get out!"

I popped another half slice of cheese in my mouth and then picked up the boiling pot of noodles, dumping them into the colander.

I decided to go to Trevor's party after all. I enjoyed the day with my parents and figured I got the whole day tomorrow and Christmas with them. If I went to the party, I could use that to hold the old friend group over until next time I was home.

I hadn't spent any time with Jessica and Trevor since they became a couple and I'm sure there was plenty more I'd missed out on in the last few months.

I grabbed my phone from the counter and saw that I had a message from Dean.

It was actually a picture—a selfie of him and Otis in front of their TV. I zoomed in, seeing Yoshi's iconic losing face on the Mario Kart race results screen and scoffed through a smile.

Dean: Maybe it's not you . . . Maybe it's Yoshi.
We miss you, baby! (Me the most)

Poor Yoshi, but my heart squeezed from his sweet message.

Me: I miss you too!! So much! About to head out to the party—ugh. I'll call you on my way home. Tell Otis I say hi :)

I dropped my phone into my purse, noticing my mom curl up on the couch and the DVD menu for *Annabelle's Wish* appeared on the screen.

"You're watching it without me?!" I whined.

It was one of my favorite Christmas movies. It was a cute, animated movie about a calf named Annabelle. She and the other farm animals are gifted a Christmas voice from Santa every year and Annabelle ultimately gives her voice to her best friend, Billy, a non-verbal boy that lost his ability to speak in a barn fire when he was little.

I actually considered flaking out on the party but then my mom said, "You know we'll watch it again tomorrow!" She took a sip of her wine. "And the next day."

I hesitantly slid on my coat, nodding. "They should have taught Billy ASL."

"You could write the remake!" she said with the utmost seriousness.

I laughed, slinging my purse over my shoulder then went over to the couch and hugged her.

"Be safe! Call if you need a ride!"

"I will!" I hollered back, walking out the door.

Just in and out. I was going to put in some face time, then be back home eating a slice of pastitsio on the couch before I knew it.

chapter forty-two

otis

I stick my key in the lock to Evelyn's studio, pushing the door open and immediately I see Evelyn writing on her bed.

Dropping my bag, I quickly move toward her and as I get closer, I notice her face is dark red with anguish, her mouth tightly clenched.

Shit.

I gently try to move her rigid limbs and lightly touch my hand to her face. Her movement becomes more violent as a tear rolls down her cheek.

"Evelyn," I say her name a few times, running my thumbs along her cheeks, trying to relieve some of the tension.

Suddenly, her eyes bulge open, her pupils are so dilated that her eyes almost look black. She heaves, springing to her feet, running toward the bathroom and I follow behind her.

She makes it to the sink and vomits instantly.

I close in behind her, rubbing her back as she continues to retch until she's got nothing left. She turns the faucet on, cupping her palm under the water, trying to drink some, but spits it back out when she coughs, her body still convulsing.

I keep rubbing her back, kissing her shoulder, just once. She holds the pedestal sink, taking a series of deep breaths that I can feel against my hand.

Finally, her breathing evens and she slowly stares up at me in the mirror.

I'm with you.

I stay put behind her, helping the only way I can. Her gaze stays fixed on me through our reflections.

Wherever you just were, you're back. This *is real.*

She holds my hand on her shoulder, her haunted eyes starting to change back to their earthy color as she takes a stuttered inhale. I keep my hand there as she brushes her teeth quickly, then gargles some mouthwash.

I watch her carefully in the mirror as she keeps her head down, holding a firm grip on my hand, before she turns and falls into my chest. Holding her tight, I kiss her hair until I feel the tightness in her shoulders fall.

My grip loosens, but I keep my hands on her shoulders, asking, "Are you okay?"

She holds my wrists there, keeping her head down and nods through a hard gulp. Her grip on my wrist tightens but when she looks up, she actually does look okay. Shaken up, but okay.

We walk out of the bathroom, toward her bed and she sits. I take the spot next to her, wrapping my arm around her shoulders. Her fingers spell between us but then she raises her hand to my jaw, scratching my scruff and I feel her exhale against my neck.

She drops her hand from my jaw, but she keeps her face tucked. We stay just like that for minutes. Just breathing, before her hands raise just slightly in front of us.

"It's the anniversary," she signs.

My arm tightens, still wrapped around her, kissing the top of her head then resting my cheek on top of it.

I'd do anything to take this pain from her.

A sad sigh escapes. "My beautiful Evelyn," I say against her temple.

She pulls back from my neck, tilting her chin up toward me and I steal a small kiss from her heart shaped lips, then press a peck to her nose.

She wiggles it back and forth, staring up at me from my shoulder.

It's such a sweet gesture that I can't help but smile down at her. I push some hair back from her forehead, getting lost in her pretty eyes, aching to see her smile.

"I want to do something with you," I sign. "But you can't laugh."

Curiosity fills her expression as I pull my phone out of my pocket. I tap the screen to find the music file I saved earlier. Clicking it, "Merry Christmas, Baby" by Otis Redding starts to play.

There it is.

Her smile stretches wide as I stand, holding my hand out to her. She eagerly takes it and I wrap my arm around the small of her back like I've seen other people do when they're dancing.

I've never done this before, but I know she likes to dance. She loves music in general, but I think she avoids it with me, and I don't want her to.

Though, at the moment, I'm pretty sure I look like Tarzan at prom.

But Evelyn doesn't seem to care. She looks up at me with sparkling adoration, wrapping her arm around the back of my neck, gently tapping the pads of her fingers at the base—I assume to the beat of the music.

After a few beats, I'm able to match the rhythm of her sway, following her taps, giving her a small kiss on her forehead. Loosening my hold just to look down at her again.

"Perfect," she says, stretching up on her toes, pressing her lips to mine.

Suddenly feeling bold, and honestly not even caring if it's dumb—I spin her away from me, then pull her back in. Her head falls back, laughing, before her hand resumes its spot on the back of my neck while our foreheads touch.

My first dance. And it's with her.

"Merry Christmas, baby," I say, my throat feeling raw.

I feel her hands tighten around me and it feels like a shockwave to my heart.

She's the best gift I've gotten in my entire fucking life.

My only hope is that *this* is what she starts to think of on December 23rd, from now on.

The train ride to Rockford takes almost twice as long as it does to drive. But spending an hour and a half in the car with Dean sounded about as much fun as shoving an onion into my open eyeball.

Evelyn has been jittery all morning. I keep trying to reassure her that everything will be okay, but the truth is, I have no idea what to expect from Dean. Marnie—the buffer—will be there so I'm hoping that will at least keep him civil.

The train slowly pulls up to the Rockford station and I see Evelyn's knee bouncing frantically as she stares up at the ceiling of the train car like she's contemplating trying to jump through it.

I take her hand in mine, kissing her knuckles. "We've got this."

Her knee slows, looking over at me. I can see through the window that my mom and dad are already here.

As we step off the train, Mom practically tackles Evelyn, who is still holding my hand. She quickly moves to me, but then back to Evelyn and my dad laughs off to the side. He eventually wraps me in a hug, but quickly lets go, knowing my mom is coming back for seconds.

From Mom's tight squeeze, I see my dad in front of Evelyn. He takes her bag, pulling her into a hug and Evelyn's eyes close as they embrace, sending a wave of calm through me.

This was the right decision.

The ride back to my parent's house from the train station is short. My mom keeps her seat belt on but spends the whole ride twisted toward Evelyn and me in the back seat.

She's telling Evelyn about the show her and Dad saw the other night at the performing arts center downtown and Evelyn's eyes light up.

"The lead girl was nowhere near as good as you, honey!" Mom signs.

Evelyn smiles. "That's really sweet, but I'm way out of practice."

"You guys have seen her perform?" I sign to Mom.

She nods. "We saw that show her senior year," Mom signs, wiggling her fingers, thinking. "What was the name, again?"

Evelyn swallows, her eyes faltering just a bit before she signs, "*The Last Five Years.*"

"That was it! You were so good, honey," Mom signs.

Evelyn looks a little wistful, managing a gracious smile toward my mom and I take her hand in mine. My mom sees since she refuses to turn around and smiles at our linked hands.

My eyes float to the roof of the car. It's a relief that she's so happy for us, but I could do without the giddy looks that resemble the same encouragement she gave me when I learned to write my name for the first time.

We pull up to the house and quickly make our way inside. There's a sweet, slightly spiced smell wafting as soon as we step into the house, making my mouth water.

Dad claps my shoulder, then signs, "Why don't you kids go get settled and then we can all eat some food—catch up."

Evelyn and I make our way down the small foyer, turning toward my bedroom. She walks slowly, stopping to look at a picture on the wall and smiles but it doesn't reach her eyes. I peek over, seeing a picture of Dean and I from when Dad first built the tree house. I'm hanging out the window and Dean is in a pirate captain pose on the ladder.

I take her hand, ushering her toward the bedroom, and I can practically feel her guilt radiating into my palm. I rub my thumb back and forth as I open the door.

Goddamnit.

I don't know what's worse: the spelling bee plaque on my dresser from fourth fucking grade or my old teddy bear sitting on my bed, propped up against the pillows.

Fuck my life.

At least there's some Cubs memorabilia—evidence that I wasn't a complete dweeb. I mean, I was, but at least my room is trying to help a little. Evelyn drops her bag, looking around like she's *Aladdin* in the cave of wonders.

She picks up the teddy bear. "Who's this?"

No use in pretending I don't know; she'll just call me out on it.

"That's Catch," I sign.

I slowly inch my way toward the dresser, hoping to slyly hide the spelling bee plaque when I see her hands move.

"Already saw it," she signs and slips her shoes off before sitting on my bed, placing Catch in her lap. "And we're keeping him, by the way." She points to the teddy bear.

I laugh but my cheeks heat. I haven't had a girl in this room . . . well, since high school.

That one time.

Evelyn spots the bulletin board I have hanging on the wall and scoots over the bed to get a closer look.

My heart picks up as I try to remember if there's anything unbearably embarrassing on there, but it's too late now.

She runs her hand along a piece of paper, and I look over her shoulder to see what it is:

"Lucky me, lucky mud
I, mud, sat up and saw what a nice job God had done.
Nice going, God."- Kurt Vonnegut, *Cat's Cradle*

Evelyn smiles, looking over at me. "I love that book."

Huh. Her taste in books is . . . fascinating. It has no pattern, which is pretty cool because it leads me to believe she'll try any author, at least once. Her eyes wander to a small spotlight article I had written about our principal in high school. He had chased down a guy who stole a girl's purse on her way into the building.

Her mouth tilts up her cheek, signing, "I think I would have had a crush on high school Otis." She loops her arms around my neck.

"Trust me. You would not," I sign back at her.

Her smile falters but she rises to her tip toes, pressing her lips to mine. When she lowers back down, she glances around the room again, sighing.

"I love you. Thank you for bringing me here for Christmas," she signs.

My chest tightens, pulling her back into me. I'm so happy she's here. It kills me to know that she's spent Christmas alone for so many years.

"I love you too," I sign, kissing her once more, then take her hand and lead her back out to the hall, toward the dining room.

Mom has already put out a large plate of salami and cheese with crackers, some kind of dip that looks fucking amazing, and a gingerbread loaf already cut with butter sitting next to it.

I load up a cracker while Evelyn grabs a few cubes of cheese and Mom brings out some wine. She pours Evelyn and herself a glass while I go to the kitchen to grab a beer.

My Dad is already in the fridge, fishing two out for us and hands me one.

We pop the tops off, clinking our bottles, then each take a sip. He puts his bottle down on the small sliver of counter next to the fridge, giving me a once over.

"You look good, son," he signs. "Love suits you."

I nod, keeping my eyes on the floor, suddenly feeling a little self-conscious.

It's kind of weird that I'm thirty and haven't had this kind of exchange with my dad before. I haven't had a lot of girlfriends, and I've *never* had a girlfriend that I brought home to meet my parents.

She's already met them.

I inhale sharply, clearing my throat. "Thanks Dad," I sign, glancing back out toward Mom and Evelyn.

They're laughing about something and my blip of anxiety settles at the sight of her smile.

My dad smirks at me, knowingly. "That's how you know it's right, Otis." He picks up his bottle, clinking it with mine one more time before he walks out to the dining room.

We spend an hour leisurely lost in conversation. Evelyn tells them about Bohemia closing and my mom immediately suggests that she move it to Rockford. The woman will try anything to get us to move out of the city.

I tell them about my book. My dad wants to read the draft I just finished but I don't feel like it's quite ready yet.

"Soon," I sign.

He chuckles. "Always the perfectionist," he signs back at me and I shrug, taking a sip of my beer.

"Evelyn, I'm so impressed with your signing. It's come a long way since we met all those years ago," Mom signs.

Evelyn smiles shyly. "Thanks. I really love it, and I've gotten lots of practice." She squeezes my hand under the table.

I see all of their heads move in the direction of the door and I know that must mean Dean and Marnie are here.

Here goes nothing.

My parents walk over to meet them and Evelyn's hand tightens in mine under the table, craning her neck to look back toward the door.

I lean toward her, hovering over her ear, saying, "I love you," before she turns her head back toward me, smiling and pressing her forehead against mine.

Dean walks into the dining room and sees us. I lean back from my moment with Evelyn, noticing his mouth flatten tightly.

We don't greet each other since our parents must be preoccupied with Marnie in the foyer and we don't need to keep up any appearances.

Evelyn stands abruptly, twisting, awkwardly stuck between the table and the chair she was sitting in.

"Hi, Dean," she signs, nervously.

"Hey, Evie," he says, pulling her in for a hug.

Evelyn's hand ineptly pats his back, his face contorting into a smug smile over her shoulder and my body tightens, narrowing my eyes at him.

Where is the fucking buffer?

My mom pulls Marnie into the dining room as Dean releases Evelyn and I stand up a little too eagerly to hug Marnie, noticing her belly has grown since I saw her last.

She leans back, smiling up at me. "Elmo! I'm you!" she laughs.

That can't be right. I look just past her, to Evelyn who signs, "I know. I'm huge!"

My eyes widen, not wanting Marnie to think that I thought she was, in fact, huge.

I shake my head quickly, signing, "No, you look great! Almost there!"

Marnie wraps an arm around Evelyn, giving her an awkward side hug.

"Congratulations, Marnie. I haven't seen you since I heard the news," Evelyn says while signing.

Marnie says something back, but I don't know what because she's facing Evelyn, rubbing her belly.

Dad comes back into the dining room. "All right kids, dinner is in an hour!"

Holy fucking God, I need more beer.

Mom made lasagna and I'm eating it like I haven't eaten anything in years. In my peripheral, I notice Evelyn watching me with amusement, sipping her water. I give her a puffy cheeked smile, knowing she gets a kick out of me and my "gusto eating," as she calls it.

Her face is a welcomed contrast to my brother sitting across from me, staring a hole through my head. He must say something to Evelyn because she looks across the table at him. Her eyes flick to me, but then back to him.

"Yeah, Bohemia's closing in January. It really sucks," she signs.

I look over at Dean because I have to if I want to know what he's saying to her.

"Sorry, Evie. I bet we could find you something at Red Line if you're interested," he signs.

Marnie is lost in her lasagna and probably wouldn't have understood what he signed anyway, but I'm sure she wouldn't love that idea any more than I do.

"Thanks, but I'm sure I'll figure something out," she signs back.

He nods, sipping his beer. And for the first time since he got here, I lock eyes with him, shooting him a quick glare.

I know he didn't actually expect Evelyn to be interested in working for Red Line—it was just another dig at me.

He returns my glare with a dark grin, then redirects his attention back to his plate.

It was quick, but it felt like one of the blows I took in that alley. It's an expression I'd seen him make plenty of times when we were younger—usually when he was fighting with some asshole—but I wasn't used to being on the receiving end of it.

Evelyn takes my hand under the table and I peek over at her. She gives me a reassuring smile and I squeeze her hand in mine then look down at my plate, but I've suddenly lost my appetite.

Back in my bedroom after dinner, I lay on my bed as Evelyn grabs Catch, snuggling in next to me. She presses herself into my side for a second then sits up.

"That wasn't *so* bad," she signs.

I snort a laugh. "What table were you at?"

She sucks her bottom lip into her mouth, her big hazel eyes filling with sympathy.

I gently pull her lip, rubbing my thumb along it. She has no reason to feel guilty.

She lays back down, snuggling back into my side. I wrap my arm around her, pulling her closer and she links one of her legs around mine with Catch squished between us.

I breathe her in with a sigh. I don't care what Dean throws at me. *This* is worth every bit of his bullshit.

There was a time when I would have done anything for him. Now, when I think back about some of our childhood memories, it feels like they're a completely separate existence from our adult lives.

"I'm so sorry, Otis. I promise I'll come back."

My eyes close, trying to shut it out.

I don't want to remember the reasons I once loved him because it doesn't matter. It doesn't fucking matter that he looked out for me when we were kids because . . . we grew up. We grew up, he left, I fell in love with Evelyn and now he hates me.

chapter forty-three

evelyn

I 'm heading to bed!" Marnie announces, patting Dean's knee. Paul and Gloria retired about an hour ago and the four of us decided to put on *A Christmas Story* and have a drink. Well, Otis and I had a drink. Marnie had hot chocolate and Dean had . . . a few.

Otis stands, taking my hand, pulling me toward the hall. I turn back around and see Dean staring at us as Marnie folds a blanket from the couch.

"Goodnight," I mutter over my shoulder, then walk down the hallway to Otis's room.

Closing the door behind us, I exhale hard.

This whole day has been a bit surreal. It's not like I came here a lot when I was with Dean, but I was *with him* when I had come here in the past.

Dean was surprisingly pleasant to me tonight, but it only made it more uncomfortable witnessing how *unpleasant* he was to Otis.

I'm trying to convince myself that they will work it out, that it will just take some time and things will go back to normal.

Whatever that is.

My eyes dance around the room, trying to steer my thoughts in a different direction.

I try to imagine a teenage Otis, in his room. I think about him reading a book or writing some clever story only he could think up on his bed—maybe a love note.

A love note from Otis would be epic.

But a grimace pulls at my lips, remembering that it was a note from a girl that set off a chain of events that made his life hell in high school and my body goes stiff with anger.

If I had gone to high school with them, that bitch wouldn't have teeth.

Hard to talk shit with just your gums.

I know he dismissed the idea earlier, but I definitely would have had a crush on him in high school—I'm sure of it. I know his experience was awful and I just wish I could have known him then. I could have been his friend, I could have . . .

I have an idea.

I may not be able to turn back time, but I can replace *one* shitty high school memory with a good one.

I'm still leaning against the door, watching Otis pull his shirt over his head. He catches me staring and a shy smile pokes his cheeks, making me swoon.

Closing the distance between us, my hands trace the soft curves of his biceps, kissing the scar on his chest. He flinches, but runs his fingertips up my arms, settling them at the nape of my neck.

He gently tugs, angling my face toward his, fusing his mouth to mine. My tongue parts his lips and he opens, deepening our kiss. Lightly running his knuckles along my cheek, our tongues swirl one another's slowly.

He breaks the kiss, inching my shirt up over my head. His amber eyes shine staring down at me, feathering his fingers over the cup of my emerald green bra.

Wanting to give him and his room what they deserve has me signing, "Where do you want me?"

Who is this woman?

His eyes drift from my breasts up into my eyes with surprise, a devious smile stretching across his face. His gaze wanders over to the far wall of the room and mine follows to his desk against the window. My teeth tug my bottom lip because apparently, with Otis, I'm a heroine in one of my smutty romance novels.

Suddenly, I'm scooped under my thighs, pushing a surprised squeak from my mouth, giggling as he carries me a few feet across the room.

Luckily, the only thing on his desk is his high school diploma which still topples over when he sets me down. He starts to unbutton my pants and hovers over the zipper, glancing up at me.

I nod and he leans in, kissing my cheek, then whispers over my ear, "My beautiful Evelyn," as he unzips my pants.

His breath on my skin, his voice in my ear—floating like a feather falling deep down to my stomach. He kisses down my neck, pulling one of the straps to my bra down, moving his lips over my shoulder.

Lowering to his knees, he pulls my pants and panties down my thighs slowly, like he's savoring me.

After dropping my bottoms to the floor, his soft lips trail up my inner thigh, hitching my breath from the slow, light touch.

His hands latch to my waist, pulling me closer to the edge of the desk before his face lowers between my legs. He licks *there*, once, and I jerk, whimpering out at the quick sensation. I look down at him and he keeps his eyes locked with mine, grinning, then licks just once, again and I have to suck my lips into my mouth to keep from moaning.

He teases my entrance with his soft, warm mouth, making me pant desperately.

More.

He suddenly stands back up, placing his arms on each side of me, smiling as I stare back at him with ragged breath.

He leans in, saying with a rasp, "Payback, baby."

My eyes squint in confusion but a slow smirk tilts my lips. He's trying to get me back for my loveseat challenge.

It's on.

I move my hands to unfasten his pants but notice they're already around his ankles. He must have taken them off through his teasing.

He's distracting me through the sound.

I crash my lips against his, deciding to save my rebuttal for another time.

I've never known desire like this. I've never wanted anyone like I want him, and it makes me feel bold.

Dominant.

Our lips break as I unclasp my bra, tossing it to the floor. Just as his grip slides to my breast I turn around, bending slightly over the desk, wiggling my hips.

I guess I can't help but mess with him a little bit.

I swear I can feel his smile behind me like a flashlight on the back of my head as he presses his chest into my back.

His arms snake around me, pulling my hips back to meet his as his other hand travels up, kneading my breast. He gently pinches my nipple, squeaking a small whimper from me and then moves his hand up to brush my hair off my shoulder.

Sprinkling his soft lips along my neck, I hear the package of the condom rip. He covers himself, settling between my legs, his chest still pressed firmly against my back.

I bend slightly, giving him more access and he gently pushes into me. Once he's inside, he pulls me back upright, thrusting slow and deep from behind. His thumb pulls my chin, kissing me over my shoulder.

So, so good.

When our lips break apart, I take the hand that was holding my chin and pull his thumb into my mouth. He buries his face in the curve of my neck, stifling a moan, as his pace quickens. My teeth lightly bite on his thumb, my body rising from him moving in and out of me.

It's not even five seconds later that I completely come apart and he follows right behind me.

Ha, literally.

I guess our fun against the desk wore my sweet man out. Otis lays next to me dead asleep, but I need to pee and I could really use some water.

Throwing some pajama pants on, I shuffle out of the room and across the hall to the bathroom. I look in the mirror as I wash my hands, noticing that I have that, post-blow-your-mind-sex glow and I swear, I don't even recognize the person staring back at me.

A satisfied sigh escapes me as I flick off the bathroom light, walking down the hall to the kitchen. As I'm filling up my cup, I see through the window above the sink that the patio light is on. I stand on my tip toes, spotting Dean.

He's sitting alone, smoking a cigarette. I lower back to my heels and turn off the faucet, taking a sip.

I should probably just go back to Otis's room, but there's a nagging thought that maybe I should go talk to him. That thought carries me to the kitchen door and I open it before my other thoughts can argue their points.

Dean straightens, dropping the hand holding his cigarette down to his side and turns around quickly. His shoulders sag and he pulls his hand back up, taking a drag when he realizes it's just me.

"Hey," I say in a hushed voice.

"Hey," he says, staring straight ahead into the backyard.

I shuffle my feet a bit. I'm only wearing one pair of socks and the cement floor doesn't have any insulation.

"What are you doing up?" he asks, still staring out into the yard. "Figured you'd be worn out."

My mouth drops in horror.

He heard us?

"That train ride is a bitch," he adds, flicking some ash.

Oh . . . thank God.

I walk around the table, placing my water down, then pull the chair out and angle it beside him.

He looks over at me quickly, then back to the abyss of the backyard.

If I hadn't seen him knock a few beers back, I'd have known it by the glassy film over his eyes. Still, he has another one sitting on the table next to the ashtray.

"What are you still doing awake?" I try. "I always heard you're supposed to sleep as much as possible *before* the baby gets here," I laugh nervously.

Dean doesn't laugh. He doesn't smile. He just looks down at the ground, taking another drag.

A long moment passes and I'm about to get up and call this all a wash when Dean's eyes slowly drift up to mine.

"My *brother*, Evie?"

I sink further into my chair—an overwhelming heaviness setting in. It feels like his eyes are choking mine, so I swallow hard and break the contact.

"It's not meant to hurt you, Dean . . . it just . . . happened," I offer. "But I *do* love him."

Dean hisses out a humorless laugh, shaking his head. When he raises his head back up, he narrows his eyes at me.

"God. Evie. I mean, what the *fuck?!*"

I jump at the aggression lacing his voice. It's a quiet intensity but it sends a chill down my spine, nonetheless. He scratches his beard, putting his cigarette out in the ashtray.

This was a mistake. I shouldn't have come out here. He said awful, nasty things to Otis when he told him and I should have known better.

I nervously play with a loose string from a fallen button on my sweater, wanting to leave but also knowing that now I *can't* leave, and the notion has my heart picking up speed.

"I'm really sorry that this is hard for you . . . I am. But I don't know why you're acting this way . . ."

That only seems to piss him off more and he stands suddenly, giving me a hard stare, causing me to gasp.

"Because I never fell out of fucking love with you, Evelyn!"

My breath catches in my throat and my body stuns, paralyzed by shock. I can't move; I can't even blink.

The only thing I can do is lift my eyes and I'm met with his intense gaze towering above me. I sit and stare for what feels like hours, not seconds, and my mouth becomes dry. My shock slowly morphs and the currents buzzing through my body light with fire.

Bullshit.

Regaining control of my legs, I stand. My eyes glare back at him as I close the distance between us with one enraged step.

Take it back, you prick.

He doesn't. His shoulders straighten, holding his ground and a roll of fury crashes through my chest.

"You . . . are full of shit, Dean! You're pissed. I get it. But don't pretend for one second that it's because you still *love* me." My tone is chastising, and I pace away, needing to put some distance between us but quickly turn back around. "You *cheated* on me and *left* me seven fucking years ago. And when you finally did come back to Chicago, you weren't crawling on my doorstep, begging for another chance. You met Marnie and got *married*. What about *any* of that concludes love?"

My heart is pounding and my limbs start to shake. I breathe deep and pull my hand behind my back, allowing my fingers to spell for a moment while I try to reel myself back in.

Dean just stands and stares at me, his face is tight but the anger it held just a few minutes ago has dissipated into quiet distress. For just a moment, I see the Dean I met ten years ago, and it feels like a thorn slowly pushing through my chest.

"I know I fucked up . . . believe me, I do. But when you . . ." he stops, shaking his head defeatedly. "I was just as scared and clueless as you were after it happened."

My fists curl at my side, my knees visibly shaking.

He can't be serious.

"Well, lucky for you, you could easily hop on a plane and leave it all behind." I cross my arms over my chest.

I clearly struck a nerve because his eyes widen and he advances on me, again.

"*Lucky?*" He steps closer. "*Easy?!*" His voice rises. "No, Evelyn, it wasn't *easy*. That's the whole *fucking point!*" His voice booms and I jump back, away from him.

His eyes squint for just a second, slowly filling with remorse as he takes in my frightened stance. A deep sigh pushes through his lips and when he speaks again, his voice is quiet and hoarse. "It was the hardest thing I've ever had to do."

Turning away, I rub my palms up and down my face.

I had seen Dean lose his temper on a few occasions when we were together, but he *never* lost it with me and witnessing it right now is overwhelming. I breathe deep, clasping my hands behind my neck when I suddenly hear him speak just above a whisper from behind me.

"I couldn't help you."

I cautiously turn, my eyebrows furrowing.

He takes a couple of careful steps toward me. "I wanted to. *So badly.* But I couldn't." His voice is low and gravelly, grating my insides to dust.

His eyes lock with mine and I can't look away. "But make no mistake about it, Evie. I never *stopped* loving you. That's not why I left, and it's not why I stayed away."

My feet wobble at his words and I plant my hand on the table, trying to steady myself but Dean catches my waist.

I slam my eyes shut, feeling like my mind is in a tilt-a-whirl, my stomach turning from the smell of tobacco and beer.

Why are his hands still on my waist?

My eyes open, slowly rising to meet his, widening when I see his expression.

I know that look. I remember that look.

His hands tighten on my waist and I instantly push off of him, stumbling back, spilling my water and grabbing the edge of the table to keep from falling.

"Evie . . ." Dean says, taking a step toward me but I hold up my hand and he stops.

I keep my hand out in front of me, trying to breathe through my anger.

"I'm—" he starts, but I stop him.

"You . . . are fucking *drunk,*" the words stutter out of me, fighting the tightness in my throat. "And we are going to pretend *that* never happened."

His eyes are full of regret as he nods, running his palm down his face. My knees shake, standing still a moment more, waiting until I'm sure I can move without falling.

My muscles tighten and I quickly grab my empty cup, practically running back inside. After dropping it in the sink, I take hurried steps back to Otis's room and then crawl into bed, latching on as gently as I can without waking him as I press my face into his back.

I'm so sorry, Otis.

chapter forty-four

otis

fourteen years ago

Christmas break had just started but I was in my bedroom reading Aldous Huxley's *Brave New World*. It was required reading but I thought it was a pretty cool book, so I found myself getting ahead of the assigned chapters.

My overhead light flicked on and off and I went to open my door. Dean stood just outside, brushing past me quickly and I closed the door.

Goddamnit.

His eye was swollen, and a bruise was forming at his temple.

Mom and Dad were going to kill him for getting into another fight. Dean had always been a little bit of a hot-head, but he seemed to be really going after people lately. I had no idea why—I had pretty much severed myself from any gossip at school.

"What happened?" I signed.

He sat on my desk, resting his feet on my chair. I tried to ignore the loose mud scraping off his boots and falling to the mesh fabric. He noticed anyway and rolled his eyes, gently nudging the chair out from under his feet.

"Dean, you've got to reel it in. UIC can still back out," I signed, walking closer to him.

He scooted past me, signing, "Well, they should meet all the assholes we go to school with," then picked up the book I left on my bed, adding, "I definitely didn't read this."

I snorted. I didn't tell him it was only required in AP English. It didn't matter, anyway. Dean rarely did his reading assignments—or any assignments for that matter. But he was really smart. He was smart in all the important ways, he just didn't try at school.

Still, he managed to write a good essay and maintain a decent enough GPA to get into UIC and I was determined to see him go. In another year, I planned on being in Chicago too and life would be fucking sweet.

"Haley and I broke up," he signed.

I tried not to look too excited. He was clearly pissed about it, but I was relieved. I really didn't like Haley. She was one of those people that seemed annoyed and dissatisfied by everything, all the time.

"I'm sorry, man. Did she do that to your face?" I pointed to his shiner, deepening in color before my eyes.

He chuckled, signing, "Asshole," while shaking his head. "Whatever, right? I'm leaving at the end of summer and it'll be nice to not have to do anything long distance. Find me a hot college co-ed." He wiggled his eyebrows, and I rolled my eyes.

"I don't think anyone says 'co-ed' anymore," I signed.

I could tell my brother was more hurt than he was letting on. He opened up to me more than anyone, but he was still a pretty private sulker.

"Mom and Dad have that Christmas party tonight. We can raid the liquor cabinet and get drunk in the treehouse?" I suggested.

He smirked, then signed, "Great fucking idea, Otis." He clapped my shoulder, shaking it in excitement and I laughed. "But first, we have work to do."

I nodded. *Work to do* meant Zelda to play.

Mom and Dad had left for their party a half hour ago and it was just getting dark. Dean stole a handle of tequila and schlepped it up into the treehouse, rolling it to the middle of the floor as he pulled himself up the last of the ladder.

"They're going to notice a giant fucking bottle missing!" I signed, shaking a little from the cold.

Dean gave me an offended look. "My brother, you forget who you're drinking with." He pulled a salt shaker out of his pocket, signing, "I'll replace it with water. They'll never know. Plus, they almost never drink it. They've had this bottle since last Christmas."

"Genius," I cracked.

We sat in the middle of the floor. I brought a blanket, even though I was layered up because it was fucking December. But the treehouse was our favorite spot. And it felt like we could both use a night in a place that helped us escape.

He poured two shots and handed me one. He licked his hand and I copied him, then he shook some salt where I licked.

"Aren't we supposed to use limes too?" I signed, immediately spilling the salt off my hand. He rolled his eyes, gesturing toward me to give him my hand again, sprinkling more on.

We clinked glasses, licked the salt on our hands and took our shots. And goddamn, it burned.

I had brought a water bottle up, so I took a sip and swished it around in my mouth trying to get the taste out and Dean laughed.

I didn't really drink. Only a couple of times, with him, just like this.

When we were younger, we used to camp out up here. We'd stay up all night telling scary stories and making shit up, watching out for One-Eyed-Willy.

It was the best.

"Tequila is gross," I signed, and Dean shook his head.

"It gives a great buzz, though. Different from other alcohol. Try not to chase it with water this time," he signed, pouring another shot for us each.

The second one went down a little easier, so I listened to my drinking coach and didn't drink any water, pleasantly surprised at the heat that spread through my stomach as the shot sunk down.

Dean nodded. "See?"

We sat for a few minutes and took in the space of our treehouse. It had two windows—one facing the house and one facing the back—toward the woods. We had tons of maps and drawings on the walls that Dean had drawn when we were younger.

I chuckled at the sign we made: "NO GIRLS ALLOWED! EXCEPT MOM!"

It was like a museum of our childhood.

I looked over at my brother and even in the dim light I could see the bruise on his temple. We were able to hide it from Mom since she was getting ready for the party, but I knew it wouldn't be long until she saw it.

Dean didn't really talk about things that were bothering him, but I could always tell. He was a textbook deflector. When something was off, he'd always distract himself and it usually involved me.

I didn't mind, though. He was my best friend—actually, he was my only friend—but we liked to do the same shit.

He had a big fight with Haley about a month ago, which I only figured out from the multiple times his phone would light up and he'd hit the ignore button, and we basically made a whole comic book in one weekend; I wrote and he drew.

But it wasn't like him to not tell me who or why he was fighting. *That's* something he usually did let me in on.

He poured us another shot and I let the warmth sink down again, cautiously looking back up at him.

"What happened today?" I signed, nodding toward his bruise.

He took a deep breath and patted his chest, then took out his cigarettes. He stuck one between his teeth and pulled the lighter out of his pocket, lighting the end.

"It was nothing, man. Just had to put an asshole in his place," he signed.

"Was it something to do with Haley?"

"Dude. I'm not harassing you about Jen! Why do you care? You hated Haley," he signed, taking another drag.

"I didn't hate her," I lied. "I just didn't think you guys had much in common."

That was true. Dean was a free thinker and Haley was a preppy cheerleader who went to church every Sunday.

"Yeah, well, I guess I was her 'bad boy' phase," he signed, bitterly.

"You'll find someone way cooler at UIC," I signed back to him, pouring us two more.

I was going to throw up that night. No doubt about it. I took a sip of water, trying to avoid the inevitable and let my shot sit there for another minute.

"There is something I want to talk to you about though, O," he signed.

I could tell it was a heavy topic just by the look in his eyes, so I sprinkled some salt on my hand and took my shot. I pointed at him while I winced from the burn trailing down my throat.

"Why aren't you talking anymore, man?" he signed.

I gasped involuntarily and a hiccup escaped. Sitting there for a few beats more, I kept my head down toward the floor until my hands finally moved.

"You know why . . ."

There was no way he hadn't heard. The whole fucking school knew.

"I know what the dick holes around school are saying but I want to know what actually happened," he signed, pouring himself another shot.

He tilted the bottle toward me, silently asking if I wanted another and my chin dipped in a lazy nod. I was already buzzed but I needed more if we were going to have *this* conversation.

We took our shots, and I wiped my mouth with the back of my hand when a gross burp crawled up my throat. I took a sip of water and stared at the floor.

"We had sex. She hated it, and she told the whole damn school just how much."

"Well, Jen's a cunt, but that still doesn't explain why you stopped talking."

The alcohol was officially leading the charge at that point. The moment itself didn't feel real, but the embarrassment felt like an itch under my skin. I didn't want to talk about it, I just wanted it to stop.

"Because I don't want to exist there anymore. I already know I sound fucking different . . . weird," I signed, not drunk enough to not feel pathetic. "I just don't want to give them any other reason to . . ." I paused, taking a steadying breath. "I just want to forget it ever happened."

Dean jerked his jaw from side to side then closed it tight. He breathed deeply through his nose before leaning toward me.

"Otis. Fuck them," he signed. "I know a year seems like a long time, but in just a year, you'll leave that place and never have to deal with a single one of those losers again."

He leaned back against the wall, putting his cigarette out on the bottom of his boot. "Did you even like Jen?"

I shrugged. "She was cute. I don't know . . ."

Dean stared at me thoughtfully. "The right girl is going to bring you back one day Otis, and I want you to remember that I told you this. That girl that you meet in the future? She won't be just a cute girl. She'll be the reason to *want* to exist again," he signed. "So, it's fine that you don't want to talk. But I refuse to let Jen Saggy-Tits Bernard be the reason you stop talking forever. You're better than every last one of those assholes."

I tried to take in what he was saying but all I could do was snort a laugh. "She doesn't have saggy tits!"

Dean laughed, nodding. "Dude, yes she does."

We laughed so hard for the rest of the night. The buzz from the alcohol made everything funny, but mostly, it just felt really good to laugh.

We went back to school after New Year's and I noticed that my plan to disappear was finally working. The nasty pictures on my locker had stopped and I hadn't seen any speculative eyes on me.

The one activity I still participated in was the school newspaper because I could still mostly keep to myself and I wanted an extracurricular activity for college applications.

I was sitting at my designated desktop next to Brad, who I actually didn't mind, given that he also tried to fly under the radar at school due to his unimpressive social status.

He wrote something in his notebook sitting between our keyboards and elbowed me.

> Hey man. Your brother is a legend! I heard he
> knocked Brandon Weaver flat out right before
> Christmas break.

I tried to pretend I'd at least heard about it, hoping he'd give me more details. Dean never *did* tell me what happened.

> Yeah. I don't really know what happened though.
> He wouldn't tell me—probably because I suck at
> lying to our parents.

Brad read what I wrote. He shifted uncomfortably, looking up at me. I nodded, encouraging him to tell me and he hesitantly wrote another note.

> Apparently, Brandon was talking shit. You
> know, about the whole Jen thing and Dean
> hunted him down. He knocked him clean out
> right outside the convenience store on State.

Damn. *I knew it.* My stupid, reckless . . . fucking awesome older brother.

chapter forty-five

evelyn

S oft lips trail down my neck, waking me up.

A smile stretches my mouth, as I pull Otis's arms tighter around me.

He buries his face in my neck, inhaling deep, pressing one more kiss right behind my ear. A chill runs through me as I wiggle and turn my neck to look back at him.

"Merry Christmas," he says before his lips take mine.

Our kiss is sweet and tender—so warm that I wish I could live in this moment forever. We pull apart, but my eyes hold onto his.

God, I love him.

Waking up next to him this morning *feels* like a gift. He's so much more than the shiny car wrapped in a big red bow in the driveway. He's the engine that makes my heart race. He's the airbag that saves my life. He's the stereo that sets my soul free.

I drape my leg over his thigh, kissing him with everything in me.

"Merry Christmas," I say against his lips.

He smiles and leans up on his elbow, staring down at me with the same adoration I feel in every bit of me right now.

Dean's eyes staring down at me.

A pang of guilt jolts me—remembering what Dean almost did last night.

I still can't believe it. The Dean I knew wouldn't have done that to his brother. Although, I really didn't think the Dean I knew was the kind of guy to cheat, either.

I press my face into Otis's chest, breathing in his woodsy warmth. A comfortable sigh escapes me, and I smile back up at him, shoving my unease down deep.

It's Christmas. And for the first time in a really long time, I want to enjoy it.

We finally mosey out of Otis's room, hand in hand, walking to the kitchen. Gloria is Mrs. Claus incarnate with her heavy, red velvet robe and green pajama pants. Her slippers even curl up at the toes and have little bells on them. She turns around as she hears us enter and charges us.

"Merry Christmas, babies!" she signs, pulling us both in for a hug.

The height difference between Otis and I causes her to lean down into my head as she holds us both around the neck. Paul walks into the kitchen from the living room, signing, "Merry Christmas," and we do the same, then make a beeline for the coffee pot.

I pour us each a mug, noticing the familiar smell of Red Line coffee. My heart dips as I remember the fate of Bohemia in just a short week. Otis tucks some hair behind my ear then brushes my jaw with his thumb, noticing my mood shift.

A throat clears behind us and I startle at the noise. Knowing it's Dean, I turn around but avoid eye contact, moving out of the way of the coffee pot but Otis stands still.

He doesn't look angry, but impatient, as he glares back at his brother. Otis takes one sip from his mug before coming to meet me and walking into the living room where Paul has already started a cozy fire.

We sit on the couch and Paul sits in the recliner doing a crossword puzzle.

"Four letter word for 'deviously clever,'" Paul signs, looking at Otis.

I think, OTIS in my head, but that's not right. Still, it makes me giggle. Otis thinks for a moment then signs, "Wily?" at his dad.

Paul points his hand, shaking it at Otis in thanks, then fills in his boxes.

I snuggle closer into Otis's side, taking another sip of my coffee as Dean plops down on the other side of me.

Goddamnit.

There's nowhere else for him to sit, but it doesn't make it any less awkward. I press harder into Otis and he winces.

"Sorry," I mouth, staring up at him and he smiles, kissing my temple.

Paul looks up at us, again. "African tree cultivated for coffee," he signs.

"Arabica," Dean and I both sign.

I don't look over at Dean, but I can feel his eyes on my profile as I take big gulps of my hot coffee. Otis's arm moves from behind my neck to drape over my knees, hugging them possessively.

Good fucking God! Can someone die from being uncomfortable?

Paul continues, totally oblivious to the palpable tension vibrating just a few feet away from him. My free hand is tucked under my legs, starting to spell.

Fireplace, couch, tray table . . .

Five minutes pass and I've spelled nearly everything in the room, twice, when Marnie waddles in. I pop up abruptly.

"Here, Marnie. Take my seat. I need a refill, anyway," I say and Otis eyes me as I shuffle my way back to the kitchen.

Gloria is cooking eggs and bacon crackles on the stove top. She's sipping orange juice from a holiday flute and smiles up at me.

"Don't judge me, honey. Mimosas are elf juice. True story," she says, tilting her glass toward me like she just gave me a lesson in Christmas 101.

"Not at all," I laugh. "I'll join you, if you don't mind."

Her smile widens, grabbing the bottle of champagne from the fridge and pouring some into a flute for me, adding a dash of orange juice.

"Just for color," I joke, and she chuckles.

We clink our glasses, each taking a sip. The bubbly sensation down my throat immediately releases some stiffness in my shoulders.

Gloria tends to her eggs and takes the bacon off the pan, then puts it on a paper towel to soak up the grease. She breaks a piece of bacon in half, handing me one half.

Well, the kitchen is the place to fucking be.

"Thanks." I smile, taking a bite of the salty, fatty goodness, pretending that the living room is another planet for a minute.

Otis suddenly walks in, immediately looking at my hands—one with mimosa, one with bacon—making a "what the hell" face.

Gloria and I crack up. Otis chuckles too but comes over, stealing the last of my bacon.

Not cool.

But I'm still laughing as Gloria calls out, "Breakfast!"

After we eat, I pull my boots on, excusing myself to go make a phone call on the back patio.

As I hear the call start to go through, I glance around the space, seeing no trace of my confrontation with Dean last night. The ashtray is gone, no beer bottle, and the water I spilled is no longer there.

I try to convince myself it was all just a dream when I hear my mom, squealing, "Pumpkin! Merry Christmas!"

"Merry Christmas." I say, trying to match her enthusiasm. "How has your day been?"

"Oh, it's good. We miss our baby, though. But guess what?" she asks, in the same way she's always asks whenever a certain thing happens on Christmas.

"It's snowing?" I answer, tears pricking my eyes.

"Mhm," she sighs. "It's never the same without you, though."

"I know, Mom. I miss you guys too."

So much.

"Maybe one of these years you and Otis can come here for Christmas?" she asks.

Suddenly, there's a rustling through the phone. "Evie Bear?"

"H-Hi Daddy," I squeak.

I hate that talking to them has become this painful. And it's all my fault. It's become a fear that feeds itself. I couldn't bring myself to visit after it happened. I couldn't go back to that house, sleep in the bed where my light slowly went out hours after it happened, or eat a meal in the kitchen I sat in while I tried to pretend I wasn't dying inside the day after.

That fear became worse the longer I stayed away, and the longer I stayed away, the more difficult it became to talk to them at all.

"How are you?" My dad's voice sounds a little strained, weighing my heavy heart further down.

"I'm good. Did mom tell you about the Bohemia?"

He sighs. "Yeah, she told me. But don't worry about it too much . . . these things have a way of working themselves out."

"It is what it is?" I laugh, quoting his iconic phrase.

He said it to me all the time as a kid and it drove me crazy.

"Yep. It is what it is," he laughs. "We're always proud of you, you know that."

I nod like he can see me, the tightness in my throat constricting my voice.

"And I'm just going to have to insist that you and Otis come here for Christmas, sometime. Your mom is making me watch the damn cow movie, *again.*"

I laugh. "*Annabelle's Wish*. It's a good one."

He clears his throat, again. "Well, anyway, Merry Christmas, baby girl. Come home soon."

"I will, Daddy. Merry Christmas."

I end the call, taking some steadying breaths. Looking out the screen and into the backyard, I try to focus on something else when I notice the treehouse.

Both Dean and Otis have mentioned it before, and I've seen it from the kitchen window but this view, in the daylight . . .

It's a badass fort.

Looking back through the sliding door, I only see Paul in the recliner. I open the door to the screened porch, walking the small distance to the giant tree, holding the Roberts' boys treasured hideout.

I peek back toward the house one more time, feeling a little guilty about trespassing but still find myself climbing up the ladder.

Pulling myself into the house, I stand up and dust myself off. The floor is littered with leaves and dirt, but the walls are covered with drawings, secret code keys, and maps. Some of the drawings are childlike but some of them are really good.

Dean used to draw.

I walk the edges of the room, admiring the old artwork, studying the drawings like they're hieroglyphics—most of them make no sense to me, but it tugs at my heart to see that the two of them had their own little world up here.

It's then that I see the ashtray Dean was using last night, tucked into the corner and a small pain aches in my chest.

Imagining Dean up here, sitting among the memories, in the place that he and Otis spent so much time together growing up.

He was so drunk last night, so . . . desolate.

I quickly climb down the ladder, feeling guilty about . . . well, *everything* at the moment. I scurry back through the patio door, then back through the kitchen, the heat doing nothing to relax my tense body.

We open gifts in the living room, around the tree. Marnie opens the onesies I got for the baby. My favorite one says, "I'm the reason it's not DECAF."

"These are so cute, Evelyn! Thank you," Marnie says, and Dean smiles over at me, but quickly averts his eyes down to the baby clothes.

Otis and I got Gloria and Paul a gift certificate to their favorite restaurant in Rockford, and theater tickets in Chicago.

Gloria hands me a package and I'm a little surprised. It was nice of them to invite me into their home, yet again for another holiday, so I certainly didn't expect them to get me anything.

I open the package, pulling out a large, bell shaped mug with thick purple paint dripping down the sides, lightly dusted with gold on the handle and around the base and lip.

"Wow . . . this is . . ." I'm speechless. It's really beautiful—so unique. I turn it over to see who the potter is then look back up at Gloria.

"I made it with my wheel," she signs, smiling. "Otis told us you . . . stole a chair from a park?"

I laugh, nodding, tears brimming my eyes. That's *exactly* what it reminds me of—my favorite chair at Bohemia.

"Thank you so much," I sign, hugging her, then Paul.

I cozy back up to Otis, admiring my new, favorite mug. He opens his gift from his parents, which are collector's editions of C.S. Lewis's *Chronicles of Narnia* and Kurt Vonnegut's *Breakfast of Champions*.

My smile stretches at the idea that if Otis and I ever share a living space, it will be full of mugs and books.

After the gift exchange, Otis and I go back to his room to pack up our bags. I wish we could stay a little longer, but this is my last week with Bohemia and I really want to open every day I can.

He pulls a small package out of his bag and I pinch my eyebrows.

"I thought we agreed we'd do gifts at home," I sign.

He smiles, shrugging. "This one's small and kind of goofy."

Somehow, I doubt that.

I open it, finding a small, beaten up piece of paper. Unfolding it, a quiet gasp escapes me.

> *I took ASL in high school but I really want to get better. Will you teach me?*

> *I'd love to!*

> *Thanks Otis! Let's do lessons here. Coffee on me!*

"You saved this?!" I sign, the girliest of tears pricking my eyes.

He nods, his mouth tilting into a self-conscious smile.

Holding this paper in my hands, something we wrote ten years ago when we barely knew each other feels sacred.

Why did he keep this?

Staring up at him, searching his face—all that stares back at me is love.

I look down again at the note that he's kept safe for our entire friendship and then back up at the man that was right in front of me this whole time.

It's the safest, most beautiful feeling I've ever had.

I hold our note in my hand while Otis holds me. "I love you," I whisper against his mouth.

He doesn't say it back this time, he just pulls me closer, like he knows I've just realized something he's known all along.

We've *always* had each other.

chapter forty-six

otis

My parents offered to take us back to the city, which is great because it takes way less time by car.

Evelyn's face has kept its glow the whole ride. I had no idea she'd love the note so much. I actually thought she might make fun of me for keeping it for so long.

Of course I kept it.

We pull up to my building and my dad throws his flashers on as we all spill out of the car. My mom stands on her tip toes, hugging me tight and bouncing, like a gas nozzle shaking every last bit of motherly love out.

"I don't care how tall you get, you're still my baby boy and I love you," she signs, then kisses me on the cheek.

"I love you too, Mom. Thanks for driving us back," I sign, pulling her in once more.

She gives me one more tight squeeze then moves to Evelyn and my dad gives me a firm hug.

"I love you, son,' he signs, angling himself toward the street, away from my mom and Evelyn. He nervously looks down, then back up at me. "Your brother's head isn't straight right now. He's struggling, Otis."

He glances back toward my mom, who still has Evelyn wrapped in her arms.

"Just . . . try to remember . . ." he stops, sighing. "Just reach out to him when you're ready, okay?"

I'm shocked that Dean talked to him about any of this. Dean was impenetrable when it came to admitting something was bothering him—*especially* to our parents.

I'd bet just about anything that my dad doesn't know the extent of my fight with Dean. If he did, I'm not sure he would be asking me to do this. But I can't say no to him, so I nod tightly, giving him a parting pat on the shoulder.

Walking over to Evelyn, I wrap my arm around her, watching my parents drive away. She looks up at me, flinching suddenly and our eyes drift up.

It's snowing.

My favorite Evelyn smile shines up at the sky.

She smiles, I smile.

She lowers her face to look at me, pulling my coat collar until our lips press together and she sighs.

After a moment, she pulls away, signing, "I have to run home and get your present."

"Let's stay there tonight. I just need to run upstairs."

She nods once, telling me she'll wait down here. I peek back at her right before I go into my building and see her glancing around the sky, enjoying the flurries dancing around her and I quickly pull out my phone to snap a picture.

Her back is to me, but her serene smile is angled up toward the sky, over her shoulder, lit by the streetlamp just a few feet away.

So fucking beautiful.

We decide to sit down in Bohemia and have some coffee. Evelyn christens her new mug from my mom and I grab my ugly-ass mug, and then place it on the pick-up counter.

She's just finished steaming some milk, pouring it in small circles, wiggling the pitcher then making one sweeping motion across the top.

Looking down, I see she's made a pretty wave pattern on the top of her latte.

"It's called a rosetta," she signs.

"You make that work of art and I'm still stuck with that?" I jerk my head toward my mug and she laughs.

She leans over, grabbing it. "I still stand by this masterpiece."

"Right. That's why you always take mine and leave *this one* for me," I tease.

She smirks, signing, "Well, I have a new mug now, so yours is . . . all yours," then laughs, starting to make my drink.

I'll still use her ugly mug.

After she pours the shots over the hot water, she hands the drink back to me and we go to my spot. She sits in the corner, her back against the wall, settling her legs over my lap on the bench.

After a few seconds under her speculative stare I finally sign, "What?"

Her mouth quirks up to the side, breathing a laugh. "I don't know. I just . . ." she pauses, thinking. "It's funny that we never had a 'talk,' you know? A 'where is this going—what are we' talk."

I knew her head was in the clouds. Ever since I gave her that note she's had this dreamy look on her face. I can't even really put my finger on it but there's something about her that feels closer to how she was when we first met.

A lightness.

I place my mug on the table, scooting closer to her. "We can, if you want."

She shakes her head. "That's just it, though. I don't feel like we need to, it's like I already know. I mean, I don't, obviously, but sometimes . . ." she signs, then tucks some loose hair behind her ear, lost in thought. "I just can't believe that after all this time, all that's happened . . . we found our way to each other."

"She'll make you want to exist again."

I startle a bit, remembering the words Dean said to me when we were kids—when I felt hopeless and alone. Never in a million years could we have known that the girl who made me want to exist again would be a girl he once loved too.

I was so defeated when he said it to me, I didn't actually believe it would happen. My mouth flattens into a tight line and I breathe deep, looking over to Evelyn.

"After what happened in high school, I really wasn't sure I'd ever be with anyone," I sign. "I was just a kid, but I really believed that some version of what happened with Jen was what I could expect from relationships."

She sighs, nodding wistfully, a deep understanding in her eyes.

"But something changed," she signs.

I nod. Something *did* change. I could have died in that alley. She could have too if things had gone a certain way and either one, or both of us would have been gone. I would have never known what it was like to kiss her smile, I would have left the world never knowing her favorite book . . . her darkest secret.

"You and I survived that night. You're the only thing that kept me conscious toward the end . . ." I sign, stopping suddenly as I remember my last thought before I passed out that night.

Evelyn looks at me with questioning eyes.

"My last thought before I went unconscious was how beautiful you were . . ." I sign, and her eyes glisten. "What we've found together, Evelyn . . ." I don't even know how to put into words what I've found with her.

Evelyn stares back at me with absolute understanding. Her smile tilts, eyes sparkling, as she signs, "You brought me back too, Otis. You brought *my life* back to life, too."

I crash my lips against hers. I kiss her like I'm kissing every version I've ever known of her. I kiss the girl I met in college who's smile made me weak, I kiss my best friend for being the beautiful, compassionate soul that always found a way to connect with me, and I kiss the woman I'm so in love with, *now*. The woman whose love I can't live *any* of life without.

She grabs the sides of my face, pulling me closer, then settles one leg on each side of me, sinking down on my lap. Her tongue pushes inside my mouth, moving slowly against mine. We kiss until our lips are swollen and she finally pulls back, then lays her head on my chest.

Koala in a tree.

I hug my arms around her tight, resting my chin on the top of her head.

Another prophetic moment. The night that we both discovered we were living fully again—together.

And it's *Christmas*.

"Baby, do you want your presents?" I say over her ear.

She slowly leans back with her arms linked around my neck, a shy smile inching up her cheek, but it morphs into an excited one as she quickly nods.

I chuckle. "It will require you getting off of my lap."

Her lips press together, like she's really not sure if it's worth it, making me laugh more, before she wiggles off my lap and goes back behind the counter.

I sift through my bag as she settles back in the corner of the bench, taking a sip of her latte.

"You go first!" she signs, a giddy glint in her eyes.

My lips pull up, taking the gift she put on the table and unwrapping it. It's an amber colored, leather bound book but there's nothing on the cover.

I open to the title page and gasp.

THE EARLY WORKS OF OTIS ROBERTS

I page through the book and she's had everything I've written—professionally or otherwise—bound into this book.

My eyes drift back up at her in disbelief and her smile is so big my heart feels like it could burst.

"How?" I sign, feeling at a total loss for words.

She fidgets in her seat, placing her mug back on the table.

"I've saved some of your articles from the paper for a few years and emailed your boss for help to find the rest," she signs. "And I started to snoop a little after I had the idea and found some stories on your laptop when I was staying at your place."

I reopen the book and turn just past the title page where I see a Kurt Vonnegut quote.

"People have to talk about something just to keep their voice boxes in working order so they'll have good voice boxes in case there's ever anything really meaningful to say."

I look back up at Evelyn, singing, "Cat's Cradle."

"I told you I love that book," she signs. "And I know that quote is supposed to give credence to the idea that everything is meaningless in context. But it means something different to me—to *us*—I think."

I place the book on the table and kiss her, again. I'll never tire of it.

"Thank you, Evelyn. This is amazing." I smile and my body reignites with nervous energy.

Handing her the first present, she gets a child-like excitement in her eyes, making me chuckle. She unwraps the gift and tears immediately fill her eyes.

It's a framed collage of pictures documenting Bohemia. There's some of the space itself, some of the customers. There's a photo of her and Mary working at the farmers market, and one of her outside the front door holding up the keys right after Sal gave them to her.

"Otis . . . I love this. Thank you," she signs, wiping an escaped tear.

My heart starts to race as I hand her the second present—I actually feel a little queasy. She unwraps it so slowly I feel like I'm about to explode by the time she finally opens the small box.

Pulling out the key, her eyebrows pinch but then quickly shoot up on her forehead.

"Are you asking me to move in with you?!"

I nod and she nearly tackles me in the seat we're sharing. I laugh as she peppers kisses all over my face, eventually landing on my lips and a squeal vibrates against my mouth, making me laugh more.

She sits back up, picking up the key again. "This is sweet, but I already have a key to your place," she signs.

My heart rate picks up, again. The idea seemed so romantic at the time but here, in the moment, it has me slightly terrified.

I nod, swallowing hard. "That's to a *new* apartment," I sign, cautiously. "It's in that building on Winthrop you always stare at when we get fancy snacks at Whole Foods."

She looks stunned, breathing a surprised laugh as she shakes her head. Holding the key with a tight fist against her chest, another tear trickles down her cheek.

"The boy who notices everything," she signs, smiling before burying her face into my neck, inhaling deep. I feel like she takes a piece of me with her every time she breathes me in like that.

I kiss the soft spot right below her ear, releasing a relieved exhale. "You're impossible not to notice," I say against her hair.

I once read that the light we see here on Earth was actually created tens of thousands of years ago. But once the light reaches here, it's a quick eight minutes until our eyes see it.

That's how it feels to be in love with Evelyn. Actually, that's how it feels to know Evelyn loves *me*. We spent years becoming friends and eventually family, that when our relationship evolved, it was like light hitting the Earth.

Years of unseen love and longing, and then suddenly, our light hit and we quickly saw everything.

chapter forty-seven

evelyn

three years ago

I was somewhere between wanting to run around the building like Kevin in *Home Alone* and wanting to flee to the airport and book the first flight out of Chicago.

I had actually done it. Papers were signed, keys were given, and people actually expected me to do something with this place now. It was no longer an idea; it was a real building that needed real money to actually become something.

I looked around the sparsely decorated space. None of the furniture matched, the walls were mostly bare, and I had a bunch of used equipment I found online.

The city had just finished its final inspection and said I could open for business when I was ready.

When I was ready.

A very dangerous offer to someone that's never ready for anything.

Otis and Reggie stood on both sides of me as I swam through my anxiety pool. My very own man-sized floaties, keeping my head above water.

"We should have a slumber party here tonight," Reggie said.

A nervous laugh blew through my lips and I looked up at Otis who was looking around the place with quiet pride.

"I live upstairs now, Reg. I'll be sleeping here every night," I signed.

Reggie slumped onto the built-in bench in the corner of the seating area and gave me a wry smile.

"Until you meet a hot, rich man," he signed. "Then you can just use the studio for storage and snacks," he teased and I rolled my eyes.

Otis smirked and shuffled his feet, then looked over at me from underneath his lashes. He was checking on me; something he'd become used to and honestly, quite good at.

I managed to give him a tense, closed-mouth smile.

"Okay. I signed up for the farmers market this weekend. I think I'll use that as a soft opening to get the word out, and then open early next week," I signed, looking at my friends for approval.

Reggie nodded, impressed.

"You could hand out promo tickets at the farmers market for a free coffee on opening day? It might get a few extra people to show up, or even just stop by your booth?" Otis signed.

"Yes!" I nodded, pointing at Otis. "Great idea. How does one make a promo ticket?"

He laughed. "Super easy. I'll make it for you tonight."

I hugged my friend tight. Otis wrapped his arms around my waist and I saw Reggie suppressing a smile as he tapped around on his phone behind Otis's shoulder.

"Hey, Helter Sexter, you good to come to the farmers market on Saturday?" I asked, still wrapped in Otis's arms.

Reggie glanced up, a devious smile curled on his lips as I felt Otis release our embrace.

"Hell yeah! Try to get a booth near the jam man," he signed, wiggling his eyebrows. "I want to learn how to jam."

Otis and I looked at each other and laughed.

The farmers market was fucking insane. There were so many people there and it was still early; only the vendors had arrived.

Reggie and I finally unloaded all the urns and cups and started to set them up on the table at our booth.

I took out the small sign that Dean had given me that read, "Proudly serving RED LINE COFFEE" and placed it on the edge of the table. I put the promo tickets Otis made in the cash box and set up small stations for drip coffee, cold brew, and a specialty pour over station.

We didn't have a choice what booth we ended up at, so we were nowhere near the jam man, but Reggie quickly started to chat up the produce guy in the tent next to us.

I looked across the way, seeing a small woman with salt and pepper hair and a tall lanky man with wispy gray hair and a warm smile.

"Jesus feck, it's splittin' the stones out here! This is the last year I'm doing this, I swear," the woman whined, wiping some sweat from her forehead as she arranged some flowers in different pales on her table.

She had a hint of an accent. I thought maybe it was Irish or Scottish, but I couldn't tell. The man with her just laughed and soothingly rubbed her back, then caught my eyes from across the small gravel path between us.

I darted my eyes down at my table, mindlessly rearranging things that didn't need to be rearranged when the man walked over to me.

"Hi, I haven't seen you here before. Is this your first market?" he asked.

He had kind eyes and still wore the same warm smile he had just a few moments before.

"Yeah. I'm opening a coffee shop in Edgewater and heard this market was a good one, so I thought I'd give it a shot."

He nodded, an impressed expression on his face. "You're so young to be opening up your own place!" he said, glancing back over toward his tent, then back at me as he extended his hand. "I'm Jim."

I shook his hand. "I'm Evelyn. Nice to meet you."

He had the face of someone wise but not preachy, like people probably sought him out for advice because he had never steered them wrong before.

His wife, I assumed, marched her tiny figure toward us. "Trading me in for a younger model, are ya?" she said playfully, and I snorted a laugh.

"Mary, this is Evelyn. She's opening a coffee shop in Edgewater. This is her first market, so don't scare her, okay?" He kissed the top of her head and gave her an affectionate hold on her shoulder, adding, "It was great to meet you, Evelyn. I have a good feeling about your place."

He was a total stranger, but his words carried some weight with me for some reason.

"Thanks, Jim. Stop by any time!" I said as he moseyed back to his booth.

"Hi Evelyn, I'm Mary. The other half of that guy." She hooked her thumb back toward Jim. "Tell me about your shop!"

She had icy blue eyes, like a dark sea, but they glittered with genuine interest.

"It's in a small, black brick building off Granville. It used to be an Italian restaurant years ago, but it's sat vacant the last couple years." I tried to gauge if I'd bored her yet, but her eyes were imploring me, so

I continued to tell her about the business but quickly ended up giving her the slightly abridged version of my life story.

"Wow," she said once I finished. Her eyes studied me, and I started to feel awkward.

"Sorry. You just have one of those faces that invites people to over-share," I said. "Ever think about bartending?"

She laughed. "I don't listen to everyone, love. Just a worthy few."

I smiled. She had a no-nonsense attitude, but her eyes held such sincerity that I believed what she was saying.

"Oh, with a smile like that . . . you're gonna have the boys lining up around the block for that, alone."

Heat flushed my cheeks before I saw Otis walking down the gravel path. They must have opened up to the public and I waved as he got closer to our tent.

"Oh, she's already taken," Mary mused as she spotted Otis.

I laughed and shook my head. "Mary, this is my friend Otis," I said while signing.

Mary looked up at him with swooning eyes. "I want a friend that looks like him," she said to me and pulled him in for a hug.

She was so small that he awkwardly bent without reaching around her to hug her back right away. He signed over her shoulder, "Crazy?"

I laughed. "I think so. In the best possible way," I signed back to him and he gave her a small pat in return.

I hurried to the cash box, grabbing two of the promo tickets Otis made and gave them to Mary.

"Please stop by if you can, Mary. I'd love to see you and your taller half again."

Mary took the tickets and waved them appreciatively. "Oh, we'll be there, love. Wouldn't miss it."

She tucked the tickets in her pocket as she went back to her tent, immediately scolding Jim about his flower arrangements.

They were the kind of people that you felt like you knew immediately. They had this instant familiarity that made me feel comfortable. My tent was across from Mary and Jim, and something about that fueled me with confidence.

"I love them," I signed to Otis, but my eyes lingered over at Mary and Jim a moment longer.

Otis chuckled. "You love everyone."

"Not true," I signed, giving him a knowing look.

He rolled his eyes. "The woman at the sandwich shop doesn't count."

"Why do I have to beg her for more cheese?! She layers yours on!" I signed, rolling my eyes. "Penis privilege."

He laughed. "Don't get me started on all the things you get because you're pretty. Let me have the cheese, woman," he signed.

A strange flutter danced through my belly at Otis calling me pretty. I smirked up at him, then noticed the throng of people starting to pile into the market.

"Here we go!" I signed.

Otis walked to the front of the table and handed me a five-dollar bill.

"Cold brew, please," he signed.

I rolled my eyes signing, "Otis, you don't have to pay. Just take a damn cold brew," then snorted a laugh.

"I want to be your first customer," he signed, then stood patiently waiting. I shook my head and smiled back up at him. He really could be charming when he wanted to be.

I poured him a cold brew and slid it back to him on the table, signing, "You paid just so I'd have to get it for you, didn't you?"

"It didn't suck." He took a sip of his drink, nodding appreciatively.

"Not too strong?"

"It's perfect," he signed back.

He stood there a couple seconds more, and a few people started to approach my tent.

"I've got to go, but I'll catch you later?" he signed, and I nodded, giving him a quick, nervous wave.

I knew he had a busy day, but it was sweet that he stopped by. A couple of people walked up to my tent and I tried to shake my nerves, channeling them all into an inviting smile. I caught a glimpse of Otis one more time near the entrance, his lips tilting as he stared back at me just before he left.

The farmers market was a success! Mary and Jim sent everyone that went to their tent over to mine, and it was so crowded that I used up all the product I made and gave away all my promo tickets.

I took the last urn out of Reggie's car and into the back room of Bohemia. Tripping over my own damn foot, I dropped the urn and it tumbled to the floor.

"Fuck!" I whined, crouching down to inspect the damage.

A small corner of the floor tile cracked and I groaned, knowing I'd have to pay to fix it. I checked the urn, noticing a small dent in the side but nothing cracked so I figured it was still usable.

It made sense that I'd cracked the floor and put a dent in the equipment on the first day I'd actually sold anything. It sounds weird, but it actually felt like a good omen.

Reggie quickly stuck his head through the door. "Are you okay?"

"Yeah, just breaking shit already," I moped.

"Want to get dinner or something?" Reggie asked.

"No, I'm beat. I think I'm just gonna crash," I said as I stuck the urns in the three-compartment sink.

But Reggie lingered by the door and I suddenly realized what he was doing. "Reg, I'm fine. Promise."

Dean got married today and Reggie thought I was going to lose myself in a night of boxed wine and weeping at posts online about the big day. If he was as good of a friend as he thought he was, he'd have known that I already did that last night when the rehearsal dinner pictures got posted.

Tonight, I was a grown-up with a business that just had an exhausting and successful day promoting the place and I would be showering then going to bed.

"All right," he said skeptically. "Call me if you change your mind."

"Thanks for helping today. Sorry about the jam man."

"Baby girl, I found myself a giant zucchini today. Jam man is yesterday's news," he drawled before winked and left.

I kept my promise to myself and Reggie and took a shower, then crawled under my sheets to go to bed. My body felt like it ran a marathon but my mind felt like it was only at the starting line.

I heard my phone ping from the windowsill by my bed. The studio literally only had a bed so the windowsill was the only surface I could charge my phone on and still reach it from bed.

Otis: How'd the rest of the market go?

My lips curled up. The vindictive side of me found pleasure in the fact that Otis was at the stupid wedding and still thought to text his brother's ex-girlfriend and see how her day went.

Take that new wife, his brother still likes me more than you!

But I immediately felt guilty for reducing my friendship with Otis to such shallow standards. Otis was my best friend, not Dean's brother. Not to me.

Me: It was good! Sold out of everything :)

I waited a moment more.

Me: How's the wedding?

Otis: Ugh. Kill me now.

Me: Haha! It can't be that bad. Find yourself a cute bridesmaid!

I tossed in my bed nowhere near sleep for another hour when I heard a knock at my door.

I knew it was Otis because he was the only person I gave my extra key to, so I opened the door and found him standing outside with a plastic bag and a bottle of champagne.

"What are you doing here?" I signed, laughing in surprise.

He walked past me and put the bottle and bag on the small counter in the kitchenette, then turned back toward me.

"I stole some cake and grabbed a bottle to celebrate," he signed.

He looked handsome still dressed in his tux, his wavy hair styled but still messy.

"Otis . . ." I signed, truly touched. "It's your brother's wedding. Don't you think he'll notice that you left early?"

"Everyone was dancing," he signed simply.

I nodded, still feeling a bit guilty that he left such a big event to come hang out with me.

"I'm right where I want to be, Evelyn," he signed, then started to unpack the cake.

Superpower intact.

I grabbed us some paper plates and mugs since they were all I had, and we sat on the floor.

We celebrated my first day of business with champagne and stolen cake from my ex-boyfriend's wedding on my empty apartment floor. And it was fucking perfect.

chapter forty-eight

otis

I t's strange how grateful you become for small, mundane things only when you'll no longer get to have them. The smell of the coffee, the cozy ambiance, the wide variety of purpose that people had to come here. It will all be over after tomorrow.

Evelyn decided to host a get together for our small crew here tonight. A party for the new year, but mostly a final send off to Bohemia.

I spent the morning packing at my apartment since Evelyn and I decided we would move into our new place January 2nd; only two days away.

My eyes search for Evelyn through the packed café when Mary hurries over to me, throwing her arms around my neck.

We finally pull away from each other and she beams up at me, saying, "Hello, love."

"Hi, Mary," I sign back at her.

Evelyn walks up behind Mary and I sign to her, "I want to give Mary a name sign."

Her eyes light up, telling Mary, and Mary's face turns to me with surprise.

"M. Hug," I sign and Evelyn verbalizes.

Mary starts to repeat the sign but then cups her hand over her mouth, tears springing to her eyes. She pulls me down, squeezing me again and Evelyn stands just behind us with an adoring smile as she wraps her arms around herself.

I feel Mary's grip loosen and she steps back, holding my face with her palm.

"You're a sweet man, Otis. Thank you," she says, collecting herself then giving me a knowing look. "Americano?"

I nod, already missing our familiar exchange.

Mary gives my arm one more squeeze then turns on her heel, heading toward the mug wall.

I take Evelyn's hand, pulling her close to me. "You okay?" I ask quietly.

Her eyes close for just a moment, shoulders falling. "Burning leaves," she signs up at me, standing on her toes to press her lips against mine.

She suddenly jerks away, looking over toward a table of people. They're raising their mugs in our direction and I look back at Evelyn, confused.

She laughs, shaking her head. "Shut up, Joe!" she says while signing but continues to laugh as she rolls her eyes. "We have an audience."

Taking my hand, she leads me back behind the counter and through the swinging door.

I glance around the back office and it feels sterile. The contrast between this room's emptiness before she opened and today is stark. One was waiting to be filled and one is being booted out. Grimacing, I shuffle my feet, then look at Evelyn, watching her sad eyes scan the room, too.

I run my knuckles over her cheek, saying, "It'll be ok, baby. I promise."

She gently nods then burrows her face into my chest.

Tightening my hold around her, we stand like that for another moment before I feel her phone start to buzz.

She digs through her pocket to pull it out and her eyes widen slightly at the screen then immediately her eyebrows pinch.

"Who is it?" I sign.

She shakes her head, slipping the phone back in her pocket.

"My mom. I'll call her back later," she signs, releasing a heavy exhale.

That's weird. I've never seen this kind of reaction when her mom calls. Sometimes she looks guilty or sad, but never nervous.

I search her face. "Is everything okay?"

She nods, signing, "Just a tough week."

I'm still not convinced but let it go for now. I know this week has been hard for her. Not only is the café closing, but she has no idea what she wants to do for work, and I can tell it's wearing on her.

Sal made sure the buyers paid Evelyn for her business—so at least financially, she won't be struggling. But I think she'd be in better spirits with some direction rather than having the money.

"I better get back out there," she signs, and I follow.

Evelyn walks toward the register and I find Mary standing just outside the swinging door, holding my hideous mug and smiling.

I graciously take the drink, immediately taking a sip. My eyes float to Mary still standing idly by my side.

"It's pretty great, isn't it?" she says and my eyebrows pinch, unsure of what she's talking about.

She looks over at Evelyn, then back at me and the corner of my mouth quirks up, nodding as I glance at Evelyn.

"She's loved you for a long time," Mary says. "Poor thing fought it so hard. But I knew it would happen."

"How do you know that?" I sign but mouth the words.

"I'm a wise old woman. I know everything," she jokes, and I breathe a laugh. "You're part of each other, love. She's always had a beautiful heart, but *you're* her pulse. You're the pounding in her chest. You bring her to life."

I stare down at Mary with such deep love and appreciation. I know she looks at Evelyn like a daughter so for her to say these things to me means . . . well, it means everything.

I clear my throat, saying, "Thank you, Mary," and a surprised smile inches up her cheeks, clutching her chest at the sound of my voice.

Evelyn has put out every kind of dip imaginable. There's salsa, guacamole, three different kinds of queso and a French onion dip that I think clogs your arteries just by looking at it.

Naturally, it's the first one I dip my chip into and it's fucking delicious.

Evelyn pushes through the swinging door and rounds the counter to meet me in the seating area but clips the corner with her foot and stumbles forward.

She recovers before actually face-planting on the floor, which is good because my hands are full of chips right now and I'm too far away to try and catch her.

She gives a dramatic and frustrated stare at the ceiling, signing, "Why do things always get in my way?"

Dropping the chips, I laugh, walking to meet her. "You're so pretty," I sign and she snorts, smirking up at me.

She really has no idea how gorgeous she is—effortless beauty with her wavy, wild hair and a casual sweater and jeans. I cup her face with my hand, noticing she's wearing the same earrings with the leaf pattern and a small grin pulls up my mouth.

She gives me a timid smile back, but it doesn't reach her eyes; it hasn't all day, and I miss it. I press my lips to hers, feeling the tension in her jaw fall as her hands hold my wrists.

The moment is broken when I feel her body pull back, her head turning toward the door. Mary and Jim walk in, and I notice Mary's mouth curl into a surreptitious smile.

They dole out their usual hugs, but everything feels muted. Mary starts to unload the bag she has with her and I try to sneak a peek—*there's definitely something good in there.*

Jim stands in front of me. His eyes crinkle at the corners—his eyes are always smiling. "Mary says you kids are moving in together," he says.

I nod, pulling out my phone to show him a picture of the building. Jim takes my phone and looks at the picture then looks back at me before affectionately clapping my shoulder.

"I can see it," he says. "It looks like the place you two will have all your 'firsts' in."

Just then, everyone's heads turn toward the door. Reggie saunters in, dressed to impress with a bottle of champagne in his hand as he looks around the room, shaking his head.

"Oh, hell no," he says, putting the bottle of champagne down on the table with the rest of the food. He shrugs out of his coat, slinging it over one of the chairs and narrows his eyes at Evelyn.

"I did *not* blow off an epic party in Boystown to sit in the dark and cry," he signs.

His serious expression and determined stance make us all laugh and everyone settles into seats around the long, rectangle table.

The night is a series of food, drinks and laughing, with only a couple tears from Evelyn. We spend the night reminiscing about all the good times and all the funny mishaps along the way—like the first time Evelyn thought she saw a cockroach under the sink and said we'd have to move and start all over. It ended up being a peanut butter cup wrapper, so luckily, we stayed.

Mary yawns, tapping the table. "I never make it till midnight anymore," she says, starting to get up.

Mary and Jim leave, and the three of us stand in the seating area, held by a weighted moment. The irony of it just being the three of us here at the end, just as it started, feels right.

I catch a glimpse of Reggie, who's eyes have the slightest shine over them, but he blinks it away quickly. Evelyn leans her head on his shoulder and hugs his arm. He holds her hand on his bicep and leans his head down, planting a kiss on the top of her head.

He says something to her, and she looks up at him and smirks, then gives his arm one more squeeze before she lets go.

Their friendship is the kind that people write books about. Neither one of them have siblings and it's like they give all of that loyalty and love to each other. My heart sinks a little, knowing it was something I once felt with my brother too.

Reggie claps his hands together, then rubs them back and forth.

"All right, I love you both but I'm a man on the prowl tonight," he signs, walking over to the table and pouring the last of the champagne into each of our mugs.

"But one more toast, before I go," he signs. "To the wanderers. To the socially unconventional, artistic people and the areas they frequent. *To Bohemia!*"

Evelyn's eyes fill with Reggie's direct definition of the word—the name she settled on because she believed it captured the idea of somewhere that everyone was welcome.

Reggie leaves and I start to pack up the left-over food on the table. Mary left the rest of her buffalo chicken dip, which I'm fucking pumped about. I'm pouring the rest of the chips back in the bag when I see Evelyn's phone light up on the table. My eyes squint but my heart drops as I read the message.

Dean: Evie, we need to talk about what happened.
Please call me back.

chapter forty-nine

evelyn

I turn around to see Otis standing eerily still by the table. My head tilts as I walk toward him, trying to get his attention. Getting closer, I notice his face looks a little pale and his expression is queasy.

I put my hand on his shoulder, trying to bring him back from wherever his mind has taken him and he looks up at me with unmistakable pain.

"What's wrong?" I sign.

Picking up my phone, he hands it to me, and my brows furrow before I click the lock screen, seeing a message from Dean.

Shit.

I wanted to avoid telling him about this. I thought if he knew, there would be no chance of reconciliation between them and that thought kills me. But *this* makes it look so much worse. This makes it look like I was complicit.

Placing the phone on the table, I put my hands on each side of his face, trying to meet his eyes, but he continues to look pretty much anywhere *but* at me.

God, the look on his face is breaking my heart.

"I love you, Otis." I move closer, pushing some of his wavy hair back and thread my fingers through it, holding them there as I press my forehead to his.

We stand there for a few beats before I pull back and release his hair. Taking a deep breath, I swallow the lump in my throat.

He's honest with you, even when it's hard.

"Dean and I talked on Christmas Eve," I sign, my nerves rising. "He was angry but then he . . ."

He what?

He didn't kiss me; he didn't even lean in . . . but I knew he was only a moment away from crossing that line.

Otis's eyebrows pinch and his mouth forms a hard line. His breathing is slow and hard through his nose as he shakes his head.

"What happened?" he signs.

I swallow hard and explain the whole conversation. After I've recounted everything, I exhale, sinking to the chair just beside me. I cradle my face in my hands and massage my temples with my thumbs as I try to steady myself.

The chair screeches against the floor and I look up to see Otis dropping to the seat across from me at the table. He looks less angry than earlier. Still agitated, but it's mixed with something else.

Disbelief . . . betrayal?

"He said he's still in love with you . . ." he signs, not as a question but like he's processing.

I nod but I still don't believe that's true. It's the one thing that has given me some peace in all of this.

After we got home and I obsessively thought about that night, I realized that this seems to be a pattern for Dean. It's obvious that he's struggling and if history has proved anything it's that he makes rash, impulsive decisions when he feels out of control.

First Haley and now me.

Otis drags his palms down his face, then shakes his head again as his hands cradle the back of his neck. He anxiously scratches his jaw and my lips unconsciously pull up at the sound.

He stares at me like he wants to say something but isn't sure if he should.

I raise my eyebrows, silently asking him and he grimaces, looking at the floor then slowly dragging his eyes back up to me.

Suddenly, he signs, "Is Dean the reason you like that sound?"

My eyebrows pinch and my neck pulls back. It wasn't what I was expecting him to ask me.

But my head lulls to the side, sighing deep—wondering how long he's been worried about this. I stand up, taking the couple steps between our chairs to sit on his lap. My hand cups his face, giving a gentle scratch to his jaw and goosebumps ripple down my arms.

"*You're* the reason I love that sound," I sign, pressing a kiss to his cheek.

It's true. Otis scratching his scruff is how I discovered my love for the sound, and I think it might be specific to only him.

"Dean didn't even have a beard when we were together," I remind him.

His eyes still hold some sadness, but his mouth pulls up at the corner before he studies me for a few seconds, his expression slowly evolving into something devious.

He pulls my mouth to his, groaning low against my lips, tickling me down deep. Lifting me up, our mouths move possessively against each other's and our tongues tangle as he holds me tightly under my thighs. My feet slowly meet the floor before we finally break apart.

Raggedly breathing, he signs, "Upstairs?"

We hurry up the stairs and as I start to situate the key in the lock, I feel Otis's hand snake through the front of my pants as he kisses my neck. A whimper squeaks through my lips as I clumsily turn the key, finally pushing the door open.

Otis removes his hand as we walk through the doorway and then kicks the door shut with his foot behind us. I pull off my shoes, and he does the same as I stumble gracelessly toward the bed. Starting to lift up my shirt, his hand catches mine.

"I like undressing you," he says quietly.

Holy hell, hearing him say that does something to me.

I smile shyly, lying back on the bed, lazily letting my arms fall above my head—inviting him to take my clothes off. His eyes are locked with mine until they drift to my nightstand. My eyes follow to see what he's looking at and I slap my hand over my face.

He leans forward and I feebly try to stop him, but he picks up the purple vibrator, examining it and then looks at me with lustful curiosity.

Well, isn't this just fucking great! I was going to throw it out since I don't really need it anymore but since I've been obnoxiously sentimental about everything, I waited.

"That's Melvin," I sign, then fold both of my arms over my face, laughing nervously. I hear Otis chuckle as he tries to pry my arms away from my face.

I finally let them fall to the sides of my head and Otis stares down at me with no trace of judgment. His eyes are burning . . . hungry.

"Will you show me?" he asks.

Oh my God. I'm mortified *and* horny and I never thought I'd be those things at the same time. But the sound of his voice saying such sexy things to me has me nodding, despite my embarrassment.

He sets the vibrator on the bed and leans down to kiss me, his mouth moves slowly against mine as his hand cups my jaw while his other hand slides down to unbutton my pants, telling me he loves me as he unzips my pants and pulls them down my legs.

His fingers lift the hem of my sweater over my head and he kisses down my neck and collar bone, picking up the vibrator and handing it to me. Pulling his own shirt over his head, I take a minute to appreciate all the cut lines of his muscles contracting from his heavy breathing.

My cheeks heat as I turn to look at him. His stare is worshiping me and that alone sends heat deep between my thighs.

"Only you," I say to him and I mean it. I would only ever do this for him.

He nods like he's caught in a trance. I am too. I flick the vibrator on and move it down between my legs, slowly massaging myself.

My eyes close and my head rolls back on the pillow as the pleasure intensifies, but I feel Otis's hand gently touch my face and pull it back to look at him.

The way he's looking at me.

My hips start to thrust as I move the vibrator between my legs, never breaking my eye contact with him. I moan as he lightly traces his thumb around my lips, then I pull his thumb into my mouth, gently nibbling on it.

"So fucking beautiful," he says.

I moan again as his hand retreats to pull his pants and boxers down, starting to stroke himself next to me.

My legs start to quake watching him touch himself and I practically rip my panties off and drop Melvin to the floor, quickly mounting Otis as he chuckles at my neediness.

Lying beneath me while I straddle him, he sits up and unhooks my bra, tossing it somewhere. His hands pull and massage both of my breasts, while his lips kiss and suck over them making my head fall back.

He leans back slightly, starting to move for the nightstand drawer but I catch his hand.

My lips tilt self-consciously, signing, "I went on the pill."

His eyes widen, letting out a staggered breath. I settle him between my legs, glancing back at him to make sure he's okay with doing this bare. He nods emphatically, causing a quiet laugh to fall from my lips.

I sink down on him slowly and he groans, loud and deep. Sitting back up, he wraps one arm around my lower back while the other one holds the nape of my neck as we meet each other's hips.

There is nothing between us now, and I can feel it. We thrust slowly, our eyes locked as we sink deeper and deeper into each other. *So, so good.*

Our pace quickens, chasing our climax. I tug on his bottom lip with my teeth and his mouth possesses mine once again as we swallow each other's moans. I feel the tightening low tickle deep in my stomach and my hands grip his back tighter. A few more thrusts and we release together.

I stay wrapped around him; his face buried in my neck. Our hearts are beating hard and fast, pressed together so tightly that I don't even know which beat belongs to whom.

We pull back just slightly to look at each other. I push a loose curl off his forehead, kissing his damp hairline, then lose myself in his warm amber eyes.

"So, who's better—me or Melvin?" he chuckles tiredly.

I push him back and wiggle off of him, kissing his chest, then his stomach, making my way further down to show him just how much I prefer *him.*

Always him.

I've been mourning the end of Bohemia for three and half weeks and now that the day is here . . . I'm feeling a bit numb. I was able to sell some of the furniture and donate the rest, so people have been stopping by to collect them.

The spool table is being carried out the front door when some unfamiliar faces walk in. It looks like a family; a mom and dad and their daughter, who looks like she might be about thirteen or fourteen.

I manage a smile, walking back behind the counter. "Sorry about that. We're closing today so I have people stopping by to pick up some of the tables and stuff." I look up at them and they collectively give me uneasy smiles.

The man hands me a piece of paper:

Two large coffees and an iced mocha, please.

I look back up at them and the man taps his mouth and then his ear. *They're deaf.*

My smile stretches. It's kind of insane that in the three years I've had this shop, I've never had any deaf customers.

Just the one. I smile just thinking about him.

"Thanks for stopping in! It's always nice to see new faces. Even on the last day," I sign, and they all look at me with pleasant surprise.

"You know sign language?" the girl signs.

I nod, giving her a kiss fist. "My boyfriend's deaf."

Turning around to pour the two coffees, I hand them to the man and woman.

"I'm Evelyn," I fingerspell my name, then show them my name sign.

"I'm Jackie, this is Dave, and that's our daughter, Jenny," Jackie signs, smiling brightly.

"It's nice to meet you guys. Are you new to the neighborhood?" I sign, starting to make the iced mocha.

"We just moved from Michigan, actually. It's a shame you're closing. There's not many places we go where people can communicate with us," Jackie signs.

"Literally nowhere," Jenny signs, bitterly.

I slowly slide the iced mocha across the counter, grimacing as I sign to Jenny, "That really does suck."

Dave hands me a twenty but I put my hand up, politely denying it. "Please enjoy," I sign.

Otis pushes through the swinging door and I wave him over. "This is my boyfriend, Otis," I sign to the family and introduce Otis to them.

"Let me give you my email. I'd be happy to meet up for coffee or give some restaurant recommendations. Chicago is a really cool city if you know the right places," I sign toward Jenny and she fights a smile.

Jackie writes her email down for me too and the family collectively raises their cups in thanks, leaving Bohemia.

A heavy sigh releases as Otis rubs my shoulders. I turn around, sighing again. "They would have loved it here."

He kisses my forehead. "They got to meet you. It was still a good day for them," he signs.

Giving him a half-hearted smile, I decide that that family should be my last customers. I drag my feet a bit, walking to the door. My eyes well up once again, flipping the sign on the door to CLOSED.

chapter fifty

otis

Otis,

I don't know what to say . . .

I'm sure Evelyn's told you about Christmas and I'm sorry. I can't seem to stop apologizing lately.

Marnie, you, Evelyn . . .

Even when you and I were close, we didn't really get into the emotional shit. But . . . I'm fucking drowning, man.

I know you looked up to me when we were growing up, counted on me . . . but I don't think you ever realized how much I depended on you.

You always helped me through my shitty choices. You hid bruises when I'd get into fights, you covered for me when I'd sneak out of the house. You told Evelyn about Haley when I was too much of a chicken shit to do it myself. You've always cleaned up after me.

I thought it was kind of strange that you thought so much of me. But it's also what fueled me.

I saw the shift happen after you caught me with Haley and it fucking killed me. I've never cared what anyone thought of me. No one, except you.

I really thought the news of the baby would help me turn a corner. I even thought it might help you and I get back on track. But I've felt the weight of your absence more and more since I found out and I just can't stop fucking up.

The things I said to you at Thanksgiving . . . I can't believe I said that . . .

When you told me about you and Evelyn . . . I just snapped.

Honestly, I was pretty sure my suspicions were true, but I hoped to God that they weren't because I knew if you two were together, then that was really it for us.

You two are in love, and you'll both always hate me. And I have no one to blame but myself.

I feel stuck with no way out. But I shouldn't have taken it out on you.

I really did know you liked her back when we were together. She didn't. That was a lie—but I knew. And you both deserve to be happy so, I'm sorry for the way I've acted.

But I want you to know that nothing, and I mean absolutely nothing guts me like what's happened between you and me. You've always been my moral compass and living without it these past seven years has officially turned me into the worst fucking version of myself.

I'm just so sorry, Otis. I still love you, and I'm sorry.

-Dean

Staring at the email I've avoided for the last few days burns through my eyes, setting my mind ablaze.

All I can focus on is . . .

He's right.

He's the worst possible version of himself and I'm still too angry to care about the rest.

I click out of the browser and tug a deep breath through my nose, closing my laptop. I need to calm down before I respond to him.

If I respond.

Adrenaline pushes my legs out of the chair and toward our bedroom. I clip my foot on one of the boxes still scattering our place, walking to the dresser to change for a run.

Evelyn and I have only been living here for about a week and unpacking has been a slow process between work and . . . other things.

I jog down the two flights of steps, then briskly push through the door and out the security gate of the building.

My legs take off in the direction of Lake Shore Drive at a slow, steady pace. It's windier as I get closer to the lake, but I like running alongside it.

The smell of Lake Michigan, the familiarity of the block, the endorphins—none of them are able to stop the freight train running through my mind and my pace quickens trying to chase away my mounting memories.

Dean had somehow convinced me to sneak out to Chicago for the day. He had a way of getting me to do stuff I would never do, like lie to our parents and tell them we were going to his friend's house all day to play video games but really sneak off to the city so he could show me around UIC without them.

"We wouldn't blend in with Mom clutching our arms and pointing at everything she sees," he signed.

"I know, but what if they find out? They might actually kill us," I signed back.

Dean laughed. "You worry too much."

We went to UIC and walked around. It felt so fucking good to actually see life outside of high school.

It had been a shitty year and I wasn't looking forward to another one—especially one without Dean around. But walking around the campus, witnessing all the kids who had survived high school was tangible proof that things would be better as soon as I graduated and got the hell out of Rockford.

We went to Portillo's and got hot dogs for lunch and there was a comic bookstore that Dean wanted to check out, so we stopped in there as we explored the city.

Dean said he had one other place he wanted to go to before we went back home, and I was riding the high of imagining what life would be like one day when I lived here. The last time I had been to the city was a couple years ago and I remember thinking I wanted to live here someday, but it felt like a pipe dream.

Today, it felt like an inevitable reality and it had my body buzzing.

We walked for half an hour when we finally approached a large brick building with a light green roof that had giant owl statues adorning each corner and peak..

As we walked to the door there was a gold plaque that read: Harold Washington Library Center.

I smiled, looking over at my brother appreciatively. I'd always loved libraries, but this one looked epic.

It was more than just a library. It had tons of books, of course, but there were art galleries, music rooms, and a courtyard on the top floor with a glass ceiling that made the room feel like you were outside. I imagined myself wandering down here to study or just browse the stacks whenever I wanted, and it felt like it was breathing new life into me.

We left the library, grabbing another hot dog on our way back to the train to head home. It was the best day I'd had in a long time, and I never would have gone if Dean hadn't made me.

We boarded the train back to Rockford, taking our seats. I sat across from Dean and couldn't help but grin.

We didn't get mushy and shit very often, but I felt so grateful for him. Not just for bringing me along today, but for the unwavering loyalty he always had for me. There were definitely some challenges to being the deaf kid, but it's overlooked how tough it can be to be the deaf kid's brother.

He always invited me along and never once made me feel like he was doing me any favors with the extra effort it sometimes took to be inclusive. I didn't have a lot of friends, but he always let me hang out with his friends. When he was dating Haley, he'd let me tag along when they'd go out for pizza. I think it pissed her off sometimes, but Dean never let that stop him.

I really looked up to him. He truly didn't give a fuck what other people thought about him, which ironically, made him well liked by a lot of people.

He looked over at me with a smug smirk, shaking his head.

"Don't get all sentimental on me," he signed. "I'm gonna kick your ass in Mario Kart when we get home."

I laughed, signing, "Yeah right, Dean, I'm gonna knock your ass right off Rainbow Road. You'll cry and break another controller."

He rolled his eyes. "Don't you think it's time you gave me a new name sign?" he signed, raising his eyebrows with slight hope.

I shrugged. "When you stop farting, we can change it."

I round the block, running back in the direction of our apartment—practically sprinting—fueled by the memory of that day in Chicago. I don't have a single bad memory of my childhood with him, and *right now* that's pissing me off.

My legs move faster, the cold air burning my lungs but for some reason it doesn't stop me. People look at me like I might be running for my life and in a way, I feel like I am.

I finally start to slow my legs as I get closer to our building and the lack of oxygen finally catches up to me, making my vision spotty as I struggle to take in enough air. Holding the gate just outside our building, I try to steady myself.

As soon as my heart rate evens out, I punch in the gate code and slug my way up the two flights. My body feels heavy but also like it's vibrating, making my limbs shake.

Opening the door, the smell of rosemary and sage instantly floods my nose. My steps stagger toward the kitchen for a bottle of water but as I reach the entryway, I see Evelyn dancing wildly—singing as she cooks—and my heart tightens, squeezing the rest of my unease out like a wet sponge.

Even after she sees me, she keeps up with her performance as I grab a water bottle from the fridge. It only takes an extra couple of steps to reach her and press a small kiss to her temple.

She scrunches her nose. "You're sweaty," she signs.

I snort a laugh. "Is that your way of telling me to take a shower?"

Her mouth presses into a line and her cheeks puff out as she shrugs, and I chuckle again.

"I think I'm going to take a shower," I sign.

"Great idea!" she signs. "Dinner in ten."

Our new apartment came with a bay window that Evelyn immediately claimed for a Christmas tree. But until Christmas comes around again, we've set it up as a reading nook with a hammock, the windowsills holding our favorite books.

Evelyn and I are lying in the hammock, reading. It's a good way for us to actually read together. The hammock can't sustain the . . . *physicality* our reading sessions have taken in the past.

We've nearly finished *The Alchemist,* and I can see why this is her favorite book. It's got a little bit of everything—there's treasure, dreams, a love story. It's whimsical, but profound.

Evelyn taps a line on the page we're reading.

"And when you want something, the whole universe conspires to help you achieve it."

I kiss the top of her head, squeezing her a little tighter. She leans up, resting her chin on my chest, her eyes floating up to meet mine before they nervously dart back down.

"We can't have sex in the hammock," I warn.

Burying her face into my chest, she laughs, then lifts her head back up and shakes it.

She pulls her bottom lip between her teeth before she signs, "I think I know what I want to do next."

I sit up as much as I can, looking at her eagerly.

Her finger absentmindedly taps a button on my shirt, right over my heart as her eyes stare down at it, then glide back up to me.

"I think I want to be an interpreter," she signs.

Wow. I'm surprised, but not. I don't know how either one of us didn't think of it before now.

"That's . . . perfect, baby."

Her eyes light up and she crashes her lips against mine. Her fingers ball the fabric of my shirt before she pulls away signing, "We need to go to bed," before tumbling out of the hammock.

chapter fifty-one

evelyn

I traveled down to the Loop to meet with an advisor and go over some options for entering a Sign Language Interpreters Program.

She thinks I can test out of the language classes since I'm already fluent and some of my credits from my existing degree will transfer over. But it still looks like it will take me about two years to complete the program.

I had applied to a few coffee shops up in Edgewater, but until I hear back from them, I still have an abundance of free time, so I decide to hop into a small café to grab a snack.

Walking up to the counter, I order a coffee and a muffin when I see familiar strawberry blonde hair at the pick-up counter. Her back is to me, but I see her face as I round the counter, waiting for my order.

She notices me and gives me a strained smile. My appetite fades as my stomach twists.

"Hey, Marnie," I say nervously. "How's it going?"

"Oh, it's going," she says through a heavy sigh.

She looks worn out, though I'm sure being pregnant tires you out plenty so I can't assume it has anything to do with her husband making a pass at me a couple weeks ago.

Still, the air feels thick.

She clears her throat. "I heard you and Otis moved into a new place," she says, taking her cup off the counter.

"Yeah, we'll have to have you guys over once it's put together," I lie, knowing that will probably never happen.

She nods. "That would be great," she says, and I can tell she knows its bullshit too.

I've never given much thought to what Marnie thinks of me. Well, nothing more than the superficial thoughts I've had about her, at least.

I don't know if it's my anxiety or what, but right now I feel like she's thinking, *"Couldn't make it work with one brother so you're trying the other one, huh?"*

I see her eyes drift over my shoulder to a table by the window. Turning my head, I see a woman with the same pale blue eyes as her, then turn back.

"That's my sister," she clarifies. "Trying to soak up my personal time while it's still *mine.*" She laughs nervously and rubs her belly.

"Oh, well I won't keep you," I say, thanking the stars and moons that this awkward exchange is coming to an end.

"Not at all! It was nice to run into you," she says. "What brings you down to this part of town, anyway?"

I'm too on edge for this. Red Line's headquarters isn't far from here and now I'm wondering if she's trying to sniff out whether I was down here to see Dean or not.

"I had a meeting over at Columbia. I'm thinking of going back to school for sign language interpreting."

She nods considerately. "That's great! Good for you."

The barista slides my coffee and pastry bag toward me on the counter and I thank her.

"It was good to see you, Marnie," I say, giving her a small, awkward hug.

We pull away from each other and I push my way through the door but glance back at Marnie one last time, seeing her shoulders hunch and her head fall as she sits at the table with her sister.

The sight sinks my insides and now I'm almost certain something's wrong.

Holding my bagged, uneaten muffin in my hand, I trudge up the steps inside our building. I unlock and open the door to find a fur-rowed brow Otis sitting at the desk.

His eyes soften when he looks over at me, but they pinch back together when he notices what I'm sure is a distressed expression on my face.

"What's wrong?" he signs, standing from his chair.

"I don't know . . . maybe nothing," I sign back to him. "Want a muffin?"

He takes the pastry bag, putting it on the coffee table, then pulls me toward the couch. I sit down on one side while he sits next to me, pulling my legs up to rest on his lap as he takes off my boots.

My head falls back as he starts to rub my feet and he chuckles softly. I straighten back up and look over at him as the corner of my mouth pulls up.

"Have I told you how good you are with your hands?" I sign, trying to wiggle my eyebrows.

He smiles, continuing to knead my arches. "Did everything go okay at Columbia?" he asks, and I feel the tension in my neck relax.

His voice is like a magic sound machine for me, like the song you put on to lighten your mood, times a thousand.

"It went well. The advisor thinks I can finish everything in two years," I sign.

He nods, looking optimistic. "So, what's the problem?"

It's a gift and curse, this superpower of ours.

"I stopped in a café by the school and ran into Marnie," I sign.

His lips pull back at the corner, sympathetically.

"She seemed . . ." I'm not really sure how to describe her demeanor. "I don't know—just not her usual, cheery self."

"I doubt Dean told her anything," he signs.

I don't miss the resentment in his expression, or the tick in his jaw that follow. I can't blame Otis for feeling unbearably angry with Dean, but it still hurts my heart.

It's hard to have had a front row seat to the deterioration of their relationship. I remember feeling so damn lucky that they made room for me in their seemingly unshakeable bond. But in more recent years, I've felt more like *I'm* the thing that broke it.

Guilt starts to consume me, and my right hand mindlessly starts to spell.

Hammock, laptop, mug . . .

Otis's hand gently covers mine. My eyes drift up to meet his and he sighs.

"Love you," he says.

"Love you," I sign.

I lie my neck back on the arm of the couch, trying to calm my thoughts while Otis continues to rub my feet.

I decided to wear my olive green dress with sleeves that landed just above my elbows. I completed the look with some rose gold chandelier earrings and brown slouchy boots—willing the fall weather into existence.

It was early September, so it wasn't quite boot weather yet, but they were comfy and I didn't know what Dean had planned.

I tried to tame my wavy hair, but it had a mind of its own. I stared at myself in the mirror and put on a natural color lipstick, deciding this was as good as it was going to get.

Our first date.

I wanted to look cute, but I didn't have much fashion sense. Actually, I didn't have any at all, but I figured it was good that he learned that quickly.

I heard a knock at the door and took a deep breath, opening it.

He was . . . so hot . . . so very out of my league.

His thick brown hair had some wax product in it that made it look styled but still not slick and his sweet brown eyes made my insides feel like pudding. His shirt was a simple black three-quarter length tee that was just tight enough so you could see the cuts of his muscles.

I was already blushing. "Hi."

His eyes scanned my face appreciatively and his mouth tilted into a sexy smirk.

"Goddamn, you're even prettier than I remember," he said, shoving his hands into his pockets nervously.

There was no fucking way that I was making him *nervous. There was just no way.*

Still, I found myself coyly looking down at the floor.

"Thanks. You look great too," I said.

Evelyn, this is your vagina speaking: Don't fuck this up for us.

I listened to her, or tried to anyway, and straightened my posture, determined to play the part of Cool Evelyn.

I meant to run my hand through my hair in an alluring way but I'm pretty sure it looked closer to how one might react to a bug flying directly into your head.

"So, where are we going?" I asked.

I imagined my vagina sitting at her desk, massaging her temple, looking at me like I was a lost cause.

Dean smiled, lacing his fingers with mine and lead me out the door.

We had a picnic, right there on campus.

I loved it! Restaurant dates always felt stuffy, and movie dates sucked because you didn't get to talk.

We were both broke college kids. It was sweet and romantic.

Our conversation had been easy and playful through the whole evening. It was just starting to get dark when I popped the last of the cheese and crackers into my mouth.

"What's your favorite cheese?" he asked.

I finished chewing, then sucked in air through my teeth, admitting, "Well, the stinky cheeses are my least favorite."

"Ugh—those are the best ones," he shot back.

I laughed. "We're doomed."

He sat next to me on the small blanket and leaned in, pinching my chin between his thumb and index finger before gently pressing his lips to mine.

I reached up and held the back of his hand, the one still holding my chin, and rubbed it with my thumb.

He released my mouth, smiling sweetly. "I'm sorry, I know you're supposed to wait till the end of the date, but I haven't been able to stop thinking about these lips for a week." He tapped my mouth with his finger.

I'm sure I turned the color of a cranberry as my lips stretched across my face, beaming.

"You have the prettiest smile I've ever seen," he said, looking at me with adoring eyes.

I felt like I was living in a goddamn Sandra Bullock movie.

How was it possible that this insanely hot guy was saying these things to me?

He kissed me again and I swooned. I didn't even care if it was a line, I ate it up like a non-stinky cheese.

Stirring on the couch, I hear a faint buzzing as I wake.

I don't even remember falling asleep. Otis is sitting at the desk as I roll over, grabbing my phone. It's a number that I don't recognize but I answer it, thinking it might be one of the coffee shops.

"Hello?" I answer, trying to sound like I wasn't sleeping at five in the afternoon.

"Evelyn, it's Marnie. Is Otis with you?"

I sit up quickly and that gets Otis's attention from the desk.

"Yeah," I croak. "Yeah, he's right here. What's up?"

"It's Dean," she stutters through a cry. "Can you guys meet me at the hospital?"

chapter fifty-two

otis

A nd for that, I fucking hate you."
The words ricochet around my head like bowling pins. It was the last thing I said to Dean. And now we're back here—at this fucking hospital.

Drunk driving. Car accident. Medically induced coma.

I clamp my eyes shut, trying to shut it out. *All of it.*

The smell of this place is bitter and sterile, sending me back to just a few months ago when I was the one lying in a hospital bed.

"I'm fucking drowning, man."

My eyes reopen remembering the email he sent.

Bouncing my knee as my heart rate picks up again, I feel a soft pressure on my thigh, stilling me. Evelyn is sitting next me with her hand holding right above my knee.

"He'll be okay. We'll get him help," she signs, then gives me one more reassuring squeeze.

My head wants to nod, but it doesn't.

I don't even know what kind of help he needs.

For as close as Dean and I once were, he never needed help—or at least, he never asked for it.

I noticed his drinking at Thanksgiving.

Why didn't I say something?

Just then, Marnie walks back into the waiting room. Her pale blue eyes are filled with tears and her steps are slow. I stand quickly to walk toward her, noticing her face is sunken and dried tear streaks run down her cheeks.

"He's still out. The doctor said it could be hours, or even another day," she says.

Evelyn is standing beside me, signing for Marnie. She rubs Marnie's shoulder before leading her back toward the chairs and I follow.

Marnie wobbles a bit as she sits, then rubs her belly through a hard exhale. Her head dips and gently shakes as her shoulders shudder. My hand moves to her back, circling between her shoulders when Evelyn disappears. She returns a moment later with a small cup of water and hands it to Marnie.

The two of them share a familiar glance that I don't understand, but Marnie thanks Evelyn and slowly sips from the cup.

"I feel terrible," Marnie says. "He's been staying with a friend of ours this week."

My eyes peer up at Evelyn as she interprets for me, but my hand continues to move around Marnie's back.

He hasn't been staying at home?

"It was just . . . too much," Marnie says, sniffling. "The drinking . . . the outbursts . . . I didn't know what to do, but I never thought . . ." She cradles her face in her hands.

I swallow the lump in my throat and look up at Evelyn who is staring down at me, comforting me with her eyes and I let out a shaky exhale.

"I'm going to call my sister, give her an update," Marnie says, stifling her tears. "You should go sit with him, Otis. Just for a little bit."

Giving my knee a pat, she pushes her way out of the seat, still wobbling from the extra weight she's carrying and walks outside. I rub my palms down my face. Everything feels painfully real *and* like a dream, all at the same time.

Evelyn takes my hand in hers and I stand up, wrapping my arms around her. I hold her tight, and she anchors me.

She stretches onto her toes, pressing her lips to mine and I take in her warmth, her wildflower scent. She keeps her hand on the side of my neck after she releases my lips and I look down at her. Her hazel eyes are strong and steady, like ancient moss giving me air.

"You should go see him," she signs. "I'll stay out here with Marnie."

She runs a hand through the side of my hair, then rubs her thumb back and forth over my jaw.

"Should I call your parents?" she signs.

Shit. My parents.

"Not yet," I sign.

Evelyn nods and we walk to the reception desk where she helps me figure out what room Dean is in. Her hand holds mine, giving it a quick squeeze, and it takes me a minute to let go of her.

She's the tether to *this* world; the one where Dean's condition is just an idea.

I walk slowly and linger just outside the door for a moment, my heartbeat quickening as I hold the doorknob. My body wants to rip off the band-aid and go in, but my mind is screaming, begging for another minute.

I slowly turn the handle, keeping my head down but gasp when I finally see my brother's lifeless body in the bed. His mouth has tubes attached to machines and abundant bruising spans from just above his left eyebrow, over his eye and down the top of his cheek.

I see that his left forearm also has a large white bandage tied around it.

My feet stagger toward him and as I get closer, I notice more bruising and scratches littering his neck. Suddenly feeling queasy, my hands grab hold of the bed bumper for balance.

My chest starts moving rapidly, my vision beginning to tunnel. I try to sit, but instead stumble back into the chair situated by his bed. My torso bends forward, between my thighs, trying to take a deep breath.

Adrenaline bounces my knees as I rest my elbows on them, clasping my hands together. I hesitantly look back over to his bed and I don't see my estranged brother. I see the seventeen-year-old Dean who was my best and only friend. I see the Dean that was my hero.

Fuck.

Emotion rises in my throat and I cough trying to clear it.

I sit and stare, caught somewhere between who we used to be and what we are now.

I would have done anything for him when we were kids. He may have never asked for my help, but he knew I was there for him.

Didn't he?

My mind races with all the times he seemed upset but brushed it off. The fights at school, the weekends he'd hide away and avoid everyone but me, his break-up with Haley . . . he never talked about *any* of it.

The heartbreak he went through when Evelyn was assaulted.

Sitting, staring, thinking. It's all I can do.

A groan escapes when I feel like I've memorized the sight of him like this and I pull out my phone to distract myself.

My lock screen is the picture I took of Evelyn outside in the snow on Christmas and the sight relaxes the building tension in my shoulders.

Scrolling through my photos, I see a picture I took of Evelyn and Reggie one night when we all went out for trivia and won. My eyes fall on an old picture; it's from my first year at Northwestern, right after I moved to Chicago.

Dean and I at a Cubs game.

My restlessness returns and I click out of the photo app. I open my email and delete all the junk when I see Dean's message still sitting in my inbox.

Hesitantly, I reopen it. The one I ignored—I actually meant to delete it all together—and the idea of reading it now has my heartbeat pulsing my temples.

The doctor has made no indication that Dean won't pull through this, but if things had gone differently, this could have been the last thing my brother said to me. He could have died thinking I hated him.

I did hate him.

Truthfully, even now as he's hooked up to machines, beaten and bruised, my anger for everything he's done still lingers, but it's different. It's an anger for how we've ended up here. How the series of bad decisions and withholding truths allowed us to become *this*.

Scrolling through the email again, my mind latches onto different words than the first time I read it.

"I feel stuck with no way out."

"I still love you and I'm sorry."

I stare down at the message, reading it over and over and over again.

It occurs to me now that he left nothing unsaid, which tells me he really believed this message was his last shot at trying to make things right with me.

He needed me. He still does.

I don't know if this hurts so much because of the relationship we once had, or because it took something as severe as *this* to make me realize how dark of a place he's been—or if it's the kid in me realizing that my big brother needs me too.

Maybe the hero complex I had for Dean was the root of our downfall. Heroes aren't human. They don't have weaknesses and they don't screw up.

The pressure he must have felt to keep that status kept him from being human with me. And when he did finally fuck up, I vilified him.

I didn't even think about how out of character it was for Dean to have an affair in the first place.

Actually, I did think about it—I just didn't care.

I don't know if it was my love for Evelyn or the fact that he had never let me down before, but I started to desensitize myself from him after that. I didn't think about his pain or where it was coming from. I didn't try to understand why he would be unfaithful and then leave when both things were so outside of his normal behavior.

He did a shitty thing when he cheated on Evelyn. But he let me believe he was just a horny prick in order to keep her secret. He made a bad decision because he's human and felt completely helpless, and then he left when he felt like he'd already lost the only two people he cared about.

Standing up, I lower the bed bumper, timidly placing my hand around his arm but my grip tightens as the repressed emotions start to boil through me.

This arm.

It's the arm that hit my bullies, the arm that shoved me while we played video games. The arm he uses to communicate with me. The arm that helped me walk out of this fucking hospital a few months ago.

I look down at him, feeling like I'm seeing him for the first time in years. Maybe for the first time *ever*, and an overwhelming sorrow crashes through me.

If he would just wake up, I could tell him all of this. If he would wake up, I could tell him how sorry I am for not trying harder to understand.

If he would just wake up, I could tell him that he's not alone.

Wake up, Dean.

I hold his arm tight; my body starts to shake and I fucking cry.

It's still dark when I wake up. I start to lift my head and a small groan escapes from the stiffness in my neck. Rubbing my eyes, I click the lock button on my phone to check the time and see a text from Evelyn.

Evelyn: Marnie and her sister are in the waiting room. I ran home to grab us a change of clothes and I'll pick up some breakfast on the way back. I love you.

My heart lifts, feeling a relief I've only recently come to know.

Sharing trauma or heartache with someone isn't about getting it off your chest. It gives some of it to someone else to help you carry.

Something Dean never did.

Another bout of guilt surfaces as I check the time on my phone. 7:08 a.m.

I glance up at Dean and see his eyebrows flinch. It's the first movement I've seen from him since I got here.

Standing up, I take the couple of steps between the chair and his bed. His eyes are still closed but there's movement behind the lids. I gently put my hand on his shoulder and a few moments later his eyes flutter open, quickly bulging with panic.

I keep my hand firm on his shoulder, trying to calm his body since he's still hooked up to all of these machines. My eyes fill as I look down at my brother's fear stricken, bloodshot eyes.

Clearing my throat, I tell him, "It's okay, it's okay." My throat is tight, likely making my voice hoarse. "I'm here."

The panic dissipates from his eyes, replaced with shock at the sound of my voice. Our eyes stay locked as his body stills before he slowly brings his hand up to mine on his shoulder, holding it there as a tear slides from the corner of his eye.

chapter fifty-three

evelyn

E very day for the last three months has felt surreal. The world, as I knew it, was flipped on its axis and I've been trying to find my footing day after day ever since.

Today, in this bizarre new reality, I'm walking from the L to Dean and Marnie's townhouse.

Dean was released from the hospital a week ago and had to spend a mandatory six hours in jail immediately following his discharge. He's found a lawyer to help him with the charges and thinks he'll be able to avoid more jail time—a minor victory in an otherwise horrendous experience.

Marnie is staying with her sister until she and Dean can figure out where they go from here.

As I approach the steps to their quaint home, my nerves start to get the better of me.

I insisted on coming here today. Otis has been coming over to spend time with Dean every day since he was released, but he had a staff meeting and a deadline for the paper, so I thought it would be a good opportunity for Dean and I to talk.

But my maturity and resolve waver as I ring the doorbell, bouncing in place, trying to steady my rising anxiety.

Dean opens the door, forcing a small smile. "Hey, Evie."

His eyes are sad and bruised and I guess the same can be said for the rest of him, too. My mouth only manages a nervous tilt as he moves to the side of the doorway, inviting me in.

I scan the small foyer as I take off my coat and then hang it on the banister while Dean stands to my side, leaning against the archway to the dining room.

After a long, awkward pause, I glance around the foyer again, finally saying, "Your house is nice," through a tight smile.

"Thanks," he says, running a hand through his disheveled hair and scratching the back of his head.

A shiver runs through me; it's so weird to see him and Otis do the same nervous ticks.

"Want some coffee?" he asks, starting to walk through the dining room.

"Sure."

I follow him, taking in the *adultness* of his house. It's tidy, there's wedding pictures on the wall and even a collection of candles in the hutch.

A strong contrast to crooked tapestries and a beat-up old chair.

The sound of the coffee grinder jolts my mind from our former life together and I see him filling a tea kettle. He picks up a small stainless steel brewer and places it next to a container of ground coffee.

"A Moka Pot?" I ask in surprise. "Fancy."

His lips twitch ever-so-slightly as he turns the heat on the kettle.

"I broke my drip brewer," he says, turning around and leaning against the counter.

411

His face is just so fucking sad that my body moves before I even have time to think about it.

I wrap my arms around his torso and hug him. I hug the sad man I used to love because he broke his coffee pot and because I haven't hugged him since he didn't die a week ago.

His arms hesitantly wrap around me before he releases, leaning back against the counter.

It's like he's trying to make sure that I know he's not going to try anything. But I already knew that. I wouldn't be here if I was worried about it.

Otis told me about the email Dean sent him. I guess they talked a bit and Otis seems like he really wants to work through their issues. And *that* makes me so goddamn happy.

The tension recharges as I sit down at the small, round table in the kitchen and nervously trace the patterns in the wood.

"You doing okay, Dean?"

It's a dumb question, but I need a jumping off point. This conversation is well overdue, but that doesn't mean I'm ready for it.

He snorts. "I've never been so *not okay* in my life."

The tea kettle hisses, and he turns around to prepare the coffee while my knee starts bouncing and my hand starts to spell below the table.

He pours us each a mug and then gingerly sits down in the chair across the table, placing one of the mugs in front of me.

I give him a closed-mouth smile. "Thanks."

We both take a sip, making identical "ah" noises before we laugh, but the moment passes quickly. His fingers trace the rim of his mug and his eyes slowly float up to mine. Pools of chestnut brown hold a weighted stare across from me and I can't look away.

"What's going on?" I ask, keeping our eye contact.

"I don't know. This is weird," he says. "You're in my kitchen."

I burst into laughter. I slap the table and gasp for air as my inappropriate outburst rumbles through me like a manic earthquake.

Dean's mouth curls up, but his eyebrows pinch until eventually his chest starts to shake with infectious laughter.

Tears start to form at the corners of my eyes and my laughter calms, but slowly transforms into nervous crying.

I've actually lost it.

Dean's smile drops, his eyes filling with concern.

I'd be worried too if a crazy woman was sitting in my kitchen acting hysterical.

"Evie . . ." is all he says.

I wipe my eyes, trying to compose myself. "I'm sorry, I don't know *what the fuck* . . ." I clear my throat. "It's just been . . . a crazy few months."

His gaze finds mine again, and it's heavy.

We sit in another staring contest for a few beats, his eyes slowly filling before he swallows hard.

"I'm so fucking sorry, Evelyn." He shakes his head, closing his eyes for a second, then pinches the bridge of his nose.

"You weren't in your right mind at Christmas. I understand that now," I say, jaggedly.

He winces, like the memory actually hit him. "I guess I have a lot to apologize for," he says, scratching at his unkept beard. "I *am* sorry for Christmas. I wasn't thinking straight, but..." He takes another shaky inhale. "That's not what I was talking about . . ."

He keeps his head down and I study his agonized face. His bruises pale in comparison to the pain I see in his eyes. They look so full of despair that it makes me wonder if they even remember joy.

My heart dips and I sigh, understanding what he's apologizing for.

"It was a long time ago—"

"Please," he cuts me off. "Please, let me try to get through this." He takes in a steadying breath and sits up a little straighter.

"My ex, Haley? She cheated on me."

My eyebrows pinch. *How did I not know that?*

"I never told anyone—not even Otis," he says, answering my silent question. "I don't know . . . I just . . ." he exhales, shaking his head.

"What?"

His eyes meet mine and he releases a frustrated sigh. "I've just never felt like my shit was big enough to complain about, honestly. Not compared to—" he stops but continues to stare at me cautiously.

Is he talking about Otis? Me?

But a heaviness settles in my chest. It's clear that no matter who he's referencing, Dean seems to think that his problems are unimportant, and *that* swells my heart.

"I wish you would have told me . . ."

Pain is pain. The severity doesn't really have a scale because it all hurts. But it's real and *it matters.*

Dean's eyes soften at me from across the table. There's a glimpse of relief to his expression but it's overshadowed by the sadness still etching his face.

"Do you remember that one night?" he says, shifting uncomfortably. "The night where you couldn't wake back up right away?"

I nod slowly, still haunted by the memory.

"I wanted to be dead after that night," he says, and I choke on my breath, but he puts a steadying hand out. "I'm not saying I was thinking of killing myself or anything. I just didn't . . . want to be alive anymore. I know that doesn't make sense, but it's true." He shakes his head and then rubs his palm over his forehead. "The way you looked at me . . . I . . ." he trails off as a sob breaks through, sufficiently cracking my heart.

"I'm so sorry," I squeak out and his head jolts up.

"No, please don't apologize," he says. "I just unraveled. Seeing you look at me like *him.* I don't know—some twisted part of me really started to believe I *was* as bad as that piece of shit."

"You're no—" I start to refute but he cuts me off again.

"I'm not blaming you, Evie. I'm *not*," he says firmly. "Nothing that happened between us is your fault, understand?"

I nod but my eyes slowly fill.

"I'm just . . . so sorry I left you alone." He takes my hand in his. "I'm sorry I made you feel like I didn't care—because I did," he cries. "What happened to you broke something in me, Evelyn."

Dean is just a blur behind my tears now.

I was understandably trapped in my own trauma when it happened that I wasn't capable of seeing how much it took from him too. Before he left for Christmas break, he had a girlfriend who adored him and when he came back, she was gone.

I didn't tell him who it was, I didn't lean on him for support, I denied his comfort.

I disappeared.

He may have been the one to physically leave but I was gone months before he left Chicago.

Something inside me softens.

Dean had become the vessel for all of my anger surrounding that time in our lives and he took it. He strapped it on his back and carried it with him.

He's still carrying it.

My shoulders rise as I take a deep inhale, then release a healing breath.

"I forgive you," I say, watching his body sink with relief.

Dean lets go of my hand and I wipe under my eyes, trying to pull myself together. Another second passes before he clears his throat.

"There's one more thing . . ." he says.

I look at him with unease—what could there possibly be left to say?

His expression is tight, timid. "Otis is the best guy I've ever known. He's always been selfless, loyal . . ."

415

I nod, still not sure where he's going with this.

"But . . . his love for you really tested that loyalty," he says and my eyebrows pinch, suddenly defensive.

"Otis *was* loyal to you, Dean. We only got together a few—" I'm stopped by his surrendering hand.

"Evelyn," he says. "I'm not talking about his *dis*loyalty to me because you guys are together now. I'm trying to tell you that . . . Otis has loved you for years—since you and I were together."

My mouth gapes. *That can't be true, right?*

"I'm only telling you because . . . I want more than anything to be a good brother to him. And you should know that he's not only the best guy I've ever known, but he's someone who loved you for ten years and never said anything because he loved me too."

I shake my head, at a total loss for words.

But hope fills my chest with his admission. Dean has no reason to be telling me this—he won't gain anything from it.

He's just being honest, even though it's hard.

Our history, their childhood—these things I believed would haunt us forever, all seem to be falling into place.

Not gracefully or easily, but . . .

It's a start.

Looking up at Dean, I feel trust rebuilding.

I believe he wants to find his way back to who he was and repair his relationship with Otis. We both suppressed the past, hoping it would just disappear, but we still ended up here. We got the chance to have this conversation and I can't help but smile, softly.

His eyebrows pinch as he shifts his weight.

"What?" he asks.

I shrug, feeling emotionally spent and maybe just a little delirious. "I think we're gonna be okay," I say, then sign, "D. Fart."

I went with Dean to his first sober meeting, then made the journey back up to Edgewater, deciding to stop by the Thai place below my old apartment building to pick up some dinner.

Pushing my way through the door, I see Otis lounging in the hammock, reading. His eyes widen when he sees the bag of food in my hand, making me chuckle.

He clumsily pushes his way out of the hammock, and I laugh some more. There's just no *good* way to get out of that thing—but I still love it.

He closes the distance between us and presses his lips to mine, stroking my cheek with his thumb.

"The kisses are always a little sweeter when I bring food," I sign, putting the takeout bag on the coffee table.

He laughs, sitting down on the couch while I plop onto the floor.

He opens the drunken noodles I got for him and I open my Pad Thai, taking a minute to enjoy the warm ginger smell that wafts up.

"How was he today?" he signs, taking a bite.

"Good," I sign. "He wanted to join a sober group, so I went with him."

He nods approvingly and I watch him dig in.

Gusto eating!

My smile pulls as I stare at him with new adoration blooming in my heart. Not because of what Dean told me, but because if it weren't for Otis, I could easily still be stuck as my *lesser self.* My plight wasn't as outwardly destructive as Dean's, but I still spent so many years less happy than I could have been because I was stuck.

My past kept a tight grip on me, holding me stagnant, unable to move forward. The night Otis kissed me, I felt that grip loosen, and each thing I've had to confront because of our relationship has been a breakthrough. But I feel like my conversation with Dean finally gave me the ticket to cross a new threshold.

I don't even feel a need to talk to Otis about his feelings for me back then. It's touching beyond words to know he loved me all those years ago, but that love was different; it was an idea. The love we have now is real. It's stronger because of the love we had before. It's the truest thing I've ever felt.

I close my eyes, feeling a resounding peace hum through me.

Otis looks at me with curious eyes, signing, "Where'd you go?"

A warmth spreads through me and I smile. "I'm right here."

chapter fifty-four

otis

four months later

Springtime to Chicagoans feels like surviving a *Game of Thrones* battle.

I've just reached the block of Dean's new apartment. A cozy two-bedroom in Lincoln Park—a way easier trek from Edgewater.

My phone buzzes and I see the notification that another copy of my book has sold and I swear, every time it happens, I have to look at it over and over again to convince myself it's real.

I decided to go the self-publishing route. I don't have an agent, and it seemed like the best option to actually put it out there. The e-book has been selling regularly and it feels fucking great. Honestly, there's undeniable satisfaction and pride that I finished it at all.

I reach Dean's building, walking up the single flight of steps, to the end of the hall. I knock and a moment later, Dean creaks the door open like I might be the monster in a horror film, and I snort a laugh.

He looks like a mess, but the good kind. The single dad with a newborn kind of mess.

He's wearing a white t-shirt with some kind of dried gook on the shoulder, sporting a burp cloth on the other one.

I walk into the apartment, which is still a work in progress. He moved in right after Ava was born about a month ago and he's been slowly trying to get the place set up.

I look around at the space, still seeing some unpacked boxes, but the living room is in order and he finally put together the small high-top table I got him.

"It's coming together," I sign.

He chuckles, shrugging. "I guess so."

I'm proud of Dean—really fucking proud of him. He's made some big and difficult changes in the last few months and it's slowly reminding me of why we were so close before.

He and Marnie amicably decided to get a divorce. It was still a hard decision, but it showed real growth for him to confront his issues and take responsibility for his missteps.

Dean leans into the small bassinet, hoisting up my tiny niece. He cradles her in his arms, staring down at her like she's treasure and my heart swells.

Watching him fall into fatherhood with complete devotion has been . . . well, kind of incredible.

I admire him for stepping up, but it all still worries me a bit.

Adjusting to life with a kid is difficult enough, but Dean and Marnie are also in the early days of their divorce. They're learning to co-parent before they've parented at all and I'd be lying if I said it didn't worry me that it will all become too much for Dean.

I hold out my arms, silently asking if I can hold her and Dean smiles, handing Ava to me.

"If you wake her up, you're taking her with you," he signs, and I roll my eyes, then glance down at the tiny baby with chocolate brown hair, and a nose that reminds me of a small mushroom.

I look back up at Dean, leaning against the wall, his eyes glued to Ava.

His steady gaze does something to calm my worry. It's soft and loving but also fierce and protective, like the sense of purpose for being her dad and taking care of her has the power to override any weakness.

"She's really fucking cute," I whisper.

He nods, signing, "Especially when she's sleeping."

"Love you, Ava," I sign, my left arm still cradling her little body.

Dean slowly pushes off the wall and rummages through one of his moving boxes. After another moment passes, I finally see what he was looking for as he holds the small gray cartridge up in my direction.

Mario Kart.

"Want to lose a race?" he signs, waving the game, tauntingly.

I snort. "Won't it embarrass you to lose while I play one-handed—holding your daughter?"

He shakes his head, taking Ava before he tosses the game to me.

"Fire it up," he signs.

It's late afternoon by the time I make it home. Today was Evelyn's first day of classes and I have a special night planned so I stopped by the store to grab supplies for dinner.

She won't be back for another hour, so I hop in the shower and then get to work in the kitchen.

As I chop some broccoli, I see her walk up to the kitchen archway and lean against the wall.

She crosses her arms, unabashedly staring and my heart does a quick flip. Sometimes it still doesn't feel real—that Evelyn looks at me like I'd only ever dreamed she would.

She shakes her right hand out, signing, "Wow," and I chuckle before she takes a couple steps more to plant a kiss on my cheek. As her head rests on my shoulder, I take a moment to nuzzle my face into her hair, inhaling deep.

Wildflowers.

I kiss the top of her head and she gently pushes off my shoulder but looks back up at me.

"How was class?" I ask.

Her smile inches up her face. "Good," she signs. "It just feels right, ya know?"

Nodding, my mouth quirks at the corner. *I really do know.*

I turn around and open the cabinet to pull out two wine glasses. Evelyn's eyebrows perk up as she opens the fridge, finding her favorite bottle of wine sitting on the shelf.

She's pretty easy to please; her favorite bottle is only ten bucks at the grocery store. She pours us each a glass and we clink them together.

"Go relax, dinner will be ready in twenty," I sign.

Her eyebrows raise again as she takes a sip of wine. "Yes, sir," she signs with a small salute.

Now that hibernation is over, there are plenty of people out as we walk around the neighborhood.

It's early evening and the sun is slowly setting, giving the streets a soft amber glow. The air is warm but there's a refreshing lake-side breeze gently whirling around us.

We approach the block we once walked so regularly, and my heart rate quickens. My hand is linked with Evelyn's, so I work hard to not tense up as my nerves start to pulse.

Stopping in front of the old, familiar storefront, we take a minute to look at the black, brick building. The inside of Bohemia is dark. The counters are covered in plastic tarps and the floors are dusty.

I look over at Evelyn who is staring at the place like an old friend. I glance back inside and notice that the vintage light bulbs she hung along the ceiling are still there. My eyes squint and look toward the back wall, seeing they haven't taken down her mug wall yet.

She's still in there.

My breath catches in my throat as I turn to Evelyn. My heart feels like it might actually blow through my chest, but I give her hand a tight squeeze and she looks over at me with a sweet expression that brings me to my knees.

Well, one knee.

I kneel down in front of her and pull the small box out of my back pocket, holding it up to her. Her mouth slowly drops, her big hazel eyes widen and immediately fill with tears—turning them greener by the second.

"Evelyn . . . you're my light and my heart." I swallow, nervously. "Will you marry me?"

I practiced saying the small collection of words a hundred times today but I'm still shaking. My nervous eyes watch her, knowing I'm looking at my whole world, wrapped up in the most beautiful woman I've ever seen.

She pulls me up, off my knee and crashes her mouth against mine. Her hands pull the fabric of my shirt like she's actually trying to make us one being.

"Yes, yes, yes . . ." I feel her chant against my lips.

Finally pulling away so I can actually give her the ring, I slide the rose gold band with a woven leaf pattern of diamonds decorating a green sapphire center stone onto her finger.

She looks down at it, then back up at me as another tear falls.

"Perfect," she says through blissful tears, smiling.

My favorite Evelyn smile.

chapter fifty-five

evelyn

My fingers fumble to unbutton his shirt fast enough. I have him pinned against the door since I basically mauled him the second we finally got back inside our apartment.

My lips press hard against his, high on his woodsy scent as I finally unfasten his shirt. I break away from our kiss to pull the sleeves down his arms before my mouth is everywhere.

The sight of the crescent-shaped scar on his chest slows my hunger and I trace it with my thumb. It seems like ages ago that the attack happened, but *this* will always be here.

My mind tries to reorganize the memory. Instead of being the night he was viciously attacked, it can be the night that we became something different.

My eyes float back up to meet his.

My future husband's eyes.

His expression is uneasy with my attention on his scar, so I move my palm over his heart, beating steady against my hand.

I look back up at him, starting to unbutton his pants, never breaking our eye contact before I press my ear to his chest and my hand sinks down into his pants, slowly stroking him.

I want to feel what he feels when he touches me.

One of his hands fists the back of my hair as I continue my movement up and down, but the thumb from his other hand finds the ear that's not pressed up against him and he gently presses his thumb against it.

Superpower intact.

It's not completely silent, but all I feel is his heartbeat. My hand moves faster as my own heart races, feeling him thump hard against my cheek. It increases, along with a shudder in his chest and suddenly his hands are grabbing both sides of my face before his lips fuse to mine.

His arms scoop me up, under my thighs, pushing an involuntary squeal from me and I feel him smile against my lips. He kicks his pants off the rest of the way and carries me to our bedroom, then lowers me onto our bed.

I sit on the edge of the mattress as my eyes drink in the sight of him, completely bare, my lips tilting up as he stares down at me.

"This feels unfair," he signs, playfully.

My hands reach down, balling the fabric of my shirt but he kneels down in front of me and catches my hands.

He likes to undress me.

Amber eyes gleam at me as he pulls my shirt up and over my head before dropping it to the floor. He runs his finger under my copper-colored bra strap from my shoulder to the crown of my breast as his gaze dances across my chest.

"This is new," he says.

Good fucking God, his voice coupled with the burning in his eyes has my stomach swirling.

All I can do is nod, swallowing hard while I stare at him.

He presses his soft, full lips to my collar bone, then feathers them down over both of my breasts as he starts to unbutton my pants.

"My beautiful," he murmurs, kissing down my stomach. "Sexy," he breathes, unzipping my pants. "Evelyn," he finishes, pulling them down my legs.

His lips trail up my thigh and goosebumps domino across my body. He smirks, pulling my panties down, then slowly moves his mouth between my thighs and I'm already so worked up that I fall back and moan, catching myself on my elbows.

One of his hands moves up to my breast and massages it as he continues to work his mouth between my legs. My eyes peer down at him as he tortures me in the best possible way, and I see that he's watching me.

The sight makes my legs shake and my insides tighten, crying out with release. He's wearing his adorable, smug grin as I practically haul him off the floor and devour his mouth—teeth collide, tongues tangle and he pushes into me.

He rocks slow and steady as our mouths ebb and flow. He pushes up, gazing down at me with such deep love and longing that my goosebumps return.

This is what making love means.

We made our love through years of friendship. We made love by counting on each other. We made love by trusting each other. We made love by knowing what each other needed without words.

And tonight, we make love by basking in the love we already made.

After three rounds of mind-blowing love making, we lay in the hammock together, naked, wrapped up in my favorite fuzzy blanket.

I've sent obligatory texts to all of our people, letting them know about our engagement and each of the responses has kept the warmth I've felt all night burning through me.

Reggie: OMG!!! Dibs on maid of honor!
Congrats, baby girl. Love you both!

Mom: We already knew :) he emailed your dad
a month ago. The message had me bawling like a
baby—can't wait to start planning!

Mary: What a beautiful love the two of you are!
So happy for you! Let's have dinner soon. Jim is
working his way through Julia Child's cookbook.
Got to get creative as you get old. Hugs!!

Otis sent texts to his parents and Dean.

Gloria: The neighbors just put their house
on the market. Just sayin' . . .

Dean's response was a sweet surprise. He sent a picture of a smiling Ava in her baby swing with a paper laying over her little body that read:

"Congratulations, Uncle Otis and Aunt Evie! We love you!"

That one got me.
I'm really proud of Dean. I'm really proud of how far we've all come. Never in my wildest dreams did I think *this* would be my life.

My dad told me this story once, about a planet where the beings had no eyes. *No one* could see so they never even knew sight existed. But, once these eyeless beings died, they were given the gift of sight.

They marveled at this new concept—something they never knew they were missing. They reveled in the beauty of seeing faces of their loved ones, admiring the colors of flowers they smelled, watching someone sing a song they loved.

But they had to die first, Dad reminded me.

Now, obviously I haven't died, but there have been times where it felt like I was in peril. Moments I truly thought that life was going to finally crush me in its fist and drop the broken pieces of myself to the ground, turning me to dust.

But when I think of all of my most treasured moments—opening Bohemia, deciding to become an interpreter, falling madly in love with Otis—they were all born from these desperate moments. Each one of them was life giving me a precious gift that I had no idea I was missing.

It sounds simple and cliché, but that's all it takes. It just takes pushing past that desperate moment. If you're given the gift of sight but keep your eyes tightly closed out of fear, you'll miss it.

I run my hand through the top of Otis's wavy hair, as his head lays on my chest. I start to quietly sing in the soft warm light of our cozy reading nook.

It would be a damn tragedy to miss this.

Otis's arms tighten around my waist as he feels the vibration from my voice, his ear still pressed against my chest, and I swear I feel his love seep into me from his fingertips.

It's easy to feel appreciative in these moments—the good ones. But it's the strength his arms have given me in the hard moments and the courage his warm, brown eyes give me in the fearful times that make me feel invincible. It's the sound of his voice telling me "It will be okay" that makes me believe it's true.

Burning leaves.

I *finally* see it. I get to feel *everything*. And that's the real gift.

epilogue

evelyn

two years later
december 23rd

As I make the way down the steps of my childhood home, the house is still dark. I round the banister then walk the small hallway, noticing the dim light in the kitchen and my lips curl.

I hear the coffee pot bubbling and see my dad sitting at the island with his back to me. Continuing toward him, I hug him around the neck from behind and his hand holds my arms linked around his chest, releasing a heavy sigh.

I know, Daddy. It's been too long.

I hold him a little longer. "Are you ready for our business meeting?" I ask, giving him a parting squeeze before I walk over to the coffee pot.

"Evie Bear, if I didn't love you so damn much, you'd be fired," he jokes.

I snort, knowing he's right but pour us each a cup, both black. I brought some Red Line beans from Chicago so it's good without anything added.

Plopping on the stool next to my dad, we each take a sip, savoring the familiar moment before he asks, "So, whatcha got?"

I smile. "Well . . . you know that family I've been working with? The one I met on Bohemia's last day?"

His eyebrows pinch but then he nods, remembering.

"Jenny, the daughter, really wants to get involved in theater. But it's hard because not a lot of theaters put deaf-friendly shows in their seasons. In fact, not many even have regular interpreters at all for *any* of their shows."

The corner of my dad's mouth pulls back. "That's a shame."

I nod. "It really is. But I'm corresponding with a theater I worked for after I graduated, and they seem interested in getting involved!"

Sipping my coffee, I add, "I want to find deaf playwrights and actors to showcase sign language. It'll be a lot of work, but I'm really excited about it."

The combining of two of my passions. Excited is an understatement.

"Jenny seems really excited too, which is awesome because she's *quite* the moody teen."

My dad laughs, nodding emphatically. "I had one of those," he says. "Like monitoring a damn hurricane."

I laugh and he smiles warmly at me, saying, "But that sounds perfect for you, Evie-Bear."

"I think so," I say through a yawn.

"Tired?"

"A little, but I wasn't about to miss another business meeting."

Otis and I got in late last night and I'm still on Central Time. That one hour makes all the difference sometimes.

"Well, I'm happy you made it this year, baby girl." Then he signs, "I've missed you."

My heart tightens. Both of my parents have been trying to learn sign language and it means so much to me, and Otis.

I lean my head on his shoulder and he rests his head on top of mine.

"I've missed you too, Daddy."

Dad and I go out for breakfast to keep up with our reinstated tradition before I go back up to my room to find my husband sleeping in my old bed.

Curling up behind him, my arms wrap around his torso from behind and he stirs. A smile curls my lips against his ear, seeing the picture of us from our wedding that my parents put on the nightstand.

We got married in the Winter Garden at the Harold Washington Library Center. It was a small gathering. Mary officiated, with a small group of everyone we loved in one of our favorite places.

I trail kisses down Otis's neck, then nuzzle my face in the nook between his shoulder and his chin.

His shoulders shake as soft, sleepy laughter spills from his mouth. "That tickles," he says, his eyes still closed.

He rolls onto his back, but I stay propped up on my elbow.

"Good morning," I say through a smile, and he traces my lips with his thumb.

"How'd you sleep?" he asks.

"Not enough," I sign, slumping my head onto his chest.

He chuckles, running his fingers through my hair, and we lay together for a few moments as I glance around my room.

It's definitely strange being back here but I think that's just because I let so much time pass. Memories have been swirling through me all morning and surprisingly, they've been more comforting than triggering.

I've only had one moment that brought me back to *that* night. It happened shortly after we arrived here. Otis held me through it, and it passed, eventually. But otherwise, I've had glimpses into fun family memories.

Mornings like I just had with my dad in the kitchen. The night my mom tried to get us to watch *True Blood* as a family in the living room. *We didn't. Thank God.*

That's the trade-off with trying to shut things out. Sometimes you unwillingly push aside all the good that happened, too. I had convinced myself that coming back here was a sure way to fall back into the endless, hopelessness of that one night but I actually feel empowered being back here. A reclamation.

My pride halts as I wince, feeling a sharp cramp in my abdomen—reminding me that I have shitty news. My arms tighten around Otis and he presses a kiss into my hair.

My smile falls as I turn to look up at him.

"I got my period," I sign.

He sits up, leaning against the headboard, his mouth tilting with disappointment. His hand cups my jaw and he pulls my lips to his, sighing against them. Our mouths release, but our foreheads stay pressed, breathing each other's strength.

"It's okay, baby. We'll keep trying," he says, still holding my face.

I gently nod, my forehead still against his, sighing my sadness.

We've been trying for over a year. We've both been checked by our doctors and they haven't seen anything wrong or irregular. It just hasn't happened for us.

I became obsessive a few months ago. I would get carried away with any possible pregnancy symptom, which ironically—and cruelly—are also PMS symptoms.

I would be *sure* that *that* was our time.

But all it would do is leave me devastated when I got my period.

So, I've tried to distance myself a bit. I'm staying off the fertility blogs and I've stopped tracking my symptoms, but there's still disappointment when it doesn't happen.

But it's December 23rd. *It's my favorite day,* and I won't let things I can't control ruin it. Not again.

I lean back from Otis, giving him a tilted smile. "At least the trying is fun?"

We both chuckle at the unhelpful phrase many have said to us through this process before he flips me on my back, covering my face in kisses and I giggle beneath him.

It isn't *not* fun.

Otis hovers above, staring down at me with the same adoring eyes that light me up, lowering himself until our noses touch.

"My beautiful wife," he says, his thumb brushing my cheek before he presses a sweet kiss to my lips.

We pull apart but he stays leaning over me, holding his weight on his elbows. I push his wavy hair back; I'll never tire of his handsome face.

My heart is in him.

Mary's phrase stuck. I've never felt it more.

My heart is safe. In life's most difficult moments, I don't have to worry about it breaking because it's no longer mine to guard.

Otis leans toward the nightstand, grabbing his phone, tapping the screen a couple of times before Otis Redding's "Merry Christmas, Baby" starts to play.

My smile stretches as he stands, pulling me up and wrapping his arm around the small of my back, holding my hand in the other.

We sway, pressed against each other, our eyes connected, reading each other's thoughts.

We'll always have this.

It's the first tradition we started of our own when we spent our first Christmas together. It's the first thing that gave this day back to me.

He gave it back to me.

My hand comes up to meet his jaw and my fingers gently scratch his reddish scruff.

"Merry Christmas, baby," I sign.

the end

author's note

Dear Reader,

From the bottom, middle, top—from my whole heart: thank you for reading this story.

Have you ever met someone and wondered how you existed before you met them? A moment concocted from the unique combination of fate and intuition that creates a literal shift in your being?

That's how I felt writing this.

When I started learning ASL two years ago, I immediately fell in love with the language, but learning about Deaf culture and community was . . . well, inspiring.

Otis's story is only one kind of experience. He is surrounded by hearing individuals. The people in his life all learn ASL and that's incredible, but sadly, this is not always the case.

I wrote the first draft of this book in two months. As readers, I imagine you know the power of a story that just needs to be told, and it just poured out of me.

It was cathartic, it was heartbreaking at times, but overall, it was healing.

We've all lived through *something*.

Simply existing can feel so hard sometimes, but just like Evelyn said, if we can push past that desperate, hopeless feeling—just an inch past it—sometimes our greatest reward awaits us on the other side.

And sometimes it doesn't.

Life, unknowable as it is, can revolve around what we choose to hold on to: despair, glory, indifference.

I'm a hopeless romantic; I always have been. Evelyn and Otis are the story I wish for everyone. Despite the issues of their past, they are people that have always given each other the permission to be exactly who they are—and I think truly incredible things can happen when we're given that safety.

To screw up, to be imperfect, to be human.

And thusly, if we don't have that safety net, like Dean, our lives can become uncontrollable. (Oh, by the way, Dean's story is coming! Poor guy had a rough go of it in this book but—fire emoji, pepper emoji, eggplant emoji—I'll leave it at that.)

I wrote the first draft of this book believing no one would read it. From that belief, I was able to give myself permission to be imperfect and I think it gave me the courage to write from a place of truth.

The book is a work of fiction but still, as a writer, you write what you know. And I *know* that true love can give us the strength to be our best selves. I know that we're all capable of rising above.

It's always in our hands, friends.

Sincerely, thank you for reading.

Love,

Larissa

acknowledgments

First and foremost, I need to thank my wonderfully supportive husband, Drew. I woke up one Sunday morning with this idea simmering and told him I thought I was going to write a book.

This man supports every crazy, wild, farfetched idea I ever have—he simply smiled and said, "That's awesome, honey! I can't wait to read it."

Little did he know he would read it over and over and over again. Deepening moments, developing characters, proofreading—and romance isn't exactly his genre of choice. He is my favorite person, and I couldn't have done this without him.

To my friend, Morgan Dennis, an avid reader of the romance genre and a general pain in my ass—thank you for keeping it real with me and telling me when things aren't working. I love (and hate) you for it. And you'll always be my favorite person to work with behind the coffee counter.

My ASL teachers. Thank you for teaching me something so invaluable. Not just the language, but the culture and the community that comes with it. I'm infinitely grateful to keep learning and promise to get better with my receptive skills!

My beta readers: Annie Charme, Jo Nundy, Becky Fisher, Rebecca Shoemake, Cat Wilkinson, Madi Peppell, Katie Walsh, and Andrea Méndez Iguartua. Your feedback and discussion helped me nuance moments and round out these characters. Thank you for your time and guidance.

Catie Hinshaw, thank you for creating Bohemia's logo for me. It's so cool that we once worked at a coffee shop together and Bohemia is such a staple in the story, so having something tangible to claim for Evelyn's shop only makes the place feel more real.

To my time spent in the great city of Chicago. It's still one of my favorite cities and living above a great Thai restaurant is something I'd love to happen again in my life.

Lastly, to my family and friends: thank you for always giving me the permission to be me. Without it, I'm not sure this book would have ever happened.

All the thanks, all the love.

WANT TO LEARN ASL?

Good news! There are so many online resources and classes taught by Deaf teachers. I was ecstatic when readers asked if I had any recommendations to learn sign language—and I definitely do, so if you want to learn this beautiful language, please message me on Instagram @sincerely_lovelarissa and I can give you some recommendations!

resources

If you or anyone you know is a victim of rape or sexual assault, please reach out. You are not alone.
National Sexual Assault Hotline:
1-800-656-4673

If you or anyone you know struggles with PTSD, know that there are people who care and want to help. If you or a loved one is battling addiction, be gentle with yourself and talk to someone.
Substance Abuse and Mental Health Services Hotline:
1-800-662-4357